NO BODIES

Robert Crouch

Published by RWC Publishing

ISBN 978-1-5498441-2-6

Cover by String Design, Eastbourne
(http://www.stringdesign.co.uk)

Other books by Robert Crouch

No Accident – the first Kent Fisher mystery
Fisher's Fables – the perfect companion to the Kent Fisher mysteries

For all the environmental health professionals who work hard each day, often without recognition, to protect public health and make your world a safer, better place.

Acknowledgements

While the writing of a novel can be a solitary occupation, the preparation, research, revision and promotion of the work often involves many people, who willingly give their time, knowledge and experience to help me produce an accurate and credible story.

My grateful thanks go to

- Lisa Harvey-Vince, Public Health England, for her extensive knowledge and guidance regarding the investigation of E. coli O157 and infectious disease control

- Sgt David Kent of Sussex Police for explaining the workings of the Custody Suite and arrest procedures

- Nick and Debbie Flude for investigative insights and for opening doors

- Jim van den Bos, Communications Officer at Wealden DC, for his ideas and help with promotional work

- Will Hatchett, Editor of Environmental Health News, for supporting and promoting my work

I'd like to offer special thanks to Caroline Vincent of Bits about Books, for supporting the Kent Fisher mysteries and for organising the promotion of this novel with a blog tour. Special thanks also go to the bloggers who are working with Caroline to review and promote *No Bodies* through their blog sites and social media. These lovely people are passionate about books and work tirelessly to help authors bring their work to a wider audience.

And last, but by no means least, special thanks must also go to Jane Prior, of String Design, who translated my vague ideas into the stunning cover for *No Bodies*.

ONE

I don't like the way the undertaker looks at my stepmother.

But she does.

Not that I blame Niamh. She's an attractive woman. She deserves a little happiness. From what I've heard, the undertaker's a considerate man with a business he takes great pride in. And you have to admire people with a passion for what they do, though his enthusiasm for embalming seems wrong on so many levels. Thankfully, it's a well-kept secret.

But who am I to judge? I have a flair for trouble, which is why we're gathered at St Mary's church on an unseasonably warm Friday afternoon in October. It looks like the whole of Tollingdon wants to pay their respects to our local MP and Cabinet Minister, the Right Honourable William Kenneth Fisher. His heart attack at a murder scene two weeks ago saved him from scandal and a right dishonourable discharge, but it hasn't saved him from media speculation.

"Vultures," Niamh says, glaring at the barrage of telephoto lenses, poised on the flint wall of the cemetery. "There's nothing left to pick over."

Thanks to his gambling, she's lost pretty much everything, including their spacious home in Herstmonceux. It's a bit of a squeeze in my flat, but we'll manage. If she stops tidying everything and criticising my clothes, I promise not to walk around in my underwear. When I find where she's put it, that is.

We'll work it out. We have no choice. William Fisher betrayed us both. She wants me to keep quiet about it, but as the coffin hovers above the grave, she nudges me forward to say a few words.

A couple spring to mind, but there are women and children present.

Father Michael commends William Fisher to the mercy of God and steps back, blotting the sweat from his forehead with his sleeve. Everyone looks at me, but I have no idea what to say. All around me the gravestones and plaques edit people's lives to a few select words. Death sanitises the past, turning sins and transgressions into shiny marble tributes, but I can't lie. I won't lie.

Neither can I tell the truth. Not yet anyway.

I clear my throat.

"Charismatic, and with a personality larger than the cigars he enjoyed, the Rt. Honourable William Kenneth Fisher touched our lives in different ways. But I wonder how many of us knew the person behind the public façade."

Niamh's grip tightens on my arm. Her green eyes flash me a warning.

"For those of us who knew the private person," I say, "things will never be the same. His unexpected death denied us the chance to express how we really felt."

I glance at Gemma. She's a few inches away, but it might as well be miles.

"That's why we should be honest with those who matter most," I say, stepping back.

The next thirty minutes plod by in a ponderous procession of platitudes. Everyone has something to say, a memory to share. Niamh remains solemn and dignified, saying all the right things. Not once does she let go of my hand, well aware that I'd rather be running over the green hills of the South Downs to clear my frustration and anger.

When the last mourner moves on, she turns to me, her voice sharp. "What was all that about being honest with those who matter most?"

Once again, I glance at Gemma, who's waiting beneath a yew tree. She's the most attractive woman I know with heavenly chocolate brown eyes, a sly smile, and a voice that's as soft and rich as velvet, even when she swears. She looks amazing in a black cotton jacket, worn without a blouse, and a complementary short skirt that shows off her tanned legs. A trilby, perched on waves of glossy hair, makes me think of Audrey Hepburn.

I wrench my thoughts back to Niamh. "How could a man with such high principles have such a low opinion of us?" I ask. "Didn't we deserve the truth?"

"He still loved you, even though …" Tears fill her eyes and she wraps her arms around me. Her cheek, hot with tears, presses against mine. "He raised you to be what he aspired to be, but …"

"He wasn't my father," I say, still not sure how I feel about it. "But I'm talking about the lies and deceit, Niamh, not biology."

She pulls back and looks at me, her eyes filled with bewilderment and sadness. "He found it difficult to express his feelings, but he loved you."

"Yeah, that's why he left me to rot with my mother for ten years."

"Let it go, Kent. Please. Don't we have enough to contend with?" Her eyes plead with me. "Play the hand you're dealt. Isn't that what you keep telling me?"

It doesn't mean I'm any good at it.

I want to tell her I'm trying, but she's already on her way. Alasdair Davenport, who claims to be Tollingdon's most respected funeral director, straightens his tie and checks his appearance in the wing mirror of the limousine as she approaches. He opens the rear door for her and then scowls when she stops to talk to Gemma.

"How's your arm?" Niamh asks.

"Sore, but much better. I'm back at work on Monday."

"Is that wise after only two weeks?"

"I'm bored at home."

"With that gorgeous fiancé of yours, waiting on you hand and foot?" Niamh's disbelieving expression seems exaggerated. "Richard's such a charming, thoughtful young man."

Unlike me, she means. I'm the one who investigated a work accident and uncovered a murder. While she hasn't accused me of contributing to her husband's death, there's a prickly undercurrent to her words sometimes. I've no idea what Gemma thinks. Today's the first time I've seen her since she was shot.

"The undertaker's waiting," I say with a nod in his direction.

"You go with him," Niamh says. "I'm travelling with Gemma."

"We're taking the back roads to avoid the cameras," Gemma says, turning towards the gravel path. "Why not come with us? There's room in the back."

The path passes the Fisher mausoleum. The simple granite portico wraps around two oak doors, built to resist a battering ram. Inside, generations of Fishers lie stacked on top of each other in a crypt carved out of the chalk. A smugglers tunnel once ran from the back of the tomb to Downland Manor, where contraband was stored and dispersed. Customs Officers never ventured into the tunnel or the crypt, unsure of which spirits they might find.

Colonel Witherington, the Leader of Downland District Council, stands like a sentry in front of the doors. A ghost of his former self, he's struggling to defy the stoop of old age, curling his shoulders against a world he no longer recognises. His skin appears almost translucent over knuckles, swollen by arthritis. When our eyes meet, he raises his tweed cap, revealing patches of grey stubble and a forehead marbled with liver spots.

He shuffles towards us, clearly in pain. "Please accept my condolences, Niamh. I know how it feels to lose someone you love dearly." His flint grey eyes give the reporters a stony glare. "Don't let those parasites contaminate William's achievements."

The sleeves of his jacket can't contain the cuffs of a shirt that looks as weary as him. The collar, padded out by a silk cravat, looks three sizes too big. Only the silver moustache, bushier than ever beneath his gnarled nose, looks healthy.

"Are you coming to the wake?" Niamh asks.

He shakes his head. “There’s nothing lonelier than being with others.”

“Lonelier than rattling around in that huge house of yours?”

“It’s empty without my Daphne,” he replies, a wistful look in his eyes, “but I came to pay my respects, not burden you with my troubles.”

Niamh shakes her head as he shuffles away. “He called on William about a month ago,” she says in a low voice. “The police found Daphne’s engagement ring among some stolen jewellery, but they refused to reopen the investigation. He asked William to have a word with the Chief Constable.”

“What investigation?” Gemma asks.

“Daphne ran off with a younger man. The Colonel won’t accept it, of course, and after your recent heroics, Kent, I suspect he wants your help.”

“Me? I don’t know the Chief Constable. And I don’t have the right handshake.”

“But you solved a murder,” she says. “Look, he may well change his mind and pester us at the wake, so I suggest you deal with him right now. I’ll tell Alasdair we’re making our own way.”

The Colonel’s stopped by the church to catch his breath. When Gemma and I approach, he flourishes a jewellery box that contains a slender gold ring with a cluster of three large diamonds.

“You’ll have to go down on one knee if you want me to marry you,” I say.

Gemma smirks. “I’m surprised you know what an engagement ring looks like.”

"This ring belonged to my grandmother," he says, his voice dry and humourless. "She gave it to my mother, who bequeathed it to me, her only child. I gave it to Daphne when I proposed, seven years ago on this very day."

I nod, but I'm watching Davenport. He's standing too close to Niamh, who's smiling and toying with her hat.

"She's dead, Mr Fisher," the Colonel is saying. "He killed her and sold the ring."

"Who did?"

He snaps the box shut. "The man who took my Daphne. She would never have parted with this ring."

If she needed money, she might. "What do the police think?"

"They think I'm a fool."

I could say the same about Davenport, who seems to have forgotten he's an undertaker. When Niamh starts laughing, I wonder if he's told her one of his jokes. The one about how he ends his letters, 'Yours eventually', had me in stitches for weeks.

I look the Colonel in the eye. "What if they're right?"

His snort is dismissive. "Come to my house this evening and you'll see I'm no fool."

I turn to leave. "This is between you and the police, Colonel. I can't help you."

"But you know about catering," he calls.

Gemma turns on me when we're out of earshot. "Did you have to be so blunt? The guy's clearly upset."

"Do I look like Hercule Poirot?"

I can't keep the frustration from my voice. Two weeks ago, I uncovered a murder and now I'm super sleuth, ready to investigate any old nonsense.

"More like Lieutenant Columbo. This is almost as old as his raincoat." Her thumb rubs at a faded stain on the lapel of my jacket. "Why not humour the Colonel? He could help you."

I'm well aware of his influence, but if I don't give him what he wants, he could just as easily turn against me. "Niamh needs me more."

Davenport steps back a couple of paces when we approach. His eyes, the colour of dirty washing up water, look like they hide a lot below the surface. His complexion, which is the colour of bone, suggests he spends too much time in his windowless embalming room.

"I understand you no longer want me to chauffeur you to the Downland Arms," he says, as if it's my fault. "While I admire Miss Dean's resolve, perhaps it's a little soon to be driving after her ordeal."

"I drove here," Gemma says.

"All the same, I will make myself available to take Mrs Fisher home should you feel tired or wish to leave early."

I can't stop myself. "You're coming to the wake?"

Niamh takes my arm and leads me away. "It's the least we can do after Alasdair's kind offer."

We leave in silence and cross the road to the Volvo estate that Gemma's borrowed from her mother. Though battered and more used to transporting sick animals, it's reliable and never lets her down, unlike me, apparently.

"Did you deal with the Colonel?" Niamh gets into the front, oblivious to the intense heat inside the car. We could have cremated William Fisher in here and saved a fortune.

I wind down the window before getting in the back. "I did."

We're soon skimming through the outskirts of Tollingdon where the modern housing estates have flooded the countryside. The considerate developers squeezed in a small parade of shops to provide some facilities for the new residents. Unfortunately, the primary school opposite can't cope with the extra children and had to add several portacabin classrooms in the staff car park. Displaced teachers now fight for parking spaces in the surrounding streets. Their favourite is the slip road that serves the shopping parade, where a small knot of people have gathered. From the way they're peering into the back of the car, I know they're not protesting about the lack of parking spaces.

"Pull over, Gemma," I say, unbuckling my seatbelt. "By those people."

She swings into the slip road and stops. As it lurches to a halt, I'm out of the car and running. The people shuffle back as I reach the old Vauxhall Astra with faded paintwork and a stump where the rear windscreen wiper should be. With my hand shielding my eyes, I peer inside. A champagne-coloured cocker spaniel shares the space behind the back seats with a sports bag, a cardboard box filled with books and a small water bowl that's empty. Shrinking into the only shade available, the poor dog's panting seems laboured. I try to open the hatch, but it's locked, like the doors.

I stare at the exercise books, strewn across the back seat, wondering what kind of teacher would go into school and leave a dog in a hot car.

I turn to the people. "Do you know whose car it is?"

An elderly man in a blazer steps forward. His voice has authority. "A scruffy young man went into the betting shop about ten or fifteen minutes ago."

"Can you fetch him?"

Blazer Man nods and marches across the grass. I pull out my phone to take some photographs.

"Are we in time?" Gemma asks, peering into the car.

I glance at the bookies. "Do you have a wheel brace?"

"Do I look like a mechanic?"

"Okay, can you and Niamh get as many bottles of water as you can from the shop? We need to drench the dog to cool it down."

I return to the Volvo. The rear's a mess of carrier bags, soil and the remains of various plants and weeds. I remove the clear plastic container that holds Gemma's white coat, probe thermometer and antibacterial gel and lift the carpet. The recess for the spare wheel is filled with oily rags. Luckily, one is wrapped around a bottle jack, which I take with me. With no sign of the owner or Blazer Man, I position myself beside the driver's door and raise the jack.

"Oi, you! Stop!"

A thin man with greasy hair, and at least two days of stubble, charges down the steps. From the shadows beneath his eyes, to the remains of curry on his crumpled shirt, it looks like he spent the night on the sofa and woke late. The whiff of stale lager, cigarettes and body odour greet me as he stumbles to a halt. His hand grabs the waist of his jeans, which look ready to fall around his ankles.

"What the hell are you doing?"

I keep the jack raised. "Your dog's cooking in there."

"I've been gone a few minutes, no more." He struts to the rear of the car and looks inside. "Now get lost."

I would pull out my ID card and tell him I'm an environmental health officer, but as I'm suspended from duty, I need to appeal to his better side.

"Just open the hatch and give the dog some air, will you?"

Nicotine fingers extricate some keys from his jeans. He opens the hatch, averting his face from the rush of heat. The dog raises its head slowly, staring at him with pained eyes. I can't believe someone so unkempt could have such a well-groomed dog.

"She's fine, see."

"She needs to cool off," I say, moving closer. "Let's take her over to the shade."

"Get lost!" he says, reaching up to close the hatch.

As I raise my hand to stop the hatch closing, the bottle jack slips through my fingers and glances off his foot. He cries out in pain and staggers back, catching his heel on the kerb. As he tumbles over with a chorus of expletives, I nudge the jack under the car with my foot. Then I scoop the spaniel in my arms and carry her to a shaded area beneath a cherry tree.

I set the spaniel down and run my hands along her flank, feeling the heat beneath the fur. Her heart's hammering against her ribs and she can't seem to pant fast enough.

"Hang on, Morgana," I say, checking the name tag.

Her owner's on his feet now, phone pressed to his ear. "He attacked me and stole my dog. He broke my foot, that's what. And it looks like he's going to attack me again, so get here fast. Turners Parade, opposite the primary school."

He ends the call and gives me a self-satisfied smile as he limps over to a bench and sits with a thud. He raises his injured foot onto the slats, wiggles his toes inside his Nike trainers, and pulls out his cigarettes. When Gemma arrives a few moments later with bottles of water in a carrier bag, he winks and takes aim with his phone.

"How about a smile, darling?"

Niamh makes a snatch for the phone, but she's too slow.

"He's not worth it," I call, wishing bottle caps were easier to unscrew. I tell Gemma to trickle water over the dog, making sure it penetrates the fur. "Do you have your ID card?"

"I'm on sick leave, remember?"

While we wet the dog, Niamh stands in front of the owner so he can't film us. He continues to smoke and enjoy the sunshine until a patrol car pulls up. He rises and puts on his best limp as he staggers towards the police officers.

"Did you call them?" Gemma asks.

I shake my head.

She's on her feet in an instant. "Why don't men ever tidy up?" she asks Niamh as she strides past.

After a brief chat with the owner, the police constable walks up and towers over me. He's in his forties, with silver hair at the temples and eager blue eyes. He straightens his stab vest with pride and beckons me to stand so his body camera can get a better view of me.

Police Community Support Officer, Avril Gardner, who was Downland District Council's animal welfare officer before they made her redundant, steps up beside him.

"I might have known it would be you." She sighs and then bends to greet the dog. "And you must be Morgana. You're a little underweight, but I think you'll make it."

While the owner looks relieved, his voice remains indignant. "There was nothing wrong with her to start with. He's the one with a problem. He assaulted me."

"Leave this to us, Mr Baxendale," the constable says before turning to me. "Could you confirm your name, sir?"

"Kent Fisher."

"The super sleuth environmental health officer?" His tone is mocking, but good natured. "I didn't notice any bodies."

I get the feeling I could be hearing comments like this for some time.

"Another few minutes and you might have had one," I say, nodding at Morgana.

"The owner left her while he was in the betting shop," Niamh says, stepping forward. "You have plenty of witnesses to confirm this. Maybe you should be speaking to them."

"I was only gone a couple of minutes," Baxendale says, searching for something in his pocket. "I placed one bet. When I came out, *he's* breaking into my car. When I tried to stop him, he drops something heavy on my foot."

"Is this true, Mr Fisher?"

Niamh places a hand on my arm. "Kent's only concern was the welfare of the dog."

"It must be under the car," Baxendale says, turning. "I'll show you."

The constable follows him back to his car, leaving Avril with me. "You could find trouble in an empty paper bag," she says.

The moment her colleague finds the bottle jack, I'm in trouble. Niamh realises too, judging by her anxious glance. Baxendale's on his knees, looking under his car. His angry voice and body language suggests he can't find the bottle jack. When he gets to his feet and jabs a finger at Blazer Man, the constable intervenes.

"You won't get away with this," Baxendale calls, pointing at me.

"Calm down," Avril says, stepping in front of him. "You should be more concerned about Morgana. Your vet needs to examine her."

"I'll take her off your hands," I say.

He ignores me and attaches a lead to Morgana.

"You can't leave him in charge of the poor dog," Niamh says, watching as he tugs Morgana to her feet. "Look at him."

The constable makes calming gestures with his hands. "We could investigate further, Mrs Fisher, but then we'd have to interview witnesses and you never know what they might say."

She nods and steps back, allowing Baxendale to pass. She helps me flatten the empty water bottles and push them into a carrier bag, keeping an eye on Baxendale. When he drives past, he wishes me well with a middle finger before speeding off.

"I can't believe he's a teacher," Gemma says, waiting by the open doors of the Volvo.

I can't believe the bottle jack vanished. I want to thank Blazer Man, but he's gone. Once settled in the back of the car, I offer to buy Gemma a new jack.

"Forget it," she says, starting the car. "I didn't know I had one."

"You don't," Niamh says with more than a hint of irony. "Thank goodness someone's looking after you, Kent, or you'd be facing an assault charge."

I settle back and stretch my legs. My feet collide with something solid beneath Gemma's seat and I reach down. My fingers encounter something oily and metallic in a cloth.

"Must be my guardian angel," I say with a smile.

TWO

Back at my animal sanctuary, I breathe in the familiar smells and shield my eyes against the dipping sun as it casts long shadows over the land. My small slice of nature nestles at the foot of the South Downs, about half a mile down a bumpy track that leads to the busy A27. The village of Wilmington lies a mile to the west. Knots of woodland and bustling hedgerows shield me from the traffic noise and the encroaching housing estates of Tollingdon to the east.

It takes several trips up the stairs from the car to my flat above the barn to transfer the leftover food from the wake to the kitchen.

"Why did you bring so much back?" Niamh asks, catching her breath.

I slide the final tray of sandwiches into the fridge. "Why did you order so much?"

She picks up the kettle. "We're never going to eat all this."

"It's not for us."

She casts me a worried look. “You’re not going to feed it to the animals, surely?”

“I won’t if you stop slipping cocktail sausages to Columbo.” I reach under the table to ruffle the fur of my West Highland White Terrier, who’s still licking his lips. “Mike and I are going to sell the food at the farmers’ market tomorrow.”

It takes her a few seconds to realise I’m joking. While I may be suspended, I’m hardly going to breach the hygiene laws I enforce. “We have some children coming over tomorrow, so we’ll treat them to a party.”

She stares out of the window as she fills the kettle. She looks lost, caught between the funeral and an uncertain future. While she’s only seven years older than me, the laughter lines that radiate from her eyes and mouth seem deeper now. A frown’s embedded itself in her forehead, giving her an aggressive, almost threatening air. Even her Irish lilt has gone flat, depressed by deep sighs and melancholy silences.

The water floods over the top of the kettle. As she pulls the kettle away, water splashes over her skirt and shoes. She stares down, tears gathering in her eyes. I can only imagine the tangle of mixed emotions, threatening to burst out, but she manages to capture them all in one angry, but weary word.

“Damn!”

For two weeks she’s faced friends, well-wishers and the media with a stoic resolve and dignity that’s bordered on insensitivity. She’s busied herself, helping Frances with the animals, cleaning and disinfecting my home to within an inch of its life, and making lists of all the unfinished business she needs to resolve. William Kenneth Fisher died without a will, life insurance, or any tangible assets, thanks to the Blackjack tables. I keep hoping we'll uncover a secret stash of money or a lottery ticket for an unclaimed jackpot.

I'm dreaming, of course, like he did when he played cards.

I turn off the tap, place the kettle on the drainer and slide my arms around Niamh.

"Don't worry," I say. "I won't give all the cake to the children. I'll save some Victoria sponge for you."

After a few minutes of sobbing, the tears fade. She retrieves a tissue from under her sleeve and dabs the corners of her eyes, smearing mascara that's already run.

"I know I'm a burden," she says, "but I'll keep out of your way."

She's referring to Rebecca, who I met while solving the murder of Sydney Collins at Tombstone Adventure Park. She's young, attractive, has a terrific sense of humour and the sexiest Scouse accent.

So, why do I feel bored already?

"Don't worry," I say, taking control of the kettle. "She has a flat of her own."

"Will you be seeing her this evening?"

Rebecca's going to a hen party in Brighton. "No, I'm here to take care of you."

She kisses my cheek. "They breed us tough in Dungannon. I can easily lose myself in a pile of washing and ironing. You sure you want to be helping me with that?"

If I stick around, I might get some idea where she puts things. She's reorganised my wardrobes, linen cupboards and drawers, blitzed the bathroom and filled my freezers with meals. I dread to think what will happen if she starts on the sanctuary.

"Not that I can do much with your clothes," she says, handing me a couple of mugs. "They ought to go to the charity shop, but an antique dealer might be more appropriate."

She's referring to my electric blue shirt, which I refuse to part with.

"Why don't we go for some retail therapy tomorrow?" She laughs as my expression says more than my mouth could ever manage. "Seriously, Kent, you should make yourself scarce in case Colonel Witherington pops round. He pestered William at least three times before he got the message."

Once I've made the tea, she takes her mug to her room, trailed by Columbo. About half an hour later, she emerges in jeans and a sweatshirt and announces she's off to walk the dogs with Frances. In the kennels beneath my flat, we have four dogs for rehoming. Until recently, Columbo was the fifth. Though he lives with me now, he still enjoys his afternoon walks with the other dogs.

Alone in the kitchen with a fresh mug of tea, I sit at the table. The cakes remind me of Colonel Witherington's comment about catering. If he turns up, I'll ask him what he meant – not that I want him on my doorstep. Our politics are light years apart and I can't ignore how, as Leader of Downland District Council, he's implementing government spending cuts with such vigour. No doubt, my impending demise will contribute to the savings.

Or he could quash my suspension if I do his bidding.

While I consider the possibilities, I drift off, woken by the phone half an hour later.

"We need to talk," Gemma says in a stern tone. "I'll pick you up at six."

My stomach tightens as I recall the crazy moment in Tombstone Adventure Park. In the split second before I left to rescue William Fisher, I wondered whether I would return. As I stared into her dark brown eyes, wondering if I would ever look into them again, I told her I was hopelessly in love with her.

Then I almost got her killed.

I drag myself to the shower, remembering how I hovered outside her room at the hospital. Each time I went to see her, Richard was there. I couldn't face seeing them, holding hands, gazing into each other's eyes. When she was discharged, I drove over to her flat and found his car outside. No matter which day or time I called, he was there. One week became two and then it was the funeral.

Now she wants to talk.

I take a long shower, working out possible excuses, determined to explain away my foolish outburst as a moment of stress and panic. But within seconds my thoughts have drifted back seven years to the crazy week we spent together. While we showered together, Gemma told me she loved me.

The following morning I ran. I want to run again.

When she pulls into the yard at six, the sun's burning fiery streaks into the sky as it plunges behind the South Downs. Clouds will soon gather, determined to end the long, dry spell that stretches back into August. With any luck, we'll get enough rain to fill the water butts and replenish the underground storage tanks.

When I'm nervous, I think about practical things like this.

Niamh pulls away from the lounge window. "You never said Gemma was coming over."

"We're going out."

"Dressed like that?" She follows me to the kitchen. "We're definitely going shopping in Brighton tomorrow. You need to make a good impression on Monday."

"Niamh, it's a disciplinary hearing, not a job interview."

She shakes her head as if I'm a hopeless case. "Where are you going with Gemma, in case I need to contact you?"

In the pocket of my fleece, I find a treat and toss it to Columbo. "You have my number."

She puts on her frail voice. "But what if I have an accident while I'm on my own?"

"Then you'd be better ringing an ambulance."

I head down the stairs to the yard below. Gemma's waiting, enveloped in lengthening shadows. She's dressed in tight jeans and a pastel blouse, with a stylish crochet cardigan to mask the scarring to her upper arm. As usual, she's wearing diamanté sandals with no arch support.

I should tell her how lovely she looks, especially as she's swept her hair back on one side to reveal her slender neck and an ear pierced with a diamond stud. That's new. A present from her fiancé, no doubt. Her dark eyes seem to glow beneath long lashes as the majesty of the Downs weaves its spell on her.

"I love it here," she murmurs.

"Not seeing Richard this evening?"

"Boys' club," she replies.

"I didn't know the Lodge met on Friday."

"Let's not discuss your prejudices," she says, getting into the car. "I know that doesn't leave much to talk about, so maybe you could listen for once."

She grimaces as she reaches for the seatbelt. She pauses, grits her teeth, and then stretches again. Once she has the buckle in her fingers, she slides the belt across her slim waist.

"Arm still sore?"

"What do you think?" She starts the car and pulls away. "No Rebecca tonight?"

"You heard then."

"I heard her proposition you at the hospital. The door was open."

She accelerates down the lane that winds its way to the A27. The Volvo creaks and groans as it swings through the bends, scuffing the verges at least twice. I'm not sure why she's transformed into Lewis Hamilton, but I have to admit to a moment of concern when she brakes late at the junction with the A27. We lurch to a stop inches from the stream of traffic pelting towards Brighton.

I pull on the handbrake. "Something bothering you?"

She turns and glares. "Why didn't you visit me in hospital?"

"I didn't want to intrude on you and Richard. He was always there."

"Not all the time."

"He was during visiting hours."

She sighs. "You could have rung or sent me a text."

She rams the gear lever into first and revs the engine. She looks both ways, releases the handbrake and swings across the road and right towards Tollingdon.

"In case you're wondering, my arm looks like someone's run a cheese grater over it, but the charity shops are queuing up for my vest tops."

The traffic lights turn green as we approach and she takes a right onto the road that leads to Eastbourne, five miles away. At the next lights, she takes the right hand lane for Jevington and the Eight Bells, I'm guessing. I often meet my friend, Mike Turner, there. He likes to chat up the young barmaids. They like to make him think he's in with a chance.

It's difficult to appreciate the flint cottages as we speed along the narrow road. We fly past the pub and head out of the village into the dark, where the sky blends into the land in an impenetrable black, punctuated only by the headlights of distant cars.

Maybe she's taking me to Birling Gap or the cliffs so she can throw me off.

After a couple of miles, the road rises into Friston, which commands views over the South Downs to the coast during the day. At night, there's a sprinkle of lights, flickering in the distance.

When Gemma takes the sharp left onto Willingdon Old Road, I wonder whether she's taking me to meet Richard. As a solicitor, he could probably afford one of the grand houses. Or maybe he lives with his parents.

"Colonel Witherington's expecting us," she says, easing off the accelerator.

"Why didn't you tell me?"

"Would you have come?"

I smile. "Of course not."

"Aren't you in the least bit curious about what happened to his wife?"

I'm relieved she's not going to ask me if I'm hopelessly in love with her. "I'm curious to know why you are," I say.

She drives slowly, checking the illuminated houses, set back from the road. While many have security lights along their drives, not all of them have nameplates at the roadside.

"We have a list of mobile caterers on our database."

So that's what the Colonel meant by catering. "He thinks his wife ran off with someone who cooks burgers?"

Gemma taps her nose a couple of times. "I thought you weren't interested."

THREE

I've passed 'Belmont' many times on my runs over the Downs, but I didn't know Colonel Witherington lived there. Though it sounds palatial, it's a modest house tucked among the trees to isolate it from the newer properties. Flint walls fortify either side of the garden to stop people and dogs wandering through. At the front, security lights spring into action as we drive onto the gravel. They're mounted on a two storey annex, which has a double garage on the ground floor. I doubt if the gleaming Nissan Micra parked there belongs to the Colonel.

We walk the few yards to the house, which has solid flint walls, reinforced at the corners with earth-red quoins, which also run around the Edwardian-style casement windows. Bars, painted white, protect the windows against intruders, or people jumping out of the first floor. Tall chimneys, crowned with pots, thrust through the orange roof tiles like shotgun barrels. Even the sweet scent of a climbing rose can't disguise the rugged oak beams of a robust porch, protected by small cannons on either side of the sturdy door. With its huge iron hinges and studs, it looks like it came from a castle.

The ‘No cold callers’ sign seems rather ironic.

Gemma runs her fingers along the rough oak. “Richard showed me details of a house not far from here with six bedrooms, a games room and an indoor swimming pool.”

“He must be doing well if you’re thinking of living out here.”

She laughs. “He was doing the conveyancing.”

“You mean his articled clerk was.”

“Just like me, doing all the paperwork and running around,” she says, tugging an imaginary forelock. “Would you like me to ring the bell, master?”

Moments later, a thin woman, right out of an Agatha Christie novel, opens the door. Dressed in a Tweed suit and sensible shoes, she’s in her 60s, with silver hair wound into a bun and eyes that miss nothing. She studies us over the top of half-moon spectacles.

“I’m Miss Hewitt, the Colonel’s housekeeper,” she says in a mellow Scottish accent. “You must be Mr Fisher and Miss Dean. The Colonel’s in the conservatory.”

We brush past the Barbour jackets and coats on the oak hooks, and sidestep the walking boots and wellingtons that nuzzle up on a mud-free rack. Unless the Colonel has small feet and a taste for pink wellingtons, the footwear can’t be his.

“I get enough exercise managing this place,” Miss Hewitt says, noticing my interest. “They belong to the mistress of the house.”

She guides us into a vast reception area that leads to a magnificent staircase lined with carved newel posts and balustrades. It doglegs to a gallery that runs around all four walls. On either side of the room, open panelled doors reveal glimpses of spacious rooms, decorated in Georgian reds and yellows, with polished parquet floors and oriental rugs. The plush oak and mahogany furniture reeks of polish.

"Awesome," Gemma says for the third or fourth time.

It's a good word to describe the chandeliers that seem to float above us. They cast an even light, which leaves few shadows on the white walls, framed with oak beams and enhanced by family portraits and pictures of battle scenes. I run my fingers along a dust free oak dresser with chunky drawers, pierced by solid metal handles. Even the suit of armour gleams like it was polished this afternoon.

Gemma peers into the dining room, dominated by a long mahogany table with seating for twelve people. "Awesome."

"Och, we had some dinner parties, I can tell you." Miss Hewitt smiles as she remembers. "Your father came here on many occasions, Mr Fisher. I was saddened to hear of his passing. He was a gentleman. One of a kind."

I wonder what she'll think when the truth comes out.

We follow Miss Hewitt past the staircase and through a door that leads into a lounge, which overlooks the rear garden through casement windows and French doors. An inglenook fireplace, large enough to accommodate a rugby team, dominates the wall opposite. Beneath the soot-stained oak beam stands a wood burning stove, flanked by symmetrical pyramids of chopped logs. The pots of pampas plumes and a sturdy aspidistra attempt to disguise the emptiness of the inglenook, but it still beckons me across the polished floorboards. They creak and groan like old sinews as we walk past plush armchairs, arranged in a semicircle to face a large flat screen television. Smaller chandeliers cast their even glow over walls lined with more portraits and battle pictures. All we need is a grand piano for a sing song.

"Awesome."

I whisper in Gemma's ear. "Just like the electricity bill for all this lighting. It must come to more than my salary."

"I didn't know you were that well paid," she says.

A door to our right leads into a smaller room, filled with stuffed animals and birds in glass cabinets and a stag's head mounted on the wall. I inch around the tiger skin on the floor, glaring at the muskets and rifles that inflicted cruelty and death in the name of sport.

"Not now," Gemma says, tugging my arm.

She leads me through more French doors into a huge conservatory, built around a framework of oak beams that wouldn't look amiss in a Tudor cottage. Earthenware pots host sprawling Swiss cheese plants, bayonet–sharp Mother in Law's Tongue, and a small lemon tree with polished leaves.

The Colonel rises from a cane sofa, disturbing the sleeping Bassett hound beside him. His velvet smoking jacket, trimmed with black collar and belt, hangs loosely over the open neck shirt and cravat he was wearing earlier. His black trousers wrinkle over shiny shoes.

He gestures to the sofa opposite. "Tea for our visitors, Miss Hewitt."

"Do you have a preference?" she asks. "Earl Grey, Darjeeling, chamomile?"

"Builder's tea for me," I reply.

"And me," Gemma says, going over to the Bassett. "What's your name then?"

Surprisingly, the dog doesn't reply. He looks at her through bloodshot eyes and then settles his head back on his front paws.

"Monty's antisocial." The Colonel sits and pats the dog on the head. "Ignored me for 14 years now. Probably slept for 12 of them."

His clipped military sentences suggest he's more at ease delivering reports than engaging in conversation. I suspect he spends most of his time alone, based on the lack of family photos or anything to suggest his wife, Daphne, ever lived here. I wonder how she felt about such a masculine environment, maintained by the organised and efficient Miss Hewitt.

Gemma sits beside me and places her small white handbag on her lap. When her knee brushes against mine, I ignore the tingle of electricity and look out at the garden, illuminated by ground lights. "You have a fine show of anemones, Colonel."

"Keen gardener, are you?"

"Kent loves digging around," Gemma replies. "Was your wife a keen gardener?"

The Colonel plucks a manila folder from a small glass table beside him. "Everything you need to know is here."

I shake my head when he thrusts the folder at me. "I haven't agreed to help."

"Agree terms first, you mean? Good man. Bring Daphne's killer to justice and you can name your price."

"That's a job for the police and Crown Prosecution Service, as you well know."

"Then just find the man, dammit, and name your price."

"I don't want your money."

"Payment in kind, you mean?" He strokes his moustache the way Blofeld strokes his cat. "Consider your problem at work resolved."

I shake my head. "I'll sort my own problems, thank you."

"Will you?" His back becomes ramrod straight, his voice domineering, as if he's addressing an insolent squaddie. "Seen the evidence against you?"

Why am I surprised that he knows more about my disciplinary than I do?

He counts on his gnarled fingers. "Illegal entry into an empty property. Taking a member of the public on an official inspection. Breach of confidentiality. Failing to attend briefings," he says, chuckling at this one. "That's the single-mindedness and tenacity I want you to apply to my problem."

"I haven't said I'll help."

"Then why are you here?"

"You mentioned catering," Gemma says, easing the folder from his fingers. "What did you mean?"

Miss Hewitt enters, pushing a small trolley that bears a teapot and some delicate looking cups with blue floral designs. There's a matching bowl with sugar lumps, two small jugs containing milk, and a second, smaller pot of tea. Royal Worcester, I guess, having watched too many editions of the Antiques Road Show on Sunday evenings.

How sad is that?

"Yorkshire's finest for our guests," she says, picking up a strainer. She pours the dark tea into the cups and looks to Gemma. "Skimmed or semi-skimmed milk?"

"Dammit, woman, you can't offer our guests coloured water."

"Skimmed," Gemma replies. "I rather like the taste."

"And me," I say. I rather like the absence of fat.

Once tea is poured and the cups passed around, Miss Hewitt leaves, saying she'll pop back shortly to see if we need anything further. I'm delighted she brewed the tea strong. I've never understood people who dip their teabag into milky water for a few seconds.

"Catering," the Colonel says, settling back with his cup and saucer. "Classic case of fingers burned. My Daphne set up a business with a man called Colin Miller. My contribution was £20,000." His hand shakes, spilling tea into the saucer. "He ran off with the money and my wife."

"What kind of catering?" Gemma asks.

He shrugs. "Your domain not mine. You have records."

If Daphne or Miller registered the food business with the council, we have. "You can check on Monday, Gemma."

"Yes, master. Would you like to scrutinise the file now?"

While we drink our tea, we flick through the contents of the manila folder, which contains letters and reports from Sussex Police and a few short cuttings from the *Tollingdon Tribune*. The details are factual and minimal, with only a physical description of Daphne Witherington. Apart from her walking boots, I've seen nothing in the house to suggest she lived here.

"Colonel, was there anything unusual or different about the day your wife disappeared?"

He jerks out of his reverie, spilling more tea. He places the cup and saucer on the table and stares at the damp patch on his trousers. "Golf club on Tuesdays. I don't play anymore, but I'm treasurer. Had lunch there as per, came home about four."

He rubs at the stain on his crotch. "My Daphne played bridge. Usually came home between five or six. At seven, I rang Dorothy Forsythe," he says, looking up. "Daphne cried off. Tummy upset. Never saw her again."

"Didn't you realise she'd gone when you got home and found her things missing?" I ask.

His face creases with pain as he coughs. "She only took her handbag and the clothes she was wearing."

The coughing intensifies and he doubles up, rousing Monty. Miss Hewitt rushes in with some kind of spray. Though he tries to fend her off, she talks him round as if he's a little child. The spray seems to have some effect, but the Colonel's pale with pain. Monty drops to the floor and slinks off to the study. Gemma and I follow.

"I can cope," the Colonel protests between rasps.

"You need to rest," Miss Hewitt says. "Let me see your visitors out and then I'll settle you down."

"Leave me alone, woman!"

I hear something thud against the double glazed window and drop to the floor. Miss Hewitt joins us, explaining how he gets frustrated and short tempered because of his poor health.

"Let me take your cups," she says.

"Why don't we bring them to the kitchen? You can tell me about Daphne."

Miss Hewitt glances back. "I need to make the Colonel comfortable."

"We'll only take a minute."

"Do you really think you can find her, Mr Fisher?"

"With your help," I say, ushering her around the tiger skin. "Maybe you can show me her room."

"I'm not sure I should do that."

"You want us to help the Colonel, don't you?"

"I want to know that Mrs Witherington's all right."

She leads the way to the kitchen. Maybe it's the heat from the Aga, but there's a warm, homely feel that's absent from the rest of the house. Dried hops hang from a dado rail that runs around the room. Their golden foliage complements the oak of the cupboards and Welsh dresser and the rich lustre of the parquet floor.

The kitchen at Downland Manor looked like this when I arrived from Manchester. After ten years in a damp basement flat with my embittered mother, the manor seemed vast. While it had a cold, efficient feel like this place, the kitchen smelt of hot buns and cinnamon. Flour coated the table, the worktops and Niamh. She was 24, married to a politician over twice her age, and as sexy as hell to my 17 year old eyes.

With a smile, I stroll over to the bookcase. It's too much to expect a copy of Mrs Beeton's *Book of Household Management*, but there's a healthy collection of English cuisine.

"You have a delightful kitchen, Miss Hewitt."

She places the crockery beside the enamelled Belfast sink. "Please, call me Alice."

"Because you're a wonder?"

"That's what my parents said." She blushes and coughs into her hand. "They had me late in life, I mean. They thought they'd never have children."

"How sweet," Gemma says, peering through the window. "Is that your car?"

"Yes, I live above the garage. I asked Colonel Witherington to convert it into an apartment when Mrs Witherington came to live here."

Gemma turns her attention to the fridge magnets. "How did you feel about the marriage?"

"I was pleased Colonel Witherington had found someone at last." Alice checks the temperature from the tap and pushes a bowl under the flow. "I didn't feel threatened, if that's what you're thinking."

The lady's protesting too much. "How long have you been with the Colonel?"

"Nigh on 40 years. I was housekeeper to the previous owner and the Colonel kept me on. I've lived here since I was eighteen."

And never married, it seems. "Did you ever feel tempted to spread your wings?"

"I've always preferred the company of a good book." She laughs as she washes the cups. "Men want to make plans for you, don't they? That would never do."

"Maybe you could take us to Daphne's room," I say, before she gets too immersed in the washing up.

She nods, dries her hands on a tea towel, and then leads us up a steep, narrow staircase at the back of the kitchen.

"Alice, were you here on the day Mrs Witherington went missing?" Gemma asks.

"I go shopping in Eastbourne on Tuesday mornings. She was here when I left and I assumed she was playing bridge when I returned."

"Did she have a car?"

Alice shakes her head. "The Colonel took her everywhere, but on Tuesdays she got a taxi."

There was no reference to checking local taxi companies in the folder.

She opens a door that leads to a short landing. The door on the right hides a bathroom, I imagine, judging by the smell of disinfectant. The corridor leads onto the gallery that overlooks the reception area. Up here, close to the chandeliers, I'm amazed at how clean they look.

"Maybe Mr Miller gave her a lift," Gemma says.

Alice gives her a cold stare. "He never visited. Well, not to my knowledge."

"Not even to collect the money the Colonel offered him?"

"He gave the money to Mrs Witherington." She stops at a door painted pastel blue, her hand on the knob. "I suggested we could run the business from here, using my kitchen."

"Why didn't she?" I ask.

"Regulations, Mr Fisher. Your province, I believe."

Pastel heaven greets us when we step into the room, dominated by primrose walls and carpet. From the wisps of net curtains to the trims around the bedding, lace adds a delicate edge to the soft tones. With teddy bears on the pillows and an easel by the window, it could be a young girl's room. But the watercolour paintings of local Downland scenes were painted by Daphne Witherington, not a child. I count at least 20 paintings that include views of the Seven Sisters on the coast and landscapes along the Cuckmere River, winding like a blue ribbon between the chalk headlands. Familiar scenes from Alfriston and Jevington High Streets contrast with the fields of poppies or the stark quiffs of the hawthorn bushes in winter.

"She's talented," I say, studying the unfinished painting of a flint barn and paddock on the easel. The bristles of the brushes on the windowsill have set solid with paint. The paint box and rest of her brushes are spotless, reclining in a jam jar.

"Mrs Witherington was an art teacher once." Alice straightens one of the paintings on the wall. "Colonel Witherington organised an exhibition at the Towner Art Gallery in Eastbourne for her."

I wonder what else he organised.

"She saw beauty in everything," Gemma says, pointing to a picture of the Long Man of Wilmington. The chalk outline of a man holding two staffs looks benign as it stands guard on the hills above the village.

I've run across the hills many times and the slopes are brutal.

"Indeed." Alice straightens the teddy bears on the double bed. She runs a finger along the delicate ironwork of the bedstead, checking for dust. "She believed in fairies and magic and the eternity of the soul."

I only believe in what I can hold in my hands.

I slip past the trunk at the end of the bed and open the louvered doors to reveal a walk-in closet. Floral dresses line one side. Most are cotton and delicate. All have price tags attached.

Gemma squeezes in beside me and pulls open a drawer filled with lingerie. "I'm surprised you didn't spot these."

"Please don't disturb anything," Alice says, a worried look on her face. "I really shouldn't have let you in here. Colonel Witherington doesn't want anything disturbed."

"Did Daphne wear any of these dresses?" I ask.

"No, she preferred those leggings women seem so fond of these days. She wore them with old jumpers and blouses, telling Colonel Witherington that no one wore gowns and dresses for dinner."

"So, who bought the dresses?" I ask, knowing the answer.

She slides back a door on the opposite side of the closet to reveal sumptuous evening gowns, protected by clear plastic wrappers. "The Colonel gave her everything she could want."

It looks and sounds like he treated her as one of his hunting trophies. Only she refused to comply, wearing what she liked, leaving him in the house while she painted and played bridge. She slept in a separate room, refused to wear the dresses he bought, and took his money to start a catering business – or not, as the case may be.

"Were they happy?" I ask.

"Are you asking me if I think she ran away with another man?"

"Did she?" Gemma asks.

"Colonel Witherington can be demanding," Alice replies, beckoning us out of the closet, "but he's generous to a fault."

I step out of the closet and glance around the room, not sure what I'm missing. The Colonel's preserved the room as it was on the day she left. Maybe he hopes she'll return to finish her painting. But why would she if he wanted her to be something she wasn't? Apart from the teddy bears and paintings there's nothing personal in the room. Even the clothes in the closet are not really hers. Where are the photographs of her family and friends?

"Thank you, Alice," I say, heading for the door. "We've taken enough of your time. Let the Colonel know we'll be in touch."

She hesitates, as if she wants to say something, and then escorts us to the front door. When we reach the car, Gemma says, "I don't think there's a catering business, do you?"

"I want to know why she didn't clean and dry her brushes before she left."

"What's that got to do with anything?"

"She loved painting, Gemma. Why did she leave her brushes and an unfinished painting behind?"

FOUR

On Saturday afternoon, I'm distracted by the cries and laughter of the children returning from their ramble in the woodland and foothills of the Downs. Frances leads them home, her beaded dreadlocks swinging in time with her arms as her Doc Martens pound the flinty path. She's surrounded by boys, all talking at once as they jostle and prod each other with sticks. Niamh, in designer leggings and running jacket, follows at the back with the girls, who are more orderly, though still talking over each other. During the morning, they had a couple of hours exploring the sanctuary. They learned about the dogs we rehome, the injured badgers, foxes and small mammals we nurse back to health, and the horses, donkeys and goats we rescue from either the slaughterhouse or a slow death from neglect.

It's a little after one and the children will be hungry.

Columbo, who's asleep on the bed, jumps to his feet and barks in one brisk movement. After a glance at me, he barks once more, rising on his hind legs to look out of the window. I lift him up and he settles in my arms to watch the children, the growling noise in his throat becoming a whine as he starts to wriggle and struggle, eager to join the party.

"You want to go outside?"

I set him down and follow the sound of scampering paws to the kitchen. After letting him out, I switch on the oven and fetch the sausage rolls from the fridge. Moments later, Columbo flies back through the door. He stops at the table, rising on his hind legs to sniff the food.

Frances follows him in, her cheeks glistening. She grins and says, "I hope you've washed your hands. Niamh will be checking your fingernails."

"How's she doing?"

"She's strict with the children, but every one of them washed and sanitised their hands after petting the goats and donkeys. You trained her well."

If I know Niamh, she'll take over the sanctuary the way she's taken over my wardrobes. "How are you getting on?"

"Fine. She's a big help. She's even …" Frances pauses and looks down, her voice almost a whisper. "She's taking me shopping this afternoon."

She picks at some fluff on a khaki-coloured top that's almost faded to a dusky white. Combined with combat trousers, this is what she wears, whether working or off duty. Not that she goes out much, unless you count buying animal feed and bedding or delivering animals and birds to more specialised rescue centres.

Then I recall the Downland Ranger who flirted with her earlier in the week. "Have you met someone?"

She raises her head and looks at me, unable to stop a self-conscious smile.

"You'll want a rise next to pay for the clothes."

I say it as a joke, but she works for virtually nothing as a volunteer. She lives in a caravan on site and sleeps in my spare room during the cold winter months. She has no family, having grown up in care, and like me, prefers animals to people. Her whole life revolves around the sanctuary, but sooner or later she had to take an interest in someone. She's far too serious for a 20 year old.

"I got a bonus," she says, fiddling with her braids. "From Miles. I mean, Mr Birchill. I didn't ask for it or nothing. I thought if you'd accepted a bonus, why shouldn't I?" She stares at me and then sighs. "He hasn't given you a bonus, has he?"

Birchill gave me money to cover the sanctuary's running costs for a few months. At the end of October, he wants to discuss the future. He means a proper access road that extends beyond the sanctuary to the woodland where he plans to build a holiday village. I've opposed the idea for the last five years, refusing ridiculous sums of money to sell my land.

Turns out he owned my land all along.

Once again, William Fisher deceived me. He didn't parcel off my land from Downland Manor next door. He put up everything as security against a loan he would never pay back, handing Birchill a country estate to add to his casinos.

"Go and buy some clothes," I say, placing a tray of sausage rolls into the oven. "I'll look after things. Nothing happens on Saturday afternoons."

"I'll be back in time to feed and walk the dogs."

The last of the children leave about two thirty. Minutes later, Niamh and Frances head out of the door, leaving me to clear the disposable plates, cups and cutlery. Columbo sticks to my heels, nudging the backs of my legs from time to time, hoping for leftovers. He looks at me as if he hasn't eaten for a month, even though Niamh feeds him enough treats to double his body weight. I dread to think how much she'll feed him when I'm back at work next week.

That's on the basis I thwart attempts to dismiss me for gross misconduct and insubordination. While my investigation into Syd Collins' work accident was flawed, everything hinges on whether my boss, Danni, wants to get rid of me. Though I'm not a member of Unison, our union rep, Lucy, has offered to defend me, but I don't want her, or anyone else in the council, knowing too much about my escapades.

"Gemma won't talk," I tell Columbo, more to convince myself than anything. "That's the trouble. Neither of us want to talk about what matters, do we?"

He tilts his head from side to side, listening to every word. If only he could give me an opinion.

By the time I've washed up and cleared everything away, it's gone three. Columbo dozes on my bed while I sit at the computer, reading my presentation for Monday. I'm so impressed I print a copy and stride around the bedroom, doing my best Perry Mason. Columbo watches and listens for a short while before jumping down from the bed, unimpressed by my American accent.

"You're right," I tell him. "Human Remains won't be moved by passionate pleas."

Bernard Doolittle, the aptly named Head of Human Resources, is an expert on policies and procedures. It makes no difference to him whether the media brand me a super sleuth, whether my father died, or whether I'm too good an officer to lose. He'll concentrate on whether I breached council policy and rules.

That's what I'm hoping anyway.

A noise outside draws me to the window. In the yard below, two young children are running around. The boy is chasing a girl, trying to beat her with a stick. Then he spots a wood pigeon on the fence and tries to decapitate it as it flies off. Close to the entrance, a young woman with jet black hair, dressed in leather trousers and jacket, locks an old BMW with pink alloy wheels. She takes a thoughtful draw on a cigarette, tosses it to the ground, and then spits into the bushes.

Columbo races down the steps, pausing only to pee on the corner of the barn before running towards the children. He stops when the boy brandishes the stick like a sword.

"Here, doggy," the boy calls, tucking the stick behind his back. He stretches out a hand. "I've got a surprise for you."

"You should never taunt dogs," I call, rushing down the stairs. "They could bite you."

The boy looks up at me with the malevolent, brooding stare of a teenager, even though he looks about eight or nine. Chocolate smears embellish his chin and a Star Wars t-shirt that's seen better days.

"He's friendly though," I say as the girl approaches. "His name's Columbo."

The boy wrinkles his nose. "Why?"

"He likes the name. Do you like your name?"

He thinks for a moment, shrugs and turns away.

My natural rapport with children never fails. Thankfully, the mother, who looks just as bored as her children, wanders up. She has dark, insolent eyes and an expression that says, ‘what are you going to do about it?’ Her fingers, tipped with black fingernails, adjust the piercing above her left eye.

“Where’s the party then?” she asks in a voice that could curdle milk.

“It finished over an hour ago.”

She fixes me with a stare. “What d’ya mean, finished?”

“Finished as in ended, stopped, all over.”

“Don’t get smart with me. That’s smart as in superior, patronising and condescending.” She smirks, obviously pleased with her riposte. “I paid good money to come to the party.”

We both know that’s rubbish. The parents make regular donations to the sanctuary throughout the year, more than covering the cost of a party.

“In that case you’ll have a ticket.”

“What ticket?”

“The one that says the party runs from ten in the morning until two.”

“I promised Sam and Charlie they could stroke the animals. Sam was ill and missed the school visit this week.”

I should tell her to come back during the week, but her daughter looks up at me with angelic blue eyes.

“Would you like the special tour?” I ask her.

She nods. Sam whoops and swooshes the stick through the air, startling Columbo. He growls and the girl rushes behind her mother.

“You need to keep that dog under control,” the mother says.

I could say the same about her son. “Sam, you need to take care around animals. If you startle them, they can kick or bite.”

"Whatever. You got any snakes?"

I'm saved by the phone, ringing in the kitchen. "I'll be back in a minute," I say, scooping up Columbo. "Wait here for me."

Once in the kitchen, I close the door so Columbo can't escape and pick up the phone. Gemma wants to know if I've looked at Daphne Witherington's folder.

"I haven't had a chance."

"Do you want me to pop over and take a look?"

Again, her curiosity intrigues me. "Are you after my super sleuth crown?"

"I thought we could get a head start."

"It's not a priority."

"Not for you, but I can check the files Monday morning while you … you're busy."

"That reminds me," I say. "Cast your mind back to the day we snuck into Collins' house. I know you didn't tell Danni, but did she question you about it?"

"No, she never asked."

"Did she ask anything else about that afternoon?"

"No," she replies after a pause. "She said nothing was my fault as you were lead officer. Are you still trying to find out who told her?"

"Just covering all bases. Look, I've got a tour to do. Frances and Niamh are out buying clothes."

"Frances never goes shopping. Unless she's taken a shine to you now you're a hero."

Below, the mother's also on her phone. I can't see her children.

"See you Monday, Gemma."

I shut Columbo in the kitchen and hurry down the stairs. "Where are your children?"

The mother blows cigarette smoke down her nostrils and turns her back. Hearing Sam whoop, I hurry around the back of the barn and spot him in the paddock, swishing his stick at a retreating goat. He ignores my call and sets off after the goat. I vault the gate and intercept him within a few strides. As he raises the stick, I wrench it from his hand.

"Didn't I tell you to be careful with animals? Now, let's get you out of here."

He kicks me in the shin. It hurts far more than expected, allowing him to land a second kick. As he takes aim once more, I sidestep and sweep him off the ground. He's heavier than I expected, especially when he kicks and struggles. His flailing arms and legs catch me a couple of times as I carry him to the gate. His sister, who's stroking one of the older goats, runs over.

"Let him go," she cries, wrapping her arms around my thigh.

I drag her with me and manage to open the gate, losing my grip on Sam, who stumbles out and falls to the ground.

"Get your hands off my effing kids!"

The mother flings her cigarette to one side and rushes over. Charlie rushes to her, hiding behind her legs. When the mother looks at Sam, he clutches his arm and bursts into tears, setting off Charlie.

"No one assaults my kids," the mother says, pointing an accusing finger.

I take my time closing the gate, determined to keep my anger in check. "If one of the goats had turned on Sam, you'd be calling an ambulance right now. And don't let

Charlie put her thumb in her mouth. She needs to wash her hands. She stroked the goats."

As if to spite me, Charlie slides most of her fist into her mouth. The mother drags Charlie's hand away. "If my kids are ill, mister, I'll have you."

"Just wash her hands," I say. "Sam's too. There's a basin by the barn."

Sam cries out. "Mum, he hit me. You saw him."

Before the mother can shoot more vitriol, Columbo bounds around the corner. Charlie screams and clings to her mother. Sam stumbles to his feet as Columbo homes in, growling and baring his teeth. I manage to grab him as the mother aims a kick.

"You should wash your hands and go," I say, struggling to restrain Columbo as he growls and wriggles to break free.

"You'll pay for this." The mother ushers her children away. Sam turns and gives me a malicious grin that makes me shudder. This child attacks animals for pleasure.

"Don't forget to wash your hands," I call as they reach the basin.

She acknowledges with her middle digit, almost colliding with Birchill, who steps out from behind the barn. At least I know how Columbo got out.

"Was it something you said?" Birchill asks when I reach him.

He's dressed in his standard black jeans and shirt, with the sleeves rolled up to his elbows. His polished shoes reflect the sun and his mirrored sunglasses hide his eyes. Since he dumped the knuckleduster of gold rings and cut his dyed hair short, he looks more businessman than cowboy.

But he still wanders in as if he owns the place – which he does, of course.

If it wasn't for the fact I need his money to run the place, I'd …

I don't know what I'd do.

He ruffles Columbo's fur. "He shot out of the kitchen like a bullet. What's going on?"

We watch the mother bundle her children into the back of her BMW, slamming the door behind them. She's texting as she climbs in behind the wheel. With an angry roar of the engine, she spins the wheels and squeals away, missing Birchill's Mercedes by inches.

"What were you doing, going into my flat?"

"Columbo was barking and scratching at the door. I couldn't see anyone around so I let him out. Where are Frances and Niamh?"

"Why did you give Frances a bonus?"

He gestures towards the kitchen. "She's got some great ideas for this place."

At the top of the steps, he goes straight into the kitchen and pulls a bone-shaped biscuit from his pocket. He's on a charm offensive. Bonus for Frances, treat for Columbo. I can't wait to find out what he's going to give me. Grief, I imagine.

"What do you want?" I ask.

He checks the kettle for water. "Tea?"

While he makes tea, he runs through his plans for a carbon neutral holiday village. His architect is sourcing the latest green innovations and technologies, including earth source heat pumps, sheep wool thermal insulation, and reed bed sewerage systems. He wants to power the site using solar panels and wind turbines, discreetly located, of course.

"There's nothing discreet about a solar farm," I say. "Unless you plan to site the panels underground."

He hands me my tea. "I can see why you wound that woman up," he says, a hint of frustration in his voice. "Look, we both know I can build the village at a fraction of the cost using conventional methods."

I look through the window at the woodland he wants to ruin. "You could throw me out tomorrow and save even more money."

"Or we can work together to build something ground breaking and original." He continues to watch me closely as he sips his tea. "Wouldn't that be better?"

I wish he'd get out of my life, but that's not likely now he thinks he's my father. A simple DNA test would settle the matter, but it might prove he's right. Without the test, there's always hope.

"Why don't you build your access road and leave me to run this place?"

"I can't have paying guests passing this ramshackle collection of old barns." He pauses and smiles. "Why don't we make it part of the village experience?"

Columbo paws his leg, after another treat.

"Why can't you leave the woods as they are? How much money do you need?"

"It's not about money." He takes a sip of tea before continuing. "I built everything I have to show the world what the son of a lowly groom could achieve. Nothing else mattered. Now I have someone to leave it to, I want to do things right."

“Then give me the land and let me run the sanctuary.”

“Hey, I know it’s not easy and I’m not expecting you to like me,” he says, sitting at the table, “but at least let me help you. We could start with your disciplinary hearing.”

Now I know why he’s here. “You’re offering to use your wealth and influence?”

He shakes his head. “I have something far more devious in mind.”

FIVE

Kelly looks like a blousy barmaid, with thick blonde hair tumbling over her shoulders, plump red lips and big blue eyes, crowned with false lashes you could shelter beneath. She flirts shamelessly and plays the dumb blonde routine to perfection. Her wide-eyed naivety encourages senior male managers and councillors to tell her more than they should. During her interview, Bernard Doolittle asked her why she wanted to work in local government.

"It doesn't pay as well as lap dancing," she replied, "but you get your own chair."

She closes the door and saunters across Danni's office, her scarlet stilettos sinking into the carpet. She reaches the sofa where I'm sitting and stops to straighten her short black skirt.

"Danni will go nuts if she finds you here." A sly smile creeps over her lips. "Or are you hoping to unsettle her before the hearing?"

That's what I like about Kelly. She's one of the smartest women I know. Her disguise is so good, no one realises she's never set foot in a lap dancing club.

"I need to strike first," I reply.

"You make it sound like a war, Kent."

"It's not one I started."

"You reckon?" she asks, sitting on the armrest. "You're too used to getting your way, lover. But now you're father's gone, a bit of humble pie won't go astray, even if it makes you choke."

She loosens my tie. "You need to embrace power dressing, Kent. Wear a sharp suit, not this old jacket and trousers. Buy some long-sleeved shirts with cufflinks, but not the two-for-a-fiver ones from the supermarket. Finish it off with a smart tie and a discreet knot."

She's more or less repeated what Niamh said an hour ago, but I only need one suit. Short-sleeved shirts are more comfortable and practical in summer. And I already own three ties - black for funerals, blue for interviews, council meetings and court cases, and my Scooby Doo and Shaggy tie for people with no sense of humour.

"You know my money goes into the sanctuary."

"Sure," she says, undoing the knot, "but Danni will dress to impress, especially as Dr Doolittle has the hots for her."

He'll be out in the cold if I can circumvent the hearing. I glance at the door, knowing Danni could walk in at any moment. I whisper in Kelly's ear, explaining what I want her to do.

She sighs. "You're not going to tell me why, are you?"

"I may not need your help, but …"

"I love it when you get devious, Kent."

She knots my tie and slides it up tight to my collar. She holds it there like a noose, staring into my eyes. "And while

I have your undivided attention, lover, lose the Hush Puppies."

My hands go to her waist. "We could have so much fun, Kelly."

She wriggles free and gets to her feet. "We will when you grow up."

I should never try to get the better of Kelly. "Say, can you check our records for a mobile caterer called *Grub on the Go*?"

While I doubt it ever existed, it's the name of the business Colin Miller set up with Daphne Witherington, according to the Colonel's file.

"I'll check food registrations, closed premises records, and enquiries," Kelly says, heading for the door. "Just like Gemma asked me to."

With a little wave of her fingers, she's gone.

I get to my feet and check my appearance in the mirror. My tie looks so much smarter, thanks to Kelly. Maybe I should take her advice and grow up instead of pining after Gemma.

I'm tempted to take a sweet from the bowl in the middle of the oval meeting table to quell the hollow feeling in my stomach. Why do I feel nervous when I have an answer for every question? Maybe it's the ill-feeling I'll leave in my wake. Maybe I'm worried that Danni knows something I don't.

I wander over to her Motivational Pinboard, fixed to the wall behind her desk and executive chair. The pinboard contains quotes from her desk calendar. She types the quotes on sheets of A4 and posts them for us to read when summoned.

'You never get a second chance to make a first impression' remains her favourite. She points me to it at least once a day – more if I'm paying homage to Scooby Doo.

"Everything in its place and a place for everything," I say, tempted to move something on her desk. A docking station and monitor, with keyboard and mouse neatly stashed where the laptop should be, occupy the centre. In the right hand corner, her internet phone and message pad align to the edge of the desk. A Downland District Council pen and pencil are poised to one side of the pad. Two letter trays occupy the left hand corner – In and an Out, as nothing is ever pending.

Hearing Danni's voice outside, I glide over to the window. Moments later, the door bursts open. If she's surprised to see me, she hides it well, striding across to her cupboard to park her executive wheeled trolley bag. She looks confident and full of authority in a designer suit, comprising a sharp blue jacket, and a skirt that finishes above the knee. Her cream silk shirt, unbuttoned at the top, costs more than my entire ensemble.

"You really shouldn't give me more evidence of insubordination," she says without looking at me. There's a slight tremor to her voice, but otherwise she sounds confident. "You were instructed to attend the hearing in the Leader's Room in 20 minutes."

The hesitant, mousy-haired woman who was fast tracked into management has matured into the confident, smartly dressed Head of Environmental Health and Waste (HEHaW). Or Donkey, as we prefer to call it.

"Unless you're handing in your resignation," she says, checking her drawers to make sure they're locked. "No? Then I suggest you leave."

I slide my hands into my pockets. "I'm going nowhere."

She smirks and walks around to the front of her desk. She perches on the edge, folding her arms as she regards me with a mixture of amusement and disdain.

"I wouldn't pin your hopes on Colonel Witherington," she says, unable to mask a smile. "He wasn't sure which internal matters he could influence, but I clarified things for him."

I must ring the Colonel and thank him for undermining my case. His unrequested intervention makes it look like I'm clutching at straws. Back at the meeting table, I reach into the bowl of sweets.

"Soft or hard centre?" I ask, swirling them about. "Which are you, Danni?"

"I think your time would be better spent preparing for the hearing."

"I'm not attending your hearing." I remove the wrapper from a toffee. "I promised Tommy Logan of the *Tollingdon Tribune* an exclusive."

"If you fail to attend the hearing, it means you accept the charges against you."

"What action are you planning to take?"

Her smile is immediate. "Oh Kent, you should follow your father into politics. You're a natural, trying to get me to say I've planned your punishment already. That would hardly be impartial, would it?"

"Talking could save a lot of time and expense, but have it your way." I drop the sweet, pull out my mobile phone, and call Kelly. "Hi, Tommy, it's Kent Fisher. You were right. They're determined to get rid of me. I'll come straight round."

I end the call, push the phone back into my pocket and stroll towards the door. I pause, wondering whether Danni will bite. She waits until the door is half open.

"Choose your words carefully, Kent, unless you wish to face action for libel."

I close the door and turn. "There you go, threatening me again, Danni. Just like you did outside the barn at Tombstone."

"I never threatened you." She's on her feet, closing the gap between us. "I've given you every chance to account for your behaviour."

"Did I miss the informal hearing Council policy dictates?"

"Not needed for gross misconduct and insubordination."

Her smug smile doesn't distract me from the beads of perspiration on her forehead.

"You had a letter prepared when you confronted me at the barn," I say. "You'd already decided on the charges before I had a chance to explain."

"You've had two weeks to raise your concerns. Why wait till now?"

"The small matter of bereavement and a funeral, a close colleague seriously injured, police interviews." I stare straight into her eyes. "Nothing important."

She can't stop her index finger ticking me off. "Then why didn't you ask for the hearing to be postponed?"

"Why didn't you offer?"

"You managed to contact the *Tollingdon Tribune* in the midst of all this distress."

"Tommy Logan rang me. When he rang the council, you wouldn't talk to him."

She strolls back to her desk. "If you go running to the press, Kent, my hands are tied."

I wait, wondering what's keeping Kelly. Then, as Danni settles into her chair, the phone finally rings. She listens for a moment, a frown etching into her forehead. "What do you mean she's been delayed?" She looks up at me. "Why have you invited Adele Havelock to the hearing?"

I pound my forehead with the heel of my hand. "Shit! I forgot to ring her."

"You can't bring her into a hearing."

"I'm allowed to have someone with me."

"A colleague to advise you, not a journalist. Anyway, I thought you were off to talk to Tommy Logan."

"Looks like I'll have to attend the hearing as I forgot to cancel Adele. She witnessed you confront me with your ready prepared letter, so I can prove you planned to dismiss me."

"She was in the barn with you." Danni slams the phone down on the desk and jumps to her feet. "You took her on an official health and safety inspection."

Softly, I say, "Danni, it wasn't a health and safety inspection."

She smirks. "You arranged it with the site manager. I have a statement from him."

"What time did I arrange it for?"

"You know what time. One o'clock."

"And what time did you see me come out of the barn with Adele?"

"What's that got to do with anything?"

"I came out at half past one, still on my lunch break."

"I saw the two of you at lunch earlier. You were on duty, investigating a work accident."

I take my time. "No, Danni, I was investigating a murder."

Her mouth opens, but no words emerge. She walks back to her desk and drops into her chair. She stares at me, shaking her head in frustration. "Why didn't you tell me at the time, Kent? You handed over your ID without a fight."

"You would have laughed at me if I'd said murder."

"You could have tried."

"When you couldn't wait to dismiss me?"

She massages her temples. "You've had two weeks to tell me, Kent. Why wait till now? Are you trying to humiliate me?"

"We had all the fallout to deal with. We were grieving, but you pressed on regardless."

"That still leaves your other misdemeanours," she says, rising. "You broke into an empty house, you bullied staff."

"Is that what Gemma told you?"

"She didn't need to."

"You never asked her, did you? Someone else told you. Well, I want this person at the hearing. I intend to cross examine him – or her."

"You know I can't do that."

"Then let me see the statement you took from this person. If you took one …"

She turns away. "What's it like, being right all the time? No, don't answer that. It was bad enough when your father was alive. I couldn't touch you because everyone was afraid of him. And now he's dead and still I can't touch you."

"Then don't make it a battle."

"Then stop undermining my authority."

I want to tell her she left me no choice, but I came here to save my job, not create a bitter enemy.

"Okay," I say. "I'll let you brief Bernard Doolittle."

"This isn't over," she says, pointing a finger at me. "From now on, you follow the rules and procedures. Is that understood? When you're out on district, I want you catching up on your inspections, not nosing around crime scenes. If you miss your target by as much as one inspection, I'll … oh, get out and stay out." She swings around so her back's facing me. "For eternity preferably."

"I'll need my ID and written authority."

"In my trolley bag."

While she phones Bernard Doolittle, I find my ID and associated paperwork in a clear plastic folder. Behind it, I spot a manila folder with the paperwork for the disciplinary hearing. Unable to resist, I open the folder.

At the front, I see my letter of dismissal, dated today, and signed by Danni.

SIX

Lucy and Nigel look surprised when I walk into the Public Protection Team office.

"That was quick," Nigel says.

Lucy checks her watch and nods. "Too quick. You'd never accept a written warning, so what happened?"

"You didn't resign, did you?" Nigel asks, looking worried.

"Did you tell them where they could stick their stupid reorganisation?"

What's Danni been planning in my absence? More efficiency gains, as she likes to call them. Fewer staff equals less management, less confusion, less repetition, and less mistakes. Fewer mistakes, surely, I pointed out, spoiling yet another of her mantras.

No wonder she had a dismissal letter ready.

I should feel angry, but she's handed me another bargaining chip, which I'm bound to need sooner or later. I don't go looking for conflict or trouble, but I refuse to be pushed around or remain silent when someone's treated unfairly. And yes, I once chained myself to trees and sabotaged foxhunts before they were banned because I can't stand by and do nothing.

"We resolved a few misunderstandings and there was no need for a hearing," I say, knowing they'll want the gory details. Thankfully, Kelly's beside me.

"I'll email everyone to let them know," she says. "When I say everyone, I mean the guys from Pollution Control. No one else in the council knows we exist, do they? When I strolled past Building Control a moment ago, they were still discussing last night's TV."

"*Grantchester* was ace," Nigel says, nodding.

"We're talking *QVC*," Kelly says. "Shall I ask Mutton Geoff to do a media release?"

"The man who put the twit in Twitter?" Lucy shakes her head, her feelings about our Communications Officer well documented. "Forget him. I want to know why Danni dropped the charges. She wanted your head on a plate, Kent."

"And your sweetbreads," Nigel says. When Kelly gives him a quizzical look, he blushes.

Lucy sighs. "He means dangly bits. Now, come on, Kent, tell all."

I'm tempted to head out onto the district, but she won't let me off that easily. As Unison rep, she's interested in anything that could undermine management – like her dress code, which tests Danni's patience more than I do.

Lucy has a collection of waistcoats that run from the intriguing to the plain bizarre. No one knows where she gets them from, but today's offering is a gold and red Paisley motif on a dark green background. She wears it with a lilac shirt, weary-looking purple corduroy trousers and scuffed

Doc Martens. Like her clothes, she often looks frayed and has a lived-in face, as my friend, Mike, would say, thanks to too many cigarettes and pints of real ale.

"As you know, disciplinary matters are confidential," I tell her, heading for my desk.

"But you weren't disciplined, were you?"

"No."

"I said they'd never sack a hero, didn't I?" She's on her feet now, striding towards the high moral ground. "Which means one of us will get the chop now, as I predicted, didn't I?"

Nigel shrinks back as she slaps her hand on his desk to make her point.

"As environmental health officers earn far more than us humble technical assistants," she says, eyes gleaming, "it looks like you'll be leaving us."

"B… b… b… but we can turn our hands to anything," he says.

"Then redundancy should be a breeze." She gives him a playful slap and returns to her desk. "I'm glad you kept your job, Kent. It means we don't have to do your work as well as our own now."

She carries a stack of folders from her desk and thuds them onto mine. "I've got a pile for Twinkle Toes too. Where is she?"

"Gemma's on a job," Kelly replies, adding another folder.

"Buying cakes to thank us for covering her work, I hope."

While Lucy returns to her desk, Nigel slides into the chair beside mine and leans closer. He can barely contain his excitement or the hairs that thrust out of his nostrils like bristles on a broom. He must notice them when he shaves, surely. Maybe he doesn't care. Like me, he's not worried about appearance.

In his fifties, widowed, with two daughters who have children of their own, he's financially secure and loyal. Part of the furniture, some would say, Nigel Long is sometimes called Chaz, corrupted from chaise. Danni thinks he's more of a Lazy Boy, preferring the line of least resistance to confronting wrong-doers. He can become agitated and nervous when things get difficult, analysing every angle. But if he seeks reassurance from me, it's because he wants to get things right.

"So," he says, rubbing his hands together, "what's it like to solve a murder?"

"I can't say too much because the police are still making enquiries," I reply. It's the same answer I gave Tommy Logan, even though I promised him an exclusive for the *Tollingdon Tribune*. "I'm the main prosecution witness."

"When did you realise it was murder? I mean, it's not like y… y… you get out of bed and think, maybe I'll find a body in a freezer today."

It still seems surreal. One minute it's a work accident, the next a murder. Someone should turn it into a novel or film.

"Do you ever watch Columbo?" I ask.

"The scruffy detective with the cigar? Haven't seen it in years."

"He was always intrigued by details that didn't quite fit or make sense. That's how it was. One detail led to another until …"

"You worked it out," he says, sounding a little disappointed. He gets to his feet and then lowers his voice. "I never thought Danni would sack you, whatever Lucy says."

"Thanks," I say, pulling my phone from my pocket. I take another look at the photo of my dismissal letter and email it to my personal account for safe keeping.

The folder Kelly left contains a food registration for *Grub on the Go*. The mobile catering business was registered 18 months ago to Colin Miller, who gave his address as the Travellers public house at Boreham St, where he kept the vehicle overnight. An attached note from Nigel says the business intended to sell sandwiches and savouries around Tollingdon's industrial estates, but there's no indication whether it started trading.

"Nigel, do you remember *Grub on the Go*?"

He shakes his head. "Sounds like a mobile trader. Is the inspection overdue?"

"Leave it with me," I reply, wondering if Gemma's already beaten me to it.

If she has, I hope she checked the file for the Travellers first.

Gemma seems subdued when she returns at 12.30. Nigel and Lucy are on district, driven out by the endless stream of people who want to welcome me back – or find out how I kept my job. Geoff Lamb offered to set up a video interview that could be made available on DownNet, Downland's unpredictable staff intranet. When he started talking podcasts on Twitter, I glazed over.

"How did it go with Danni?" Gemma asks when I stroll over.

"I'll tell you over lunch."

"I'm not in the mood." Her gaze returns to the monitor and the list of emails that await her.

"Where were you this morning?" I ask.

"Out."

"At the Travellers?"

She frowns. "Why would I go there?"

"You asked Kelly for information on *Grub on the Go*."

"I haven't looked at it yet. How does the Travellers fit it?"

"I'll tell you after you tell me what's troubling you."

"I'm fine," she says, staring at the monitor.

"I only want to help."

She shoves the mouse away in frustration. "Well you can't."

"There's no such thing as can't."

She stares at me, her angry eyes filling with tears. "Are you a plastic surgeon?"

I back off, wanting to tell her the wounds will heal, but she blames me for the injury. Not as much as I blame myself.

Her hand goes to her injured arm. "I'll have to pay for cosmetic surgery as the wound's superficial. That's pretty much what they told me at the hospital."

I persuade her to come to lunch and we leave the town hall in silence.

For a small provincial town, Tollingdon manages to pack in more eateries, antique shops, pubs and hairdressers than the national average. While it's managed to avoid concrete for the most part, the town centre's ornate brick buildings look dull and tired beneath the leaden sky. A stiff wind whips the desiccated brown and yellow leaves from the cherry and mountain ash trees that line the pavements. Litter sprawls in the gutters. Weeds fill the cracks between the flagstones, which are more uneven than ever. The predicted downpour for this afternoon won't wash away the neglect of a town that's not as exclusive or prosperous as it thinks.

Nor the cuts in public spending that have hit Downland hard.

The proliferation of SALE signs contradicts the high price tags in the antique shops and galleries. Young mothers with their buggies march straight past, heading for the cut-price stores in the precinct, while the wealthier residents congregate in mutinous groups in the tearooms and restaurants to discuss the drop in standards. The Vietnamese nail bar, due to open in a couple of weeks, gets top billing. Complaint letters have doubled since the *Tollingdon Tribune* ran a full page advertisement for the place. Disgruntled residents would normally write to their MP, but he died recently and the by-election is months away.

Gemma turns into 'Tasse de Tollingdon', a local coffee shop that's trying to compete with the national chains. There's nothing remotely French about the bold brown lettering above the shop or the large coffee beans stickers that smother the window. But as the owner thinks the name means 'A Taste of Tollingdon', that's hardly surprising. Once past the smell of coffee beans and the noise of milk being foamed, we weave through the low sofas to the counter and watch the baristas autograph the froth on their cappuccinos.

"Two teas," I tell the young woman with the false smile. "Do you fancy a treble chocolate muffin, Gemma? A six-mile run later will burn off the calories."

While I wait for the tea, Gemma sits at a small table at the back. It's dark, cramped and in need of a wipe with one of those magic cloths that never seem to get washed. She remains silent while I pour, only perking up when I tell her about Colin Miller.

"I could go straight to the Travellers from here," she says.

"You're on a phased return. Mornings only."

"I wasn't working this morning. I was in Outpatients."

"Nice try, but you're going home this afternoon."

She shakes her head. "This isn't work, is it?"

"If there's a mobile catering business on the premises, it is."

"But you're barred from the Travellers."

I smile, realising she doesn't know. "So are you."

Councillor Gregory Rathbone, Portfolio Holder for Environment, Waste and Communities, dislikes both of us, but especially me. I stop most of the businesses he starts because he ignores safety and hygiene rules. He's bound to be ecstatic when he hears I kept my job.

"Mike and I are visiting this evening," I say, aware she's having dinner with Richard.

Mike won't be happy about it, but he'll help. On an unofficial visit, we'll have more chance of getting information from Rathbone. If I visit with Gemma, he'll complain to Danni.

"Does that mean you're taking Colonel Witherington seriously?"

"The trail may lead nowhere."

"What if it leads somewhere? What do we do then?"

"We can't do anything during work's time, obviously."

"I'm not working afternoons, am I?" She leans closer, her voice low. "I'm bored stupid at home. I need to get out and do something. Let me do the legwork."

"You're on a phased return," I say, aware of her frustration. "If HR find out, you'll be in the brown stuff."

"I'm not an invalid, Kent."

"You were shot, Gemma. That's got to play on your mind."

"But not yours, clearly." She glares at me with cold eyes, but the tears still run down her cheeks. "Then again, you're not the one permanently disfigured."

I don't know what to say. I think back to that night, wondering if I could have done things differently.

"It's my fault. I should never have taken you with me, Gemma."

She looks up. "I don't blame you," she says, grabbing my hand. "You saved my life."

"But you said …"

She shakes her head. "Ignore me. I'm all over the place. The consultant said the scars will fade and I can move on."

A hollow feeling fills my stomach. "Move on?"

Her grip on my hand tightens. "I thought I was going to die. I thought …" She takes a deep breath. "I'll be fine, honest. But what about you? What happened at the hearing?"

"Danni dropped the charges."

She looks surprised, yet relieved. “That’s great. No really, it’s great,” she adds, dabbing the corner of her eyes. “Now you can move on.”

“I’m not going anywhere.”

“I meant with your life. You’ve got Rebecca now. Birchill will help you develop the sanctuary. Niamh can use her contacts and influence to raise your profile with the people who count. It’s everything you wanted, Kent.”

If only.

SEVEN

I'm in my underwear when Niamh breezes into my bedroom.

"Isn't it time you stopped taking advantage of Frances?" She sits on the end of my bed to fuss Columbo. "And you shouldn't allow dogs on the bed. They start thinking they're human and as important as you."

I'm not sure what's encouraged her critical review of my lifestyle, but she's more like her old self, looking elegant in a pastel green blouse and black skirt. Her trip to the hairdresser and beautician seems to have restored her self-confidence ahead of Davenport's visit this evening.

That's why I'm off to the Travellers with Mike.

"Maybe you'd like to advise me on which clothes to wear," I say, opening the wardrobe.

"Don't be so childish. I'm simply suggesting you take more responsibility around here. Take your dog," she says, tickling Columbo behind the ears. "Frances looks after him while you work. Then, you expect her to carry on in the evening while you go out with …"

I slide a pair of stone-coloured chinos from a hanger. "Rebecca, as you well know."

Niamh shakes her head when I pull on the chinos. "Do you want to look like a vagrant when you meet Rebecca?"

She makes the name sound like an unpleasant medical condition. "Black's much more forgiving," she says, reaching into my wardrobe. "I'll press them for you."

"I don't have time. Mike and I have business to attend to."

"Oh, you're out selling catering equipment," she says, sounding even more critical. "Is that wise with all the trouble at work?"

Danni would go ape if she found out about my second hand catering equipment sideline, but it helps to fund the sanctuary. It started by accident when Mike took early retirement and wanted to start a mobile catering business. He couldn't afford a new van or equipment, so I used my contacts and local knowledge to source cheap alternatives. I always knew when a business was struggling or about to close.

"It's Mike's business, not mine," I say.

Niamh sneers. "And your manager's going to believe that? You don't need me to tell you what she'll do."

"Oh, I don't see why not," I say, stepping out of the stone chinos. "You're already running my life."

She hands me the black trousers. "Like you listen to anything I say."

"I always listen," I say, pulling on the chinos.

"And ignore my advice," she says, giving me the hurt look she does so well.

"If it makes you feel better, Mike and I are not selling equipment. We're checking out someone linked to Daphne Witherington."

"I thought you'd refused to help the Colonel?" She sighs and looks at Columbo. "No one tells me anything around here."

Columbo barks, his tail wagging as if he expects a treat.

"You're not wearing that," she says, looking aghast.

I have no intention of wearing my electric blue shirt even though we've had some great times together. With a grin, I put it back in the wardrobe and pull on the white shirt I've worn all day. "We're off to see Gregory Rathbone."

"How's he involved? He and the Colonel don't exactly see eye to eye, now do they?"

"The Colonel invested in a mobile catering business for his wife before she vanished. Her business partner kept the vehicle at Rathbone's pub."

Niamh looks thoughtful as she strokes Columbo. "What changed your mind about Daphne?"

"I haven't changed my mind. It's a catering business and it's easy to check out. Not that I expect to get anything from Rathbone."

"Why didn't you check this caterer out while you were at work?"

"I thought you'd want me out of the way when Davenport came over."

"Alasdair's allergic to dogs, I'm afraid." She ruffles Columbo's fur once more, looking into his big, dark eyes. "I'm sure he'd love you, but his eyes start streaming and he can't breathe. A few strands of fur set him off."

I can't help smiling at this unexpected bonus. "So, you're going out too," I say. "Now who's taking advantage of Frances?"

As the name suggests, the Travellers is more hotel than public house. The accommodation takes up one side of the site. At the back, where the land slopes away, the guest rooms overlook the nightclub, which opens onto a terrace and ornamental gardens. The views across the marshes to the coast make the Travellers a popular wedding venue, in spite of the wide screen TVs and sports channels. Fortunately, these occupy one of the bars at the front of the building, well away from reception and the visitors' lounge.

Window boxes and hanging baskets, spilling over with colourful annuals, brighten up the black Tudor beams that suggest great age and character, but only at night. During the day, it's clear the beams are plastic, despite all efforts to disguise them with flowers, banners and bunting. And that's the problem. The tasteful gold letters that spell out Travellers suggest class, but the menu board offers an extensive range of burger and chip meals, 'two for one' offers on steaks and free bottles of wine for group bookings.

"How do kids afford BMWs?" Mike asks, extending his long legs out of my Ford Fusion. He lights a cigarette and walks around the cars, appraising the wide tyres, chrome exhaust extensions and spoilers like aircraft wings.

"They must cost a fortune to tart up and run," he says, shaking his head. "My ex-wife claimed I was high maintenance. I thought she meant tall, as I explained to her solicitor. When you're as tall as I am, you look down on everyone."

He laughs at his joke, but he's never recovered from the day his wife ran off with the kitchen fitter. "He could have plumbed in the appliances," was all Mike said at the time.

Inside the Travellers, we're treated to a world of black that covers the walls, ceiling and bare floorboards. Within minimal soft furnishings, the music from the jukebox bounces around, making conversation difficult. The lighting is furtive, relying on the bright screens of gaming machines and plasma TVs to boost illumination. I doubt if it's enough to spot whether you've been short-changed. Then again, people who like to pay double to have their beer in long thin glasses probably don't mind.

We walk through to the saloon bar, where regulars shoot pool and try their hand on the quiz machines. The décor remains predominantly black, but the wear and tear exposes plenty of light pine to offer some contrast.

"Why have you brought me to this fleapit?" Mike asks.

"Over 50s disco night." I automatically peer over the bar at the shelves and floor behind, which look clean enough. "They limit the numbers to give you more space on the dancefloor."

"Are you saying I'm overweight?"

He pats the large girth that epitomises Mike's Mighty Munch, the roadside burger van he runs. For someone who spent his working life in Sussex Police, he's not a bad cook, blending his Caribbean culture into the hearty fast food he serves. He's a bit spicy for some people, but I love his plain speaking and no-nonsense attitude. His zest for life is incredible for someone who spent most of his time poking around crime scenes for evidence.

"I'm saying you could pull if you're lucky, Mike."

He smirks. "You know me. If I fell in a barrel of boobs …"

"You'd come out sucking your thumb," we say in unison.

Our laughter attracts a young barmaid with a pale complexion and startled black hair. No wonder. The tight top she's squeezed into must be cutting off her circulation. She trots up with short staccato steps, thanks to high heels and skin tight leggings. Her gothic makeup does nothing to lift her sullen expression and bored eyes.

With banter at a premium, Mike concentrates on her chest until she places his beer on the counter. "So, what time does the action start?" he asks.

"What action?" She takes the money, deposits it in the till, and returns to the far end of the bar to watch the pool players.

"Does she work here because she likes people?" he asks. "Or is it some form of penance?"

We settle in a small booth with padded seats and a table that's stickier than an unwashed frying pan. "Have you come across Colonel Witherington?" I ask.

"I know he chaired one of the joint working groups with the police."

"What about his wife?"

"What about her?"

I give him a brief overview of her disappearance and the link to Colin Miller. He drinks his lager while I explain, only letting his gaze drift once as the barmaid collects some glasses from an adjoining table.

"So," he says, putting his empty glass down, "you reckon the Colonel's wife did a runner with the money and Colin Miller, who might have kept his van here. Why don't we wander round the back and see if it's still here?"

"They ran off about a year ago. The van won't be here."

"So, why do you need me?"

"I want your help with Councillor Gregory Rathbone," I say, gesturing to the man who strolls into the bar as if he's about to receive a standing ovation. He has shiny black hair, slicked back and combed behind his ears. His narrow face seems to come to a point, thanks to a long, sharp nose and protruding chin, tipped with a goatee.

"Isn't he behind every new scheme the council launches?"

"Only the ones that fail," I reply.

To win 'Downland Pub of the Year', Rathbone designed voting cards that looked almost identical to his customer services cards. Then he got his cronies to fill in hundreds of them with different coloured biros. Unfortunately, an EHO who shall remain nameless voted using the customer services cards. Rathbone was rumbled and disqualified.

"The competition hasn't run since," I say, concluding the story. "And I won't mention the rules and laws he breaks. Let's just say he never sends me a Christmas card."

"Like most people," Mike says, play punching my arm. "So, you want me to be a witness in case he gets difficult, is that it?"

"I want you to intimidate him."

"Me? You're the one with the food horror stories."

"I'm not allowed to have any official dealings with him. Don't ask," I say, remembering the pressure Rathbone heaped on me after closing one of his cafés. "Colin Miller owes you twenty grand and you've called to collect. If Rathbone plays dumb, show him your nasty side. You always said you'd make a great villain."

"Yeah, but I haven't got my violin case, have I?"

"You can't act either, but that's never held you back."

He wags a warning finger at me. "Do you want my help or not?"

We return to the bar, where Rathbone gives me his best cloying smile. If he could get his eyes to join in, sincerity would be within his grasp.

"May I offer my sincere commiserations over the death of your father, Mr Fisher? William was an inspiration to us all, serving the community for … well, until he died, obviously. What a shock." He shakes his head as if he's lost a dear friend. "And poor Niamh. Please send her my condolences and best wishes. She must miss him terribly. As I'm sure you do," he adds quickly. "Let me offer you a drink on the house to toast his memory."

I decline, having drunk only half of my St Clement's. "This is Mr Brown," I say when Mike pushes his glass forward.

"Gregory Rathbone, owner of this establishment." He fills Mike's glass with the cheapest lager. "Have you started evening hygiene inspections to keep us on our toes?"

"I'm here to ask a favour."

"Always happy to help our colleagues in enforcement, you know that."

"Mr Brown's an entrepreneur like you. He invested in a mobile catering business about a year ago."

"*Grub on the Go*," Mike says, right on cue. "You might have heard of it."

Rathbone shakes his head. "Good name for a business. How can I help?"

"It's not his business," I reply. "It's owned by Colin Miller, who kept the vehicle here."

"Are you sure?" Rathbone asks.

"His food registration says he kept the vehicle here."

Rathbone laughs. "People say all kinds of things on forms, don't they?"

"When they bother to register," I say.

His smile vanishes. "An innocent mistake, Mr Fisher. One anyone could make."

Mike leans forward. "Miller owes me twenty grand, pal. So, if you know where he is, or anything about the van, I'd like to know."

"Since when did EHOs become debt collectors?" Rathbone leans closer, giving me a hint of what his garlic bread might taste like. His voice is low and menacing. "If you've revealed confidential information about my business to a third party …"

"Food registration details are public, as you know. Mr Brown's owed money and I thought you'd be happy to help a fellow entrepreneur."

"Sorry to disappoint you, gents, but I have no recollection of the man."

Mike drains half his beer. "If he stayed here, you'll have a record of his home address, credit card."

"That's confidential."

"But you can check to see if he stayed here." Mike's evil smile scares me as he pulls himself to his full height. "Or I might start to wonder whether you're hiding something. And if you're hiding something from me, who knows what you're not telling the tax inspector."

Rathbone's perspiring. "How dare you question my integrity?"

"Would you rather I helped myself? I mean, you must make twenty grand plus on a Saturday night, pal. You'd hardly miss it, would you?"

"Hang on," I say in my best horrified voice. "I didn't bring you here to threaten people."

Mike stares at Rathbone. "Colin Miller has convictions for deception and fraud. If you're helping him, that makes you an accessory. I can talk to my friends in the force if you prefer."

"There's no food van here. Never has been. Take a look if you don't believe me."

I put a hand on Mike's arm, worried he's taking his role too seriously. "I told you Miller was unlikely to be here."

"But he was here, wasn't he?" Mike leans forward as if he's about to grab Rathbone by the lapels and haul him over the bar. As much as I'd like to see that, I have to calm things down.

"Mr Rathbone, if you recall anything about Colin Miller, please tell us," I say.

Rathbone looks up at a security camera and then at me. A slow, sly smile smothers his lips, suggesting I've blundered. Still smiling, he helps himself to vodka and returns, looking smug once more.

"A year ago, someone wanted to make and sell sandwiches," he says. "I let him use the kitchen. He left early and came back late, so I hardly saw him."

"What about his van?" Mike asks. "You let him park it here."

Rathbone takes a slug of vodka. "He drove a black BMW. An unusual choice of delivery vehicle, don't you think? I mean, would you transport knocked-off meat in the boot of your car? Not that I ever took any," he adds quickly. "I have a reputation to maintain."

Mike finishes his lager. "How long was he here?"

"A month, maybe two?"

"What was he like?"

"He was a middle-aged bloke with a comb over, strutting around with one of those aluminium briefcases. He never carried anything it. Not even the leaflets he had printed."

"What leaflets?" I ask.

"For *Grub on the Go*. Someone came round with five boxes of them, but he'd already scarpered."

Mike plants both elbows on the counter. "Where did he go?"

"How would I know? He took off without paying his bill."

"And why would he do that?"

Rathbone takes his time, stroking his goatee. "Miller had a thing for some woman he used to know. A real looker, he said. A singer or dancer, I think. She worked for him until she met some deadbeat from around here."

"And Miller tracked her down?"

Rathbone nods. "Her husband came round and scared my receptionist into giving him the room number. He left a right mess, I can tell you. Took me days to clean it up."

"Did you report this to the police?" I ask. "You have CCTV, right?"

When Rathbone doesn't answer, Mike leans forward. "Does this deadbeat have a name?"

"I never met him. I think he ran a shop, if that's any help."

"What kind of shop?"

"He didn't say."

"Where?"

Rathbone shrugs. "I wasn't here at the time."

Mike stares at him for a moment and nods towards the door.

"I'll catch up with you in a moment, Mr Brown."

Once Mike's gone, I thank Rathbone for his help, aware he could still complain to Danni. "If I knew Mr Brown was going to lose his temper, I'd never have brought him here."

Rathbone laughs. "I've no idea why you're interested in this man, Miller, but why the charade with your friend? Why didn't you ask me?"

"I didn't think you'd tell me."

"You're probably right," he says, collecting the empty glasses from the bar. "The bastard stitched me up. He had the full use of my kitchen and my stock and never paid a penny. He paid for the room for a month, but nothing after that. Then he cleaned the room out when he left." Rathbone bangs the glasses down. "If you find him, let me know where he is."

"He's long gone and I'm not going to look for him."

"And I'm not going to say anything about tonight," he says, looking smug. "Now you owe me a favour, Mr Fisher."

I can't believe I walked into that.

Back in the car, I congratulate Mike on his performance. "You should take up amateur dramatics. You're a natural heavy."

"Do you have to keep going on about my weight?" He pulls on the seatbelt and sighs. "I'm not sure we got much from your oily friend, mind. Someone who runs a shop with a woman doesn't give us much to go on."

"You're forgetting the printer."

"What printer?"

"Someone printed the leaflets. He had five boxes, remember? It's bound to be someone local, a company on one of the industrial estates."

"Or someone in Eastbourne or Lewes. Please don't ask me to give you a hand."

I start the car and pull away. "I'll start with the cheapest. That's what Miller would have done. And if he didn't pay for the leaflets, someone might remember him."

"You've got it all figured out, haven't you?"

Yeah, just like this evening.

EIGHT

On Tuesday morning, Niamh wanders into the kitchen in her dressing gown and slippers. Her tousled hair, lack of makeup and weary expression can't disguise the dreamy smile on her lips or the glint in her eyes. Columbo, who's resting beneath the table, scrambles to his feet. She bends to fuss him, resting a hand on my chair to steady herself.

"Why are you up so early?" she asks, glancing at the laptop screen. "Not working, I hope."

"Sorry, if I disturbed you. I know you got in late."

"Keeping tabs on me, are you now?" She laughs and heads for the kettle, filling it from the filter jug. "I know you don't approve of Alasdair, but it's really none of your business, is it?"

"I don't want you rushing into anything."

She seeks out new mugs from the cupboard. "That implies I'm looking for something. For someone as fickle as you, that's ironic. Or should I draw any conclusions from that?"

"Of course not," I reply, surprised at how defensive I sound.

I bundle up the notes scattered across the table and shut down the laptop while she makes tea. When she joins me at the table, my efforts to identify local printing companies are tucked inside the folder the Colonel gave me.

She slips Columbo a treat. "Did you learn anything from Gregory Rathbone?"

I give her a sanitised overview. "Now I need to find the company that printed the flyers."

"How will that help?"

Like many of my investigations at work, I follow a trail. "I'm trying to get a handle on Colin Miller. Did he seduce Daphne Witherington or rip off her old man?"

"Or both," Niamh says with a smile. "Be careful you don't get too involved, Kent. Daniella Frost hasn't thawed yet."

As Danni will be watching everything I do, I'm planning some overdue food hygiene inspections in businesses close to printing companies.

By half seven, I'm in the office, studying the team's inspection programme. As we start on 1st April, we're just over halfway through the year and almost 20 per cent behind our target. While we always catch up in the last quarter, we'll struggle to close the current gap.

And I'll be held responsible if we fail.

Maybe I should drop the Daphne Witherington inquiry. People disappear all the time. Some go abroad. Many don't want to be found. Some are never found.

"I'm glad to see you in bright and early," Danni says, peering around the door. "Let's slot your performance appraisal review in before Cabinet meets. Shall we say 15 minutes?"

She's gone before I can reply. The new, efficient Danni has cut everything from her dowdy hair to the length of her skirts. Conversations have become bullet points while she trims the budget with a chainsaw. 'New Approaches for New Challenges' proclaims the lengthy briefing note. Roughly translated, it means get rid of expensive managers and buildings. As I escaped sacrifice on the altar of efficiency, someone else will have to take my place.

Fifteen minutes later, my appraisal review rewards me with a list of new projects I can't possibly deliver. If she's setting me up to fail, she's succeeding.

"Remember," she says, pointing to her Motivational Pinboard. "There's no room for slackers on the Efficiency Express."

"Shouldn't it be slow coaches?" I ask, glad she still knows how to motivate her staff.

Back in the Public Protection Team office, Gemma's arrived. The change in the weather has prompted her to ditch beachwear in favour of a sensible but stylish blue jumper and matching skirt that just about reaches her knees. Brown suede boots have replaced her trademark diamante sandals.

She gestures at the bundle in the crook of my arm. "Got your assignments?"

"The first station for the Efficiency Express is Agile Central," I reply, dumping the papers on my desk. Aware that Lucy and Nigel are listening from behind their screens, I hold up the briefing note. "In a hotly contested battle, our team lost, which means we're leading on Agile Working again."

"I thought Facilities said it was impossible," Gemma says.

Lucy comes out of hiding. "They said hot desking wasn't feasible. This is about working from home."

"For those who can be trusted," Danni says.

When I look round she's gone. Maybe I should communicate with her on the new Enterprise Social Network we're piloting for the council. Instead of talking to each other, we will converse on the office equivalent of Facebook, but without the cute animal photographs. That project also receives hearty support from the team, especially Lucy, who photocopies the briefing notes so she can share them with her Unison colleagues.

"So much for consulting with the union," she mutters, returning my notes.

I signal to Gemma and we head for the vending machine at the end of the corridor. There's no tea or coffee due to a hot water malfunction, so I settle for fizzy orange.

"Danni's agreed to let you take on more food inspections," I tell her as we look down at the High Street. "You'll take on the lower risk businesses to free us up for the higher risk."

"When can I do some real work?"

I understand her frustration, but I can't bend the Food Standards Agency's competency standards. "You know the rules, Gemma. Once you've done the Higher Certificate in Food Premises Inspection –"

"If I do it." She sighs and looks away. "Danni promised to enrol me months ago. Now, when I mention it, she fobs me off."

She's unaware that two businesses complained about her aggressive and inflexible attitude. Like many officers who come from outside environmental health, she struggles to accept the law is a minimum standard that's not as high as most people imagine.

"I'll help you," I say. "But right now, concentrate on easing yourself in gently while you recover from your injuries."

"My mind wasn't injured."

"You were shot, Gemma."

"Grazed," she says, her voice rising. "I'm not going to burst into tears or go off with stress, if that's what you think. I'm sick of moping around the house every afternoon when I could be doing something useful."

"Maybe I can help with that."

I explain about the flyers Colin Miller ordered and give her a list of print firms to check in Eastbourne. "If you find someone who remembers him, we'll check it out."

"You just don't want to let go of my hand, do you? How sweet."

Not as sweet as the news Kelly delivers when I'm on my way out of the door an hour later. "You've been summoned to Cabinet, lover. Gregory Rathbone has requested your presence at midday when the meeting finishes."

I should have known he would never keep quiet about last night.

"You okay?" she asks.

"How long do you think I can stay out of trouble, Kelly?"

"Long enough to jump on board the Efficiency Express?"

We both shake our heads and laugh.

The aroma of polished oak panels and self-importance fill my nostrils as I stride across the sumptuous carpet in the Leader's Office. Portraits of the Queen, Winston Churchill, and Isambard Kingdom Brunel watch me from the walls. The aldermen, mayors and leaders, who served Downland District Council and its predecessors have their names etched in gold letters on several oak boards. They provide an unbroken chain to a grand and imposing past, when working for the council meant something.

The Leader and Deputy Leader of the council, along with four Portfolio Holders, make up the Cabinet. They're seated on one side of a large oval table. Danni sits at one end, next to Gregory Rathbone. The Chief Executive and his PA, who should be at the other end of the table, have left. Colonel Witherington gestures to the gold-coloured chair with deep green velvet upholstery that faces him.

All eyes are on me. The Colonel and Rathbone I know, but the remainder are names on the internal directory. At least there's one woman at the pinnacle of local politics. Geraldine Hammond, Portfolio Holder for Planning, has a benign expression, but piercing eyes that dare you to mess with her.

"Please accept our condolences on the death of your father," she says. "We all knew William personally and feel his loss, as I'm sure you do. The shock and turmoil of his death may have caused a few misunderstandings, which we regret."

Danni shifts in her chair, slapped down for trying to discipline me. No wonder she looks like she's swallowed a wasp.

"If we can help or support you and Niamh through these difficult times, let us know," Geraldine says.

"Thank you," I say. "I appreciate your concern."

"You must be wondering why we summoned you." The Colonel straightens his papers and then looks up. "I know you disapprove of accolades, Kent, but you have become something of a local hero, if we're to believe Tommy Logan at the *Tollingdon Tribune*."

He pauses for polite laughter, allowing Geraldine to add to my discomfort. "You're an inspiration to your colleagues in times of great turbulence."

"Just like Hugo Carrington," Rathbone says.

"Did he solve a murder?"

"The Hugo Carrington Award has only been presented three times since its namesake passed away," the Colonel says. "By a happy coincidence, its first recipient was your father, so it seems rather fitting that we present the award to you."

Their spontaneous applause catches me by surprise. Danni too, it seems, as she's a couple of seconds behind and rather lukewarm with her clapping. The councillors rise and come round the table to shake my hand and add more congratulations.

"It's a cheap and vulgar plaque," the Colonel tells me when everyone has left, "but the cheque for £1,000 makes up for that. Now tell me how your investigation's progressing."

He's delighted with my summary, even when I warn him not to build his hopes up about finding Colin Miller

"I've waited a year for someone to take me seriously. My expectations are already low."

My expectations take an unexpected hit when news of the award appears on DownNet. On Wednesday morning, it takes Lucy seconds to hit her stride.

"The council's cutting services and getting rid of people to save money, but they found £1000 for you. I hope you told them where to stick it."

The money will pay a few veterinary and feed bills. "The cash comes from a trust, not the Council's budget," I reply.

"And what about Twinkle Toes?" she asks. "Where's her award? You're a man, so you get the credit. She's a minion who gets shot and she's overlooked. Doesn't do much for your credibility, does it, Kent?"

Or Gemma's morale, I suspect.

She rings me at 11.40, interrupting my hygiene inspection of Tollingdon Tearooms. The owner has already apologised for not having a body in the freezer. He has no idea he's at least the third person to say that this week.

"I've found the company that printed the flyers," she says.

"What are you doing in Eastbourne?"

"I checked Eastbourne yesterday afternoon. I'm at the Flintlock Industrial Estate near the bypass. I inspected *Sweet Sensations*, a confectionery wholesaler next door to Tollingdon Business Supplies. The owner remembers Colin Miller."

"I'll be with you in 25 minutes."

It takes me 45 minutes to answer questions, write out a summary report of my inspection findings, and give the owner of Tollingdon Tearooms a new 5-rated hygiene sticker for his window. I needn't have worried about being late as Gemma's taking coffee with three mechanics at a motor repair unit. No wonder it takes so long to get a car repaired.

She walks over and hands me a sample pack of chocolate bars. "They give these to businesses as a taster."

"Must bring my car here for a service," I say, eyeing the 80% cocoa chocolate bar.

"No, they came from the wholesalers …"

She pulls a face and then laughs. Once the chocolate's in the car, we walk over to Tollingdon Business Supplies, which has a dent in its roller shutter door. The small door to its side leads into a short, concrete block corridor and staircase to the first floor.

'Stationery moves us', proclaims a large banner on the wall.

It moves me straight up the stairs to a reception area, overwhelmed by a rampant Weeping Fig. Slotted in beside the plant is a receptionist with a tiny head mic to match the proportions of his insignificant desk. A young man of few words, he nods Gemma through into an open plan office crammed with desks and computers. A woman with a loose ponytail and baggy sweatshirt eats an egg mayonnaise sandwich as she listens to a caller on her headphones.

"The rest of the sales team must be out selling," I say, stepping over some electric cables.

Multifunction devices that scan, email, copy and breakdown with monotonous regularity line the walls not occupied by old-fashioned filing cabinets. Desks, overflowing with papers and notes, contain computers with flat screens and phones that seem to have cornered the dust market. Heaven help anyone with asthma, especially the women with rather large lungs who adorn posters for all manner of stationery products and technology.

"The machines must generate a lot of heat," I say, admiring a rather lovely brunette, bending over a printer. "I can't think why else these women are scantily clad, can you?"

Gemma rolls her eyes. "You wait till you see the owner."

"Is she in a bikini too?"

"He's a relic from an old sitcom. When I walked in he was driving the forklift. He tried to pick me up."

"I expect you raised his blood pressure."

A short, balding man with a self-important chest emerges from an office in the corner. Dressed in trousers with no creases and a brown and white tank top over his shirt, he struts over, giving Gemma a huge smile.

"Miss Dean," he says, addressing her boobs. "You're a fast mover. I wasn't expecting you back so soon. Maybe something took your fancy?"

His attempt at a self-conscious laugh fades quickly when he turns to me. "You must be Kent Fisher. Terry Ormerod, owner of this palace of paper products. No freezers here, you'll be glad to know."

His sticky hand feels like a slug. "Come into my sanctum, please. I'll get Wendy to make us some coffee."

While he gestures to the woman eating sandwiches, I follow Gemma into the small office. It smells like a locker room, so I open one of the windows, but the roar of traffic on the bypass puts paid to any hope of ventilation.

"Refreshments should be here in a minute," Ormerod says, dropping into his vinyl executive chair. He looks at

Gemma's legs. "I should have asked if you take sugar, Miss Dean. Or maybe you're sweet enough."

"I understand you did some work for Colin Miller," I say before he can talk to any more of her anatomy. "*Grub on the Go*?"

He looks at his computer screen. "We produced the artwork and printed 5,000 flyers for his business."

A laser printer in the corner produces a copy of the flyer. Apart from the logo, the artwork consists of a list of products. No pictures or photographs. No address or email, just a mobile phone number. *Grub on the Go* supplied sandwiches and rolls, all freshly made, with fillings including prawn, pâté, cheese and chicken. The prices were cheap, which probably meant the sandwiches were as tasteless as the logo. In small print at the bottom of the page, Miller offered burgers, sausages and fresh meat at 'prices your mother will remember'.

I pass the flyer to Gemma. "What was Miller like?"

Ormerod shrugs. "I only saw him once when he delivered sandwiches on the estate. He kept them in a tray in the back of his BMW. That's not legal, is it?"

"If they're wrapped and delivered within four hours of manufacture, they should be."

He looks surprised. "Miller's sandwiches were three days old at best. Well, that's what the mechanics told me. And they were supermarket sandwiches with his label stuck over theirs. Tell me that's legal."

Wendy comes in with our drinks, saving me an explanation. Once she's left, I ask him to describe Miller.

"Total poser," Ormerod says with a smirk. "Black BMW, metal briefcase and a wink for the ladies. But he was thinning on top. Bit like his suit. That had seen better days." He pauses and frowns. "Say, isn't it the law to wear a white coat when you deliver food?"

"The food's packaged, so there's no risk of contamination." Gemma's rewarded with a lingering look at her legs.

I take a sip of weak tea. "When did you produce the flyers?"

He looks at the screen. "Monday, 30th August last year. We printed them on the Friday and he collected them the following week."

That's about a week before Daphne Witherington disappeared. Yet Rathbone said the leaflets were delivered after Miller had left.

Ormerod leans forward. "Is he back? He never paid me, see."

I put my cup on the windowsill and rise. "Thanks for your help."

"Always happy to help," he says, almost knocking his chair over as he scrambles to his feet. "Why don't you leave me your card, Miss Dean? In case I remember anything else."

She hands him a standard Downland District Council card. He looks at it and says, "If you ever want something with more class, give me a call."

Outside, she bursts into giggles. "He won't be printing my wedding invitations."

"That's quick. I hadn't realised things were moving so fast."

She studies the flyer, pretending not to hear me. "What now?" she asks.

"Try the mobile number at the bottom."

"Miller won't be using that, surely?" She punches it into her mobile and listens. "Unobtainable," she says in a 'told-you-so' voice. "Looks like the end of the road."

"Not quite. Someone supplied him with cheap meat."

"And you know who."

"No, but I know a man who will."

We reach Mike's Mighty Munch shortly after two thirty. Business tails off after lunch, but the dull skies and threat of rain have killed it for the day. With at least four laybys along the Uckfield bypass, competition is fierce, which may explain why Mike hasn't gone home.

"I could go home and defrost the freezer," he says, putting down his smart phone. "Or wash my white coat. If you ask me nicely, I might even copy some documents from the police investigation into Colin Miller."

I smile, surprised and pleased at the same time. "Cheers, Mike. I wasn't expecting that."

"Of course you were. That's why you're here, isn't it?"

"What documents?" Gemma asks.

He reaches for a couple of large mugs. "If you're not still averse to my refreshments, I might tell you."

Last time we visited, she criticised his appearance, the state of the van, and his attitude to hygiene.

"I'll have decaff tea," she says.

While he makes the tea, Mike tells us what he's learned. "I spoke to DI Briggs. He's certain Daphne Witherington ran off with Colin Miller. There's been no activity on her bank account or credit cards since the day she left, but Miller has form for fraud and deception, including cloning credit cards. They're probably using new or faked cards and accounts."

"Does that mean she's changed her identity?"

Mike hands me a mug of lukewarm tea. "Briggs told me her husband had a short fuse. He thinks she's escaped an abusive marriage and doesn't want the Colonel to find her."

"He beat her?" Gemma's surprise is tinged with distaste.

He shrugs. "It could explain why she disappeared."

While Colonel Witherington likes to be in control, I'm not sure he'd strike his wife. And if he did, would she leave her paints and paintings behind?

"What if she wasn't abused?" I ask.

"What if she doesn't want to be found?"

Mike clearly believes his former colleagues. "A dog walker noticed a black car in the lane on the morning she disappeared. Tuesday, 8th September, wasn't it? Didn't Rathbone say Miller drove a black BMW?"

"Lots of people have black cars."

"With a *Grub on the Go* sticker in the rear windscreen?"

"Our printer friend never mentioned stickers," I say, glancing at Gemma for confirmation.

"There's more. Miller took Daphne for a meal in La Floret the evening before she disappeared. And guess who saw them? Your favourite undertaker."

"Davenport?"

Mike picks up his smartphone. "I photographed his statement. I'll email both pages to you. Interestingly, his description of Miller doesn't tally with the one Rathbone gave us."

I consider this new information, wondering why the Colonel never mentioned it. Why isn't the statement in the file he gave me?

"Do you think Rathbone was spinning us a line?" I ask.

He laughs. "Who would you trust?"

Neither of them, but I keep it to myself. I finish my tea and put the mug on the counter. I'm about to leave when I remember why I called.

"If I wanted some cheap meat, Mike, and I wasn't too fussy, where would I go?"

He gives me a suspicious look. "Why don't I like the sound of this?"

"Miller sold cheap meat."

He pushes his chest out. "Daphne Witherington ran away from an abusive husband."

"That's speculation."

"Based on strong evidence."

"Circumstantial evidence. The Colonel was out, so she had ample time to take clothes, her paints and paintings. Why didn't she?"

"Now who's speculating?"

He turns away, so I usher Gemma back to the car. As I'm about to climb in, Mike calls out. "Todd Walters."

"Who's Todd Walters?" Gemma asks when we're on our way.

"An unsavoury butcher in Mayfield."

NINE

I drop Gemma at her flat and decline a sandwich. It's already 3.30 and I want to talk to Davenport before my final food inspection of the day. With a chunk of 80% cocoa chocolate in my mouth, I drive into the centre of Tollingdon and past the Town Hall. A left at the mini roundabout, followed by a right at the next, takes me down a lane that runs behind the shops. At the end of the lane, I pull up outside the rear of Tollingdon Funeral Services.

In the time it takes to eat another chunk of the dry, bitter chocolate, the photos of Davenport's witness statement download to my phone. He's factual and to the point, describing Miller as loud and offensive after too much champagne. He's average height with thick brown hair and a moustache.

"Not quite the Miller described by Rathbone or Terry Ormerod," I say, thinking aloud.

Witnesses often describe people differently because they're not trained observers, Mike once told me. Rathbone and Ormerod's descriptions are based on memories, embellished even. Davenport's statement is a record from the time. I'm sure he's a reliable witness, even if he spends more time observing the dead.

On the second page of his statement, he says Daphne Witherington looked embarrassed, especially when Miller told waiters he was leaving dreary Sussex for sunnier climes with the most beautiful woman in the world.

The Colonel must have seen this statement, so why didn't he give me a copy? Was he afraid I would dismiss his suspicions or doesn't he want to accept his wife went abroad with Miller? If she did, why didn't she take her paints?

I grab the ring binder that contains my inspection forms and records and pop it in the carrier bag with my white coat. After I've spoken to Davenport, I'll head around the corner to the High Street and inspect Tollingdon Kebabs, which opens at 4.30.

The wide iron gates, topped with spikes, are folded back against a brick perimeter wall about ten feet high, topped with razor wire. Security cameras, mounted on the wall of the main building, survey the large yard, which contains several outbuildings, including a garage for the limos. The digital locks on the doors make me wonder if there's a roaring trade in stolen hearses.

A smart but old, red MGB with polished chrome bumpers catches my attention. It belongs to Yvonne Parris, according to the nameplate on the wall. Hopefully, she's as sporty as her car, but not as old. Davenport's Ford Mondeo has a tow bar and window stickers from his trips to the Cotswolds, Yorkshire Dales and the Lake District.

I can't see Niamh on a caravan site, queuing for the showers while Davenport cooks bacon on a stove.

"You lost, guvnor?"

A stocky man in dusty blue overalls steps out of a timber building and slides his safety goggles to the top of his bald head. He skirts the rows of headstones, stacked like dominoes, and stops in front of me.

"Environmental Health," I reply, holding up my ID. "I'm on a transport at work survey for European Health and Safety Week. You have a well-organised yard with plenty of space to segregate pedestrians and vehicles." I point to the flapped doors in the main building. "Is that where the coffins are delivered?"

"We prepare them in there."

"You should fit a barrier around your headstones," I say, gesturing. "What if a truck reversed into them? Say, is that why the building at the end has a steel door?"

"That's the embalming room."

I give him my best shudder. "No wonder the windows are blacked out. I'll give that a miss. And the cold store next to it. I guess that's where the bodies are kept."

"Is Mr Davenport expecting you?"

"Keep taking the tablets," I reply, patting a headstone.

I make my way to a small rear door, wedged open with a fire extinguisher. I imagine it's difficult to punch numbers into the digital security locks when you're carrying cups of tea. Sure enough, inside the door there's a small kitchen with sink, kettle and microwave. A long, dimly lit corridor leads past doors on either side. At the end, one of the two panelled doors hides the stairs to the first floor.

The second door opens into a small, muted room. The olive green upholstery on the chairs and sofa matches the carpet and the curtains that hide the door to the viewing area. The pale green walls look bleak despite the subdued lighting. Only the lilies on the mantelpiece above the cast-iron fireplace bring a welcome splash of colour. I'm not including the leaflets and brochures on funeral plans, strategically placed on the low table between the armchairs.

When Niamh arranged the funeral, I stayed at home. Thanks to the cuts, bruises and swelling to my face and neck, I looked like the Elephant Man. And I was still smarting from the revelations and discoveries about William Fisher. Now, standing here in this sombre room, I'm ashamed to say my anger and frustration blinded me to Niamh's grief.

It did save us from an argument though. She doesn't like eco-friendly, biodegradable cardboard coffins.

I open the door into the main reception area, which looks out onto the street. It's much brighter and warmer than my last visit a few years ago. The Council was tendering for the welfare burials we have to carry out by law when someone dies without relatives. On that occasion, I stepped into the world of Miss Marple, complete with antique furniture and phone. Miss Penrose, who had an uncanny resemblance to the legendary Joan Hickson, sat behind an old oak desk, hammering out letters and invoices on a black manual typewriter. She smelt of lavender and had a kind, sympathetic smile that must have comforted many a grieving relative.

A woman in her thirties, with short blonde hair, inquisitive blue eyes, and a wide smile, now sits at a modern desk, complete with PC and flat screen monitor. She's dressed in a smart cream blouse, which parts to reveal a thin gold necklace and slender neck. Her long, dextrous fingers stop their hypnotic rhythm on the keyboard when she spots me. She removes her frameless spectacles and pushes her hair behind her ears as she looks me over.

"Do you always enter through the rear?"

Her deep voice and languid smile soften her American accent. Something Neanderthal pastes a grin on my lips and deepens my voice as I pause by the water dispenser.

"If you leave a door open, someone will walk in."

She sighs. "If only it was Mr Right."

"Perfection always disappoints. It's better to seize the moment."

"And trespass onto private property?"

"Can I help it if I'm intrigued by the MGB in the yard?"

"How do you restrain yourself when you pass a showroom?"

"It's a constant battle," I reply, taking a plastic beaker, "so I confine my urges to the owners of the cars. You are Yvonne Parris?"

"Since the sex change, yes. It's amazing what surgeons can do, don't you think?" She laughs as I hesitate, spilling water over my hand. "Boy, do you look mortified," she says, collapsing back in the chair. "Never make assumptions."

I shake the water off my fingers and walk over to her desk with much less swagger than before. "You're a long way from home, Miss Parris."

"And you're a short distance from the door, Mr Kent Fisher." She chuckles, enjoying my surprise. "Alasdair spotted you on the security cameras. He's busy with a client at the moment and suggests you make an appointment for tomorrow."

"I'm here officially."

"Is that why you sneak in through the rear, trying to catch us out?"

"Mr Davenport may have information on a business I'm investigating."

She pulls on her glasses. "Do you always turn up and expect people to stop what they're doing?"

"No. Well, not intentionally. But when you put it like that, I guess I do."

She begins typing once more. "Then you must be an expert at returning at a more convenient time. Alasdair's in the embalming room."

"I'll pop in on my way out," I say, placing the beaker on her desk. "I'm sure he can embalm and talk."

She rises, revealing a short blue skirt, slim legs and sensible shoes. "Why don't you let your ego cool off in the waiting room," she says, striding around the desk. "I'll see if Alasdair will spare you a few moments."

There's no way I'd enter an embalming room, but she shows no fear. She returns a few minutes later, telling me Alasdair will be along shortly.

"How long have you lived in England?" I ask to fill the silence that follows.

"Long enough to recognise bullshit."

"You're not passing through then."

"In my fascinating MGB, you mean?"

I should give up as my touch has deserted me. "Must be an expensive car to maintain."

"For a receptionist, you mean?" She removes her glasses and regards me with cold, but curious, eyes. "Has it occurred to you that the MG was a birthday present from my father? Hey, maybe I'm temping to earn a few bucks before returning to San Francisco."

For someone who's not interested, she's revealing a lot about herself. "If you were temping you wouldn't have a named parking bay," I say.

"Give the man a star. No, I'm not temping. Neither am I married, engaged or interested in men who think they can do as they please."

That put me in my place.

Davenport saves me from any further mishaps. He strides in, looking paler than ever, his forearms as white as his rolled-up shirtsleeves. When I shake his cold hand, I notice a small tattoo of a heart and the word 'Angelina' on his forearm. He'll need to remove that if he's serious about Niamh.

"Can I get you a tea or coffee, Mr Fisher?"

When Yvonne rises, he raises a hand. "I think it's my turn to do the honours, Miss Parris. We're one big, happy family," he tells me as we walk down the corridor. "No one's too important to make coffee."

In the kitchen, he tries two cupboards before finding a catering tin of instant coffee, which he places on the worktop.

"Yvonne tells me you need my help with a business," he says, staring at the mugs, submerged in dirty water in the sink. "I'm intrigued to know how I can help – unless someone has died."

"You wash, I'll dry," I say, pulling a damp tea towel from a ring on the wall. "Ever heard of a sandwich business called *Grub on the Go*?"

Davenport, who's used to handling bodies, pushes a tentative hand into the murky water, looking relieved when he pulls out a mug. "Should I have heard of it?"

"Colin Miller ran the business."

He rinses the mug under the tap and hands it to me. "It no longer exists?"

Would he answer every question with another?

"You're head of the Chamber of Commerce," I say. "Maybe you came across it."

"We don't have many sandwich rounds in our little fraternity," he says, rinsing a second mug. He looks into the kettle and turns it on. "It's a pity because the food at our meetings can be bland."

"You saw Colin Miller once."

"Was he looking up from a coffin?" His laugh peters out as he struggles to open the coffee tin.

"He was dining with Daphne Witherington at La Floret."

Finally, the lid comes off and tumbles to the floor. He pounces on the lid, scooping it up with some agility. "That must be at least a year ago. Why are you interested in him now?"

I could tell him I'm cleansing the database at work, which we do from time to time. Lots of businesses register and then don't start trading, leaving us with unwanted records that clutter up the system. But if Niamh's mentioned my interest in Colonel Witherington, Davenport will know I'm lying.

I finish drying the second mug. "You know Daphne went missing."

"And you clearly know I witnessed her last night in Tollingdon." He stops spooning coffee into the cups. "Are you sleuthing at the expense of the ratepayer?"

"No, I'm taking a late lunch."

"No need to be defensive, Mr Fisher. I'm not going to report you." The kettle comes to the boil and he fills the mugs with water, leaving little space for milk. "If you've read my statement, there's nothing more I can tell you."

"The police won't let me see a copy. That's why I'm here."

"I see," he says, pulling a bottle of milk from the fridge. "I can spare you ten minutes."

Armed with coffee strong enough to unblock drains, and my carrier bag, I follow him upstairs to a dark office that doubles as a store. A musty smell emanates from a thick layer of dust and bundles of old papers, strewn on every available surface. Old files, strapped together with thick elastic bands, fill an old coffin that's lying across a row of rusty filing cabinets. Instead of drawing back the curtains to let in light, he switches on an old lamp with a decorated glass shade, which casts uneven shadows across the jaded wallpaper.

"Our premier range," he says, patting one of the coffin lids, laid to rest against the wall. Each lid has a card with details printed on it. "Once, I could remember every make and model," he says, settling in a creaking swivel chair. "Now, I don't have the energy or the inclination. That's why this place is a mess. I had to move everything out of the cellar when the public sewer in the road flooded the basement last winter."

"That's one way to be interred."

His laugh misses his eyes. “Niamh told me about your legendary wit.”

I find a space on the desk for my mug. It’s the oak desk, inlaid with leather, which Miss Penrose used. I move a bundle of papers from a chair and sit, placing my carrier bag in my lap. Davenport picks up a paper knife and starts cleaning a fingernail while he speaks.

“From what I recall, Colin Miller was a boorish show off. He bought champagne and drank it like cheap wine. He gave large tips to the waiters and made sure everyone knew how generous he was. I didn’t know who he was at the time. In fact,” he says, pausing in his nail cleaning, “I felt uneasy as Daphne was obviously having an affair of some sort. It was only later, when I found out she’d gone missing, that I realised I could help the police.”

He keeps his observations factual, giving little in the way of opinion, despite my questions. When he finishes, he has a clean set of fingernails.

“I can understand why Colonel Witherington won’t accept what happened, but I don’t see how you can help, Mr Fisher.”

“He asked me to check out Miller’s catering business.”

Davenport takes a noisy sip of coffee, grimaces, and then puts the mug to one side. “I rather had the impression you weren’t interested.”

“Is that what Niamh told you?”

“Colonel Witherington pestered you at the funeral. You seemed rather dismissive and he looked angry. But you must admit, missing wives are a long way from environmental health.”

“Not if there’s a caterer involved. We investigate accidents and food poisoning outbreaks, following the trail of evidence, sifting fact from opinion, truth from lies.” I get to my feet. “I enjoy separating the false from the genuine.”

“Do I detect a warning, Mr Fisher?”

“A warning? What do you mean?”

“You looked uncomfortable when I spoke to Niamh at the wake.” He clasps his hands behind his head, revealing damp armpits. “I try to support the bereaved through their grief.”

“You can’t have a moment to yourself.”

He rises and strolls around the desk. “Niamh needs someone to talk to – someone who understands grief.”

“Someone like you, you mean.”

“Not necessarily, but I’m a good listener.”

“And I’m not?”

He regards me the way people look at traffic wardens. “It’s not for me to say, but you spend a lot of time investigating crimes and tending to your animals. Then, there’s your social life –”

“You’re right. It’s nothing to do with you.”

I grab my carrier bag and hurry down the stairs, kicking open the door at the bottom. How dare he criticise me? He has no idea what’s going on at home – unless Niamh confides in him, of course. By the time I reach my car, the anger and frustration have faded to guilt. She spoke to Davenport because she couldn’t speak to me.

Did I let her down?

The way I let Gemma down.

TEN

While Niamh talks about nothing in particular over supper, Davenport's words reprimand me like a conscience. I can listen without judging and I'm going to prove it.

"You put your feet up while I clear the dishes and then I'll make us both a cup of tea."

"Not for me," she says, slipping Columbo a morsel of turkey. "I'm going out."

"With Davenport?" I thrust the plates into the dishwasher and close the door with a thud. "No problem."

"Clearly there is," she says, getting to her feet.

I groan, wondering what happened to my pledge to listen without judging. "I wanted to have a chat, Niamh, but I suppose it can wait."

"If it's important, I –"

"No, no, you mustn't keep Davenport waiting."

"Don't ever go on the stage, Kent. You're a hopeless actor."

She strides out of the room, closing the door so Columbo can't follow. He stares at the door for a moment and then wanders over to me. I sit next to him on the floor and ruffle his fur.

"Yeah, I know. I'm no good at this emotional stuff. That's why I switch it off so I can stay calm and focused. I wouldn't be much good at saving animals if I got upset by the sight of blood, would I?"

He stares at me for a moment and barks as if he understands.

"That's right. I see things as they are. It doesn't make me uncaring, does it?"

He nudges my arm as I've stopped stroking him.

"Look what happened with Gemma." I cringe, recalling the moment when I blurted out my feelings for her. "Did it bring us closer? No, it put a barrier between us. I couldn't face her in hospital, so she thinks I don't care."

Who am I kidding? She's thought that since the day I ran out on her seven years ago.

"I need to clear her out of my system, little mate."

Columbo rests his head on my thigh, watching me with those big, dark eyes.

"Davenport too. I let him rattle me today. Niamh knows I care. I let her move in here, didn't I? I don't need to be all touchy feely, do I?"

He sighs and snuggles up against my leg, enjoying the attention. It's clear I'm better with animals.

I stroke his fur as he drifts to sleep, contented with his life. It wasn't always that way. That's why I can't let Davenport or Colonel Witherington deflect me from my sanctuary. There will always be animals to rescue, no matter what happens. But will it have to be on Birchill's terms?

Once again, the anger flares. How could William Fisher say he'd given the land to me when he'd already lost it to Birchill?

I sigh and nudge the anger back into its hiding place, reminding myself I have to play the hand I'm dealt, to do what's best for Frances and the animals.

I'm still on the floor when Niamh returns from her bedroom, looking smart and business like in a pale green trouser suit and sensible heels. She's pulled her hair into a ponytail, revealing new gold earrings. The glow in her eyes brightens when she looks down at us.

She brushes a hand across my cheek. "And people say you don't care."

"You look great," I say, noticing the woman not the stepmother. "I'm sorry."

She shakes her head. "No, I'm sorry. I forget how difficult it must be, having me under your feet. We'll talk later."

Columbo jolts to life when I get to my feet. I kiss her on the cheek and give her a hug. "I don't mind you seeing Davenport. It's your life and you should enjoy it."

"I'm not sure anyone enjoys themselves at a Tollingdon Hospice Trust meeting, but I'll try."

Thankfully, she can't see me cringe.

Columbo and I are curled up on the sofa, watching Inspector Morse on DVD when Niamh returns at ten. After fending off Columbo, she tosses her jacket on the armchair, releases her ponytail, and drops onto the sofa next to me. She kicks off her shoes and sighs with pleasure when she wiggles her toes. Columbo clambers over her legs and settles himself between us.

"Now he's sexy," she says, gesturing at John Thaw on the screen. "Vulnerability in a man is always appealing." She reaches across me for the remote and switches off the TV. "You know every episode inside out, Kent, so don't look at me like that."

It's more the playful way she's behaving that troubles me. Did Davenport attend the hospice trust meeting? After all, he is the next step in the process.

"Good meeting?" I ask.

She settles back, her shoulder against mine. "I'm counting my blessings, I suppose. Colonel Witherington joined us for the first time since his wife left him. He resigned from the Trust, saying he would need its services soon as the cancer was spreading fast.

"Not a word," she says, raising a finger. "He's got months, maybe weeks to live. The only thing keeping him alive is your investigation."

"No pressure then."

"Do what you can, Kent. He's not expecting miracles."

"They take longer," I say. "Have you spoken to Davenport today?"

"Please call him Alasdair. I know you feel threatened by him, but –"

"You have spoken to him then."

She puts a hand over her mouth to suppress a giggle. "He put your nose out of joint, didn't he?"

I shift, not sure how to respond. "Do you find it easier to talk to him?"

"He understands how it feels to lose someone you love."

"And I don't?"

She puts a hand on my arm. "You feel betrayed by William. You see his failings, the weakness he hid. I saw it too, but I forgave him because I loved him. When I told you how much I missed him, you said he wasn't worth grieving over."

Sometimes, I need to keep my feelings to myself.

"Alasdair doesn't judge," she says. "He knows what it's like. His wife, Angelina, died after a long illness about eighteen months ago. He still misses her as if it was yesterday. That's why we talk."

"Therapy, you mean?"

She squeezes my hand. "Gemma knows what it's like to lose a father. Okay, he walked out when she was a child, but the loss is the same."

"I'm fine," I say, getting to my feet. "If it helps to talk to Dav … Alasdair, then I'm cool with that. But what if he wants more than talk?"

She considers for a moment. "What if I do?"

At work on Thursday morning, I struggle to concentrate. My talk with Niamh resolved nothing. If anything, it made me realise how bogged down I am. Gemma needs to know I'm over her, though that might be difficult to believe after my outburst of undying love at Tombstone.

Maybe I can show her I've moved on by inviting her and Richard to dinner at the sanctuary to celebrate their engagement. And if I invite Davenport, I can make peace with Niamh.

Pleased with my idea, I focus on Todd Walters, who may have supplied meat to Colin Miller. According to the database, Walters has run his butchery business for a long time, resisting the all-conquering supermarkets. He didn't like anyone in a suit, I seem to recall. I only met him once about 10 years ago when I was a district inspector, or DI as Nigel likes to call it. When he answers the phone, 'DI Long speaking', I wonder if he's a frustrated police officer.

He's certainly frustrating me. The inspection of Walters' shop was due seven months ago.

"You awarded him a Food Hygiene Rating of '2', Nigel." We're in *Toasted*, a coffee shop along the High Street from the Town Hall. "Why have you let the inspection slip?"

His stammer frustrates him. He closes his eyes tight shut and reprimands himself with an angry shake of the head. Then he takes out his wallet and stares at the photograph of his wife, who died when their children were at school.

"When Emily was here, I … I … I never worried about anything," he says. "I knew everything w… w… would work out fine. The district was a different place then. No one challenged what we said because they knew we were helping them."

He looks up, his eyes mournful beneath their bushy brows. "Now, it's f… f… f… freedom of information requests, complaints about inspectors, smear campaigns on Facebook. Honestly, Kent, I spend most nights worrying someone's found something I missed."

"Like an overdue inspection?"

"W… W… Walters assaulted a VAT inspector. Put him in hospital."

"When was this?" I ask, wondering why it's not recorded on the file to warn others.

"About a year ago?"

"Is that why you haven't inspected him?"

"No. Yes. Well, no, not directly. Since Emily died, I've had to look after my girls. They were all that mattered."

"And you did a great job," I say, wondering where he's heading.

"Yes, but they're in Australia now. We Skype and they're coming over this Christmas, but I... I... I'm lonely." He blushes and sips more coffee. "I never thought anyone would be interested. Look at me. I look like my clothes come from a charity shop. I'm clumsy. I... I... I... can't speak when I get nervous. But she didn't care."

"Who didn't care?"

He swallows and looks at the floor. "Stacey Walters."

"Todd Walters' wife?"

Nigel shushes me as my voice rises. He leans closer, sweat beading on his forehead. "The moment I saw her in the shop... She wore tight jeans, a white tee shirt and an apron tied around her waist. She had amazing ..." His cupped hands tell me all I need to know. "She used to be a model and there she was, coming on to me while her husband chopped meat in the back room."

He thrusts his wallet back into his pocket.

"She stood so close, brushing against me. In the storeroom, she said she was hot and took off her apron."

He stares into his cup, his cheeks burning.

"What happened?" I ask, fearing the worst.

"I wanted her to pull off her top and seduce me, but all I could hear was her husband, chopping up meat. Somehow, I finished the inspection and told him what needed doing. As I left, Stacey asked if I'd be coming back to check on them."

From the flush of his cheeks, I don't need to ask if he returned.

"I Googled her," he says. "She had a different name as a model, but I found photographs of her. I spent every evening, fantasising about her. But when I plucked up the courage to go back, the shop was closed. A neighbour said Todd Walters put an inspector in hospital for messing around with Stacey."

He sighs and shakes his head. "You think that would have frightened me off, but I went back a few weeks later. Walters went ballistic when I asked after his wife. He stood there, shouting at me, cleaver in hand, going on about someone taking his Stacey away. I don't know why I said it wasn't me, but he pinned me to the wall."

Nigel runs a finger under his collar, clearly distressed. "I thought I was going to die. Then he fell apart and started sobbing, so I legged it."

"Why didn't you put a note on file?"

"What if he accused me of sleeping with his wife?"

"You didn't."

"No one would have believed me, would they? You know what management are like, Kent. Why would someone complain unless it was true?"

I nod, well aware of what it's like to have no management support. "But what if Gemma or Lucy visit? They could be in danger."

"I w… w… w… was going to tell you, Kent, but Walters rang me to apologise."

"Nigel, he put someone in hospital."

"I know. I know," he says, shaking his hands. "I thought if I did the next inspection no one would be at risk."

"But you haven't, have you?"

He shrinks into the sofa. "Are you going to report me?"

I should, but after some of my escapades it would be hypocritical. Fortunately, no one's come to any harm and he knows how badly he behaved. Danni won't see it like that, and she'd be right, of course, but with jobs on the line, I don't want to sacrifice Nigel.

"I'll do the inspection, Nigel. You need to tackle your backlog. That means working evenings for the next few weeks, okay?"

He nods and rises. "No problem. I'm sorry."

"Next time, you report it right away and put a warning on file."

He nods and slinks away.

While I wonder whether I was too lenient, Gemma rings. "Kent, you need to see this place. It's a dump."

I reach for my pen. "Where are you?"

"Walters' Butchers in Mayfield. He's not a happy bunny."

ELEVEN

Gemma's waiting on the pavement in front of St Dunstan's Church in Mayfield High Street. She huddles beside the stone wall, the collar of her pale blue fleece turned up against the wind.

"You took your time," she says, scurrying over, white coat in hand.

"Not so fast. You shouldn't have gone in there."

"Because I'm not experienced enough to inspect a butcher?"

"Todd Walters assaulted a VAT inspector."

Doubt defuses the defiance in her eyes. "There's no warning on the file."

"You read the file then."

She glares at me. "If you'd put a warning on file, I wouldn't have gone in, would I?"

"You shouldn't have gone in without talking to me first."

"I'm not psychic, Kent. How the hell can I do my job when you never tell me anything?"

"I would if you'd stop rushing off to do your own thing."

She stares at me in disbelief. "We wouldn't be here if I hadn't dragged you to see the Colonel. If I hadn't found the printer you wouldn't know about Walters."

"And if you'd spoken to Nigel, the last officer to inspect this place, you'd have discovered Walters has a violent streak."

"You won't admit you're wrong, will you?" When I don't answer, she turns. "In that case, I'm off to organise my wedding. That's one thing you can't screw up."

She marches down the street, narrowly avoiding a waste bin. When she reaches the coffee shop, she stops, mutters and then marches back. "Okay, so I forgot where I parked."

"Sometimes you need to take a breath," I say, stepping in front of her. "What did you say to set Walters off?"

"I saw how grubby the place was when I walked in. I was about to come out and call you when he asked who I was. When I told him, he blew a fuse, so I came out and rang you."

"Well done. So, do you want to hear what Walters has to say about Colin Miller or not?"

J.T. Walters and Son was established in 1951, according to the faded, traditional sign above the shop. The film of dirt on the glass, and the flaking paint, make me wonder if the windows have been neglected since that date. Inside, the stainless steel display cabinets offer a half-hearted selection of fresh meats and sausages, adding to the impression of a shop on its last legs. The battered blackboards on either side of the entrance reveal the latest offers and conceal the crumbling render on the walls. The door creaks and groans when I push it, setting off a bell as it springs open.

The smell of meat, rancid fat and damp wood greet us. A blend of sawdust, dirt, and waste food coats the bare floorboards. The painted walls are cracked and blistering, bare apart from a couple of faded posters showing various cuts of meat. Behind the counter, which consists of two glass-fronted display cabinets and a worn wooden chopping block, the walls are tiled and lined with a metal rail, used to hang game. Not that there are any birds there. There's not much meat on display either, which is hardly surprising. I can imagine some of the elderly residents, who remember Mr Walters Senior, remaining loyal, but for how much longer? It's a shame because we need independent butchers, making proper sausages and burgers, offering us meat that's to our liking rather than bulk wrapped in plastic.

Todd Walters, a short, muscular man with a neck like a bull, finishes rolling and tying a pork joint on a chopping block that's as bloody as it is old. He turns, his small, suspicious eyes studying me. He wipes his hands on his filthy white coat and winks at Gemma.

"Brought the boss, have you?"

"Kent Fisher," I say, holding up my ID.

"I know who you are." He lifts the lid of a chest freezer and peers inside. "I had a body in here, but I've turned it into burgers."

"Was it a VAT inspector?"

He thuds the lid shut. "What do you want?"

I peer behind the counter at the dirty floor, lined with greasy sheets of cardboard. Several days of sawdust and blood have accumulated in the junction between the floor and the wall and beneath the display cabinets. Mingled into this debris are a couple of pencils, some trampled polystyrene trays, and enough scraps of meat to keep the local rat population happy.

"I'm tempted to close you down," I reply.

"Then you'd be doing me a favour."

His weary voice tells me he's not joking. "Don't you have an assistant?" I ask.

"Do I look like I can afford an assistant? Unless you want to lend me yours," he says, looking Gemma up and down. "I think you'd rather like my sweetbreads."

"I prefer them warm and still attached," she says.

He grins and starts to undo his coat. "My Stacey liked my sweetbreads."

"Where is she?" I ask, grabbing the opportunity he's dangling before me. "According to the last inspection, she ran the shop."

"Well, as you can see, she's not here."

The tension in his voice and stance warns me to back off. I stroll over to the window and look down at the solitary string of sausages, alone on the refrigerated stainless steel plate.

"Must be hard working on your own," I say. "I'm surprised you're still trading."

"I have my regulars."

"Was Colin Miller a regular?"

Without warning, he grabs a cleaver from a hook on the wall. Gemma screams as he smashes the cleaver into the top of the display cabinet. The glass shatters, collapsing in a shower of fragments on the meat below. Packets of herbs and stuffing leap from the shelf to land on the floor among the rest of the broken glass.

Walters stares at the mess, his chest rising and falling. His eyes bulge as he raises his arm once more.

"Put the cleaver down, Mr Walters." I keep my voice calm and my eyes on the cleaver. "I only want to talk about Colin Miller."

"His name's Mellor. Colin Mellor. He stole my Stacey."

He brings the cleaver thudding into the Formica shelf at the back of the cabinet, missing the electronic scales by a whisker. Tongs fly into the air and clatter to the floor. The neat pile of wrapping paper cascades in a steady stream.

Thankfully, the cleaver's stuck fast in the shelf.

I glance across to check on Gemma, back pressed against the door, phone in hand. "Step away, Mr Walters," I say, crunching through the glass, "and tell me about Stacey."

He tugs at the cleaver once more, determined to wrench it free. When he fails, his thick fingers curl into a fist. A strangled sound starts deep in his throat and erupts into a despairing roar.

"NO!"

He smashes his fist down on the scales. Then he hurls them at the wall, but the electric cable yanks them back. They crash into the side of the cabinet and fall to the floor. Walters, chest heaving, his breath rasping, stares at them until he notices the blood on his knuckles. His shoulders sag and his head falls forward.

I breathe once more. "Everything's fine, Gemma. No need to ring the police."

Her expression suggests otherwise.

"Lock the door so no one interrupts us. Mr Walters, where do you keep your first aid kit?"

He looks up, a little dazed. "Upstairs. Why, are you hurt?"

"I was thinking about your hand."

He glances down and snaps out of his trance. "Shit," he says, striding towards the butcher's curtain at the rear of the shop. He pushes through the clear plastic strips, smeared with fat, grease and dirt, and clatters into something on the other side, leading to more expletives.

"It's okay," I tell Gemma, who's still rooted by the door. "He's upset about losing his wife. And this place, I guess. It must be haemorrhaging money."

"We should go. He's unstable."

"He accused Miller of stealing his wife. Sound familiar?"

"And when you mention Miller, he could go mental again."

"It's Mellor," he calls from the back.

"See, he wants to talk," I say, suddenly an expert in solving emotional problems. "He's probably bottled up his feelings since his wife left."

She glances at the mess on the floor. "You don't say."

"If you're worried, wait for me outside."

I push through the curtain into the passageway, almost crashing into a twisted stainless steel wash basin, hanging from the wall. Some of the shrink-wrapped bales of plastic trays and containers underneath have scattered across the floor. Though there's only a faint light from behind, I make out aprons, coats and hats on hooks above a wooden bench, covered with parts from a mincing machine.

At the end of the corridor, I duck under the cobwebs into a musty-smelling room that's tiled from floor to ceiling. Two letterbox windows high on the far wall cast a subdued light on a bowl chopper, and a sausage making machine, mounted on an adjacent stainless steel table. An industrial sized mincer, minus its innards, sits on another table. Though clean, it doesn't look like the room or the machines are used much.

The sound of running water takes me to the opposite side of the room, where a spider scrambles to escape one of the two deep sinks. I grab some paper towels from the dispenser above the washbasin and wipe the blood from the cold tap before turning it off. There's more blood on the side of the basin and on a couple of crumpled paper towels on the floor.

"Gross!" Gemma stops at the door, flapping her hands at the cobwebs.

"I thought you were going to wait."

"I heard a rat under the floor."

She ducks under the cobwebs, pushes her hair back and looks around. "What's this?" she asks, peering inside the bowl chopper.

"It mixes the sausage meat," I reply. "When we've got more time, I'll tell you all about butchery."

"As long as you skip the sweetbreads," she says with a grin. "I've seen plenty."

I push through the door in the corner and head up uncarpeted stairs, covered on one side with exercise books. They're Walters' accounts, going back decades it seems. They continue along the right hand side of the landing, breaking only for doors, stripped of paint. A door on the left opens into a living room, which reeks of curry, courtesy of the mountain of trays on the dining table. Two sofas, which look ready for the tip, form an L-shape that cordons off an old TV on a pedestal and a small hi fi stack.

Walters stands by the fireplace, rubbing cream into his knuckles from a container on the mantelpiece. The recess to one side contains fitted pine cupboards with louvre doors. The recess on the other side contains a frame for a cupboard. The partially stripped wallpaper and holes and cracks plugged with filler, suggest some kind of renovation, now defeated by mess and neglect.

Maybe the makeover stopped when Stacey left.

"I'm sorry about …" Walters replaces the lid on the container and stomps across to the window. He pulls back the grubby net curtain and looks out at the High Street. "I've lived here all my life. No mortgage, no loans, no debts. Then Colin Mellor turned me over."

Gemma tenses as Walters' fingers curl into fists.

"My suppliers want to take me to court," he says, turning. "I told them to go ahead. I have nothing, so they're welcome to as much as they want. Even the furniture's worthless," he says, kicking one of the sofas. "Place looks like a tip, doesn't it?"

"Do you have any refuse bags?" Gemma asks.

He points to a louvre door in the corner.

In the kitchen, she opens the cupboard beneath the sink and ferrets around, pulling out washing powder, two buckets and a pack of unused cleaning cloths. When she reaches the refuse bags, she throws them to me. "Clear the table, Kent, and I'll make some tea."

Walters remains on the sofa while I gather up the takeaway trays. It appears he likes chicken korma with pilau rice and plain naan bread. It takes one bag to contain the waste and a second for the grubby, sticky tablecloth that's soaked up curry for months. I transfer the bags onto the landing as Gemma emerges with a tray and three mugs of tea.

"Thanks for your help, Mr Walters," she says. "Couldn't have done it without you."

At the mention of his name, he stirs and struggles to his feet to take the 'World's best husband' mug from her. He walks over to the cupboards beside the fireplace and opens the door to reveal a glass cabinet, containing trophies and shields. He takes out a large framed photograph of a slim woman in a black shirt, holding a trophy aloft. She has frizzy black hair, a small oval face with a wide mouth and unusually thick lips, and sexy dark eyes that can barely contain her delight.

"My Stacey," he says with pride. "Club champion three years running."

A set of gold personalised darts fan out from a black holder, embossed with the word 'Stacey'. The pink flights also proclaim her name in the same stylised writing.

Gemma whispers in my ear. "No one that skinny can have boobs that big."

I remember Nigel saying she was once a model. "Unusual sport for a woman," I say.

Walters replaces the photograph in the cabinet. "My Stacey could do anything."

"How did you meet her?" I ask.

"She worked for Colin Mellor. He managed a private club in Brighton. He fancied himself as a big promoter with his metal briefcase and shiny suit." Walters takes a slug of tea. "If you wanted strippers, dancers or singers, he was the man. One of the lads in the rugby club had a 21st birthday so we hired a stripper. Someone knew Mellor and got in touch. He came over and offered to jazz things up on Saturday nights with a few of his girls."

"Did that include Stacey?"

He glares at me. "She was a singer not a stripper. She had an amazing voice."

He wrenches open a second cupboard door to reveal a small karaoke machine and microphone, along with a shelf filled with CDs. He pulls out a CD and hands it to me.

Stacey knew how to pose for the camera. Cocooned in a tight scarlet corset that pushed her breasts up to her chin, she leans forward, her dark, sexy eyes, peering through her tousled black hair.

He takes back the CD before I can flip it to read the track list.

"I met Stacey in Brighton," he says, closing the cupboard. "Mellor had plans to take the club upmarket. He wanted dinner and cabaret, not leering hooligans. He wanted cheap steaks to sell at the highest prices. The margins were good, so I supplied him. One day, when I was delivering, I heard a woman singing and went to take a look."

"Stacey," I say.

He swallows and nods. A warm smile spreads over his face. "I was mesmerised. When she spotted me, she waved me over, but ... I was late for a delivery and had to leave."

He drinks more tea to hide his flushed cheeks. "I went to watch her every Saturday, hoping she would notice me, but there were always plenty of men in suits in the way. Then, one night, three or four blokes kept shouting rude suggestions while she sang. When she came off stage, they crowded round her, touching her up."

He runs a finger under the collar of his shirt. "I told them to lay off. One of the blokes told me to eff off, so I decked him. And his three yuppie mates," he adds with a proud nod. "Next thing I know, Stacey's dragging me out through a fire escape. Mellor's not far behind. He grabs Stacey's arm and pulls her inside. He tells her to get back to the customers, but she refuses. That's when he slapped her."

"And you decked him, right?"

"I bust his jaw and cracked several ribs. I never expected Stacey to come with me, but she chased after me, so I brought her here."

"Did Mellor come after you?"

He shakes his head. "I expected him to show up with some of his bouncers to beat the shit out of me, but he never did. I thought Stacey would stay a few days and then go back, but she loved it here. She said I was her hero. And then last year …"

"He showed up, right?"

Walters' brows dip with suspicion. "Why are you interested in my Stacey? I thought you came here to inspect the place."

"I came to find out about Colin Miller. Or Mellor, as you know him."

"Why?"

"He ran off with my fiancée." I ignore the stunned look on Gemma's face and say, "She owned a small delicatessen in Tollingdon."

He turns to Gemma. "So why are you here?"

"She's my mother," she replies without hesitation.

"But you work with Mr Fisher."

"That's how he met my mother."

He frowns. "Why didn't you say when you walked in?"

"Mr Walters," I say, stepping between them, "I need to find out if Colin Miller and Colin Mellor are the same person. Can you describe him?"

Walters walks over to the window. "Stacey didn't tell me he was back until I spotted him from up here. As soon as I saw the shiny suit and metal briefcase, I knew it was him. He'd put on weight and lost a lot of hair, but he still drove a fancy black car."

"Did you confront him?"

Walters nods. "He said he was starting a new business and wanted a reliable meat supplier. I didn't believe a word," he says, turning. "I knew he was interested in Stacey because I found some letters from him."

He trudges across to the cupboard. "So, I supplied him with some meat and waited to see if he made a move. I asked Stacey if she missed singing in the clubs, but she said she loved being part of the village. She'd a rough childhood," he says, opening the door. "She never talked about it so I knew it must be rough."

"How long did you supply Mellor?" I ask.

"I never saw him again. I wondered if my Stacey told him to sling his hook. Then, she tells me about some new business in Brighton, looking for meat. I wondered if it was Mellor, so I drove over there, but I couldn't find the place."

He pulls out the framed photograph and stares at it. "When I got back, the shop was open, but she'd gone. No one saw her go. Someone in a flat across the road saw a black car driving away, but she also said she could see my aura, whatever that is."

"Did Stacey contact you?" I ask.

He shakes a forlorn head. "Why would she? She was gorgeous and talented. What did she see in a lump like me?"

A little boy lost, by the look of things.

"Can you remember the date?" I ask.

"I'll never forget it. 22nd September last year."

That's two weeks after Daphne Witherington disappeared.

TWELVE

"What do you make of that?"

We're in Mayfield Macchiato. I'm not sure why people think alliteration will make their business stand out, but it's preferable to the proliferation of misspelt names, like Beanz or Koffee, that seem to be sweeping the country. MM, as its coasters and place mats proclaim, still needs to update the chintz tablecloths, wooden floorboards and oak dressers from its former incarnation as a tearoom. Maybe the owners had no money left after purchasing the beast of a coffee machine that dominates the counter. I prefer the chink of fine china cups to the industrial blast of steam, hissing through milk. Maybe the locals agree as we have the place to ourselves.

Across the street, Todd Walters has closed his shop, maybe permanently.

"If Miller and Mellor are one and the same," I say, "why did he get involved with Daphne Witherington when his old flame's 20 miles up the road?"

"He needed money and conned the Colonel," Gemma replies.

"Twenty grand doesn't go far. And what happened to Daphne?"

"Maybe Miller was putting a girl band together."

She grins and slides the last mouthful of a double chocolate muffin into her mouth.

That's the problem. Are Miller and Mellor the same person? The man described by Rathbone and Walters bears little resemblance to the one Davenport saw.

Yet within two weeks of each other, Daphne and Stacey disappeared without warning, leaving valued possessions behind.

I consider this on the drive back to the office, looking for a link between the two women. Maybe they met by chance and became friends. Maybe both felt trapped in their marriages. When I start to wonder if Daphne is Stacey's mother, I know I've lost the plot.

Back at my desk, I delete around three quarters of my emails without opening them. Most are invites to courses I can't manage without. Ironic, considering I manage to live without them. I'm offered training, equipment and contract officers on a regular basis, even though I never respond to the emails. The Food Standards Agency, Health and Safety Executive, and Public Health England keep me occupied with alerts and updates, most of which are interesting but need no action. That leaves the EHCNet messages from environmental health officers around the country who want advice, information or help with problems. Danni keeps a tight control on these. We have to get her permission to send anything, and she filters incoming messages, only forwarding those she thinks we can respond to.

Apart from today.

"She's on leave until Monday," Kelly says. "You're in charge, lover."

"Does that mean you have to do anything I want?"

"Is it something Danni would never agree to?"

"Would I do that?" I ask, devastated by the slur on my character.

I dictate my message, asking for information on Colin Miller/Mellor and *Grub on the Go* and Kelly posts it on EHCNet.

"Why are you and Twinkle Toes so interested in him?" she asks. "What's he done?"

"I want to find out if he's traded anywhere else."

"What are you up to?" she asks, not fooled by my half-truth. "Danni will want a full written explanation on Monday. And a worksheet on the database."

I'd forgotten that detail. "Okay, I think he's selling dodgy meat."

"And you've been so busy catching up on overdue inspections, you haven't had time to create a worksheet." She looks up from the computer. "Shall I set one up for you, lover? I imagine you received an anonymous tip off, as usual."

That avoids having to make up a name and address for a complainant that doesn't exist. I lean over and kiss her cheek. "What would I do without you?"

"You'd get caught."

When my phone rings at five to five, I hesitate before answering, keen to get home. Thankfully, it's Gemma. "Do you still keep your running gear in the car?"

In the background, I can hear fast moving traffic. "Where are you?"

"Friston Church. I'm about to run to Colonel Witherington's house and I thought you might want to join me."

"Why?"

"I need your spare head torch. And I think Alice killed Daphne Witherington."

Twenty minutes later and changed into my running gear, I pull up next to her Volvo. The light's almost faded beneath a moody sky that's mumbling with thunder. As intrigued as I am about Gemma's assertion, I'm not sure why I agreed to run with her.

Then she emerges from the car in leggings and a running top that's moulded over her sports bra and I know why. No matter how many times I remind myself she's engaged, I come running when she calls, literally in this case. Self-awareness and logic don't stand a chance.

"Why would Alice kill Daphne?" I ask.

Gemma zips up her high visibility jacket and follows me to collect the spare head torch.

"Can you imagine how Alice felt, after all those years of loyal service? The Colonel marries Daphne and brings her home, relegating Alice to a couple of rooms above the garage. Then she has to serve and clean up after the woman who took her place."

I adjust my head torch and nod. "Jealousy's a powerful motive. But that doesn't explain Colin Miller."

"He was only after money. Alice used him to divert attention. She knew he'd vanish once he had the money." Gemma pauses to secure her head torch, taking care not to trap her ponytail. "Then all she had to do was make it look like he'd run off with Daphne. Motive, means and opportunity, I'd say."

I nod, seeing the logic. "Now tell me why we're going there in our running gear."

She switches on her torch and grins, obviously pleased with herself. "Colonel Witherington's at a meeting. Alice is home alone and won't be expecting us."

"Naturally, she won't think we're nuts, running in a thunderstorm in the dark."

"She'll be more concerned with the sprained ankle I'm going to have and want to help me. That's when we ask some searching questions about the garden."

"The garden?"

"All in good time, Holmes. First, I have to set the scene."

Another rumble of thunder encourages us to get going. It takes a few minutes to cross the busy main road, but once over, we settle into a steady pace, running in single file to give oncoming traffic plenty of room to pass. We reach the turn into Old Willingdon Road within a few minutes and run side by side. A crack of thunder booms across the valley, driving away the electrified humidity with a blast of cold wind.

"So, Watson, how did she do it?" I ask.

"Alice became Daphne's best friend and confidante. She pointed out all the Colonel's little faults and petty jealousies so Daphne wouldn't upset him. He's the most wonderful and generous man, but he has a temper sometimes," Gemma says in a Scottish accent. "Och, it soon blows over but it might seem a little frightening the first few times. He won't be mad at you, but he likes to be in charge and do everything for you. It's only because he loves you so much. Don't worry. He'll never strike you."

I can see where she's heading. "So, she starts to worry he'll hit her. Meanwhile, Alice primes the Colonel, telling him to buy his wife clothes and lavish her with gifts because she wants to be spoiled. When she complains, he loses his temper and so on."

"You're smarter than you look," Gemma says, oblivious to the latest crack of thunder, which explodes right above us. Any moment now, the rain's going to pelt down. "The stage is now set and Alice calls in Colin Miller. Having secured him twenty grand, he has to take Daphne to La Floret that night so everyone will think they're running away together. Then, when they both disappear … What do you think, Holmes?"

I'm impressed. "Where's the body?"

"Under the conservatory. Now, let's pretend I've sprained my ankle," she says, stopping at the boundary of Belmont. Alice's Micra sits in the drive and the lights are on in her flat. "You'll have to carry me from here, Kent."

"Why you think Daphne's under the conservatory?"

"The Colonel had the rear garden landscaped and replaced the old conservatory about 12 months ago. Richard's brother, Mark, supplied and built the conservatory. He said Alice watched them like a hawk. She never stopped wandering over, checking on them, asking questions about what they were doing and how long it would take. That's what made me wonder if she'd killed Daphne."

"If you're right, she's not going to confess."

"We'll see."

Gemma groans in agony, hobbles over and slides an arm over my shoulder. "Come on," she says when I don't move. "Put your hand around my waist."

Before she can demonstrate her limping skills, the clouds shower us with some of the biggest raindrops I've seen. An almighty crack of thunder shakes the ground. Within seconds, we're drenched, but laughing for some reason as we hurry to the garage. I ring the bell. Alice opens an upstairs window, peers down at us and then comes to the door. If she's surprised to see us, she hides it well.

"Let's go over to the house," she says, opening a golf umbrella.

Once in the warm kitchen, she puts on the kettle and then goes upstairs, returning a few minutes later with luxurious bath towels. She recoils as the windows vibrate from more thunder. The rain sounds like it's ready to beat its way through the glass.

"What on earth are you doing out in this weather?"

"We're running for charity," Gemma replies, wrapping the towel around her. "Every mile equals money, but we have to run so many miles each week. That's why we go out in all weathers."

Alice shakes her head as we drip on the floor. "I hope you're not expecting me to sponsor you."

While she makes tea, Gemma peers through the window. "Your conservatory's taking a battering," she says. "You might need to check for leaks once the storm passes."

"It's quite robust, I can assure you."

"Are you sure?" Gemma manages to imbue her question with just enough doubt. "Only Kent spotted some hairline cracks the other night. He thought it might be settling."

"I'm not a building inspector," I say, "so I can't be sure."

"He's too modest," Gemma says, turning away from the window. "He's got an amazing eye for things that are out of line. You wouldn't want the conservatory to sink into the ground, would you?"

"I can assure you it's built on very firm foundations. I watched them pour the concrete."

"Must have made a mess of the garden," Gemma says, taking a cup of tea. "Kent can take another look to put the Colonel's mind at rest."

"I don't think that will be necessary," Alice says, her voice sharp. "The Colonel has more important things to worry about."

"You said he looked frail, didn't you, Kent? With all that stress and responsibility I'm surprised he doesn't take it easy and stand down from the council. He could go any moment," Gemma says, looking at Alice. "And then where would you be?"

There's no mistaking the coldness in Alice's eyes as she sips her tea. "I'm not sure we should be talking like this."

"I'm just saying how fragile life can be. I mean, look at Mrs Witherington. Here one day, gone the next."

Alice goes over to the window and pulls back the net curtain. "Looks like the rain's easing," she says, though it sounds as violent as before. "I could offer you an umbrella, Mr Fisher, but I doubt whether you could run with it in this wind. I'm not trying to get rid of you, but I do have my supper in the oven."

"Do you mind if I say hello to Monty?" I ask. "Is he in the conservatory?"

"I'd rather you didn't traipse about the place in your wet trainers," she says. "I'll take the towels, if you've finished with them, and put them in the wash. I'm sure Colonel Witherington will be disappointed he missed you."

"We only dashed in to dodge the rain," I say. "There's no news about Daphne."

"But we're on Colin Miller's tail," Gemma says, a little too enthusiastically. "I can't wait to hear his version of events."

Alice holds out a hand for the towel. "I'm sure the Colonel will be pleased with your progress. There, it sounds like it's stopped raining."

Gemma hands over her towel. "I love the way a storm clears the air and lets you see things as they should be."

Alice takes the towels and follows us to the front door. Outside, there's a faint veil of rain, but the ground smells clean and fresh. The door closes sharply behind us and Gemma punches the air.

"Guilty! How prickly was she when we suggested the conservatory was subsiding?"

"You were hardly subtle."

"That's what you like about me. Now, let's get running because I'm cold."

We set off into the dark, damp clothes clinging to cold muscles. Neither of us speaks until we're back at the church.

"How much do you reckon the Colonel's leaving Alice in his will?" she asks, peeling off the head torch.

"If everything goes to Daphne, Alice won't get a penny."

"But if the Colonel thought Daphne ran off with Miller, he might have updated his will."

THIRTEEN

On Friday morning, Columbo and I have a serious talk. He never breaks eye contact while he listens, tilting his head from side to side, occasionally barking, especially when I tell him my plans. He's quick to nudge me if I stop stroking him.

Once we've agreed terms, I tell Niamh about my idea for a dinner party tomorrow evening.

"You know Alasdair's allergic to dogs," she says, giving Columbo an apologetic look.

"Frances will spoil him rotten, leaving me free to get to know Dav … Alasdair better. I'm assuming he's going to be around a bit longer."

She wags her finger. "You're fishing again. Do I ask you about Rebecca?"

She thinks I can do better than a softly spoken Scouser with hair extensions. Turns out Rebecca can do better than an environmental health officer with pretentions. She's discovered a super sleuth's life isn't that exciting when there are no cases to investigate.

"Rebecca's moved on," I say, "but I'm inviting Gemma and Richard."

Niamh sighs. "If you're on your own, we need to invite someone else."

"That narrows it down," I say with more sarcasm than intended.

"How about Alasdair's receptionist, Yvonne Parris? She's charming, witty, sophisticated, and much closer to your age."

Everything Rebecca's not, she means. "She's bound to have something far more interesting planned for Saturday evening," I say. "Or someone."

"Not at the moment," Niamh says with a grin. "Are you sure you don't want to book a table at La Floret and save on the washing up?"

She means my flat doesn't have the character or ambience for a sophisticated dinner party. And unlike Downland Manor, where a contract catering and service company used to handle the arrangements, we'll struggle to accommodate six people and the dirty dishes we'll create. Luckily, downstairs in the barn, I have a dining table and six chairs that Mike and I bought from a failing hotel several months ago.

"You concentrate on the menu," I say, "and leave the arrangements to me."

"I'm doing the cooking, am I?"

"You're the best, Niamh."

I'm out of the door before she can argue. If Yvonne Parris accepts the invitation, it will show Gemma I've moved on. That's if she and Richard can make it. When I get to work, I call her into Danni's office.

Gemma seems surprised. "Richard and me?"

"Alasdair will be there too."

Gemma reaches out a hand to test the temperature of my forehead. “Do you intend to snipe at him all evening?”

“Niamh and I had a heart to heart and I’m pleased he’s helping her move on. I thought it was time I did too.”

From the way she’s studying me, she either thinks I’m nuts or plotting something sinister. “Is Rebecca part of this moving on?”

“She’s already moved on. She’s more raves and dance music than Barclay James Harvest.”

Gemma’s brief smile could mean anything. “Are you inviting anyone to make up the numbers? I only ask because if Richard can’t make it, I’ll be on my own too.”

“Then you’d better make sure he can.”

“So, you are inviting someone.”

“Indeed,” I say, enjoying her curiosity.

With Gemma at home for the afternoon, Nigel playing a round on the golf course, Lucy on district and Danni on leave, Kelly and I are the thin green line of the Public Protection Team. The quiet allows me to catch up with reports and gather my ideas for some of the projects Danni wants me to take on. The only distractions are the trickle of emails that will build to a torrent as five o’clock approaches. As usual, everyone has something they need to complete before the weekend.

At 3.50, Brian Slade rings. An EHO with a strong West Country accent, he speaks slowly, as if there’s nothing to be gained by rushing, telling me he works for Mendip District Council in Somerset. His warm voice has the reassuring quality of someone who’s in control and happy with his work.

"I may have found the man you're looking for, Mr Fisher." He pauses to slurp a drink. "We came across him on the fringes of the Glastonbury Festival in June, selling sandwiches and soft drinks from a cool box. We had a couple of complaints, alleging he'd put his own labels on out of date supermarket sandwiches. No one thought to keep the cartons, of course, so we had nothing to follow up."

He takes another long slurp. "Then, a few weeks ago, a new burger van appears in Glastonbury. One of our admin officers makes a couple of phone calls and finds out it's owned by a guy called Colin Mellor, who keeps it at one of the less salubrious pubs in the district. He's calling the business, *Grub on the Go*."

I'm making notes as he speaks. "Have you checked him out?"

"Yes, we sit around doing nothing all day," he replies in a good-natured tone. "Mellor only trades Friday and Saturday nights, but the police tell me he's moved to a car park in the town centre. So, before I visit him tonight, is there anything you want to tell me?"

"We had similar complaints about relabelling sandwiches, but he only traded briefly in our district. He vanished about twelve months ago."

"So, why did you send the EHC Net message?"

"His name cropped up in connection with another matter."

"Anything you want to share with me?"

I can't tell Slade I'm looking for a missing woman. "We're not sure it's the same man," I say, playing for time.

"Well, according to his Facebook page, Colin Mellor has converted a Volkswagen Camper into a burger van. There are photos of it, and him, if that helps."

Why didn't I think of looking on Facebook?

I type in the address Slade gives me and bring up the *Grub on the Go* page. I ignore the good luck posts and open the photo gallery. The camper looks like 'The Mystery Machine' from Scooby Doo with a serving hatch and canopy.

The final photo shows a man in a baseball cap and white coat, standing beside the hatch. He's average height, slim, and in his 50s, I'd say. While there's no way of telling whether he's bald on top, I can just make out silver hair below the baseball cap. The shadow from the peak of the cap hides his eyes, leaving me with a broad smile and teeth below a thin nose that was broken once.

"It could be our man," I say. "Would you mind if I joined you tonight to confirm it? I could be with you by ten thirty, say."

Another slurp of tea. "What exactly has this chap done to make you scoot across country at the drop of a hat? Did he take a shine to your wife or something?"

I keep my tone light. "We're talking dodgy meat. That's why I want to talk to him."

"I'm quite happy to visit with the police and interview him, Mr Fisher. Once we know where he operates from, we can inspect that too."

"I know, but I'm worried he might do a runner again."

"And you're going to stop him?" His good natured laugh just about covers the suspicion and disbelief in his voice. "Well, if you're set, be my guest."

It takes a few minutes to agree where to meet and swap mobile phone numbers. He suggests I book a room at the Four Seasons guest house, just outside the town centre, gives me the postcode and wishes me a safe journey.

I book a night in the Four Seasons and then email the Facebook image of Mellor to the Colonel. Though eager to get going, it's only four thirty and I have to wait for Lucy to return or ring to make sure she's safe. Moments later, she walks in, looking weary. She doesn't mind me finishing early and waves me out when my phone rings. "I'll deal with it," she says.

I'm halfway down the stairs when she calls me back. "Kent, we have an E. coli O157. A four year old girl's in hospital with renal failure."

"Do you want me to ring Danni?" Kelly asks as I rush past.

"Let me get some details first."

I drop into my chair, panting a little. On the pad, Lucy's written 'Charlotte Burke, four and a half years old, E. coli, possible renal failure.' After a deep breath, I pick up the phone.

"Hi, it's Barbara Hussain, Health Protection Practitioner at Public Health England." Her voice is cool and efficient. "Has your colleague explained the purpose of my call?"

I make notes as she tells me about Charlotte Emily Burke, who lives in Tollingdon. She's four years eleven months old and a probable E. coli O157 based on DNA typing. She has suspected Haemolytic Uraemic Syndrome and is on her way to the Evelina Hospital in London for specialist treatment with her mother, Chloe, and grandfather, Steven Burke.

"We'll get confirmation of E coli from the culture in the next 24 hours," Barbara says. "In the meantime, we'll organise the interview and questionnaire with the hospital and let you know if we need anything followed up. Details are a little sketchy at the moment, but she may have started at Tollingdon Primary School last month."

I can't stop the groan as I think about E. coli spreading through the school. With only a few bacteria needed to cause infection, and Under Fives being particularly vulnerable, this could be our worst nightmare. Previous outbreaks have stretched local authority and public resources to the limit as the number of cases accelerates out of control before peaking.

"The school's closed for the weekend," I say. "What do you want me to do?"

"Leave that to us. Like I said, details are sketchy, but it looks like her mother kept Charlotte home from school last week because she was unwell. I don't know if she went back this week, but I doubt it, given her condition."

"Let's hope not," I say. "What about spread within the family?"

"We'll get all the family details and contacts when we conduct the interview. Do you have enough sample pots and forms?"

They won't last long if we have to test a whole school. "Sure. Any other cases?"

"Nothing reported by GPs or the lab so far, but that could change over the weekend. We have an out-of-hours number for your department, Mr Fisher, but it's generic. Could I have your mobile number?"

I pause, my trip to Glastonbury in the balance. "You have numbers for Lucy and Nigel, don't you?"

"Yes, and Dannielle Frost, but her phone's on voicemail, asking me to contact you."

I give Barbara my personal mobile number. "How bad is Charlotte?"

"She's in the best place, Mr Fisher. The minute we have more information, we'll be in touch. In the meantime, Charlotte's the only case we're aware of. If anything changes, you'll be the first to know."

She wishes me well and ends the call. I ring Danni and leave a message, asking her to ring me urgently. Then I turn to Lucy, who's sitting with Kelly. Both look anxious.

"Isolated case at the moment. We'll remain on alert over the weekend, just in case, but hopefully the girl will be okay. On Monday, we'll get straight to the school."

"I'll keep trying Danni," Kelly says.

"And I'm around all weekend if you need me," Lucy says. "Chaz too, so don't let this spoil your plans, Kent. You're only down the road if we need you."

A mere 200 miles down the road.

On my way to the car, I ring Brian Slade, but his phone diverts to an out-of-hours message. I should remain in Tollingdon, but nothing's going to happen overnight, is it? And I'll be back by lunchtime tomorrow. Despite my justification, my gut tells me I have to put work, and the illness of a young girl, first.

Then, as I'm about to leave a message and cancel my trip, I realise Brian Slade will visit Colin Mellor whether I join him or not. If Slade mentions my name, Mellor could disappear again.

FOURTEEN

"Welcome to the Isle of Avalon."

Slade's lazy handshake suggests he ambles through life at a steady pace, enjoying the journey. Middle-aged, overweight and reeking of cigarettes, he has the look of a man who doesn't take himself or life too seriously. With a grin as wide as his girth, he looks me up and down, his deep blue eyes tiny behind the thick lenses of his steel-framed spectacles.

"It means the island of apples," he says, thrusting his paws into the pockets of his crumpled beige jacket. "That's why cider's so popular around these parts."

Maybe my quest will be fruitful, after all.

He pulls out a packet of cigarettes as he speaks. His hands perform a familiar ritual, tapping a cigarette out of the packet, rolling it between his fingers before lifting it to his nose for a quick sniff before he lights up.

"This used to be one of seven islands on an inland sea, a place of myths and legends. In the grounds of Glastonbury Abbey behind us, we have King Arthur's resting place." He lights the cigarette, inhales and blows the smoke skywards. "Or do we?"

He laughs as I step back a couple of paces. "I know I'm not a picture of public health," he says, "but it's a job, not a vocation with me. My life's my family. I got a steady job with a good pension at the end and I get to meet lots of interesting people." He pauses to inhale more smoke. "But I never met one who comes halfway across the country for a burger vendor. What did this guy do?"

During my rush across country, I had plenty of time to consider what I wanted to do and ask when I met Mellor. I considered his possible responses, what I would do if he refused to talk, and whether I could believe him if he cooperated. Not once did it occur to me that my actions might seem unusual.

"I'm interested in what he knows," I reply. "He's already run once, so would you mind if I approach him alone? Two of us might spook him."

"If he runs, you can do the chasing." Slade might be joking about his weight, but there's no humour in his eyes. He doesn't trust me, and why should he?

As we stroll past some colourful shops, trading in magic, gemstones and the occult, I wonder if they saw the recession in their tarot cards. Not that the kebab shop opposite is short of customers. Slade tells me about the town as we walk towards the Market Cross, a tiered Gothic tower as tall as the surrounding buildings. It seems to be a focal point for the locals, drawing them over from all directions.

They're an intriguing mix. The New Age set, dressed in combat fatigues or flowing, gypsy-style clothes, sport more piercings than a dartboard, along with a colourful palette of tattoos. One or two lead bull terriers by thick ropes as they stroll among the younger people in jeans and hoodies, glued to their mobile phones. The more conventional residents seem to take no notice, enjoying the diversity that's reflected in the shops and restaurants. You can eat anything from Vegan to Vietnamese here.

"Ever heard of Joseph of Arimathea?" Slade asks, stopping to extinguish his cigarette on the top of a waste bin. "I think he was the Virgin Mary's uncle. Anyway, he was a merchant, or something like that, and he may have brought a young Jesus with him on a trip to Avalon."

While I have no views on religion, the thought of stepping on land once walked by Christ sends a tingle down my back. King Arthur produces a similar reaction.

My reaction draws a smile from Slade. "There's more to Glastonbury than the music festival," he says, setting off once more. "Not that I'm complaining. I've seen some great bands over the years. Coldplay in 2011 was my favourite."

We pass the Crown pub and some old stone buildings of various ages, including the George and Pilgrims Hotel, built circa 1452. The Glastonbury Tribunal, built from big, solid stones, looks even older. The oak door looks like it would withstand an army, making me wonder if it was a prison in the past. It's a tourist information centre now, holding visitors captive with its displays of bright leaflets and posters.

We stop at the corner of a blue rendered shop that sells crystals. "What do you make of this new age idea?" I ask.

"Returning to nature, living the simple life without chemicals and additives?" Slade laughs. "They want to return to the dark ages, but keep their mobile phones, if you ask me."

We turn left into a narrow alley between the shop and the metal railings that enclose the churchyard. A large mural on the wall of a craft shop features twisted roots, twining into a trunk that's topped by clusters of pink flowers. I've no idea what it signifies, but it seems quite at home in a town of colourful shops and restaurants.

It would generate petitions in Tollingdon.

The alley opens into a large public car park that's half empty. Straight ahead, beneath a wooden freestanding awning that could have come from an old railway station, stands the Volkswagen Camper. A small flue emits a spiral of greasy fumes that waft the aroma of fried onions our way, reminding me I haven't eaten since lunch. The hand painted sign on the passenger door says *Grub on the Go*.

Brian taps out another cigarette. "Don't take too long," he says, glancing up at the sky. "Shouldn't be surprised if you've brought the rain with you."

Two young women, dressed in short skirts and skimpy tops, are chatting to the man inside. His face is all grin as he stares down their tops. His hands assemble a hot dog with practised ease, allowing him to concentrate on his patter.

"There you go, darling," he says, handing over the food. "You said you wanted to slide your lips around a big sausage. Well, they don't come any bigger than mine." He gives her a suggestive wink and passes a cheeseburger to the second woman. "If that doesn't satisfy you, I'm here till three."

He watches their bottoms wiggle as they strut away in their high heels.

"If I were 20 years younger," he says, turning to me.

Maybe 30, I muse, looking at the shadows and sagging skin on his weary face. His long nose looks like it's slithering towards his mouth, filled with yellowing teeth. He removes the greasy baseball cap and wipes his shining crown with the sleeve of his shabby white coat. If this is Colin Mellor, then the comb-over described by witnesses has become a silver ponytail.

"You look like you could eat a horse," he says in his cheeky Cockney voice. "I don't tell all my customers I offer that kind of speciality, but my burgers are thoroughbreds."

"Environmental health." The sweep of my ID card prompts him to replace his cap. "Are you Colin Mellor?"

"Guilty," he replies, holding out his hands for cuffing. "I should have a permit, I know, but I'm only passing through, guvnor, bringing a little gastronomic pleasure to the locals. Could I tempt you with a burger, Mr …?"

"Fisher. Kent Fisher. I'm from Downland District Council in East Sussex."

"You've driven all this way to see me?" His suspicion vanishes when he gasps like a camp theatre luvvie and clasps his hands to his chest. "I didn't know my sausages were so famous."

"Daphne Witherington's a big fan of yours."

"Has she made a complaint?"

"No, but her husband has."

"Hey, it's only banter. You know how it is. You flirt with a woman to make her feel important so she comes back. It's harmless fun."

"Twenty grand doesn't sound harmless to me."

"What are you talking about?" he asks, looking confused. "And why are you here? Why aren't the local Hygiene Police checking me out? This isn't an inspection, is it?"

Either his acting's better than his chat or he's not Colin Mellor.

"No, I'm here with Todd Walters. He wants to see Stacey."

"No idea who you're talking about," he says, scanning the car park. "You've got me mixed up with someone else, but I'm sure we can sort this out. I'll be right with you."

He unfastens the white coat and slips it off as he turns to the sliding door behind him. As he leaps down, I glance back at Slade to signal success. Then I hear Miller's heavy footsteps as he runs.

For a man in his fifties, he's quick, arms pumping as he charges down the side of a modern looking stone building, heading for a junction at the bottom. With a glance back as he crosses the road, he almost runs into a car coming around the corner. The screech of brakes pierces the night air. Somehow he sidesteps and weaves past the car, ignoring the shouts from the driver. Mellor stumbles and bounces off the wall of the corner house, oblivious to the mural, proclaiming 'Too much of a good thing can be wonderful'.

I doubt if his lungs agree, but he crosses the road, picking up speed again. The smokers and drinkers in the garden of the *Who'd A Thought It* pub cheer as he rushes past. Their cheers become jeers as I chase after him.

Trust the British to favour the person fleeing.

I'm aware of something a moment before it thuds into the back of my neck. Beer splashes over my shoulders and hair before the bottle crashes to the pavement. The huge cheer from the pub garden encourages me to keep running.

The road bends to the right into a car park that stretches out on both sides. Ahead, behind a wire mesh fence and playground, is a school, decorated with another mural. I can't make out the detail in the dark. Neither can I see Mellor. He seems to have vanished. I slow to a walk and scan both sides of the road. With the school to my left, guarded by a high fence, I focus on the car park to my right, serving a DIY store. There are a couple of cars near the main entrance, but otherwise it's empty.

When I reach the end of the car park, I stop. Mellor couldn't have reached the road junction in the distance unseen. Either he's crouched behind one of the parked cars or he ran up the service road to the back of the store. I vault the yellow and black barrier and keep to the shadows. The road isn't directly lit, but there's enough light from the houses and store to see it swings right into a service yard about 50 metres ahead.

If Mellor's not hiding there, he's already running from the car park to safety.

When I round the corner, the light from the houses behind me illuminates the rectangular yard, which contains a couple of wheeled refuse bins, a pile of builder's rubble and scaffolding boards, and a compactor behind some bails of cardboard. A forklift truck sits nearby, ready to move them in the morning.

I scan the area, listening for heavy breathing or steps on the concrete, but the only sound comes from cars and distant traffic.

My senses warn me I'm not alone. He's either behind the bins, the compactor, or the forklift truck.

"Come out, Mellor and talk." My voice bounces around the enclosed space. "I want to talk about Daphne Witherington."

Something clangs against the compactor, startling me. I head towards it. Then, hearing the rumble of wheels on concrete, I stop and turn. The refuse bin deals me a glancing blow, knocking me to the ground. The sound of more wheels urges me to my feet. I scramble out of the way and spot Mellor. He backtracks as I approach, unaware of the scaffold boards on the ground until he tumbles and falls onto them.

His arms cross in front of his face when I loom over him. "Don't kill me! Please! Don't kill me! I have money."

Of all the things I expected him to say, this wasn't on the list. I step back a couple of paces and tell him to get to his feet.

Slowly, he stands, his legs wobbling a little, a hand clamped to his elbow. I gesture him away from the scaffolding boards and he steps back against the wall of the store, his eyes wide with fear.

He fishes a roll of notes from a rear trouser pocket. "£500 to say you never found me."

"You got twenty grand from Colonel Witherington."

"And I kept my part of the bargain," he says, his voice ragged. "I took the old crust's money and left, as instructed."

I raise my hand to silence him. "What about his wife, Daphne?"

"What about her?"

"Did you take her with you?"

"Why would I do that?"

"She went missing the day you left."

"Nothing to do with me. What's the old crust been telling you?"

He's such a natural liar, I don't know what to believe. I step back to give him space. "Let's get a few details straight, first. Are you Miller or Mellor?"

"Whatever takes your fancy," he replies, his back against the wall adjacent the loading area and roller shutters that reach to the roof. "I use both, but I'm Miller by birth. That's how the old crust tumbled me. He found out I had form for deception and dodgy credit cards."

"Then why couldn't the police find you?"

"I didn't know they were looking for me. I haven't done anything."

"How about conning him out of twenty grand?"

He shakes his head. "He thought I was having a fling with his wife, but it was harmless fun. She was bored and I paid her a few compliments. You saw me earlier. Put a pretty woman in front of me and I can't help myself."

"What about the money?"

"If he wanted to believe I was screwing his wife and pay me 20K to scarper, who was I to argue. I needed the cash."

"What about the meal with Daphne Witherington the night before you left?"

He shifts his weight from foot to foot. "What about it?"

"Come on, Miller, you were seen."

He shakes his head. "I never went near the restaurant. Why would I? I had the money."

I move closer, certain he's lying. "Wrong answer."

He presses back against the wall, arms shielding his face. "I didn't go near the restaurant, honest. Not after the phone call."

"What phone call?"

"Someone rang me, said I was being set up. Said the Colonel planned to bump me off that night and tell everyone I'd run away with his wife."

"Who rang you?"

He shrugs, but he won't meet my eyes.

"Come on, Miller. Who rang you?"

"It had to be the old crust, didn't it? He was the only one who knew about our arrangement."

"What arrangement?"

He lowers his arms and draws a breath. "He wanted me to take Daphne out and make it look like we were running away the next day. Then, when I don't call for her the next day, she thinks I've dumped her and goes back to her husband."

"If he intended to kill you that evening, why would he ring you first?"

"So, I'd leg it straight away. And I did, I can tell you."

"But you were seen in the restaurant."

He shakes his head. "On my life, it wasn't me."

I recall the different description Davenport gave and wonder if Miller's telling the truth. It's clear he's no hero, so why would the Colonel frighten him off and replace him with someone else? And why would Daphne play along with a fake Miller? Why would she think he was going to whisk her away from the Colonel?

"I don't believe you." I move closer as he looks from side to side, planning his escape, no doubt.

"The old crust killed his wife, didn't he? He got me out of the way so he could blame me when he snuffed her out." His confidence fades as he stares at me. "But something's gone wrong, hasn't it? He's sent you to snuff me out too."

When I say nothing, he waves the roll of banknotes at me. "Five hundred more at home to say you couldn't find me."

If he's telling the truth, Daphne could be lying under the conservatory. Then why would the Colonel ask me to trace Miller and risk me uncovering the truth?

"Daphne's engagement ring," I say, thinking aloud. When it resurfaced, the Colonel panicked. "Okay, Miller, convince me."

"I knew I shouldn't have come back from Spain," Miller says, pocketing the money. "That's where I was supposed to take Daphne. He booked the flights, everything. After the call, I thought what the heck and went straight to Malaga."

"Not without Stacey you didn't."

This seems to knock him back. "How do you know about Stacey?"

"Her husband's a huge fan of yours, Miller."

"Mr Charisma? Do me a favour. He beats the crap out of some drunk who touched her up and suddenly he's Mr Perfect. I got Stacey a recording contract, and she didn't want to know me. I took her off the streets and she dumped me for a butcher with two brain cells."

The sound of a car revving nearby distracts me for a moment. "You went to see her, didn't you?"

"When I set up *Grub on the Go*, I needed meat. I could have got it anywhere, but I wanted to see Stacey, for old times' sake."

"You went when Walters was out."

He gives me a sad shake of the head. "He spotted me in the café opposite and came over. I thought he'd smack me one, but he was fine. He even offered to get me some cheap meat. I didn't believe him until Stacey told me to get lost."

The sound of more revving, followed by a squeal of tyres and doors slamming, drowns out his voice. I look around, but there's nothing but shadows. Maybe it's kids in the car park.

"She said if I ever came back, she'd tell Walters," Miller's saying, looking deflated. "When I told her I loved her, she laughed." Then he grins. "But I still had Daphne Witherington. She couldn't get enough of me."

"I thought you said it was harmless fun."

"It was until the old crust found out. Look," he says, straightening, "I took the money and bought a share in a bar on the Costa del Sol. I'd still be there if the authorities hadn't turned against us."

"Us?"

"Me and my business partner."

"Stacey Walters? You left with her a couple of weeks after you were supposed to dump Daphne, didn't you?"

"If you say so," he replies, suddenly full of confidence. He calls over my shoulder. "Help me, guys! He's trying to mug me."

I turn and face two men in hoodies, their faces hidden by shadows. Their muscular build and posture suggests they work out, but why are they here? I pull out my ID card and move towards them.

Then I realise my mistake.

I feel the thud in my side. I don't feel any pain as I stagger sideways and crash to the ground, grazing my face and hands on the concrete. Adrenaline spins me over in time to see Miller raise a short scaffold pole above his head. It smashes into the concrete where my head was a moment earlier. The noise and vibration seem to daze me.

"Cool it, dude." One of the hoodies steps in and grabs the pole as Miller raises it once more. "You ain't killing no one, man."

My phone, lying several yards away, starts to ring.

With an angry snarl, Miller stamps on the phone. Then he smashes it with the scaffold pole. He tosses the pole to the ground and stamps off, kicking me in the back as he passes.

The hoodies stand and watch as I pull myself to my knees, aching across my back. I wipe the grit from my face, wondering what these two have in mind. Whatever it is, they're in no hurry.

I glance down at what's left of my phone.

"Not such a smart phone," the first one says, poking it with his toe.

The second one bends to pick it up. "Reception's terrible round here, dude. You need to go higher."

He hurls the phone onto the roof of the warehouse. They laugh and then swagger away. A few moments later, heavy footsteps bring Slade stumbling into view, gasping for air. When he sees me he rushes over and helps me to my feet.

"Did those two do this?" he asks, looking at my face.

I shake my head. "Miller."

"If I hadn't seen him running out of the service road, I'd never have found you. What's going on, Kent?"

I take a step forward, ignoring the aches. "We have to get back to the van before Miller escapes."

"I'll call the police. If he assaulted you –"

"No, let's get to the van."

Slade's phone rings before he can argue. Though he turns away, it's clear he's had complaints about a noisy party. He says he's busy, but agrees to visit in the next 30 minutes.

"Did you get the registration number of the camper?" I ask as we hurry back.

He nods and pats his notebook. "He won't get far."

Though aching and no doubt bruised, I'm relieved the blow landed on the soft tissue between my ribs and pelvis. Had Miller been a bodybuilder rather than an overweight caterer, he could have killed me.

The rain feels cool on my face as we hurry back, passing the deserted pub garden. Head bowed as the rain thrashes down, we reach the Market Cross before I realise we've taken a wrong turning.

"I need to get to the van," I say as Slade turns towards Glastonbury Abbey.

"You need to get checked out."

"I'm fine."

"Says the man who's limping and clutching his side. What happened back there?"

"Lead the way." I can pick up my car and drive around to where Miller left the camper. At least I'll be out of the rain.

Thankfully, another phone call distracts Slade as more complaints come in about the party.

"I'll be fine after a shower and a good night's sleep," I tell him as he hovers beside my car. "Go and deal with your party."

I drive out into Market Street before he can argue and head towards the church. When I realise there's no road into the car park from this direction, I drive around the side streets, hampered by the mist on my windscreen. Five minutes later, I find the one-way street into the car park.

Miller's camper has gone.

I'm 160 miles from home, soaked, in pain, and the details for the guest house are on a warehouse roof with my phone.

Maybe I'll hang on to my private detective application a little longer.

FIFTEEN

I've always wanted to spend the night with Kinsey Millhone.

Ever since I met the feisty private investigator in *A is for Alibi*, it's been a fantasy of mine. I didn't think it would be in a deserted car park in Glastonbury, but with only my Kindle for company, and every one of Sue Grafton's novels to choose from, it's a pleasant way to pass the time.

I'm not sure when I drifted to sleep, but now, at 7.30 in the morning, I'm wide awake, if a little immobile. The slightest movement hurts. While Glastonbury comes to life, I'm heading in the opposite direction. The left side of my abdomen, my left arm and shoulder, and the right side of my face ache. Stiffness from a lack of movement numbs the rest of me. My bladder aches most of all, until I move.

I'm not sure if my cry travels beyond the misted windows, but it reminds me to take care. I peel away the blanket and shiver as the cold air penetrates my running shirt. It takes me a few moments to remember I changed out of my sodden clothes last night. As they're not in the car, they must be in the boot.

Once my feet are on the tarmac, I pull myself into a standing position, feeling the muscles groan in my lower back. When the ache ebbs, I'm aware of the cold wind, whistling through my shorts. It appears I removed my underwear as well as my clothes. A nearby milkman stares at me. I guess he doesn't see many runners who can barely walk. But the movement eases the muscles and I'm soon moving more freely.

In the public toilets, I assess the abrasions to my cheek and forehead in the mirror. The swelling and reddening are superficial. My hair, matted with blood and sweat, will need a long shower and an industrial comb to untangle. The abdominal bruising has darkened, ready for a journey through the colours of the rainbow over the coming days.

How did I let Miller get the better of me? Where did the hoodies spring from?

Back in the car, it takes me a few minutes to orientate myself and drive to Glastonbury Abbey. Customers fill the confectionery shop at the edge of the car park, reminding me I haven't eaten for almost twenty hours. I accelerate away and turn right at the next roundabout to head out of town. Moments later, I spot the Four Seasons guest house. While the name suggests the place opens all year, the empty forecourt doesn't support that impression.

The red brick Victorian building, trimmed with honey-coloured stone on the corners and around the bay windows, rises through three floors. The dormer windows in the roof stare down like surprised eyes as I make my way to an arched porch, also trimmed with stone. I ring the bell and wait, recalling a bed and breakfast I once inspected. The middle-aged landlady took a shine to the young environmental health officer, saying, "It's a long time since anyone inspected me."

A tall, slim woman, immaculately dressed in a navy jacket and skirt, opens the door and looks at me as if I've rifled through the bins. Her unimpressed grey eyes match the colour of her wavy hair, tamed with hairspray. Keen to dispel her suspicions, I offer my ID card.

"We were expecting you last night, Mr Fisher," she says in rich, West Country tones. "We didn't realise you intended to run all the way from Sussex."

"It's a long story," I say.

"You look like you need to freshen up." She returns my ID and glides across the hall to a small reception counter, busy with brochures for local attractions, a bell, and a sign telling guests all the things they can't do.

The aroma of bacon draws me inside. "Can I still have the breakfast I paid for?"

"Of course. Did you bring any luggage?"

She wants to know if I have any clothes to change into. "My clothes got wet in the rain."

She nods and hands me a key with a black fob that says, WINTER. "We name our rooms after the seasons," she says, not realising how sharp I am.

"As opposed to Vivaldi, you mean."

"You're on the top floor, Mr Fisher, which has some lovely views across the marshes. You won't have much time to enjoy them as you should vacate the room by ten. Unless you wish to stay a little longer?"

"I need to return home today."

"Then take as long as you need, Mr Fisher. I'm Ann Summers, by the way." The twinkle in her eye tells me she's heard all the jokes. "That's why we chose the name, Four Seasons."

The attic room's clean, decorated in soft blues and cream, and a reasonable size for a single. In the en suite shower, I take advantage of the complimentary gel and shampoo, allowing the hot water to soothe and warm my muscles. Back in my running clothes, I jog down the stairs to the dining room at the back of the house. I have the place to myself, which means large helpings of grilled bacon and sausages, poached egg, mushrooms, tomato and baked beans, washed down with dark tea in a pale cup.

Ann refuses to join me for tea and toast, claiming she has to get the place ready for more visitors this afternoon. I'm sure she runs the place on her own as there's no sign of a Mr Summers or any domestic help.

Back in the room, I settle on the bed to write up what I learned from Miller. Even before he turned on me, his claims about running off the day before Daphne went missing sound lame. Why would Colonel Witherington threaten to kill him? It made no sense at all. I'm prepared to believe he loved Stacey Walters. I'm even willing to believe she went to Spain with him. Did she remain, singing in karaoke bars, flirting with the punters? Is that why he returned?

Or did he kill them both?

From the ferocity of his attack on me, he could have.

Then again, maybe nobody killed anyone and I'm wasting my time.

I'm no wiser when I wake a few minutes later, the notebook sprawled on the bed beside me. I pick up my pen, trying to recapture my train of thought. Then I spot the clock on the bedside cabinet.

I'm downstairs within a couple of minutes. Ann asks me if I slept well and charges me half rate on the understanding I return again, which I promise to do. She also lets me ring Niamh, who wants to know where the hell I am. When I suggest she cancels dinner because I might be late, her voice turns cold.

"You'd better not be after all the trouble I've gone to."

After a race across country, I arrive home around a quarter past seven, squeezing my car in between Davenport's Mondeo and a black Audi TT that probably belongs to Richard. With silent thanks to Ann's ibuprofen, I ease out of the car and spot Columbo, frantically pawing the window of the caravan. When he starts barking, Frances scoops him up and lets him out. He hurtles over, leaping up at my legs. I scoop him into my arms so he can lick my face.

"Miss me, did you?"

"He's been sulky all day." Frances gasps when she notices my injuries. "What happened?"

"You should see the other bloke," I reply.

She takes Columbo and doesn't ask why I'm wearing my running gear. "You have to stay here," she tells him when he whines. "The undertaker's allergic to dogs."

I smile. At least there's no danger of him moving in here.

The sweet aroma of garlic and rosemary welcomes me into the kitchen. Niamh ignores me at first, busy with some smoked salmon. When she turns, the knife falls from her hand and thuds to the floor.

"Sweet mother of Jesus! What happened to you?"

She hurries over, wiping her hands on the wildlife apron that covers her best green frock. Her hair, normally tugged into a loose knot, is sculpted back into a ponytail that flows in luxuriant, shining waves down her back. Her fringe is braided into a plait that runs across the top of her forehead.

"You look stunning," I say. "And that smells wonderful."

"You look shite," she says, her face close to mine. "There's calamine lotion in the bathroom cabinet and a suit for you in the bedroom. And don't you dare stop to talk to your guests, looking like that."

Naturally, I go straight into the lounge to apologise for being late. "I'm running late," I say, pointing to my shorts and vest. "And I slipped on some wet steps and took a nasty tumble," I add, enjoying their stunned looks. "Good to see you, Alasdair."

Davenport, who looks like he's dressed for the undertaker's annual ball, shakes my hand, nervous as I lean forward to sniff his aftershave. It almost masks the stale reek of cigars. "Embalming fluid smells much nicer these days.

"Smart motor," I say, turning to Richard. His handshake's gentle. "Gemma, I would love to hug and kiss you, but I need to change into something less revealing."

Davenport, whose eyes have reddened, steps back as I pass. He fumbles in his trouser pocket and just manages to push a handkerchief over his nose before he sneezes.

"Are you going down with something?" I ask, aware of Columbo's fur on my running top.

Back in the corridor, my childish grin completes my adolescent behaviour. At least it took my mind off my injuries, but not as much as Gemma's little black number.

She looked so glamorous next to Richard, who's young, good looking and much more grown up than me.

In the bedroom, I find a new white shirt with discreet pinstripes, a stylish navy blue suit on a hanger, and a new striped tie. I smear my side with ibuprofen gel before dressing. As I look at myself in the mirror, I'm tempted to swallow some gel to calm the flutter in my stomach.

I'm not afraid of Davenport. Yvonne's smart and sassy, but not my type. Gemma's spoken for and I barely know her fiancé.

So why do I feel nervous?

Maybe I shouldn't be exorcising my demons all at once.

I stare out of the window, wishing I could join Frances in her caravan and watch trashy programmes on her portable TV. I want to go back to the times when it was just the two of us, united in our struggle to make ends meet. Birchill's money may dispel our worries, but at what cost?

When the time comes to leave, I'll miss this place.

My performance is superlative when I return to the lounge. Even its transformation into a dining space, complete with the table and chairs from the barn, fails to unnerve me. Niamh's olive green leather sofa and armchairs from Downland Manor have replaced my dreary and weary, furniture. It means her belongings have arrived, turning my lovely bare walls into an art gallery.

It didn't happen in a couple of hours either.

Alasdair, whose eyes are still red and swollen, has stopped sneezing. He and Richard look comfortable in each other's company and well-mannered enough to ignore my injuries. I try to ignore Gemma, but she looks stunning and effortlessly elegant in her sleeveless black dress that finishes well above the knees. A thin, skin-toned dressing masks the scarring to her upper arm, restoring her self-confidence. Or is it indifference?

It looks like I'm history.

"I can see why you're head of the Chamber of Commerce," I tell Davenport, topping up his glass with more Prosecco.

He's overdressed in a black velvet jacket, frilled shirt and bow tie, but the creases in his trousers could slice through paper. Like the shine on his shoes, they suggest a military background I'm unaware of. When I spot the delicate white rose in his buttonhole, I want to ask if it came from a wreath. Instead, I ask if he helped Niamh rearrange my lounge.

His hesitation confirms my suspicions, but he seems surprised when I shake his hand. "Thank you for brightening the place up," I say, excelling in my role. "It's good of you to give up your time while I'm falling down steps in Glastonbury."

"You didn't get 'alon' with the Isle of Avalon," he says, looking pleased.

Richard nods in appreciation. "Nice play on words, Alasdair."

His athletic build, short hair and square jaw give him the rugged looks of someone who climbs mountains without safety ropes. He has the quiet, inner confidence bestowed by a private school education, law degree at Oxford or Cambridge, and wealthy parents. It's there in the casual gaze of his blue eyes and the understated, but expensive pinstripe suit and waistcoat beloved by the legal profession.

His wide smile and constant glances at Gemma tell me this confident young man has never been happier.

"If you want to sue anyone for the accident, Kent, I'd be glad to advise you."

Gemma wraps her arms around his. "Kent doesn't approve of people suing when they should look where they're going,"

"I was only joking," he says, raising his hands. "It's not my field. I spend my time poring over contracts and leases. It's terribly tedious. Not like your work."

"I'm sure your work has its moments."

"Divorce and litigation, I suppose. Call me old-fashioned, but I don't like to see marriages boiled down to columns on a spreadsheet."

"Me neither," I say, starting to like this man. "So, have you named the day?"

"Not yet." He gazes into Gemma's eyes. "It's hard to find a day when everyone can get together. My lot are scattered across the planet," he says, as if they're pioneers. "We're holding the ceremony in Herstmonceux Castle. It's traditional, enchanting and so romantic with the moat. And you gave the kitchen a top hygiene rating, of course."

It's good to know I'm contributing to their happiness.

Niamh walks in with a bottle of white wine in a cooler. She places it on the table and encourages us to take our places, according to the elegant name cards she's produced. "Our last guest has just arrived."

Yvonne knows how to make an entrance, strutting into the room in a strapless scarlet dress and matching stilettos. A sparkling necklace caresses her smooth, slim neck, while silver bracelets clasp her wrists. Her wide smile and confident blue eyes scan the room before focusing on me. She pushes her short blonde hair back with long fingers, tipped with red. Her American accent adds a touch of drama to her soft voice.

"Like you, Mr Fisher, I can sneak in from the rear."

She laughs, well aware she can raise more than a smile. She has the natural confidence I've found in most Americans, coupled with a desire to shock and get her way, I suspect. I can't help feeling that nothing is off limits.

"I prefer not to get beaten up when I do," she adds before kissing my injury-free cheek.

I pull away. "Let me introduce you to Richard and Gemma."

She embraces and kisses them both, swapping a few words. While Richard enjoys the moment, Gemma looks uncomfortable, especially when Yvonne tells her she has the most awesome, sexy eyes.

Niamh also looks uncomfortable. "Come and help me with the food, Gemma."

"Allow me," Yvonne says, stepping forward. "I haven't contributed anything so far."

Davenport breaks the silence after they leave. "She's self-assured, as you can see, just like her father. He passed away unexpectedly last year and she took it badly, him being in New York. I never expected her to return, but I'm pleased she did."

I can't help feeling the potted history is for my benefit.

"Even you, Kent," Gemma says, leading Richard to the table. "I've never seen you lost for words."

Has she forgotten the first time I undressed her?

Niamh and Davenport sit at opposite ends of the table. I'm next to Gemma and facing Yvonne. If she plays footsie during dinner, I wonder who she'll choose.

"I must say I'm impressed with the sanctuary," Richard says once we're settled. "We arrived early and Gemma gave me the guided tour. I don't know how you find the time and energy to work and run this place, Kent."

"He has help," Niamh says, arriving with two plates of smoked salmon and rosemary potato rosti. Yvonne follows with two more and takes her seat opposite me.

"We met Frances," Richard says, nodding. "You can't help but admire people who have a passion for what they do."

"What are you passionate about?" Yvonne asks him.

He glances at Gemma and then blushes. "Oh, I see what you mean. Windsurfing's my passion – when I'm not skiing, of course. How about you, Alasdair? Can't be easy, dealing with the grief stricken."

"I help those who've lost to find their way," Alasdair says, sounding like one of Danni's motivational mantras.

"You're very clever with words," Richard says. "What about you, Yvonne? What are you passionate about?"

"Life."

"Ironic, considering you work for an undertaker," Gemma says.

"Life goes on for those left behind," Davenport says. "We support the living."

"Surely your work's done once the coffin's in the ground," I say. "That's what people pay for, isn't it? Family and friends do the rest."

"What if there is no family?" he asks. "What if families can't or won't take that on? You've never married, have you, Kent? You don't fully appreciate what it's like to lose a partner you've loved and cherished for so many years."

"Don't tell me I don't understand loss," I say, irked by his smug superiority.

"That's enough!" Niamh glares at me from the doorway, the final two plates in her hands.

Davenport raises his hands. "It's okay. Kent feels that somehow I've taken his place."

"No I don't."

"Of course you don't," Gemma says, her voice loaded with sarcasm.

"I know how it feels," Davenport says, his tone soothing. "I lost Angelina to a long and debilitating illness. I watched her die, day by day, hour by hour, the life draining from her until there was only a shell." He pauses, his eyes tight shut. "I lost my wife, my soulmate and my best friend in February last year, but it seems like only yesterday."

I should say something sympathetic, but Davenport doesn't have a monopoly on loss.

He looks straight at me. "I'm not taking Niamh away. I'm returning her to you."

I'm tempted to throw up, but Niamh distracts me by thumping my plate on the table. There's no mistaking the fury in her eyes, though I don't see what I've done wrong. Maybe I should say something to appease her. She's already miffed because I dislike salmon. Like pretentious people, it makes me gag.

"You baked any humble pie?" I ask, my tone light. Too light, it seems.

"Death isn't a joke, you know."

"I'm sure Kent wasn't making light of William's passing," Davenport says, dragging the high moral ground even further from me. "Kent's grieving too, but he hides it behind jokes and quips. He doesn't mean any harm or disrespect, so let's hear no more about it and enjoy this wonderful food you've prepared. Let's celebrate the joys ahead, like Richard and Gemma's marriage. And Kent can do the washing up," he adds, raising his glass.

"For at least a month." Niamh raises her glass. "To Richard and Gemma."

After a polite first course, Gemma insists on helping Niamh clear the plates and serve the main course of garlic-basted chicken, served with baby leeks, carrots and parsnips. This time, Richard catches the compliment bug, saying how wonderful everything tastes as he speeds through the course. If only his profession could work as quickly.

Yvonne puts her knife and fork down after eating only half the food. "If you two are getting married," she says, looking at Richard, "how come you haven't fixed a date?"

"We had to find out when Herstmonceux Castle was available," Gemma replies. "It's so popular."

"You're getting married in a castle?" Yvonne grins, mischief in her eyes. "Perfect for someone to gallop in on a white steed, I'd say."

"Or a horse drawn carriage," Richard says, thankfully missing the point. "Can you imagine arriving in a gold carriage with glass doors, darling?"

"We haven't planned the details yet," Gemma says, pushing her half empty plate away. "Richard only bought the ring three weeks ago."

"After Kent saved your life," he says. "It made me realise how precious you are to me."

Yvonne gives me a wicked smile. "Do you save many women?"

"He prefers animals to people," Gemma says.

"Yet he saved you," Yvonne says with an air of intrigue.

Davenport doesn't allow the silence to settle. "You're looking for a missing woman at the moment, aren't you, Kent? Daphne Witherington disappeared about a year ago, didn't she?"

I nod and fork vegetables into my mouth.

Richard looks impressed. "How do you find the time, Kent?"

"He's using his work contacts to find a caterer who worked with Daphne," Niamh says. She looks relieved that Davenport's changed the subject. "Did you find him in Glastonbury?"

"Glastonbury?" Gemma looks at me as if I've betrayed her. "You never told me Miller was in Glastonbury."

Richard looks from me to Gemma. "Who's Miller?"

Niamh takes over. "Daphne ran away with a caterer called Colin Miller. Kent tracked him down to Glastonbury." She turns to me. "Was Daphne there?"

I shake my head. "Miller didn't tell me anything useful. Then, as I hurried back to the car in the rain, I slipped on some steps."

This seems to satisfy everyone except Gemma, who mentions our visit to Todd Walters and his missing wife.

Richard frowns. “Two missing women? Are they connected?”

“Miller knew them both,” she replies.

Yvonne swirls the wine in her glass. “Sounds like an intriguing ménage a trois.”

“I saw Miller and Daphne in a restaurant.” Davenport undoes his bow tie as he speaks. “They were running away together. So, where does Mrs Walters fit in?”

“Maybe Mr Miller saves fallen women,” Yvonne says, still swirling.

“He was bragging about it in the restaurant,” Davenport says. “Everyone heard him.”

“He admitted he knew Stacey,” I say, aware that everyone’s looking at me.

“And she’s missing too,” Richard says. “What a puzzle. This is like one of those murder mystery parties where everyone dresses up to play the parts.”

“Who said anything about murder?” I ask.

“You travelled halfway across the country to interview this chap, Miller,” he says. “That seems a bit much for a man who ran off with someone’s wife. He must have told you something useful?”

Their expressions may be expectant, but I’m saying as little as possible. “It’s difficult to talk when you’re cooking burgers and serving customers.”

“Why didn’t you talk to him when he wasn’t working?” Niamh asks.

“He probably doesn’t pack up till well past midnight.”

“So, you didn’t interview him today.”

“No, last night.”

“So, it was dark when you slipped.”

I nod, not liking the tone of her voice.

"Then what kept you in Glastonbury for most of today?"

"And why weren't you answering your mobile?" Gemma asks.

I feel like the accused in the dock, the way everyone is looking at me. "My phone was damaged when I fell."

"Haven't you heard of phone boxes?" Niamh asks.

"Okay, I overslept. I didn't sleep much because of the pain from the fall. After breakfast, I drifted off. You can check with Ann Summers at the guesthouse, if you like."

"Ann Summers!" Gemma can't stop herself giggling, setting off Yvonne.

Niamh's far from pleased. "You went all that way for nothing then."

"Discounting the awesome shiner," Yvonne says.

"Does that mean your investigation's over?" Davenport asks.

"But two women are missing," Richard says, looking around the table for support. "You can't leave it there."

"Why not?" Yvonne's sharp tone silences everyone. "What if they don't want to be found?"

Richard looks puzzled. "What do you mean?"

"Lots of women have abusive relationships. Way too many make excuses and put up with the beatings and mind games, but some find the courage to escape."

Gemma nods. "Walters has a violent temper."

"Colonel Witherington too," Niamh says, gathering the plates. "Wasn't he accused of bullying council staff?"

Davenport helps with the plates. "The Colonel has a short fuse when he can't get his way."

"Case solved," Yvonne says, daring me to disagree. "Do you really think they're gonna thank you for finding them?"

SIXTEEN

On Monday morning, my popularity soars when I walk into the office. While I like to think it's my natural charisma, easy-going style and super sleuth reputation, not to mention an understated modesty, it turns out Danni hasn't shown yet. With Kelly on leave for a couple of days, officers turn to me for guidance – after they ask who thumped me.

Danni's decision to take time off at the end of last week has left a number of unsigned invoices and orders that Finance can't process. When I remind them they won't let me authorise expenditure over £500, my popularity wanes. It plummets when I delegate all other financial decisions back to my manager and put the phone down.

"Did Gemma's fiancé do that?" Lucy studies my face and then casts a glance at Gemma, who looks subdued.

"You can believe what you like, but I slipped on some steps."

She laughs and saunters back to her desk, leaving me to sift through the problems reported to our call-out service over the weekend. As usual, residents sound off about loud music from their neighbours, out of control parties, people shouting and swearing when they leave pubs, and dogs howling all night. These will go to the Pollution Team for standard response letters, as will the complaint about Japanese Knotweed rampaging across a garden and breaking through a concrete patio. Apparently, we can deal with it under antisocial behaviour legislation, according to the complainant. It's comforting to realise the public know our job better than we do.

"The war on weeds has started," I tell Ruth Jordan, Pollution Control Officer. "Mr Angry from Alfriston wants immediate action."

Ruth's a dizzy blonde with a loud, excitable voice, children that are always ill, and an enthusiasm that no amount of mistakes can quash. To be fair, her enthusiasm causes most of the mistakes, especially when it teams up with her unerring ability to tell people what she thinks of them. But what she lacks in diplomacy, she makes up for in effort. Since Trevor Harmer, her manager, went off sick with stress, she's taken on his district work, including several complex noise assessments linked to planning appeals. Her colleagues believe she's the cause of her manager's stress, leading to more than a little tension in the team.

Ruth takes the messages. "Some woman from Public Health England got her knickers in a twist yesterday. Some kid's got E. coli O157 and she wanted me to rush out with poo pots and exclude him from school or something. I told her kids don't go to school on Sunday. I don't think she has children – or a sense of a humour."

She gives me a toothy grin and slides me a scribbled note from her pad. "She said she phoned you and Danni several times and left messages, but neither of you called back."

Her expression changes to one of horror, tinged with distaste. “Tell me you weren’t with Danni this weekend.”

“You think my boss whisked me off to a hotel in Brighton for some bonding?”

“Bondage more like. Anyway, we all saw her kiss you.”

“Because I saved her job. Anyway, that was months ago.”

I wonder when people will start to believe me. Not for some time, if Ruth’s expression’s anything to go by.

“But you always answer your phone at the weekend, Kent. That’s why I ring you.”

I point to my cheek. “I fell and broke my phone.”

She squints over her glasses. “Your phone did that? Were you talking to someone when you fell?”

I nod, knowing any other response will lead to more questions.

Back at my desk, I ring Barbara Hussain at Public Health England. Once we get past my broken phone and the unhelpful attitude of my assistant, Ms Jordan, Barbara tells me about the investigation into Charlotte Burke’s illness.

“It’s definitely E. coli O157 and probable Haemolytic Uraemic Syndrome.”

“Poor girl,” I say, knowing that doesn’t begin to cover it.

“She’s critically ill with renal failure. Even if she pulls through, there's a risk of kidney damage, poor mite. We need to test her brother, Liam. He's eight and attends Tollingdon Primary School.”

“Isn’t he in London with his mother?”

“He went home with his grandfather last night.” She gives me an address for one of the smarter districts in Tollingdon. “As far as we can ascertain, he hasn't displayed any symptoms, but we can't be sure. The mother became hostile when my colleagues tried to interview her. The nurses calmed things down and offered to complete the questionnaire.

"We got the feedback yesterday afternoon," she says, her voice dropping. "Chloe Burke, the mother, is convinced she'll lose the children if the father finds out. He's filed for custody, claiming she's an unfit mother because she has a history of substance abuse. That's why she won't answer any questions."

"I'll let you know what I find out from the brother and grandfather," I say.

"Mrs Burke did tell the nurses she took the children for a meal in Eastbourne, Saturday teatime, nine days ago. Your colleagues in Eastbourne are following up on that. We're not aware of any other cases at the moment, but that could change. If you exclude Liam from school and pot him, we'll keep trying with Mrs Burke. I'll forward the few details we have."

"Can you copy everything to my manager, Danielle Frost?"

"Of course."

"Copy me into what?" Danni asks as I put the phone down. She's leaning against the door frame, a dreamy smile on her lips. "Walk this way," she says, exaggerating the wiggle of her hips on the way to her office.

I'm hoping she's won the lottery because if she's in love … I stop, realising I don't want to go there. I've never thought about her having a man, or woman, in her life. It looks like I'm about to find out, judging by the way she flops into her chair.

"Looks like you lost a fight, Kent. Want to tell me about it?"

I take a seat. "I'd rather tell you about Charlotte Burke. She's four and half, confirmed E. coli O157, and in hospital with renal failure."

She switches on her computer. "Eastbourne District General?"

"No, the Evelina in London. Her condition's critical."

"Then she's in good hands."

That's management speak for not our problem. "The family live in Tollingdon, so we'll do the legwork."

"Gemma can run round with poo pots," Danni says, typing in her password. "I've got something far more important tasks for you. I've just spent the last four days devising a new, more effective and efficient way of working."

At least she's not in love. That's small comfort compared to the systems, forms and records she'll create. There's bound to be at least one matrix, supported by several decision trees and a forest of evaluation reports, all bundled within the ultimate measure of management success – a proliferation of acronyms.

"I'll email you my new PHIS so you can get up to speed PDQ. OK? Public Health Improvement System," she says, responding to my blank look.

I'm loath to spoil her moment, but I force myself. "Charlotte Burke has a brother at Tollingdon Primary School. We need to exclude him and test for E. coli."

She frowns at me as if I need constant spoon feeding. "Gemma can manage that too. Honestly, Kent, why do I pay you to be a manager when I make all the decisions? Let your team do the work. Just make sure they deliver. That's all I ask."

"This could turn into an outbreak, Danni."

"If it does, I'll expect you to run the investigation, not deliver poo pots. That's why PHIS will be such a help. Make sure you study the documents because we're meeting with Bernard at two."

"Bernard Doolittle from HR?"

"He has to agree any restructure."

Restructure is management speak for staff cuts. That means more uncertainty, people worrying whether they'll have a job or not. Not that I'm immune. Danni has left the E. coli investigation to me, so I take the flak if anything goes wrong. Past outbreaks in Scotland and Wales, where environmental health staff became overwhelmed by the explosive increase in cases, suggest we won't cope.

I'll become the first casualty of her restructure - which might be exactly what Danni wants.

"Grab some poo pots," I tell Gemma. "We need to get the shit before it hits the fan."

While she collects the pots and forms from the tiny room we laughingly call 'The Lab', I print the PHIS document Danni's emailed me and stuff it into a folder. No Kinsey Millhone for me this lunchtime.

"I'm no expert on Haemolytic Uraemic Syndrome," I say on the drive to Tollingdon Primary School, "but I thought you got it after you'd recovered from E. coli."

"Like a secondary infection?"

"No, more like a delayed reaction. You get better then it hits you. If Charlotte was ill and then recovered, we're looking at a long incubation period. If she went to preschool, who knows how many kids she could have infected?"

"But there haven't been any other cases, have there?"

That's what puzzles me. There should be other cases. "We'll get a better idea when we talk to the brother and grandfather," I say. "The mother's not very helpful."

"Give her a chance. Her child could be dying."

"I know, I know. But she wouldn't want other children to suffer, surely?"

Gemma's voice rises. "You can't imagine how she's feeling,"

I'm not sure why she's so prickly, but it could be linked to the dinner party. Most of the time she seemed subdued, as if she didn't want to be there, which makes me wonder why she accepted the invitation.

When we reach Tollingdon Primary School, I park outside the shops on the opposite side of the road, a few yards from where we found the cocker spaniel in the car. Gosh, ten days have elapsed since the funeral.

We cross the road and push through the bright red gates of a school built less than 20 years ago. The bright panels below the windows add colour to an otherwise drab single storey building. We approach along a path that cuts through flower borders made to look like miniature meadows and through double doors into a small foyer, plastered with notices and drawings. The reception window on the right reveals a small office that's used as a dumping ground for coats, toner cartridges and old computer monitors.

After signing in and getting our visitor badges, we're taken next door to see the Head. Connie Warburton's in her 30s, with a rounded, smiling face and a fondness for bright colours, if her glasses and office are anything to go by. Her royal blue suit, buttoned over a yellow blouse, matches her glasses and complements her intense eyes. Her small office walls hosts a collage of pictures the children have painted, while a table that runs along one wall is crammed with boxes, containing old mobile phones. By contrast, her desk is relatively tidy. Several photographs show a smartly dressed son and daughter, both sporting the same short, precise hairstyle their mother favours.

It's a far cry from the forbidding headmaster's office of my childhood.

I pick up a Nokia from one of the boxes. "Do any of them work?"

"We send them to a charity in Africa. If you have any phones you no longer need …"

"I have the opposite problem. I keep breaking mine."

"We might still be able to use them," she says, gesturing us to sit. "Now, how can I help you?"

"You've heard of E. coli O157, I imagine."

She pushes her glasses up her nose and leans back, waiting for me to continue. It makes a change to have someone calm and unhurried to talk to. Like the word 'asbestos', E. coli often alarms people.

"One of your pupils, Liam Burke, has a sister who's picked up the bug."

"Charlotte Burke?" Connie's expression suggests I've answered several questions. "That's why we haven't seen her for the last two weeks. Her mother never answers the phone or our emails."

"I thought Charlotte was at preschool."

Connie taps away at her keyboard and studies the monitor. "She started last month. She was with us for two weeks and we haven't seen her since. Her mother's a nurse, so you'd think she'd let us know, wouldn't you?"

I force myself not to think of all the vulnerable patients Chloe Burke could infect. "Does she work at the hospital?"

"No, she works at a nursing home in Pevensey Bay. I think it's the Beach View."

That's even worse. Between them, the Burke family could have infected vulnerable young children at one end and frail, elderly adults at the other.

"At least she'll know about personal hygiene," Gemma says. "Have you had any children off with food poisoning or tummy upsets?"

Connie shakes her head. "Just the usual bugs and colds. I'll check with her form teacher to be on the safe side." She picks up the phone. "Lisa, can you interrupt Kirk? Ask him to bring Liam Burke to my office. What? Oh, I see. Well, keep trying."

She replaces the receiver and sighs. "Surprise, surprise. Liam didn't show this morning and no one's answering the phone."

"His mother's at the Evelina Hospital in London with Charlotte. Liam's with his grandfather, so we can visit him there."

"His grandfather? She never told us she'd moved." She sighs and rises. "Let me know when you've spoken to him, will you?"

"Sure. And don't worry about the E. coli. We're onto it."

"You might want to keep it to yourself," Gemma says. "If parents find out, who knows what they'll think."

Connie smiles and nods, but I suspect she's one step ahead of us already. "There's no room in here, so let's go and talk to Kirk. He'll know if anyone else has been ill."

We follow Connie along a brightly painted corridor, lined with photographs, pictures and montages that detail projects in Africa to provide drinking water, health care and vital supplies like mosquito nets. Gemma's diamante sandals slap on the polished vinyl floor, drawing more than a couple of looks from Connie. As we approach the main hall, she stops at the last door, knocks and enters.

Gemma peers through the viewing panel. "You're not going to believe this."

It's Baxendale, the man who left his cocker spaniel to cook inside his car. He's dressed much smarter now, though his shirt and combat trousers look like they're about to fall off his skinny frame.

"I hope he doesn't bear grudges," I say, watching him limp across the classroom.

"Well, well, well," he says, closing the door behind him. "I didn't know you saved teachers from suffocating in hot, stuffy classrooms, Mr Fisher."

He leads us into the main hall and opens the door next to the serving hatch. His limp becomes more pronounced when he enters the kitchen, drawing sympathetic remarks from the women working there. They fall silent as Gemma and I follow through the clean, modern kitchen, the dry goods store and out into an enclosed yard. Here, among the bins and cardboard boxes, he pulls out his cigarettes.

"We're not allowed to smoke on school premises," he says. "But the contract caterers are responsible for the kitchen and yard. The children can't see us here."

"They can smell you," I say.

He cups his hand around the flame and lights up, taking a long draw. "So, Mr Kent Fisher, what's it like being Mr Righteous?"

"Healthier," I reply, backing away. "Did the Head tell you why we're here?"

"You want to know if Liam's been ill. No, he hasn't. I don't know about Charlotte because she's been absent for two weeks."

"Has anyone in the class been ill with sickness or diarrhoea?"

"Like Salmonella?"

"E. coli. It's –"

"I know what it is." He exhales smoke through his nostrils. "To my knowledge, no one's had food poisoning in the last week."

"How about the last three weeks? The bug can strike, die down and then flare up again."

"Three weeks?" He laughs, almost coughing as smoke pours out of his mouth. "I can't remember what I did yesterday. Look, Liam has attendance issues. We're never sure whether he'll turn up from one day to the next. Sometimes, he's gone for days."

"I thought you cracked down on truancy," Gemma says.

"He's absent. That doesn't mean he's truant." Baxendale takes an angry drag on the cigarette, which seems to calm him. "He's a bright kid in a troubled family. I'm no social worker - not that they're much use – but most marriages are a mess in my experience. You should come to parents' evening. You're lucky to get both parents with some kids."

Gemma's phone rings and she walks out of earshot.

“Wouldn’t say no to that,” he says, watching her exit through the large gate. Then he looks at me and laughs. “Treading on your toes, am I? Well, take it from me; you don’t want to get mixed up with someone at work, especially someone half your age.”

I sense the bitterness of personal experience in his words.

“I can see from your expression you think I took advantage of a pupil,” he says, his eyes flashing with anger. “Well, I married her – not that it’s any of your business.”

“Then don’t tell me about it.”

“It was her dog in the car,” he says, grinding the cigarette beneath a heel. “That’s all I have left. She left me for some kid who likes gangster rap and getting pissed every Friday night. Evenings in with a curry and a film didn’t do it for her.”

The gate opens and Gemma rejoins us. “Danni wants us to ask about farm visits.”

“We don’t take the children to farms,” Baxendale says, glancing at his watch. “But we visited your animal sanctuary the week before last. Does that count?”

SEVENTEEN

"You should suspend school visits," Gemma says.

We're weaving our way through the streets to the nearby Poets Estate, filled with smart 1930s semidetached houses with bay windows and hipped roofs. Somewhere in the midst of Wordsworth, Keats and Byron is Stephen Burke, Liam's grandfather.

"The children are supervised and they're not allowed to touch the animals," I say. "And no one's been ill. Besides, Charlotte Burke didn't get E. coli last week."

"What if Liam picked up the bug and infected his sister?"

"Then why wasn't he ill?"

"We don't know he wasn't. You heard Baxendale. Liam's in and out of school. Wouldn't it be great if he could blame Liam's absence on your sanctuary?"

I'd rather not think about what Baxendale might do.

"If I suspend school visits, people will assume the sanctuary's the source of the infection," I say, turning into Byron Avenue. "Frances is so strict with the children."

"She'll want to suspend visits," Gemma says, checking the numbers of the houses. "You should get your animals tested too. If they're negative, you've nothing to worry about."

And if they're positive, I'm loading the gun that's pointed at me.

"If there was a problem, other children would be affected. We'd have other cases. At the moment, this is an isolated case."

"Remind me who says every outbreak starts with a first case?"

I pull up outside Stephen Burke's house, taking in the neat garden and the gleaming Audi Quattro. It stands in a driveway where weeds daren't spread, unless they want to face the wrath of a pressure washer. He's even jetted the pavement outside his house. We walk up a crazy paved path that strolls between flower beds of petunias, begonias and geraniums, evenly spaced in neat rows as nature intended. Sweet peas, still flowering profusely, cling to netting on either side of the bay window. In the porch, we can't stand side by side, thanks to the pots of lobelia and fuchsias, dripping with red and purple flowers.

I ring the bell and step back, ID card in hand. A few moments later, a man in his late 40s or early 50s, with thick brown hair, Harry Potter glasses and a pleasant, smiling face, opens the door. Dressed casually in a pink shirt beneath a blue jumper and jeans, he looks like an executive on a day off.

"Stephen Burke?"

"Environmental health?" he responds in a cultured voice "The hospital said you'd be calling. Do you want to talk to Liam? Only he's in the back garden. I was told to keep him out of school until you'd tested him."

"Could we have a chat with you first?"

Inside, the house looks as pristine as the exterior with simple but tasteful wallpaper and furniture, made from 'real' wood, as the manufacturers like to say. I've yet to find unreal wood, but I live in hope.

"Would you like a cup of tea?" he asks, pausing by the kitchen door.

"White, no sugar, please."

Through the arch that leads into the dining room, I can see a child, dribbling a football and dispatching it into a small goal at the end of a long, narrow garden. Liam looks fit and healthy to me.

I stroll over to the bookcase beside an Art Deco fireplace, complete with diamond motif in the centre. I notice several fantasy novels, written by SL Burke. "Are you an author?" I ask when he returns.

He nods, placing a tray with mugs of tea on a coffee table between two sofas. "I was made redundant and decided to take the plunge. Do you like fantasy, Mr Fisher?"

I wait for a smart remark from Gemma, but she only smirks.

"I prefer crime fiction," I say, distracted by Liam, who's now waving a cane around like a sword, threatening a buddleia.

"Would you like a homemade cookie?" Burke asks.

"Yes please," I reply, noticing the family photos on the dresser in the corner.

Once Burke is back in the kitchen, I head over to the dresser. It only takes a glance to realise why Liam looks familiar. It's Sam, the child I hauled out of the goat paddock a couple of Saturdays ago. And Charlotte is Charlie, the girl who kicked my shins. Chloe is the mouthy mother, who looks nervous and self-conscious as a teenager. Someone turned her into a rebel with a yearning for tattoos. And nine days ago, she let her children run wild in my sanctuary.

When she finds out I'm investigating her daughter's illness …

I take a deep breath, surprised by how unsettled I feel. But it's no time to feel sorry for myself. I need to deal with this. Nigel has to take over, but I can't leave Gemma to carry on alone.

"Can I borrow your phone?" I ask. "I need to talk to Nigel."

"He's at the Food Standards Agency in London," she replies. "Imported Food training, I think. I can text him to ring you at lunchtime."

I glance out at the garden, my thoughts in overdrive. If the boy stays there, waging war on the bushes, we could interview his grandfather, leave the specimen pots and go without Liam recognising me. If he heads towards the house, I could make an excuse, duck out the front and leave Gemma to finish. Tomorrow morning, I'll hand over to Nigel and manage the investigation the way Danni wants me to.

"No, don't disturb him," I say, sitting on the sofa beside her. "Let's work quickly and get back to the office."

Burke returns with a plate of cookies. Unlike Gemma, I've lost my appetite.

"How's Charlotte?" I ask.

"Stable, whatever that means. Christina, my wife, went up yesterday and she's staying there until … She was quite distressed when she saw Charlotte and all those tubes… It reminded her of Chloe, our daughter. She had an accident when she was 16."

He pauses to compose himself, nibbling at a biscuit. "She became pregnant, thanks to a character called Snake. His real name was Michael Addison. He took drugs, rode a motorbike with a gang and had tattoos across his chest, back and arms. Chloe refused to have a termination and moved in with him. We didn't hear from her for months, but we knew she'd taken her exams. Then, one day, we got a call out of the blue. She'd been injured in an accident. They saved the baby, but he was born a heroin addict."

Burke lets out a long sigh, as if he's wanted to talk about this for a long time.

"We brought her home and tried to help her kick the habit, but she moved to London with Snake. We got photos from time to time, including her wedding, shots of Liam, and then Charlotte. She never told us she was expecting again."

The remains of the cookie crumble in his fingers and dribble onto the carpet. "We tried to find them, but we couldn't. We had to settle for the few crumbs she gave us. Then, in June this year, she arrived on the doorstep with the children. She left Snake almost a year earlier, but he tracked her down. Now he's demanding custody of the children."

Burke stares at the crumbs on the floor. "She's clean, though her moods aren't easy to deal with. And the children have settled. We don't need this."

"Do you know how Charlotte could have been infected?" I ask, aware that Liam's getting closer to the house.

"No idea. We take them out and eat in all the usual places. We go walking on the Downs, but we always carry antibacterial wipes. Christina insists on it. You can't be too careful with animals and their faeces, can you?"

"No," Gemma replies, casting me a glance.

"There was a fair in Eastbourne a couple of weeks ago. We had burgers from a stall. The kids loved them, but they were a bit pink inside. I swapped Charlotte's for mine, but I've not been ill," he adds. "She only had a couple of bites. Would that be enough?"

"Possibly. Bugs don't spread themselves evenly in food."

"Can you remember the name of the stall?" Gemma asks.

He shakes his head "Liam might remember. Do you want me to call him in?"

"Let him play," I reply. "Our colleagues in Eastbourne are dealing with it."

"So, if it wasn't the burger, what made Charlotte ill?" Burke asks.

"It could be anything," Gemma replies, reading off her questionnaire. "Undercooked food, contact with animals at a farm or zoo, camping or playing in a field where cattle or sheep graze. Manure could be infected," she says, almost as an afterthought. "I notice you grow vegetables."

His back stiffens. "Are you suggesting I made Charlotte ill?"

"We're not suggesting anything," I reply, wondering if his defensive response owes more to guilt than the stress of his granddaughter's illness. "We need faecal samples from you and Liam. Gemma will go through the process with you and answer any further questions. I need to ring the relevant authorities and update them."

Gemma passes me her phone and I escape through the front door, relieved to be out of Liam's line of sight. I sit on the garden wall and ring Frances.

"There's nothing to worry about," I say, fending off her questions. "No one else is ill, but we'll cancel the school visits until we establish the source of the bug."

"But the children are supervised," she says, clearly anxious. "You know I don't let them pet the animals. They wash their hands with antibacterial soap. It can't be us, can it? I mean, you can never guarantee that every surface is sterile… I'll disinfect everything, Kent."

"Slow down," I say. "If anything was wrong, I'd know, wouldn't I?"

"Sorry," she says. "I remember what happened to that attraction in Surrey."

Me too. "Ring the schools and postpone the visits."

"What do I tell them? I can't say we have infectious animals."

"Frances, there's no evidence our animals are infected. Tell them we need to do some urgent repairs."

Next I ring Noreen McIntyre at Eastbourne. She mutters something derogatory about the Leisure Team. "We keep asking them to demand food registrations from anyone who holds an event but they never do. I checked the fair's website and they're in Scotland now. So there's not much we can do, is there?"

"No," I say, certain Danni will blame the burger and pass the buck to Eastbourne. Feeling better than I did 20 minutes ago, I get to my feet. "Sorted."

"What's sorted?" a voice asks.

Turning, I look straight at Liam Samuel Burke and the cane he's holding like a light sabre.

He may not have recognised me. As soon as I walk away, he runs into the house. Five minutes later, Gemma joins me in the car.

"Did you meet, Liam?" I ask.

She nods. "Bright kid. He seems to be fine."

"But?"

She frowns at me. "Since I teamed up with you, I'm suspicious of everything. Anything that doesn't sound right or doesn't fit and I'm off looking for reasons. I don't know how you sleep at night."

"I close my eyes and drift off." I start the car and pull away. "So, what doesn't fit?"

"Every time I asked Liam a question, he looked at his grandfather like he needed permission to answer." She pulls on her seat belt and sighs. "It's probably nothing."

"You should trust your instincts, Gemma."

"I trusted you and look what happened. Sorry," she says, her cheeks reddening. "I'm on edge at the moment. Maybe it's a delayed reaction to the shooting."

I'm not so sure. "What really bothered you about Liam?"

"His grandfather said almost nothing, letting Liam answer. Then I asked if he'd been unwell in the last few weeks and he said he'd been sick. His grandfather was straight in, saying it was one of those 24 hour bugs, blaming it on a Chinese meal. He said it was probably four weeks ago. Then it was five. Then it became a couple of months."

"You think it's more recent, right?"

"Or he's trying to deflect the blame. If Liam had sickness or diarrhoea, it wasn't reported, was it?"

"If he wasn't taken to his GP then no, it wouldn't be."

Gemma drifts into a thoughtful silence that lasts until we reach the office car park. Then she becomes animated.

"Remember what grandfather said about the husband wanting custody of the kids," she says. "What if Chloe's not clean? What if she was out of it on drugs and didn't take Liam to the doctor when he was ill?"

"Burke could have taken him."

"But he didn't, did he? We'd have a lab report if he had."

"Only if Liam tested positive," I say. "If he was negative, Burke would have told you."

"Which means they kept Liam at home until he recovered," she says, looking pleased. "Mother makes up some story for the school and swears Liam to secrecy. Only he infects Charlotte and mum has to pull her out of school and keep her at home so no one knows, especially the husband."

It's an interesting hypothesis. "Then Charlotte goes down with renal failure, poor kid."

"Can we prove it?" Gemma asks.

"Not unless Chloe owns up."

I recall the antagonist mother at the sanctuary that Saturday afternoon. If she believes she could lose her children, she'll blame my goats and there's nothing I can do to stop her.

Or maybe there is.

"Can I borrow your phone again?" I ask.

Gemma heads into the office while I walk across to a small grassed area and sit on the bench. I ring Downland

Manor Hotel and ask to speak to Birchill. I'm put straight through to his office.

"Hi Kent," he says, sounding like he's eating. "How can I help?"

"Do you remember the woman with the two children at the sanctuary, a week ago, Saturday?"

"The mouthy one? How could I forget?"

I explain the situation and my theory that Chloe has been less than honest about her children's health. "There's a chance she'll claim my goats infected her daughter."

"I heard you tell her at least twice to wash the children's hands," he says. "How did they get in the paddock anyway?"

"I went upstairs to answer the phone. I asked them to wait in the yard for me."

Birchill laughs. "Would you have waited?"

"No," I reply. "When I returned, they'd gone, but I'm not sure the mother even noticed."

"So," he says, sounding like he's about to formulate a plan, "if she accuses us of infecting her children, what happens?"

"I've already told Frances to cancel the planned school visits this week."

"That could be viewed as a sign of guilt."

"Or a sensible precaution from a caring, law-abiding concern."

"If the children are supervised and don't touch the animals, where's the risk?"

"There's always a risk." I stop, aware my voice is rising. "You can never guarantee there are no bugs left on surfaces. An infected person could bring bugs onto the site."

"Have any other children been ill?"

"None, as far as I know."

"Then I can't see how anyone can claim it's the sanctuary. You have risk assessments, systems in place, and hundreds of children who have never had so much as a sneeze after visiting the place. If you start cancelling visits, people will suspect there's something wrong. Don't close," he says, as if ticking off the last item on his list.

"I'm an EHO. Doing nothing is not an option." I sigh, angry and annoyed with myself for leaving the children to run free at the sanctuary. "If Chloe Burke finds out I'm investigating the case, she'll accuse me of protecting my sanctuary."

"So, why the hell are you investigating?"

"I didn't know who the kids were until this morning. When I recognised the boy, I got out of the place and left Gemma to finish, but he may have recognised me."

"Then get someone to take over right away. Make sure you put it in writing so no one can accuse you of improper conduct. Gemma will back you up, won't she?"

"She's not the problem. Danni will insist I close the sanctuary and have the goats tested."

He pauses. "I'll deal with Danni."

"No, this is my problem."

"Then why did you ring me?"

I close my eyes, angry with myself for seeking his protection and help. How shallow does that make me? What's wrong with me? Where's my resolve?

"You're a witness," I reply. "I need you to corroborate the events of Saturday afternoon and discredit Chloe Burke."

"In that case, we need to tilt the odds our way."

Five minutes later, Gemma intercepts me on the landing of the second floor.

"Colonel Witherington's in Danni's office," she says. "He's been there for over an hour."

"Where's Danni?"

"She's at some high-powered meeting. Her email doesn't say where, or with whom," she says, emphasising her correct choice of grammar. "She's booked a meeting with Dr Doolittle at two, so she'll be back before then."

"Okay, let's see what the Colonel wants."

When I open the door to Danni's office, I hear him snoring. He's seated at her meeting table, his head drooping forward. His mouth hangs open, a dribble of saliva running from the corner of his mouth to his chin. His neatly arranged hat, gloves and walking stick rest next to an untouched cup of tea.

Gemma closes the door, making enough noise to stir him. His head jerks up and he takes a few moments to orientate himself. We sit opposite and wait. Then he points a gnarled finger at me.

"Why do you think I killed my wife?"

EIGHTEEN

"Did you kill her?" I ask, meeting the Colonel's icy stare.

"You think my Daphne's buried under the conservatory?"

"Is she?"

He slaps his hand down on the table. "Dammit, man, I'm too ill to waste time playing games. You went to Glastonbury to confront Miller. When were you going to tell me? Next week? Next month?"

I offer silent thanks to Niamh for telling him. "When were you going to tell me you paid Miller to leave?"

He shows no emotion. Unlike Gemma, who realises how little I've told her.

"You paid him twenty grand to take Daphne out and pretend they were running away together." I pause, watching for any reaction. "Then, the next day, when he doesn't show, she's devastated and you pick up the pieces, right?"

"When I found out about Miller, I was angry. No," he says, slumping back in the chair, "I was scared of losing her. I knew she had needs I couldn't meet, but Miller sounded serious, so I checked him out. He was a third rate chancer, so I made him an offer to see how much he cared for my Daphne. He practically snatched the money from my hands."

He pauses for a self-satisfied smirk. "Only he duped me, didn't he? He did everything I asked and then took my Daphne anyway. Now she's dead."

I remain silent, not sure who or what to believe. I know Daphne was at home Tuesday morning and gone by the evening. Where she went, if she left at all, or who she went with, I don't know.

I walk over to the window. "The investigation's finished, Colonel. Miller's gone. There's no evidence your wife is dead."

He slams his hand down on the table. "She's dead, dammit! I feel it here."

He thumps his chest and then gasps. His face twists with pain, his cheeks growing redder. When his hands begin to shake, I'm sure he's fitting.

"Gemma, get some water," I say, hurrying over to him. "Colonel, take deep breaths."

"Pills. In my pocket."

He points to his jacket pocket with a shaking finger. Inside, I find a small bottle of pills. I take one out and place it on the table. He pinches the pill between his fingers and then pushes it under his tongue.

"Bloody angina," he says, clearly in pain.

I head for Danni's desk. "I'll call an ambulance,"

"I don't need a hospital," he says, his tone still angry. "I need to know what happened to my Daphne."

"What if she's alive and doesn't want to be found?" Gemma asks.

"Why would she do that? She loved me."

"Then why did she fall for Miller?"

Tears fill his eyes and he lets out a mournful groan. In a quiet voice, he says, "I lost my temper with her."

Maybe the fit unsettled him. Maybe the thought of dying makes him want to tell the whole story. I raise a hand to silence Gemma and we wait while he draws deep breaths. Slowly, his breathing returns to normal and the colour returns to his cheeks. He straightens and clasps his hands together.

"I bought her beautiful dresses and gowns, but she insisted on wearing those awful leggings, or whatever they're called, and shapeless sweaters, even when we had guests. One evening, I went to her room when she didn't come down for dinner and found her gowns on the floor, like she'd thrown them there in a rage. I told her she was keeping our guests waiting and she laughed. She told me what I could do with my guests and my dresses."

He closes his eyes tight, squeezing tears out of the corners. "I wanted her to be happy and have the best. I worshipped her. I wanted to see her looking beautiful in those gowns. I wanted others to see how lovely she was." He looks up, clearly distressed as he shakes his head. "I worshipped her. I never meant to strike her."

Gemma and I exchange a glance. "When was this?" I ask.

"About a month before she left."

"She was seeing Miller at the time."

His head jerks up. "He turned her against me."

"And you offered him money to jilt her? What made you think he would?"

"Desperate times demand desperate measures."

"Didn't it occur to you that Miller could tell your wife what you were planning?"

The Colonel stares at me, his frown deepening as he realises what I mean. Then his stubborn nature kicks in. "No, she's dead," he says, struggling to his feet. He pulls on his cap and gloves as he shuffles across the office, walking stick under his arm. He turns at the door and says, "Find the man who killed her."

The door slams behind him.

"Why did you lie about Glastonbury?" Gemma asks, breaking the silence.

"I didn't lie."

"No, you didn't say anything." She pauses, expecting me to say something. "What about Stacey Walters? Did you ask Miller about her?"

"Miller said he left the day before Daphne disappeared."

"And you believe him?"

I think back to Glastonbury. Miller didn't seem to know that Daphne Witherington had disappeared. He said he didn't have dinner with her at La Floret because he thought the Colonel was going to kill him. While it sounds like a plot from a cheap movie, if it's true, then who had dinner with her? Did anyone else know about the Colonel's plan?

I shake my head, certain only Miller knew. It means he lied to me from the moment I spoke to him. So, why don't I believe he killed Daphne Witherington or Stacey Walters? He wanted to kill me, didn't he?

"I need to brief Danni about the E. coli case," I say, glancing at my watch. "Where is she?"

At five minutes to two, after several visits to her empty office, I'm no wiser. Bernard Doolittle's phone goes straight to voicemail, prompting an unwanted image of them thrashing around on his desk. But his office is also empty.

I sit at my desk, uncomfortable with the strategy I agreed with Birchill.

Then Gemma waves me over. "Todd Walters has received a letter from Stacey," she says in a low, but excited voice. "I said we'd pop round at seven."

My phone rings before I can ask her about the letter. It's Frank Dean, the Chief Executive. "Kent, would you come up to my office to discuss the E. coli case," he says. "Immediately."

I put the phone down and turn to Gemma. "Make sure you get poo pots from the Burkes."

"Don't you want to know about the letter?"

"Later."

I hurry down to the Chief Executive's suite on the first floor. The level of polish on the oak panels and the spring in the carpet increase as I walk past the Council Chamber and Committee Rooms. While I spend as little time as possible down here, I'm always impressed by the quiet and cleanliness. All the inward-facing services like HR, Finance, Legal, and Facilities Management, occupy this floor, looking after themselves, it seems.

Outside the Chief Executive's office, I draw a breath. I knock and enter, expecting to see Danni and Bernard Doolittle with Frank Wheeler, but not Colonel Witherington. He still looks weary and fragile, despite holding his head high.

Frank beckons me to the polished oval table. "Have a nibble," he says, pushing a tray of sandwiches towards me. "Coffee?"

I decline and sit facing the four of them. While Frank acts the genial host, he can't dispel the tension. The absence of any files or papers on the table suggests nothing is being written down. They must have good memories as Danni's been absent for three hours.

Frank finishes his sandwich, wipes his hands on a napkin and nods to Danni. She straightens in her chair, places both hands flat on the table and clears her throat.

"We've received an email from Rapier and Radcliffe, solicitors representing Chloe Burke. She claims her daughter, Charlotte, was infected by E. coli O157 at your animal sanctuary on Saturday, the eighth. In addition to the formal complaint against you and this Council, she's demanding a substantial sum in damages."

So much for being distressed by her daughter's illness.

"We need to carry out an internal investigation," Doolittle says. "You'll hand over the E. coli investigation to Nigel, who will report direct to Danni."

I make a note on the back of the PHIS report.

"We will examine all your activities pertinent to the case," Doolittle says, looking like he can't wait to get started. "The Head of Audit will lead and we will ask the Health and Safety Executive to inspect and report on your animal sanctuary."

I wasn't expecting that.

"It also appears you do not have planning permission for the sanctuary," Doolittle continues. "Or the first floor living accommodation you have created within the barn."

Someone has been doing their homework.

Danni picks up the baton. “You must close your sanctuary immediately and test your animals for E. coli.”

While I’m tempted to remind her I’m innocent until proven guilty, I simply make notes. This is a well-rehearsed performance that thankfully, Miles Birchill anticipated. I baulked at his suggestions on how to defend my sanctuary, but now I’m glad I listened.

“Colonel, is there anything you wish to add?” Frank asks him.

He shifts in his chair, avoiding my gaze. “Officially or unofficially?”

As the Chief Executive starts to answer, I cut him off. “Everything must be official and recorded. My solicitors will want a full transcript of this meeting, which I notice no one is recording.”

“Solicitors?” Danni looks surprised. “This is an informal meeting to advise you of a complaint that’s been made. We’re not accusing you of anything.”

I consult my notes. “What about not having planning permission for my sanctuary or living accommodation?”

“I said you didn’t appear to have planning permission,” Doolittle replies. “That’s not an accusation.”

“They have nothing to do with Mrs Burke’s complaint either,” I say, getting into my stride. “But you obviously checked with Planning. If not, you’re making an assumption.”

His back straightens. “Of course I’ve checked.”

“Even though it has nothing to do with the complaint made, Mr Doolittle.” I pause for a moment to enjoy his blustering discomfort. “And please don’t threaten me with the Health and Safety Executive. I can give you the name of the inspector, who checked my sanctuary last year. I can let you have a copy of his report that says I meet all health and safety at work requirements, unlike this Council."

Doolittle looks ready to pounce on me, but Frank makes calming gestures. "There's no need to get personal, Kent. We're –"

"Then don't tell me how to run my business." I gather my papers and rise, looking down on them one at a time. "If Chloe Burke intends to claim compensation, she'll sue me, not the Council."

"She's made a formal complaint about you," he says, remaining seated.

"And the council, you said. Maybe you'd like to put some meat on the bones."

"It's a conflict of interest," Doolittle says. "She claims your animals caused the illness and you're investigating it."

"I'm not investigating."

This causes a ripple of surprise. "You were there this morning," Danni says.

"And when I discovered who was infected, I left and rang you. But you've been incognito, Danni. Had you returned to your office you'd have seen the note I put on your desk a couple of hours ago."

She holds up her BlackBerry. "Why didn't you email me?"

"Some things are too important and complex for emails. But you've been hard to reach since last Wednesday. Just like you, Bernard, now I think about it."

"Let's not turn this into a soap opera," Frank says, rising. "These are serious allegations, Kent. The professionalism and reputation of you, your department and this council are being challenged. We need to present a united front."

"Then present it to Chloe Burke, not me."

I stride out of the room and slam the door. My heart's pounding harder than it does after a sprint, but I don't have time to catch my breath.

I need to write a note and get it on Danni's desk before she returns to her office.

NINETEEN

Gemma's late and still in her work clothes.

"I took the poo pots to Brighton," she tells me when I climb into her Volvo. "One was a bit runny and it might have leaked, so be careful."

Immediately, I lift my backside from the seat and look down. It takes a few seconds for her laughter to cut through my alarm. Peeved, but relieved, I settle in the seat.

"Fancy being mugged by your own wind up," she says.

"I'm glad to see you've perked up."

She sets off along the bumpy track. "I'm looking forward to more sleuthing. It's much more fun than poo pots."

"You should be spending more time with Richard," I say. "He's a good bloke."

"I'm glad you approve. He's kind, gentle and caring."

Unlike me, she means. Only this isn't about me, is it?

"You're lucky to have him," I say. "I like him."

"Do I detect a bromance?" She glances at me and laughs. "Jeez, you're so serious tonight."

"You were hardly singing from the rooftops earlier."

She pulls up to the junction with the A27 and swings right across the road. “I was tired, that’s all. It’s great having Richard around every evening, but I like my space.”

I nod, wishing Niamh wasn’t there wherever I turn. Maybe that’s why I’ve never wanted a permanent relationship. I like the freedom to do what I want when I want, with whoever I want. Had Niamh not moved in, my brief encounter with Rebecca might have developed.

Who am I kidding?

“He wants the four of us to go out for a meal,” Gemma says, taking a left at the traffic lights. “You and Yvonne, I mean. He loved the banter between you. So, what do you say?”

“She’s not my type.”

“Because she gives as good as she gets, if not better?” Gemma shakes her head in disbelief. “She’s exactly your type, Kent. She’s gorgeous, stylish, quick-witted and fun. Okay, she’s American, but otherwise she’s perfect.”

“Alasdair invited her to make up the numbers.”

She laughs. “You said Alasdair, not Davenport. Are you ill?”

“Maybe I’m moving on.”

“Can I have it in writing?”

“Talking of writing, what about this letter?”

“Stacey Walters is alive and well in Glastonbury with Colin Miller,” she replies.

Walters has replaced the display cabinet he smashed, cleared the mess, and bleached the shop to within an inch of its life. The fresh smell can’t quite disguise the years of neglect, but I can see the gaps between the floorboards now the grease and muck have gone. A newer chopping block has replaced the worn and bloody one, the white wall tiles are gleaming, and there's a new set of scales on the counter. While he hasn't quite managed to add sparkle to his personality, his mood's brighter.

"Mr Fisher, Miss Dean, thanks for coming. I wasn't sure you'd be interested."

His drab coat's gone, replaced by a crisp blue pinstripe shirt with white collar and cuffs. His black trousers, bunched at the waist by a hefty belt, have turn-ups, suggesting hibernation at the back of the wardrobe for a couple of decades. With his hair slicked back, and a smile to lift his jowls, he looks ready for a night out.

We follow him into the corridor, which looks wider without the clutter. "Are you going out?"

He scoops up a cardboard box from the stairs, which have also been swept and cleaned. "No. Why do you say that?"

"No reason." We follow him into his flat, which still looks like a crash pad for university students.

"I cleared so much stuff, I ran out of room in the yard," he says, setting the box on the table. "A mate's shifting it tomorrow. Stacey won't recognise the place."

I glance at Gemma, who looks equally surprised. "She's coming home?"

He nods and grins, plucking an envelope from the table. "See for yourself."

It's a standard supermarket brand envelope, bearing a first class stamp and Walters' address on a printed label. From the ragged tear, it looks like he opened the envelope with a chainsaw, almost obliterating the Bristol postmark, dated yesterday. Inside, a sheet of A4 paper has been folded into quarters. There's no address or date on the letter, which comprises one paragraph in Times New Roman, followed by a large, flamboyant signature that's unreadable.

Gemma nudges up close to read it with me.

"Dear Mr Walters,

A year has passed since Stacey and I moved to Glastonbury. We're deliriously happy and she has no intention of returning to you, so don't send anyone else to try and find us. Stacey's singing once more and I've grown my catering business. By rights, she's entitled to half your home and business, but she don't want nothing – just a divorce.'

"It doesn't sound like Stacey's coming home," I say.

"It's a fake." He laughs and takes the letter back. "And I thought you were the clever one, Mr Fisher. He tells me they're in Glastonbury and then says don't try to find us. Stupid or what?"

It appears my trip to Glastonbury prompted Miller to write. Is he worried Walters will follow? If he is, then the letter's an open invitation.

Yet Walters has declined the invite.

"It's a printed signature," he tells Gemma, running his finger over the back of the paper. "There's no indent from a pen. If he'd written it, he would have signed it. I think my Stacey wrote this. She wants me to come and get her."

And I thought I had a vivid imagination.

"Then why didn't she phone?" Gemma asks. "Or text?"

"I don't have a mobile phone."

"You have a phone in the shop."

I'm enjoying Gemma's tenacity, matched only by Walters' conviction.

"What if he overheard her?" he asks. "Or checked the last number she phoned?"

It doesn't follow that she wrote the letter, but I don't care what Walters believes. "If she wrote the letter, why does she want a divorce?" I ask.

"She wants to talk to me, obviously."

"I hate to break this to you, Todd, but her solicitor will talk to yours."

He shakes his head so hard, I'm surprised he doesn't wrench his bullish neck. "She didn't take her stuff, did she?" He points to her darts and then wrenches open the cupboard that contains her karaoke equipment. "Why not? Did you ever think about that, Mr Fisher?"

Before I can answer, he says, "No, because you don't know my Stacey. She's always had a restless spirit. She needed to get away, now she's ready to come back. That's why she wrote a coded letter to me."

"Todd, Stacey's not in Glastonbury. Neither is Miller, I suspect."

He laughs. "How do you know?"

"I was there last Friday night."

"You met Miller?" His face is now inches from mine, overpowering me with his aftershave. "Why didn't you tell me? Did you see Stacey?"

"I don't think she's with him."

"Then how do you explain this?" He pushes the letter into my face. "First thing tomorrow, I'm going to Glastonbury. Tell me where he lives."

"He attacked me," I say, pushing the letter away. I lift my polo shirt to reveal the huge swollen bruise of blue, yellow and purple on my side. "Then he ran off. He's gone, Todd."

Walters shakes his head.

"For all he knows, I called the police," I say, determined to make him see sense.

"Did you?" he asks.

"Of course he didn't," Gemma replies. "He's a bloke."

He jabs the letter with his finger. "It says they're in Glastonbury,."

"Because he's already left," she says, making no effort to hide her frustration.

Walters paces across the room, staring at the letter. He slumps onto the sofa with a thud that probably dislodges plaster from the ceiling below. Then he rips the letter into small pieces and tosses them in the air.

"You must think I'm a right mug."

I beckon Gemma to leave. As we reach the door, he calls us back. He hurries into the kitchen and returns with a bottle of champagne. "That's why I asked you over," he says, holding the bottle out. "I wanted to say thank you for helping me."

Part of me wonders if I've made things worse. "Put it on ice," I say. "You never know what tomorrow will bring."

Outside, Gemma's straight to the point. "Did you just tell Walters you were going to keep looking for Stacey?"

"I never said that."

"You can't give him false hope, Kent. It's worse than no hope."

I know how he feels.

On Wednesday morning, I find a note to call Colonel Witherington.

"You need to take the rest of the week off," he says, his tone conciliatory but firm. "In military parlance, you need to remove yourself from the crossfire."

"And let the world think I'm guilty?"

"This isn't about you, Kent."

"My sanctuary's in the frame."

"What about the reputation of the council and your colleagues? Can you imagine the editorial Thomas Bloody Logan will write?"

"And have everyone think I'm running away?"

"This is a time for discretion not valour, Kent. Get your animals tested and pray to God they come back negative."

"And if they're positive, I'm screwed."

"So put your house in order," he says. "They want the blame to fall on you and they'll do everything they can to discredit you. That includes your pretty assistant. Can you trust her?"

"Of course," I reply.

A few minutes later she beckons me to the lab. "Has someone complained about me?" she asks. "Only the Head of Audit has summoned me for a formal interview. He doesn't say why, but it must be something to do with the E. coli, right?"

"It's not about you," I reply. "Chloe Burke claims my goats made her daughter ill, but she didn't keep Charlotte and Liam under control when they visited the sanctuary."

Gemma looks at me in surprise, which quickly turns to anger. "Hang on. Liam and Charlotte visited your sanctuary?"

I nod. "The day after the funeral."

"And you started the investigation knowing this?"

Her voice is almost ultrasonic. She stares at me, mouth open, anger and disbelief burning in her eyes. It's like I've betrayed her and everything I believe in.

"I didn't know who they were until I saw Liam in the garden yesterday."

"Then why didn't you tell me right away?"

"That's why I left you to finish the interview."

"You could have told me in the car." She heads for the door, clearly hurt and betrayed. "Why don't you trust me?"

"Do you think I would have visited Stephen Burke if I'd known who his daughter and grandchildren were?"

"That's not what this is about," she replies, slamming the door behind her.

I lean back against the wall. I want to trust her, but I'm worried what she'll think when she finds out how I feel about her. What if she doesn't like what she sees? What if she pushes me away?

It's better not to know.

Moments later, Kelly enters, looking concerned. She takes one look at my face and opens her arms to hug me. "You never know what's around the corner," she says.

For a moment, I wonder why I'm hung up on Gemma when Kelly never fails to put a smile on my face. "Why don't we go somewhere exotic?"

She pulls back and looks into my eyes. "Are we talking about a caravan at Camber Sands?"

"How do you know about that?" I ask, intrigued.

"You'd be surprised how many waitresses I know."

"That was years ago," I say. "I'm grown up now."

"Yeah, grown-ups often hide in cupboards when the shit hits the fan. What's going on, Kent? What have you done this time?"

"A girl's in hospital with renal failure, fighting for her life, and it could be my fault."

She listens to my precis and makes sympathetic noises in all the right places. Then she kisses me on the cheek and tells me to keep a low profile, as Colonel Witherington suggested.

But I can't sit around and do nothing. Frances believes we're finished. No matter what I say, she's convinced the E. coli poisoning is her fault because she went shopping with Niamh that Saturday.

When I talk to Niamh, she wants to bring in the family solicitor in case there's a lawsuit even though I've notified my insurance company of a possible claim. When she insists, I explain what I've done. Unfortunately, I mention my discussion with Birchill and she lets rip.

"That bastard took everything we have! He blackmailed your father to do his bidding."

"He wasn't my father."

"He may not have fertilised the egg, but he treated you like his own, you ungrateful eejit. I can't believe you're even talking to that man, that scum who's ruined our lives. You should be ashamed!"

I want to remind her that William Fisher gambled away the family estate. He lied and betrayed us, but she'll never see it that way, even though she knows he was unfaithful to her.

"Birchill owns the land we're living on," I say, my hands on her shoulders. "He could evict us tomorrow. I have to work with him."

"You don't have to go running to him, do you?" Tears fill her eyes as she says, "You could ask me for help."

I pull her close, wondering what to do about Miles Birchill. While I don't like the man, or condone his actions, he went from a disgraced groom on the Fisher estate to multimillionaire, returning to Downland Manor to claim his prize. And he didn't lose it all gambling.

But that's not Niamh's fault either.

The next morning, I ring the office to say I'm working from home. But I can't concentrate. After a couple of hours pushing emails around, I drive to the Belle Tout lighthouse and walk along the cliffs to Birling Gap to clear my head. With the wind howling off the sea, and the waves battering the cliffs, it's wild and raw, just how I like it. The soft, rolling slopes of the South Downs mask the ferocity of nature, as it chips away at the chalk and scrapes through the bushes and trees that fight to get a foothold on the thin layer of soil.

The noise deafens my doubts and fears. In the distance, the rise and fall of the Seven Sisters, majestic above the foaming sea, draws me towards Birling Gap and the National Trust café. I could have driven to the car park, but I wanted to walk along the cliffs and clear my head. Instead, I'm reminded of Gemma.

When I left her bedsit seven years ago, I came here. I walked for hours, wrestling with my feelings as I strolled over the Seven Sisters and back, finally stopping at the café.

I looked out across the water, sparkling in the late morning sunshine, recalling the evening before when the sun streaked the sky on its descent behind the hills.

We'd made love on the grass in a sheltered nook behind the café after it closed. She looked up at me with dreamy eyes. "I'm hopelessly in love with you, Kent Fisher," she said. "I can't imagine life without you."

And I gave her Birling Gap café to inspect. How thoughtful of me.

I skirt around the remaining coastguard cottages, now ominously close to the receding cliffs, and into the car park, packed with cars despite the weather. The gravel crunches beneath my feet as I stride across to the stairs that lead down to the beach. Even on a gloomy October morning, there are still dog walkers, students and tourists strolling over the shingle to the water's edge. At low tide, the rocks beneath the chalk emerge, trapping seawater into small pools.

I rest my arms on the rail, looking along the coast, recalling Columbo's first visit a few weeks ago. He hated the shingle beach, but it didn't stop him slowly picking his way over the pebbles to the water's edge, only to jump back from the waves. Then, after testing the water was safe with his paws, he went in further, a little at a time.

Maybe I could learn a thing or two from him.

The café's busy, despite the weather. The queue shuffles towards the counter, where assistants produce mugs of foaming coffee and pots of tea for the regular customers, who present their loyalty cards for another stamp. Mine's at home, along with my thoughts.

"Good to see you, Kent."

I snap out of my daze and spot Debbi waving and heading for me. She's one of those outdoor types with no-nonsense hair, a weather-beaten complexion and rough hands from building walls and paths. Her smoker's laugh reminds me of Muttley, Dick Dastardly's faithful dog. She treats me to this every time we meet, before repeating the dodgy joke I told her the first time we met.

"What do you call a man with a sharp drop?" she says, shaking my hand.

"Cliff Edge," I reply.

And she's off, laughing like it's the first time she's heard it, much to the amusement of the customers either side of me. The women behind the counter smile politely.

"Never fails," she says, straightening her shirt. "Never fails. Oh Kent, where have you been? I thought you'd emigrated."

"I'll be here when the place topples to the beach below," I say. "I can't believe how much the cliff's eroded in the last couple of years."

She looks out of the window as if she expects to see the rocks falling away. "It's frightening how close it is. So, what brings you here? It can't be another inspection as your assistant, Gemma, was here recently. Pretty young thing, isn't she?"

I shuffle along, aware we're holding up the queue. "I only popped in for a cup of tea and a scone."

"Then you must meet our new chef. His scones are to die for."

She's tugging my sleeve, easing me away from the queue. "I'll treat you to a cream tea while we chew the fat. I hear you're a famous detective these days."

She leads me through to the back and into the kitchen, talking about her new puppies and how much paperwork she has these days. The kitchen looks as spotless and well-equipped as it did the last time I inspected it. The stainless steel gleams, the floor sparkles, and the two young women preparing sandwiches use the correct coloured chopping boards.

"I can't come in without a white coat," I say, when she beckons me to join her.

Her hand goes to her mouth and she scuttles back to join me in the doorway. "I'll get them to bring the cream teas through to the office," she says, leading me down the corridor.

The office smells of walking boots, waxed jackets and Danish pastries as we weave between the three desks. Each one sags beneath a mess of paperwork, walkie talkies and stained mugs, filling the spaces between the PCs and the letter trays. I'm about to sit in a plastic chair beside Debbie's desk, when I spot a watercolour painting of Birling Gap and the Seven Sisters on the wall next to the standard health and safety poster.

"Daphne Witherington," I say, checking the signature.

Debbie nods. "Such a talented artist. Look at the way she captures the light and shade of the cliffs. It's always changing, always shifting."

Indeed. I have enough photographs to fill several memory sticks. "You knew her?"

"She was a regular visitor with her easel and paints. We were organising an exhibition," she says, joining me to admire the painting. "Nothing elaborate, but we spent the best part of six months planning the details. Then, a couple of weeks before the event, she vanished. I still have her paintings in a storeroom."

"Didn't the Colonel want them back?"

She shrugs. "I don't think he knows they're here. I held onto them in case she returned." Debbie waits for the assistant to deposit two cream teas on her desk and depart before continuing. "Daphne must have had one hell of a barney with her old man to up sticks like that. He was always checking on her, you know."

"Really?"

We sit at her desk and she reaches for a scone. "Oh yes. He got his housekeeper to ring on some pretext, especially if he was expecting her home at a certain time. She used to stay out longer, just to wind him up. Once, she asked me to pretend I didn't know where she was, but that backfired. He turned up in his Range Rover ten minutes later to take her home, even though she preferred to walk across the fields."

I decline a scone, knowing it will take at least a five mile run to burn off the calories. "Do you think she was unhappy?"

"With her marriage?" Debbie piles clotted cream and jam on the scone as she speaks. "I'd say she felt suffocated. Not that she ever said so. No, everything was bright and exciting to her. Out here, whether she was walking on the cliffs or painting, she felt liberated. That's why I don't understand why she just left. Unless…"

I pour some tea into my cup while she savours a mouthful of scone.

"Unless she did it to teach him a lesson," she says, spilling crumbs everywhere. "Then she'd have come back, I suppose."

"Maybe she met someone else."

Debbie swallows the scone and licks some cream from her lips, clearly savouring the pleasure. "She often went walking with a Scottish chap who lives somewhere near Jevington. He has an unusual surname. He's still around, I think." She shrugs and takes another bite of scone. "Are you sure you don't want one?"

Her hand's already reaching for the second scone. While I want to ask more about the Scottish man, I sense she's repeating rumours. The Colonel might know something.

"Did her husband approve of the exhibition?" I ask, going back to the painting.

"It was his idea."

"Really? It doesn't sound like he was that involved."

"He wasn't. I think he did it to give her something to do, if you know what I mean."

I nod. Daphne's marriage to the Colonel was loveless. But was it loveless enough for her to vanish shortly before the art exhibition she'd spent months planning?

Why didn't the Colonel tell me about the art exhibition?

I consider this on the drive back to the sanctuary, wondering whether the Colonel planned to kill his wife and blame Colin Miller. Maybe the Colonel struck his wife and she fell and hit her head on the corner of one his sturdy pieces of furniture. Loyal Alice would take his side, of course, suggesting they hide the body under the new conservatory.

But if that's the case, why did he ask me to investigate? Why risk me discovering the truth? Maybe he thought I'd never find Miller, who had fled to Spain.

Before I can think about this in more detail, Kelly rings and I pull over onto the verge.

"I don't know what you've done, lover," she says, sounding unusually serious, "but there are two policemen waiting for you in reception."

TWENTY

Sergeant Tom Bowles and PC Melanie Craddock rise from their seats when I enter the interview room in reception. Their neutral expressions and police jargon tell me this is not going to be a friendly chat. After brief introductions, he advises me that a complaint has been made, accusing me of assaulting a minor at my animal sanctuary.

"If you mean Liam Burke," I say, "he was left unsupervised by his mother, who was out of sight on her mobile phone. As he was provoking my goats with a stick, and in danger of provoking an attack, I carried him out of an animal pen to safety."

Bowles, who's a big man with hands that could crush coconuts, watches me closely. He takes his time to respond. "You're admitting you laid hands on the boy."

"As he refused to leave when I asked, I didn't have much choice to prevent him from being injured."

"Or to protect your goats," Craddock says, her eyes cold and unforgiving.

"What was he doing in the enclosure with the goats?" he asks.

"You'll have to ask his mother why she let him roam around unsupervised. I had to take a phone call and left them for no more than a couple of minutes. When I returned the children had gone. I found Liam and his sister in the paddock with the goats."

Bowles makes notes as I speak. His colleague steps in. "Was the sister in danger too?"

"She rushed across to help her brother, so I got them both out together."

She looks at her notebook. "The mother alleges you set your dog on them."

I suppress a smile. "My West Highland terrier was shut inside my flat at the time. He was let out by Miles Birchill. He witnessed everything."

The officers glance at each other and close their notebooks. Bowles looks straight into my eyes for far longer than necessary before saying, "I think it would be better if we continued this at the Custody Suite, Mr Fisher."

"Are you arresting me?"

"No, you're attendance would be entirely voluntary at this stage."

It's the next stage that bothers me. "And if I decline?"

"Why would you do that, Mr Fisher?" Craddock asks. "I'm sure you want to help us clear this matter up as soon as possible."

"I need to make a phone call," I say, rising.

I nip into the IT office down the corridor and ring Birchill. His secretary interrupts his meeting to put me through.

"Chloe Burke's accused me of assaulting her son," I say. "The police want me to go to the Custody Suite for interview. It's voluntary, but I think they want to charge me."

"William Rogers, my solicitor, will attend with you. When's the interview?"

"I'd like to get it out of the way this afternoon, if that's okay."

"I'll need to make a statement too," he says. "I'm busy until three, so if you attend at two, I'll come along later. How does that sound?"

When I consult the Council's Solicitor for an opinion, it often takes weeks for a response. "Fine," I reply.

The line goes dead and I turn to my IT colleagues, who pretend they didn't hear my conversation. "Do you have my replacement phone yet?" I ask.

Armed with a new Windows phone, I return to the interview room. "My solicitor can't make it until two o'clock this afternoon. And Miles Birchill will attend at three to give a statement. I hope that's all right."

At one fifty, I pull into the car park and switch off the engine. The Eastbourne Investigations and Detainee Handling Centre lies at the end of Hammonds Drive on the edge of an industrial estate. A modern two-storey building built of brick and double glazing, framed in police blue and industrial grey, the centre looks out across the marshes that fill the centre of the town. To the right of the building, I notice a roller shutter door, where prisoners enter in a van, I imagine.

William Rogers joins me a couple of minutes later in his black Jaguar. He's young and sharply dressed in a suit and brown leather shoes that smell expensive. He swaggers across, clutching an I-pad and notebook in a hand with beautifully manicured nails. He stops next to my car and waits for me to get out.

"Mr Fisher," he says, his voice neutral but refined. "William Rogers. I have Mr Birchill's account of events, which I would like you to browse before we go inside."

I take the I-pad, aware of his cologne and soft skin. In his early thirties, he's tall and dark with thick hair in confident waves, tamed by gel. Well-trimmed eyebrows, separated by a dimple at the top of his small, but smooth nose, add to the alert, but controlled aura he emanates. Everything about him is smooth and confident, from his complexion to his assertive voice.

"That's how I remember it," I say, then I'm not sure Birchill arrived in time to see me lift Liam Burke out of harm's way.

"Anything you wish to add?" he asks.

I shake my head. "What happens in there?"

"We'll be in one of the interview rooms, which will be fitted with video. A detective may be watching as assaulting a minor is a serious charge." He removes his sunglasses to reveal eyes a curious shade of dark blue. "Don't elaborate or embellish. Only answer the questions they ask and let them draw the answers from you. If you're not sure, consult with me."

"I've interviewed suspects under PACE," I say.

He smiles. He knows that, of course. He's a well-briefed brief.

At the entrance, we announce ourselves on the intercom and we're let into an atrium that rises to the roof. It's light, airy and eerily quiet. Ahead of us, the reception desk, fortified with glass screens, is unoccupied. The posters deal with health and safety and cocaine drop points, whatever they are. We take a seat against the outside wall and look across to the opposite side. It has blue doors on both levels, with a landing running along the first floor. Somewhere behind the wall, suspects are checked in and interviewed.

"Are there cells here?" I ask.

"I think there are 18 cells in total, three for juveniles. You won't see them or the main reception area because they're beyond the interview rooms." He points to the door straight ahead of us. "The reception area's like the bridge of the Starship Enterprise. It's like a huge console with four bays where suspects are checked in and processed by the duty officers. It's modern, smart and efficient, but don't tell them I said that."

The sound of a buzzer distracts us and a young woman in a grey tracksuit strides out of the door. She's young, maybe a teenager, with short dyed hair, rounded cheeks and piercing grey eyes. Her short neck is covered with black tattoos. One of them extends down towards her cleavage, passing under a crystal necklace, which she fiddles with as she studies me.

"Hi," she says. "How are you?"

"Fine," I reply. "You?"

"I got bail." Her hair bobs as she nods. "Trouble with me ex, see. Still I got bail. That's good, init? You gotta think positive. Just need a lift back to London now. No one available," she says, gesturing back to the reception area. "I gotta wait now for me dad to come. You ain't going anywhere near Wimbledon, is you?"

William shakes his head and rises as the door opposite opens. He recognises Tom Bowles and strides across, making no noise at all. After a few words, he gestures me over and we walk through, following Bowles into a square room with industrial grey carpet and white walls. We're directed to sit on blue chairs behind a beech laminate table. Fixed to the wall above, a flat screen TV plays video footage, supplied by a camera in the corner on the opposite side of the room. There's also a second table with what looks like a DVD player and flat screen TV.

It's a long way from the small windowless interview rooms on TV police shows.

Moments later, DI Briggs strolls in, reeking of cigarettes. A dusting of crumbs trickles down the lapel of his tired jacket. He's tightened his tie without fastening the top button of his shirt, adding to the sense of indifference that pervades him. He places a folder on the table and sits, looking at us in turn for just long enough to show his dislike.

"You have some interesting friends for an enforcement officer, Mr Fisher. Then again, so did your father."

He pauses, but I say nothing, happy to let him voice his prejudices.

His world weary voice and eyes suggest he has better things to do. While Tom sits next to him, Briggs checks the monitor and goes through his set up routine, explaining the interview will be taped and could we each give our names clearly. Once introduced, he reminds me I'm here on a voluntary basis to answer questions relating to a complaint of assaulting a minor.

"You are not under caution and you're free to leave at any time," he says

He outlines the substance of the complaint and asks me to tell him about the afternoon in question. Briggs stares at something on the ceiling, occasionally cutting for clarification as I give a brief, factual account in line with Birchill's statement. William sits there, pushing back the cuticles of his fingernails.

"You left Mrs Burke and her children unattended," Briggs says after I finish. "Is that usual practice, bearing in mind you have dangerous animals on site?"

William leans forward and Briggs smiles. "Let's forget the word, dangerous."

"I had to answer a phone call. I asked them to wait for me in the yard till I returned."

"You expect children to understand the potential dangers and stay still?"

"No, but I expect their mother to."

He flicks open the folder. "It's alleged you were absent for over ten minutes, Mr Fisher."

"Two minutes max."

"And this dog of yours …"

I don't respond, waiting for him to complete his question.

"A rescue terrier, is it? Where was it?"

William looks up. "Could you be more specific please?"

"You haven't mentioned your dog, Mr Fisher. I'm informed it behaved aggressively toward the children after they'd left the paddock."

"He was excited after being shut inside the kitchen. Miles Birchill let him out."

Briggs' eyebrows rise. "Why did he do that?"

"You'll have to ask him. I was trying to save children from being injured."

He grins, well aware of the game we're playing. "I intend to," he says. "So, he let your terrier out and it ran at the children, barking and baring its teeth."

"Columbo sees strangers and he barks like most dogs would."

"Columbo?" Briggs can barely suppress a laugh. "You call your dog, Columbo? What about the goats? Starsky and Hutch? Morse and Lewis?"

"My boss is called Frost, if that helps."

He sighs, looking like he's had enough. "I think that will do for the moment, don't you? Mr Rodgers, I understand Mr Birchill will be along shortly to give his version."

William leans back and folds his arms. "Maybe I could ask you something, Detective Inspector. As Mrs Burke is at the Evelina Hospital with her critically ill daughter, can you tell me when you interviewed her about the events in question?"

Briggs closes his folder and rises. "The interview is terminated."

"Have you questioned her?" William asks, rising.

Briggs turns, his expression dour. "I spoke to her by phone, being sensitive to her circumstances."

"I look forward to receiving a transcript of that conversation, Detective Inspector. Will you be returning to interview Mr Birchill at three?"

Briggs leaves without replying. Bowles looks lost. "I'm sure he'll be back. You're free to leave, Mr Fisher."

He follows Briggs. William takes me into the room next door.

"Briggs hasn't formally interviewed the complainant. He's fishing as usual, hoping you'll incriminate yourself. Miles will put him in his place."

Birchill's early, already waiting in the atrium. "How did it go?" he asks.

"We can refute the allegations."

"Thank you, William. That leaves the goats. Do you think we should test them?"

The solicitor turns to me. "Can the council force you to test them?"

I nod, well aware it's what I would do. "It would look better if I tested them voluntarily."

"Agreed," he says, turning back to Birchill. "But we'll decide what to do with the results."

Birchill grins and nods. "Okay, we test the goats."

"Does that mean you're paying?" I ask.

He looks at me with surprise. "Are you asking for my help?"

"I know how much the test costs."

I need a long run to clear my head, but the outstanding jobs on my desk won't resolve themselves. Within minutes of checking the files, messages and complaint details, it soon becomes clear I need to perform major surgery. Armed with a cup of tea and a bar of chocolate from the vending machine, I begin to sort through the mess, making new and smaller piles to help me prioritise my priorities. Within ten minutes, I've spread from my desk to the floor, separating and ranking jobs.

New business enquiries have proliferated over the past couple of weeks, mainly because someone has stockpiled them, it seems. I know Kelly would put them on the computer straight away, so who's been taking the calls and not putting them on the system? A quick peek in Gemma's In Tray confirms my suspicions when I discover several more queries from people wanting to set up food businesses. I separate these out and place them on the desk, ready to add to the ones she must have dumped on me.

Unfortunately, as I replace the remaining files in her tray, I accidently knock the queries to the floor. While I'm on my hands and knees, gathering them up, a familiar pair of legs and diamante sandals approaches.

"No arch support," I say, pointing at her sandals.

"No management support." She plucks her jacket from the back of the chair and leaves.

I'm still pondering what she means when Tommy Logan rings.

"A little bird tells me you've been kidding around, Kent."

I sigh, in no mood for his quips. "Is that what you call a tweet, Tommy?"

"Oh, I'm sure Twitter will pick up the photographs of your goats, dear boy. They look far too cute to poison a sweet little girl, but appearances can be deceptive, as they say."

Is there anyone Chloe Burke hasn't spoken to?

"What's that supposed to mean?" I ask.

I can almost see his innocent look of surprise as he speaks. "I only called to warn an old friend about the storm brewing on Facebook. I say storm, but it looks more like a hurricane."

TWENTY-ONE

Shortly before 7.30 the following morning, the hurricane hits Downland's Facebook page. Parents are refusing to take their children to Tollingdon Primary School, claiming it's infected with E. coli. I don't have to scroll far through the posts and replies before someone blames me. This spirals into a thread about the dirty, dilapidated and unhygienic animal sanctuary I run. I never realised so many people considered the place to be a death trap.

Then I spot the second thread, which accuses me of visiting the school to blame the food for the outbreak and pass the buck. (Some people think a buck is a male goat, which prompts plenty of LOLs and Likes.) Most prefer to like a different thread – the one that says I'm as corrupt as my lying and cheating father.

"What are you looking at?" Niamh yawns and then pushes her hands through her tousled hair. "You don't normally bother with Facebook."

"Work," I say, closing the lid of the laptop.

"Wasn't that a photo of this place?" she asks, taking my cup of cold tea from the table. "You want another?"

I shake my head. I need to warn Geoff Lamb, so he can take control of the Council's Facebook page and stop the lies and unfounded accusations. I grab my phone and head into the lounge so Niamh won't hear. When his phone goes straight to voicemail, I leave a brief message and return to the kitchen.

"I thought it was a photograph of the sanctuary," Niamh says, her face close to the laptop screen. "It was only taken a minute ago."

"What?"

I rush over, almost falling over Columbo. The post is a couple of minutes old. From the window, I spot Frances remonstrating with a man in trainers and a bomber jacket, while a woman in a hoodie fires off shots with a camera.

Columbo races past me down the stairs, barking as he makes a beeline for the intruders. The man jumps back. The woman shrieks and loses her footing as she turns. Columbo's on her, his teeth clamping over her arm as she crashes to the ground. Though Frances and I both shout at him, he's not letting go as the woman flails and tries to swat him.

"No, you don't," I cry, grabbing the man as he swings a boot at Columbo. He misses by inches and falls to the ground as he loses his balance. Frances grabs Columbo and pulls him off. The photographer, her face white and her breathing heavy, scrambles back to their Ford Fiesta.

"Get off my land," I say, facing the man, who's back on his feet, checking his bomber jacket for damage. "And you can stop taking photographs."

The man looks across to his colleague. "Did you get all that?"

"Some of it," she replies, examining the tear to her sleeve.

"Are you okay?" I ask her.

She nods. "Tough little guy, isn't he? My mum has one."

Columbo growls as she approaches.

"Take him to the caravan, Frances. I'll deal with these two."

"Adrian Peach from *The Argus*," the man says, holding up a card. He's young, with unruly blond hair and piercings to both ears. The uneven prickle of stubble on his hollow cheeks can't hide the fiery traces of eczema. "And this is my colleague, Wendy Birch."

She's also young, with military hair, coloured a shade of blue that matches her devil-may-care eyes. She has a long, narrow face that's attractive in an unconventional way, despite the nose ring.

"You're trespassing," I say, my breathing and adrenaline back to normal.

"You let the public in."

"We invite them in."

"This is going round Facebook." He swipes the screen of his phone a couple of times and holds up an image of me, taken shortly after I left hospital three weeks ago. "It's not the best image for someone who's supposed to protect public health, is it?"

"You're still trespassing."

"And you look like you've had another fight," he says, talking with a confidence that worries me. Meanwhile, his colleague takes more photos. "And Wendy has photos of you attacking me and pushing me to the ground."

"I think you'll find I was defending my dog."

"Which attacked my colleague." He smiles, looking like someone about to propose a deal. "I could add the story to the one where you assaulted a child in one of your pens. Didn't your dog also attack the child?"

He's got me and he knows it.

"Anything you want to say about that, Mr Fisher?"

I can think of several responses – none of them printable – but I'm not sure what to do for the best. While I hesitate, Niamh calls from the kitchen door.

"Would anyone like a bacon sandwich? You look cold and hungry, so why don't you come up? There's plenty to go round."

Peach glances at Birch, who nods. "Who's that?" he asks, clearly taken with Niamh.

"My stepmother."

He smiles to himself. "You're living with your rather attractive stepmother?"

"Yes, I've even let her have her own room until she can find somewhere to live. It's not pleasant being made homeless when your husband dies, but don't let the truth get in the way of a good story, will you?"

"Are you always this prickly, Mr Fisher? Or can I call you Kent. Unusual name that."

I could give him the usual lie about being born in Kent. "Do you want breakfast?"

I signal to Frances, who's watching from the caravan. She opens the door and Columbo bounds down the steps, barking as he approaches. Then Niamh calls from the kitchen, holding his bowl aloft, and he races up the stairs. We follow.

Peach gets more than a story about the sanctuary and E. coli as he munches through several bacon sandwiches, doused in brown sauce. Though fresh out of university, he's sharp enough to realise there's another story about William Kenneth Fisher ready to unfold. Niamh, whose opinion of the media is marginally more caustic than mine, has taken to Peach. She thinks anyone with piercings needs rehabilitating.

"I've never seen you so friendly with a reporter," I tell her while Frances gives Peach and Birch the guided tour.

"He needs fattening up," she says, washing the plates even though we have a dishwasher. "Fast food is ruining his complexion."

"Unlike bacon sandwiches," I say, dodging a play slap. "But seriously, do you really want to talk to him about what happened?"

"We need a favourable report after the reception you gave him," she says, ruffling Columbo's fur.

"All the scandal and secrets?"

She laughs. "Of course not."

The reporters leave around nine. I ring Kelly to say I'll be late, but she suggests I work from home while Danni's in meltdown.

"You've never seen so many headless chickens," Kelly says. "SMUT came in early and they're locked away in the Committee Room, discussing strategy. No guesses for who's top of the agenda."

Senior Management (USELESS) Team, as she calls them, meet weekly to make sure the council's running smoothly, to deal with any problems and to plan for the future. In reality, they talk, eat Jaffa cakes and doughnuts, and do whatever the Head of Finance tells them they can afford. Occasionally, they have some real problems to tackle, like where to have lunch.

"Why's Danni in such a flap?" I ask.

"SMUT wants to know why she let you investigate a case where you had a conflict of interests."

As blame's normally delegated in local government, I can expect a summons before the morning is out. "No need to guess what she'll say then."

"Good job you wrote that note," she says, "because you have a serious problem on Facebook."

"I know. Someone's stirring them up."

"Chloe Burke?"

"Someone at the school," I reply, certain it's Kirk Baxendale. "I'll ring Public Health England to update them. Ring me if you need me."

"Stay at home, lover. Tommy Logan's camped out in Reception, so the rest of his reporter friends won't be far. But if you do have to show yourself, remember Danni's advice."

"You never get a second chance to make a first impression," we say together. Once the laughter abates, she says, "Watch your back, lover. People are sharpening knives."

Barbara Hussein at Public Health England takes control of the Facebook revolt. "We have letters and posts for this kind of situation. We'll calm it down. Just make sure your Communications Officer, Geoff Lamb, liaises with us before putting out any media releases. We need to be consistent."

"Of course," I say, relieved there's one less task to deal with. "Any news on Charlotte?"

"No change, I'm afraid. Mum's still refusing to discuss the case with us."

"She's happily pointing the finger at me," I say.

"You, Kent? Why?"

I draw a breath. "Her children visited my animal sanctuary ten days ago. She didn't supervise them and they came into contact with my goats."

"Thank you for telling me," she says, her tone cold. "A little sooner might have helped."

"I stopped investigating the moment I realised who the Burkes were. I also cancelled all school visits and I'm getting the goats tested."

"Good," she says, her tone still cold. "We should have an indication late this afternoon or first thing tomorrow from the family's samples. Fingers crossed."

I settle back, grateful for the mug of tea Niamh slides in front of me. She sets another three on the table, dismissing my quizzical look with a smile. Then Frances and Gemma enter.

"Does Danni know you're here?" I ask Gemma.

"She will when she checks her emails."

"Right," Niamh says, placing a pad of paper in front of her. "We need some plans to protect the sanctuary because we're out of bacon."

"Tommy Logan's on his way," Gemma says. "He wants to beat the stampede."

"When you've finished your tea I want you out of here," Niamh tells me, her tone firm. "If you're not here, the reporters will eventually lose interest."

"Or wait for me to return."

"You need to fight your corner at work, Kent. Frances and I can handle things here."

Columbo barks.

"You too," Frances says, ruffling his fur. "Just don't bite anyone."

He barks again, clearly taking no notice like a good Fisher.

"Why did you send for me?" Gemma asks. "You seem to have everything under control."

"Not quite. I need you to keep my stepson out of trouble."

"How am I supposed to do that?"

"I'm sure you have inspections you need help with."

On the road into Tollingdon, I ask Gemma to detour to the primary School. "We need to deal with Baxendale," I say. "If he's stirring up trouble on Facebook –"

"Didn't you hear what Niamh said?"

"The head needs to know how much unnecessary panic he's caused on Facebook."

"You don't know it's him, Kent."

"Who else could it be? If we can persuade the head to take action against him…"

"And convince everyone you're trying to protect yourself."

"That's exactly what I'm trying to do, Gemma. And I need your support."

"Don't make me regret this," she says, swinging left.

At the school, we're shown into Connie's office. Unlike our previous visit, she looks harassed and drawn. "Please tell me it's good news," she says, massaging her temples. "I'm afraid to look at Facebook."

"That's why we're here. We want to talk to Kirk Baxendale."

"He didn't start the furore," she says, picking up a couple of aspirins from her desk. "We have Stephen Burke to thank for that. He's already threatening to sue the school for taking children to your animal sanctuary."

She washes down the aspirins with some cold-looking tea and then mutters something about another migraine.

"Kirk's gone," she says, rising. "I don't know what you said, but he resigned straight after your visit."

TWENTY-TWO

Connie refuses to tell me where Baxendale lives, even when I assure her that Chloe Burke brought her children to my sanctuary, not the school.

"So why is Stephen Burke persecuting us?" Connie asks.

After Chloe complained to the council and the police, her father should be attacking me not the school. And Baxendale's sudden departure can't be coincidence.

"That's why I need to speak to Kirk," I say. "Liam might have said something to him that could help with the investigation."

"Then why didn't he tell me?"

Connie looks lost, caught between her duty to protect her staff's confidentiality and a desire to defend the school's reputation.

"I can require you to release Kirk's address," Gemma says. "One call to the office and –"

"I'm not being obstructive."

"What if Charlotte dies?" I ask. "What if Kirk knows something that might have helped?"

"That's not fair," she mutters, turning to her computer. A couple of mouse clicks delivers Baxendale's address to the screen.

He lives on Chalvington Road, named after a small village about five miles west of Tollingdon. Unfortunately, the less tolerant of the town's residents have renamed it and the surrounding estate, Chavington to reflect the social housing tenants who live there. While many of the houses have satellite dishes and customised BMWs parked in front, not all the residents are young single parents on benefits. Some have partners. Some have jobs. More than a few have gardens filled with shrubs and annuals rather than old cars and furniture.

While the compact and unexciting brick houses are modern, they look weary, thanks to their surroundings. The wide grass verges, mown by a contractor in a hurry, are strewn with dog poo and the contents of refuse bags, torn open by foxes and seagulls. The regimented cherry and mountain ash trees add some colour, but sadly, I don't see any birds in the branches, which is good news for car owners, I guess.

We park behind Baxendale's Vauxhall Astra. A quick survey suggests he's valeted the interior, removing all traces of cigarettes, ash and exercise books. A pine freshener hangs from the rear view mirror to battle any residual odours.

From the road, we walk down the path between the rows of terraced houses that face each other across a grassed area. Baxendale lives at the end, overlooking fields and marshes. We approach through a garden the size of a postage stamp, dodging lavender and box hedging that's in desperate need of a trim. Weeds and wild grass have smothered the rest of the garden, leaving only a solitary fuchsia to flower its heart out by the wall.

"The curtains are drawn."

Like an estate agent on a viewing, I'm stating the blatantly obvious.

The doorbell chimes, 'There's no place like home'. When no one answers, I walk around the side and follow the narrow concrete path. The garden waste bin reeks of dead and rotting houseplants, dumped on a bed of desiccated weeds. The adjacent recycling bin is overflowing with cardboard, and plastic and foil takeaway trays.

"Baxendale gets his five a day from chocolate orange and fruit gums," I remark as Gemma peers inside.

"He's not home," she says. "This must be over a week old."

"He's here," I say, pushing open the gate into the back garden. "He's having a clear out."

The gate opens into a small paved garden, littered with dried dog poo. A collection of earthenware pots hold the limp and faded remains of herbs, annuals and patio roses that died, waiting for water. Once around a rusting patio table and chairs, I'm greeted by a gathering of charity bags next to the open patio doors. The bags contain the contents of a wardrobe and a couple of dressers, it seems. Pink and black leggings, brightly coloured tops, blouses and jackets fill at least two bags. Another contains shoes and trainers, while the fourth holds underwear and lingerie.

Inside the patio door, a wedding dress, folded inside shrink wrapping, waits on the floor.

“What the…” Baxendale stops, almost dropping another full bag on me. “Oh, it’s you,” he says, pulling out the earphones from the MP3 player in his shirt pocket. He removes the remains of the cigarette from his mouth and flicks the stub over my head.

“If anything takes your fancy, help yourself,” he tells Gemma.

She holds up a bright pink blouse a few sizes too big for her.

“Marcie was all curves,” he says, dropping the bag on the patio. “Unlike me.”

His curry and chocolate diet has left him stick thin. Despite the shave and haircut, his hollow cheeks and sunken chest suggest he’s had the life sucked out of him. Disposing of Marcie’s possessions can’t be easy, triggering memories that must make him doubt his decision to move on.

“Where’s your spaniel?” I ask.

“I took Morgana back to the breeder for rehoming. She was Marcie’s dog.” He scoops the wedding dress from the floor and sighs. “Seven years of marriage condensed into six bags.”

“All crammed with memories,” I remark.

He steps outside and lays the dress on top of the closest bag. “Got time for a cuppa? Unlike the rest of my life, the milk hasn’t gone sour.”

Gemma shakes her head, but I accept. I’m curious to learn why Marcie left so much behind, especially her beloved spaniel.

Inside, the lounge diner extends to the front of the house. The pale pink walls, dark grey carpet tiles and black ash furniture add a 1980s ambience I rather like. While the cerise coloured radiators, skirting boards and architraves shout rather than welcome, the steel framed black leather sofa and chairs look stylish and comfortable.

"We're intruding," Gemma says in a hushed voice, joining me to watch the Jeremy Kyle Show without sound. "It can't be easy, clearing out all the memories. Not that you'd know much about that."

"You don't think I have a sensitive side?"

"If you have, only your animals get to see it."

I stroll across to the bookcase, filled with DVDs and CDs. Though tempted to arrange them in alphabetical order, I focus on the content, not sure what the mixture of punk, rock and 80s classics like Duran Duran and Spandau Ballet tell me about Baxendale, Marcie or their relationship.

Photographs of Morgana, the cocker spaniel, trace her life from cute puppy to adult. I wish people wouldn't dress dogs in silly knitted coats and hats to make them look like ballerinas or cowgirls, but Marcie must have spent a fortune on her dog.

"I'll bet she caused problems at school," Gemma remarks.

Marcie's a brash, in-your-face type with bold makeup, big, spiky hair and a chunky steel necklace that looks more like a watch bracelet. As Baxendale said, she's curvy, squeezing herself into leather skirts and pink tops that are much too tight. Though she wears enough eyeliner to make Alice Cooper jealous, there's something self-conscious about her bovine eyes that echoes in her hesitant smile.

"It's all front," I say, aware of the loneliness and isolation that not conforming can bring.

"I might have guessed you'd be looking at her front."

"Marcie liked to shock." Baxendale walks through, carrying a red tray with three black mugs. "She liked to rebel, but underneath she was a lonely girl, afraid she would never fit in or be loved."

He places the tray on a small glass table between the sofa and chairs. "Her mother walked out when she was a child, leaving her to look after her disabled, alcoholic father in a remote farm cottage near Heathfield."

"She must have had help from social services," Gemma says.

"I wish," he says with a sigh. "She came to school when she felt like it, which was most of the time, thankfully. She was a punk with attitude, keeping you at arm's length. Though she lacked social skills, she had a worldliness and allure that fascinated me."

I look at the photos, trying to see what Baxendale saw.

He hands me an empty black plastic bag from the sofa. "All the films and music are going to a mate of mine who runs a market stall. We're splitting the proceeds."

While he transfers the DVDs and CDs into the bag, he tells us about Marcie.

"Her father treated her like a slave, practically chaining her to the house with his needs and demands. Yet he introduced her to literature and art when he was sober. She blushed bright red when I spotted *Tess of the d'Ubervilles* in her schoolbag. Turns out she had a passion for Hardy, D H Lawrence and Graham Greene. When she asked for extra tuition in English Literature, I couldn't stop myself. Tongues started wagging, of course, but I had no idea she'd told everyone we were having sex. We weren't, of course."

That makes me wonder if they were.

"I don't think the Head believed me, but without evidence, he couldn't do anything. Kids like to shock. I was instructed to stop the extra tuition and distance myself from Marcie. I asked her why she'd spread rumours about us and she said I'd never screw her unless she encouraged me. I didn't know what to say."

He sweeps another clutch of films from the shelf and places them in the bag. "I cancelled the extra tuition and did my best to avoid her. Then her father died."

He pauses, clutching the remaining films to his chest. "That's when I discovered she'd looked after him from the age of seven. He was in a wheelchair after he broke his back in a work accident. Her mother walked out, unable to cope. He took to the bottle and pissed away the compensation on booze, cigarettes and drugs. She even bought cannabis for him."

"Couldn't have been much of a life," Gemma says.

He drops the films in the sack. "She grew up quickly, I know that. She dealt drugs, drank vodka, and *entertained* his drunken pals to make ends meet. Can you believe that?"

I look him straight in the eyes. "When did she tell you this?"

"After the funeral. She begged me to go with her, so what could I do? She was fifteen and alone in the world. We sat in the farmhouse, drinking vodka, talking about books and out it came – her whole, sorry life." Tears fill his eyes. "She said she survived by thinking of me and how I would save her. When she asked me to stay the night …"

He lights a cigarette and takes a long draw. "Not my finest hour, was it? Next morning, I told her it was over."

"How did she take it?" Gemma asks.

"How do you think?" He grabs the plastic sack and dumps it on the patio. "She missed school, got into trouble with the police. Social Services intervened, but after a few months of behaving herself, she lost control again. Eventually, the police lost patience and prosecuted her. That's when I knew I had to do something. So I married her."

Of all the solutions that flashed through my thoughts, this wasn't one of them.

"It made perfect sense," he says, staring into my eyes. "The court had adjourned the case for three months, which meant she'd be sixteen. We arranged the ceremony for first thing on the morning of the hearing, determined to show the magistrates she'd reformed."

He walks to the dresser and picks up a photo of them on their wedding day. She'd lost weight and looked self-conscious, but happy.

"From the registry office we went straight around the corner to the Magistrates Court, Marcie in her wedding dress, me in a hired suit. We thought the magistrates would be lenient, but some pompous old colonel with a big moustache accused us of playing to the gallery."

A light goes on in my mind. "Colonel Witherington?"

Baxendale nods. "He wanted to send Marcie to a young offenders' institute, but the woman on the bench – Daphne Featherstone – persuaded her colleagues to impose a suspended sentence and give us a chance to prove we could make a life together. She gave us the names of people and organisations that could help."

"What was she like?" I ask.

"She understood what Marcie had been through, having lost a soulmate herself. That's why I couldn't believe it when she went on and married that colonel."

"It takes all sorts," I say, suddenly an expert. At least I know how the Colonel met Daphne.

"Marcie and I were like chalk and cheese, but we did all right. She got a job in a nail bar and I sold double glazing. We started with a bedsit, moved up to a flat and three years ago, I got the job at Tollingdon Primary. That's when it started to go wrong."

A long tube of ash falls to the floor, but he's staring at the photograph. "We bought this place and maxed out our credit cards. We lost a holiday we really needed and Marcie became withdrawn. She started taking drugs again. She denied it, of course, but I knew the signs. I've no idea where she got the money until I realised there was someone else. She ran off with him on 18th March this year."

He goes to the door and throws the cigarette into the garden. "I came home from school and found Morgana out here with an empty bowl of water. Marcie never left her outside, so I knew something was wrong. When she didn't come home, I rang round, but no one had seen her. When she didn't come home the following day, I wondered if she'd overdosed. Then a letter arrived, saying I was better off without her, that she'd always held me back. She said she was safe and not to worry."

"Was it typed?" I ask.

He looks up, a frown wrinkling his forehead. "No, she wrote it."

"Did anyone around here see her leave?"

"You're joking, right? They're either elderly or drugged to the eyeballs. The lady opposite said Marcie left in a taxi, but she has dementia, so who knows?"

"Black cab or private hire?"

"How should I know? What's it to you?"

"She went off without any warning," I reply. "Isn't that unusual?"

"I'll tell you what's unusual," he says, ready to light another cigarette. "Marcie left everything behind."

"Including Morgana."

He stops and stares at me. "You didn't come here to talk about Marcie, did you?"

"No, Charlotte Burke."

"Of course." His smirk soon fades. "How is she?"

"Fighting for her life, I imagine."

"It can't be easy for her family," he says, glancing at his watch. "Look, I'm leaving for Scotland next week. I've got lots to do."

He strides into the kitchen, slamming the door behind him.

Back in the car, I turn to Gemma. "Another wife who's vanished without warning, leaving her most treasured possession behind."

"You think Marcie's connected to Stacey and Daphne? No way. She wrote to Kirk."

"She knew Daphne."

"They met in court."

"You heard Baxendale – Daphne helped them. What if Marcie stayed in touch with her over the years? What if Daphne confided her problems or told her about the Colonel?"

"Where does that leave Stacey? She didn't know Colonel Witherington or Daphne."

I smile, enjoying the pleasure of a solution falling into place. "Aren't you forgetting something? Who attacked a VAT inspector?"

"Todd Walters." She stares at me for a moment and sighs. "He went to court for assault, right?"

"Stacey would attend with her husband. If Daphne was on the bench, she might have struck up a friendship with Stacey. When Daphne wanted to start catering, Stacey could have supplied her with meat or introduced her to Miller."

"You know what this means," Gemma says, starting the car. "You're pointing the finger at the Colonel again."

TWENTY-THREE

On our way back to the office, Niamh rings. "Your vet can't test the goats till Saturday, but I rang Sarah and she can fit us in tomorrow."

"You rang Sarah?"

"Someone has to sort things out."

Gemma's listening, aware that we're discussing her mother.

"Sarah's independent," Niamh continues, "which means she's more credible than a man already in your pay."

I can't believe Sarah agreed.

"Anyway, you don't have a choice," she says. "Tommy Logan's hanging around with a photographer."

"What's he got to do with it?" I ask, a little slow on the uptake. "You've spoken to Tommy, haven't you? What have you said to him?"

"I had to make them a cup of tea, Kent. It's miserable out there and he wrote a lovely obituary for William. I told Tommy you had a vet coming to do the tests. He assumed it was Sarah as you two go way back, so I rang her and asked her to do it."

I can tell she's waiting for the backlash, but what's the point? The damage is done. I still can't believe Sarah agreed, but if Niamh's worried about what I'll say, maybe I can turn it to my advantage.

"While you're on a roll, Niamh, can you do some digging for me? Todd Walters assaulted a VAT inspector about 18 months ago. I'm guessing he was prosecuted in the magistrates' court. Can you check the records, find out what happened, who was on the bench?"

"I could ask Tommy Logan. He must have reported the case."

"No, I don't want him sniffing around."

"Why don't you ask Colonel Witherington? He may even have presided on the day."

"That's what I'm trying to find out, but I don't want him to know."

"Why not?" she asks. Then she gasps. "You think he has something to do with Stacey Walters going missing?"

"I don't know, so don't say anything, especially to Tommy Logan."

"As if I would, Kent."

I end the call, wondering what else she's told Tommy about my investigation.

Gemma doesn't look pleased. "Has my mother agreed to test your goats?

"Niamh arranged it."

"My mother said hell would freeze over before she set foot in your sanctuary. Why's she changed her mind?"

"Why are you asking me? I still don't know why she fell out with me."

One day we were shoulder to shoulder, resisting Birchill's bulldozers, the next she didn't show. Or the next. When I rang, she didn't answer. When I went round to her surgery, she refused to see me. I assumed Gemma had confessed to our brief liaison.

"I never told her about us," she says, "so stop fishing. I was too embarrassed to tell anyone. What was I thinking, getting mixed up with someone twice my age?"

I stare at the Downs, subdued by the leaden skies. Thinking never came into it, I recall. Or age. "Well, you've got someone your own age now."

I settle back, hoping the rain will deter the media and send Tommy Logan back to his office. I dread to think what he'll say in tomorrow's Tollingdon Tribune, especially when he learns I gave a reporter from the Argus a tour of my sanctuary.

"I'll take this afternoon and tomorrow as leave," I say. "I should be there when the goats are tested. I can't keep leaving Niamh and Frances to cope."

"But you don't mind leaving us to cope." Gemma's sharp tone matches her glare. "We're your team, Kent. You're supposed to look after us. You're not the only one affected by Charlotte Burke's illness."

She takes a deep breath and eases back on the accelerator. "There, I said I would raise it with you."

"The team put you up to this?"

"It's not a conspiracy, Kent. It's difficult for us too. We're trapped in the fallout."

"I can't be in two places at once, Gemma."

"No, but you could try talking to us."

"I'm trying to protect you from the fallout," I say, a little belatedly.

She accelerates up the hill, punishing the engine in third gear. "You haven't even asked me how my interview went with the Head of Audit."

I groan, realising why she's annoyed.

"How did it go?" I ask.

"It was horrible. He was after anything he could use against you. They've decided you're guilty and expect us to give them the evidence."

One moment I'm the proud recipient of the Hugo Carrington Award, now I'm the scourge of Downland District Council. "They want a scapegoat, that's all."

"Then why did he tell me my loyalty was to the council that employed me not an ex-lover who was using me to cover his indiscretions?"

For a moment I'm speechless. "How does he know about us?"

She slams on the brakes and swerves over to the side of the road, bouncing off the kerb as we lurch to a halt. "I didn't tell anyone," she says, wrenching up the handbrake. "Did you enjoy telling everyone how you seduced a naïve young waitress?"

I shake my head. "I would never do that."

"Well, I haven't told a soul, so one of us must be lying."

On my way to the second floor, I wonder how the Head of Audit found out about Gemma and me. Mike knows, but he'd never tell anyone. Gemma must have let something slip because we were discreet, shut away for a week together. Unless someone spotted us walking along the Seven Sisters and Birling Gap.

In the office I drop into my chair, aware of the overwhelming silence. I miss the sound of Nigel, snorting his way through a Cornish pasty. I miss the smell akin to scorched rubber that fills the room when Lucy devours rice cakes. Most of all, I miss the laughter when we speculate about what crazy idea management will dream up next.

While my computer boots, I check my voicemail and In Tray, surprised to find no messages. After a quick glance at Facebook to see how the Council has responded to the E. coli allegations, I ring Geoff Lamb. But like everyone else, he's unavailable. No doubt he's ensconced with SMUT, working on another strategy.

"Have you seen the Council's response on Facebook?" I ask Kelly when she strolls in, shaking her umbrella. She parks it in my waste bin to drain and moves closer to look at my monitor, her head inches from mine.

'The Council would like to make it clear that it has no interest or involvement in Downland Animal Sanctuary and can't comment on any allegations made against it or its proprietor, Kent Fisher.

'Downland District Council would also like to assure people that it takes allegations against its officers seriously and will be conducting a full and thorough investigation to determine if there's been any unprofessional behaviour or malpractice.'

"What did you expect?" she asks, stepping away.

"You think they'd at least offer some sympathy to the family. There's a young girl in hospital, fighting for her life. If she dies –"

Kelly's finger presses to my lips. "She's not dead, Kent. Take a walk and get some fresh air. You'll need a clear head when you meet Danni at four."

"There's nothing in my diary."

"That's why I'm telling you." She hands her umbrella to me and smiles. "She intends to spring it on you so you don't have time to prepare."

I kiss Kelly on the cheek. "Can you contact the *Guinness Book of Records*? There can't be many people who've returned from suspension to be suspended again within two weeks."

"If suspension was an Olympic sport, lover, you'd be world champion."

Outside the rain's eased, leaving a dull sheen on the pavements. Armed with a supermarket sandwich deal, I find a dry bench inside the shelter at the Princess Diana Memorial Garden. Fascinated by the way the raindrops bead into small spheres and roll off the leaves of the Lady's Mantle, I don't notice Yvonne Parris until she sits beside me.

"Pretty flowers," she says, nodding at the geraniums. She pulls a tissue from the pocket of her red raincoat and then removes her glasses to dry them. "No need to look so glum."

"I don't see you smiling."

"Bantering with the bereaved always energises me." She grins, enjoying her sarcasm. "So, I left Alasdair on the front desk. You know how he likes to be one of the troops."

I nod, remembering his awful coffee. I offer up my remaining low fat turkey salad on malted bread. "Would you like a sandwich? Or some crisps?"

"I'd prefer a latte." She slides her glasses over the bridge of her small, but cute nose and settles back, unbuttoning her coat to reveal a white blouse and tight black skirt. "You interested?"

A blouse stretched almost to transparency over a well-filled bra never fails to interest me, as many waitresses in Tollingdon have discovered.

"When I'm through with this," I say, raising my sandwich, "I'll treat you."

"Is that before or after my latte?"

She laughs and turns her attention to a blackbird that scoots across the grass and under some bushes. "Your stepmom's awesome," she says as I munch away. "I loved the way she put you in your place on Saturday night."

"She has her moments."

Yvonne nods, a vague smile wandering across her lips. "What's the score with you and Gemma?"

"We work together, that's all." I push the last of the sandwich into my mouth and flatten the packaging, ready for the recycling bin nearby.

"You must see a lot of each other, I imagine."

"At work, you mean?"

She stares deep into my eyes. "Sure, that's why I couldn't understand why you spent all evening looking at her, even when I was talking to you."

She rises, fastens her coat, and starts to walk. I push my waste in the recycling bin and catch up with her. Neither of us speaks as we stroll along the High Street. She turns into Kaff, a coffee shop with trendy décor and seating, aimed at people much younger than me. White leather sofas and armchairs mingle easily with low, stainless steel and glass tables. Along the back wall at the far end of the bar, the seats slot into booths with large photographs of coffee plantations on the wall.

The noise of grinding coffee beans mingles with the murmur of muted conversation. Inhaling the sharp, slightly burnt aroma, I glance around, my eyes adjusting to the harsh LED spotlights that pick out the tables and cast shadows on the floor. Most of the customers have hung up their raincoats and parked their golf umbrellas, large enough to shelter a family of four. The customers who brought their children seem unaware that a chocolate muffin does not stop kids getting restless, especially when their parents are glued to their smartphones.

"Decaffeinated skinny latte," Yvonne tells the young barista. "And a cup of tea."

She saunters through the tables, nodding to one or two people as she passes. She removes her coat and places it on the arm of a sofa by the window. After placing the dirty cups on a tray, she sets it down on an adjacent table for the waiter to collect.

"Gemma kept looking at you too," she says, when I'm seated next to her. "Do you two have unfinished business?"

"We got into a bit of a scrape recently. That's all."

"I know, but that's not what I meant," she says, watching me closely. "After two failed marriages, I can spot the signs. I'm not looking for a third, Kent, but neither will I become invisible when Gemma walks into the room."

"Maybe I'm not interested in you."

She grins. "Oh, I think we both know you are."

The barista arrives and places a tray on the table. He smiles at Yvonne before retreating back to the counter.

While I move the small pot of tea and giant cup closer, she tips a tube of sugar into her latte, stirring it in with the long spoon. When she's finished, she settles back in the sofa and gives me a wry smile.

"Would you talk more if we went somewhere more conducive, like La Neapolitan? It scores five on your hygiene rating scheme and they do wholemeal pasta."

I should be flattered. "Another time, Yvonne."

"Are you too busy chasing killers? Or regrets?"

She laughs and takes a few sips of her latte, clearly enjoying herself. I take one look at the weak tea in the pot and get to my feet.

"All work and no play make Kent a dull boy," she says, tucking her hair behind her ear. "If you change your mind, I'll be at La Neapolitan from eight this evening."

Before I can tell her I have other plans, her mobile rings with a blast of Taylor Swift. "Alasdair," she says, rolling her eyes. "What gives?"

She listens and nods a couple of times, raising a finger to ask me to wait a moment. "Yes, he's with me," she says, nodding once more. "I'm sure he won't mind. He'd like a word," she says, offering me her phone.

"Kent, you're not going to believe this," he says, his voice animated. "There's a body in a freezer. Déjà vu or what?"

"Where?"

"Meadow Farm, Jevington. I've just arrived to collect it for the mortuary. I can't do anything till the crime scene people have finished, but I gleaned a few details from one of the uniforms. Though the body's covered in ice, they're sure it's a woman."

From the noise in the background it sounds like the police are there in force.

"The guy living here moved out over the weekend without telling anyone. The managing agents only found out this morning and sent someone to check the place. The poor woman spotted the freezer in the barn and got the shock of her life. Hang on a moment."

I listen to the voices and noises in the background while Davenport talks to someone with a deep, officious voice. I can't make out what he's saying, but he's doing all the talking.

"Sorry about that," Davenport says. "Looks like I'll be kicking my heels a little longer. Anyway, do you know who owns Meadow Farm?"

"No idea."

"Colonel Witherington. That's why I called you."

"You think Daphne Witherington's in the freezer?"

He pauses. "It's hard to tell when someone's hacked the head off."

TWENTY-FOUR

"Sounds like she got the cold shoulder," I say.

Thanks to Mike and his graphic scenes of crime photos, I've developed a dark humour that reveals itself in moments like these. Then again, what do you say when someone tells you there's a headless corpse in a freezer?

I ask Davenport to let me know if he learns anything more and end the call. Yvonne, who's picked up the gist, wants all the details as we walk towards her office.

"Do you think the caterer dumped her there?" she asks.

My money's on the Colonel.

"We don't know who she is yet," I say.

"Oh, come on. Who else can it be?"

Maybe that's what troubles me – her certainty. There's no doubt, no room for concession or compromise.

"I'm heading this way," I say, turning at the junction with Furnace Lane.

"See you this evening," she calls over her shoulder.

With over an hour to go to my meeting with Danni, I have time for a trip to Friston.

When I arrive at Belmont, there's a patrol car on the drive. I pull up alongside Alice's Nissan and walk across to the porch, stepping over tyre tracks in the gravel that suggest a heavy van or small lorry was here. She opens the door before I can knock.

"Oh, Mr Fisher, he's had a heart attack." Her face looks pale and drained, her eyes swollen with tears. "The ambulance left a few minutes ago. She's dead, isn't she? Mrs Witherington. That's why the police called."

I'm not sure what to say, so I remain silent.

She straightens her sweater. "They're in the study, if you want to talk to them, Mr Fisher. I was going to make tea, but Colonel Witherington …" She bursts into tears again. "Is it her?"

"I don't know."

I escort her back to her warm kitchen, where she was making a fruit cake. I sit her down and let her talk while I make tea.

"I've been expecting something like this for weeks," she says. "He gets so frustrated and worked up when things don't go the way he wants. He resigned from the Council the other day," she says, looking up. "I won't repeat what he said about your manager."

"I didn't know," I say, wondering why the Chief Executive hasn't made an announcement.

"He's dying, Mr Fisher, and you finding Mrs Witherington is the only thing keeping him going. That's why he's furious with the way the Council's treating you."

"Is there someone I can call to keep you company, Alice?"

"This place and Colonel Witherington are all I need. He's made provision for me when he … passes. I shan't want for anything."

Apart from some company maybe.

"Oh, I know you must think me foolish," she says, "but I've had a wonderful life. You wouldn't believe the people I've met and the places I've been with him. I was his personal assistant before I became his housekeeper. We travelled all over the world."

It's clear she loves the Colonel and this house. Did Daphne Witherington spoil things? It's not the time to ask, but I may never get a better chance.

"What happened when Mrs Witherington came along?"

Alice looks up. "Colonel Witherington had stopped travelling by then. He became a councillor and then a JP. That's where he met Mrs Witherington – at the court. I was pleased he'd finally found someone. Men should never be alone."

"He had you."

"Och, it was never like that. He became besotted with Mrs Witherington. Like chalk and cheese they were, always arguing about things – in a good way, I mean. He believed in punishment, she favoured rehabilitation."

Alice's expression makes it clear which view she favours. "I enjoyed looking after them. It made a change to have a woman in the house."

"You got on well," I say, pouring tea from the pot.

She pauses and then smiles wanly. "They've found Mrs Witherington, haven't they? The police, I mean. That's why they're here."

"A woman's body was found earlier at Meadow Farm in Jevington."

Alice closes her eyes. "Mrs Witherington spent a lot of time there with Mr McGillicuddy. He rented the place."

I grab my notebook. "McGillicuddy as in *The 4.50 from Paddington*? Miss Marple?"

She gives me a blank look. "Ross McGillicuddy was a gamekeeper in Argyle before he won the lottery. Not the jackpot, but enough to travel around the country. He loved it here and stayed longer than he intended. He got on well with Colonel Witherington and even butchered meat and venison for us."

"Did the Colonel know his wife spent time at Meadow Farm?"

"Of course," she replies, her tone a little frosty. "He encouraged her. Ross McGillicuddy could be a forgetful man, always late with the rent. He was a big, strapping man with a bushy beard and hands like bear paws. I think he frightened the Colonel, but Mrs Witherington soon charmed the money from Mr McGillicuddy's wallet."

"They became friends, you mean?"

"Aye, but not the way you mean it," she says. "He was more interested in his hog roast."

Am I too cynical or is Alice naïve? If Daphne visited Meadow Farm, why are there no paintings of the place or the land around it in her room? And even if McGillicuddy operated a hog roast, it wouldn't take up that much of his time during the working week. In my experience, people with hog roasts attend country fayres, events and private parties, usually at weekends.

"Did he run the hog roast as a business?" I ask, certain he never registered it with the council.

"I wouldn't know."

If he ran a business, he would need freezers. But if he killed Daphne Witherington, why keep the body? And if it is her in the freezer, there's nothing to connect her to Stacey Walters and Marcie Baxendale. Even if McGillicuddy sold meat to Colin Miller, it's a tenuous link at best.

"How did McGillicuddy react when Daphne went missing?" I ask.

Alice shrugs. "I hardly saw him. Colonel Witherington visited the farm once a month to check on things."

"But he had managing agents to look after the place."

"Mrs Witherington collected the rent and dealt with any repairs. When she went missing, he didn't have the time, so he employed managing agents. He visited every month to make sure they were doing what he paid them to do."

Or the Colonel wanted to make sure his wife was safely tucked away in the freezer.

He could have killed McGillicuddy too for having an affair with her. Visiting monthly would have kept up the pretence that he was alive.

A tap on the door interrupts us. A young man in his 20s, with bright eyes and thick hair swept back from his forehead, strides in. He has the build of a rugby player under his suit, and a crooked nose to match.

"We'll be on our way now, Mrs Hewitt," he says, looking me over. "Are you a relative?"

"Kent Fisher, environmental health. The Colonel's an old family friend. And you?"

"DC Coyne, Sussex Police. Can I ask what the purpose of your visit is?"

"The same as yours, I imagine."

He gestures to the door. "Perhaps you'd come with me."

I follow him down the corridor. In the large reception area, we meet DS Fowler, another stocky detective who looks like he'd rather be breaking up fights on a Saturday night than dealing with dead bodies. He's clutching several manila folders to his chest.

"What brings you here, Mr Fisher?"

"Like you, I'd like to know who's lying in the freezer at Meadow Farm."

A flash of surprise, maybe anger, interrupt his neutral expression. "How do you know about that?"

"You can't discover a body in a village like Jevington and keep it quiet."

"Clearly, you have friends there," he says, eyeing me with suspicion. "Is there anything you'd like to tell me about this body?"

"Have you spoken to Alice, the housekeeper?"

"All in good time, Mr Fisher. We're not all expert detectives like you."

"Then you won't know that Ross McGillicuddy, the tenant of Meadow Farm, and Daphne Witherington saw a lot of each other." Now I have their attention. "She was a regular visitor to the farm before she went missing."

Fowler glances at his colleague and smirks. "I think we'd better ask the governor to hand the case over to Mr Fisher."

"Then maybe you should give me the manila folders," I say. "They belong to the Colonel, right?"

"Coyne, let the housekeeper know we're taking these."

Once we're alone, Fowler turns to me. While his voice remains polite, his eyes warn me to watch myself. "We appreciate all the assistance we can get, Mr Fisher, so we'll be sure to contact you if we feel you can help us."

Outside, I realise I should have kept my mouth shut. The detectives would have interviewed Alice as part of their investigation. They'd already spoken to the managing agent who discovered the body, so they already knew about Ross McGillicuddy.

As I reach my car, my phone rings. "Call me psychic, Kelly, but you're going to ask me where I am."

"Where are you?" Danni demands in a voice that could rattle bin lids.

"Getting my goats tested," I reply. "It's taking longer than expected, but I should be with you shortly."

"You might want to stop off and buy a copy of *The Argus*."

She ends the call, leaving me to wonder what Adrian Peach has written about the sanctuary. Before I can drive off, my phone rings again, showing Kelly's number once more.

"Sorry about that," she says. "Danni knew you'd ignore the call if she used her own phone."

"Have you seen *The Argus*?"

"Only what's online. There's a photo of you and a reporter scuffling."

"Not one of my finest moments. Well, at least I'm getting the goats tested."

"That's why I rang you. Before she spoke to you just now, Danni rang your sanctuary. Your stepmother said she hadn't seen you since this morning."

TWENTY-FIVE

In Danni's office, I decline a seat at the meeting table, forcing her to stand to deliver what sounds like a well-rehearsed critique of my shortcomings. It's my last act of protest, which is probably pointless, considering how easy I've made it for her. I'm insubordinate, disrespectful, gung-ho, a loose cannon, and obdurate.

I refute the last one.

"Frankly, Kent, you're an embarrassment to the council," she says, winding up her speech. "Have you any idea how this is affecting your team and colleagues? No, I don't suppose you have," she says, not giving me a chance to answer. "Well, unless you pull your socks up, keep your head down, and make sure your back's covered before moving forward, you're going nowhere. Do I make myself clear?"

I've no idea what she means, but I look suitably chastised as I leave her office.

Kelly looks up. "Are you okay, lover?"

"Am I causing problems for the team?"

She gives me a hesitant nod. "It looks like you don't care about their problems because yours are more important."

"More urgent, Kelly, that's all."

"Don't you end up in the same place?"

I consider what she says, knowing she's right.

For too long, I've bent the rules and taken chances, protected by William Fisher, MP. His death means I'm vulnerable. Either I curb my behaviour or turn to Birchill for protection. It means accepting he's my biological father, working with him on a holiday village that will destroy even more wildlife, no matter how green he tries to make it.

I can't do that.

The time has come to stop hiding behind others and set an example to my colleagues and my team. With local government facing austere times, struggling to survive in a world where all the good we do is undone by unfair, and often untrue, reports in the media, people will lose their jobs. People I know and care about. People I need on my side.

I lean across and kiss Kelly on the cheek. "Thank you," I say before pushing open the door to Danni's office.

Startled, Danni ends the phone call and thrusts the receiver back on the phone. Her cheeks redden even further when the receiver tumbles off and clatters onto her desk.

"Danni, I'm sorry for any trouble I've caused," I say, looking into her flustered eyes. "I know I'm not the easiest person to manage, and I appreciate it be must difficult for you at times."

Her surprise melts and for a split second I sense a glimmer of a connection between us. Then she rises, straightens her jacket, and says, "I thrive on challenges."

She grabs her trolley bag on the way to the door and forces Kelly to step out of the way. The trolley bag crashes against the door frame, but fails to slow Danni, who strides down the corridor to the stairs.

"You apologised to Danni." Kelly looks at me in disbelief. "Hey, Gemma, Kent just apologised to Danni. A genuine apology."

"A real apology?" Gemma asks, staring at me. "Are you ill?"

"Don't be so unkind," Kelly says. "He's growing up at last."

Gemma shakes her head and returns to her desk. "Exactly what did you say to Danni?"

"You don't have to look so surprised. I'm the first to own up when I get things wrong."

"Yeah, right, Kent."

Her smirk does little to ease my discomfort. It looks like nothing I say will convince her I'm serious. No wonder, after the way I ran out on her without even leaving a note. No wonder after I told her I loved her and then kept out of her way for the next two weeks. Maybe it's time to atone for my poor behaviour.

"I'm sorry if I've been a pain in the butt. I never meant to _"

"Two apologies in five minutes," she says, cutting me off. "Hey, Kelly, Kent's apologising again. People will start to think you have feelings, Kent Fisher."

Gemma's dark, sexy eyes smoulder with mockery. While there are many things I want to say, the most attractive woman I know looks anything but.

"You were about to say you never meant to what?" she asks as I return to my desk.

"Undermine morale," I reply, spotting the Post-It note on my desk. "Liam and his grandfather are positive for E. coli. Is it the same strain as Charlotte?"

"Probably. We'll have confirmation tomorrow."

"Then you need to question the grandfather again," I say. "He must have been ill."

"Or a symptomless carrier," she says.

"Then it's time we found out."

"I know," she says. "That's why I made an appointment to see him in the morning."

I should tell her she's one of the most intelligent and capable women I know. "See you tomorrow," is the best I can manage.

Back home, I walk Columbo in the rain, enjoying the water as it runs down my face. He's more interested in sniffing every blade of grass as usual, interrupted only by an occasional shake. I doubt if he understands what I'm saying. I'm not sure I do, but he wags his tail in all the right places. He even dips his head and looks sad when I tell him my feelings for Gemma are now in the dustbin.

"There's no room for regret on the Fast Forward Express," I tell him, prompting a hearty bark. He shakes the water from his fur and trots up the stairs to the kitchen, where Niamh's waiting with a towel to give him a rubdown. Naturally, it's a game and he gets the towel between his teeth and tugs it from her hands.

After a quick shower, I join them in the lounge for a mug of tea. Columbo's already on the sofa, nudging her arm for more attention.

"Charlotte Burke may have caught the bug from her family," I say.

Niamh looks so relieved, I'm surprised by how emotional it makes me. "See, prayers are answered," she says.

Charlotte could still have caught it from the goats and passed it to her brother and grandfather, but I keep that to myself. If Stephen Burke was ill, then why didn't he admit it? Did he think he was protecting his daughter in her fight to keep custody of her children?

"Do you still want Sarah to test the goats?" Niamh asks.

"As I'm not paying the bill, yes."

"You mean he is – Birchill."

For a moment, she stares at me, eyes filled with an incendiary blend of disbelief, disgust and fury. Then she lets rip. Columbo scuttles under the table as she berates me for betraying her, the memory of her husband and everything that's good on this earth.

"That man destroyed our lives. He took everything from us – our land, our heritage, our dignity. And you have the nerve to take his money. Money he stole from us. And don't you dare tell me it's because he's your father."

She's on her feet now, shouting at me. "William was your father. He loved and cared for you. He was there when things went wrong. He put you first, even when his own problems got the better of him. He saved this piece of land for you, Kent."

"He did not," I say, keeping my voice calm, but firm. "He lost this land along with the rest. He lied, Niamh. He lied to both of us."

I've never seen such a wild look in her eyes. For a moment, I wonder whether she's going to strike me. But doubt's crept into her eyes. I think she knows the extent of her husband's deceit. I can't blame her for wanting to gloss over it or pretend it never happened, but we only have a home for as long as Birchill permits.

"The man's poison, Kent," she says, tears in her eyes. "For the love of God, can't you see that?"

"We still have to deal with him," I reply, putting my hands on her shoulders. I look into her angry eyes. "I can't change that."

"You can," she says, almost pleading with me. "I know you think William betrayed you. I understand that. I do. He betrayed all of us. And it hurts. It hurts so much. But he was ill, Kent."

"Then why didn't he seek help?"

"He tried, but addiction's a disease."

"Like adultery, you mean?"

The slap stings my face, but I don't flinch. "He could have resisted, Niamh. He could have resigned from the Cabinet, but he wanted the glory."

"I don't see you resisting," she snaps. "Your father's not cold in the ground and you're inviting that man into our home. Why won't you fight him, Kent? What are you afraid of?"

"I'm afraid he's my father," I say.

She marches to her room and slams the door behind her.

Once changed into my black polo shirt and chinos, I drive to the District General in Eastbourne to visit the Colonel. Rather than pay the excessive charges in the hospital car park, I scour the housing estate opposite. Ten minutes, and as many roads, later, I find a space halfway up the hill and down a small cul-de-sac.

It takes me another ten minutes to learn I can't see Colonel Witherington as I've missed visiting hours. While the nurses sympathise and agree that it's difficult when you have to work during the day, being an environmental health officer cuts no ice. Being Kent Fisher fares no better, though one of the nurses asks if I'd like to check her chest freezer. Then the Ward Sister asks me if I've tested negative for E. coli, thanks to contact with the animals at my sanctuary, and ushers me off the premises.

I drive to Friston, hoping Alice will know more about the Colonel, but darkness fills her flat and the house. Then I realise she's at the hospital. Had I stopped to think, I could have asked to see her instead of trying to force my way onto the ward.

With a shake of the head, I start the car, tempted to nip down the road for a bite to eat at The Tiger in East Dean. Then a text tempts me back to Tollingdon.

The Prosecco's chilled. I'm hot. Yvonne.

I'm lukewarm, but what the hell? After the day I've had, Yvonne could be just what I need.

At 8.20, I leave my car at the town hall and walk the couple of streets to La Neapolitan. In Market Street, I cast a brief glance at the *Tollingdon Tribune's* first floor offices across the road. Though the lights are out, I turn up my collar in case Tommy Logan's lurking in the shadows. He often works late with only a table lamp and vivid imagination for company.

La Neapolitan wraps around the corner with Victoria Road, populated by chic restaurants, tearooms and art galleries. The three storey Victorian buildings, with their ornate gables and brickwork, tower above me like custodians of more prosperous times. Overlooked by red, green and white striped awnings, the restaurant's sheet glass windows, boast bright menus that offer Italian dishes for everyone. Inside, it's modern and noisy, with an open plan dining area that bustles with waiting staff, weaving between the tables like black and white ants. The aroma of garlic, basil and tomato fills the air, wafted by large, silent fans in the industrial ceiling.

I join the queue at the polished wood reception counter and glance around the vast space. When I spot Yvonne by the window, I peel away and almost bowl over a cute waitress with dirty plates balanced on her arm. I apologise for the third time today and pick up the spoons that fell to the floor. When I hand them back and look into those dark, Italian eyes, I almost make a fool of myself.

"She's married," Yvonne says, showing no offence at my interest in the young waitress.

She's wearing a fitted red jumper with a sparkling brooch. The sleeves stop short of her wrists, cuffed with silver bracelets, but the colour is a perfect match for her nails and lipstick. There's a touch of Meg Ryan about her hair and face – a confident assured sparkle and vitality with more than a hint of fun. As long as she doesn't do the scene from *When Harry Met Sally*, we shouldn't attract too much attention.

"Not wearing your glasses?" I ask, taking the Prosecco out of the chiller to top up her glass.

"No, I wanted to be blind to your faults."

"But you might not see my good points."

"Like your fashion sense?"

I peel off the damp anorak to reveal crumpled chinos and a polo shirt that needs laundering. "Sorry, I wasn't planning on coming here."

"You know how to make a girl feel wanted." She takes a sip of wine, studying me with eyes that seem to analyse all the time. "Should I ask for the tab?"

I ask a passing waiter for still mineral water, no ice. He offers to take my coat, but I decline, draping it over an adjoining chair. I sit and straighten the red, green and white tablecloth. Then I move the red candles in their green tumblers onto the window sill.

"I once investigated an accident where a man leaned across the table to kiss his girlfriend. The heat from the candle melted his cheap shirt, causing nasty burns to his chest."

She smiles. "I'm pleased to learn you're planning to kiss me, but I wish you'd buy better quality shirts."

"How can you tell when you're not wearing glasses?"

She leans closer, treating me to her potent perfume. "I'm not wearing knickers either."

"Because you couldn't see where you left them?"

"Maybe I want to make things easy for you."

Maybe that's the problem.

The waiter arrives with my mineral water and pours it into a glass. I look outside at a thin, elderly man with an unkempt beard. He trudges along in a trench coat that drags his shoulders into a stoop. His cold hand tugs the short length of rope attached to a small, bedraggled mongrel that's found something edible in the gutter. As if sensing my interest, he glances through the window with the staring, bloodshot eyes of a man who needs a drink.

The waiter waves him away. "Are you ready to order?" he asks.

I haven't even opened the menu, but I order what I always eat in Italian restaurants - bruschetta, penne arabiatta with extra chilli, a side salad, and tiramisu for dessert. Sometimes, if I'm feeling wild, I order a pizza with extra chilli.

Yvonne orders calamari, followed by a large vegetarian pizza and no dessert.

"Are you expecting someone?" she asks, breaking the silence since the waiter departed. "Only you keep looking out of the window."

"Do I?"

"I'm getting the impression you don't want to be here."

"I've had a bad day, that's all."

"So tell me about it."

"I don't want to talk about work."

"Does that include the body at the farm? Is it anything to do with your missing women?"

"No idea, but it was considerate of Alasdair to tell me."

"He's like that."

"So tell me about him."

She laughs. "You think he's taking advantage of Niamh, don't you? Well, he's still grieving for his wife, Angelina, who died about eighteen months ago. Not that he'll ever admit it, being a man, but it sounds like she had a rough time."

"What happened?"

"I wasn't around, but she died a long, slow death from pneumonia apparently. Yeah, I thought you could treat it with antibiotics too," she says, "but she refused treatment. She was scared of doctors and hospitals, I think. That's why Alasdair blames himself for her death."

She helps herself to more Prosecco. "That's why he understands pain and loss. That's why he connects with bereaved people."

"You clearly admire him."

"I like a man who's not afraid to show his feelings – or admit his failings."

"How did you come to work for Alasdair?" I ask, passing on the opportunity she offered.

She studies me while she takes a long drink of wine. "He buried my father and a few weeks later a job came up, so I applied, thinking it would be different and interesting."

"And is it?"

Though she skimps on the detail, she's dealt with some strange, and 'frankly freaky', requests from relatives, including the lady who wanted her dog buried with her husband.

"That was timely, the dog dying ..." I stop, realising the dog was still alive. "She didn't have it put to sleep, did she?"

"Alasdair suggested she place a photo in the casket. It's kinda like his trademark."

The waiter arrives with our starters at this point. After declining the offer of black pepper, I sink my teeth into the soft, toasted ciabatta base and let the tomato, pesto and garlic slither across my tongue, stimulating my taste buds and my thoughts.

"Did Angelina's family put photographs in her coffin?"

Yvonne leans closer. "There was an almighty ruck. They wanted her buried in the family plot in Eastbourne, but she wanted to be cremated. I'm with her," she says, jabbing calamari onto her fork. "I want my ashes scattered out to sea from Beachy Head. It's just about the most beautiful place around here, especially with the pretty lighthouse."

Having steered the conversation away from Davenport and onto the South Downs, she reveals a love of mountain biking and trail running, thanks to a misspent youth pickpocketing. Despite having wealthy parents, she dropped out of Boston University when her mother died and took to the road to become a country and western singer, marrying her manager, Duane.

"I couldn't really sing, but I loved the freedom. Not to mention the sex, liquor and drugs."

While I don't doubt she led a wild and adventurous life, there's no emotional content to her tales. She's factual and precise, more interested in dates and places than what she did there. Not once does she mention making a record or playing a gig. She talks plenty about Duane's lovers, naming quite a few before she divorced him and gave up the rock 'n' roll lifestyle.

"Then I met Jonathan." She pauses, a faraway look in her eyes. "He was a dream. English gentleman, rich and handsome, with a cruiser in the Caribbean. We married on a sandy beach in Guadeloupe and toured the islands. Then the nightmare started."

She tells me about Jonathan Jones, property developer, conman and lowlife. Turns out he didn't own the cruiser, or the house on the beach in Miami, or the villa in Antibes. He used her to rip off her father and many of his friends in a scam and took off to Columbia with the money.

"We were living in an apartment in Canary Wharf when he vanished. I didn't know he'd gone until the police broke the door down one morning. They refused to believe I didn't know about his scams and interviewed me for days, going over the same stuff. Eventually, they had to let me go. I was the lucky one," she says with a sigh. "Pa lost everything. His health declined and he went into a nursing home. He died in September last year."

"I'm sorry to hear that."

"That's when I met Alasdair and here I am – 38, single and penniless. What about you?"

"About the same," I reply, "but slightly older."

"Come on, Kent. Your father owned an estate. You must be loaded."

"I don't earn enough to sustain my sanctuary."

"So you do detective work to bring in extra cash? Come on!"

The waiter saves me from an explanation, arriving with Yvonne's pizza, on a wooden board and my pasta in an oversized bowl. The aroma of tomato, chilli and sweet peppers all blend into a heady mix that demands a liberal helping of parmesan.

"You can never have enough parmesan," I tell the waiter, refusing to let him take it away.

"Smells like sweaty socks to me," Yvonne says, tearing away a slice of pizza with eager fingers. She pushes the slice into her mouth, smearing topping on her lips and the corners of her mouth. Then she laughs and tells me to loosen up.

When I take her advice and make a flamboyant approach toward my pasta, I catch the empty mineral water bottle. It scuttles across the table and bounces off the windowsill before falling to the floor beneath the table. While Yvonne giggles, I stretch a hand down. I can't quite reach the bottle, so I slide my chair back and duck my head under the table.

Yvonne has great legs – athletic, shapely and tapering to slim ankles, charmed by fine silver bracelets. On the top of her left foot she has a tattoo of a spider's web, visible between the straps of her red, spike-heel shoe. I'm no lover of tattoos, but it's discreet, artistic and almost as tiny as her short red skirt. And she's not wearing knickers as she said, but a thong, if I'm not mistaken.

As my fingers tighten around the bottle, she ducks her head under the table. "Enjoy the view while you can, Kent, because someone's about to rain on your parade."

I look around and spot the sodden suede shoes beneath the brown corduroy trousers with frayed and dirty hems that drag along the ground. When I emerge from beneath the table, Tommy Logan raises his trilby. He gives me a Blofeld smile so sly and joyous I know I'm in trouble.

"Kent Fisher on his knees," he says in his familiar drawl, eyeing Yvonne with pleasure. "I never thought I'd see the day."

"Yeah, I was looking for you in the gutter," I say, extricating myself.

"Perhaps you'd like to introduce me to your rather delectable companion."

"I don't mix with tramps," she tells him.

He pretends to look offended, placing his hand over his heart. "You'd look like a bedraggled vagrant if you'd spent the last four hours outside a barn in Jevington in the rain."

When his photographer, a young man with gelled hair and big teeth, steps out from behind him and points his camera at me, the maître d' strides over.

"Then, on my way back to the office from my vigil, I see Kent Fisher, having fun with a comely young lady. He can't have heard the news, I thought or he'd never be out enjoying himself, would he?" A sly smile sidles across his mouth. "Then I realised you would have heard the news long before me."

"What news?" I ask, getting to my feet. "Has Colonel Witherington died?"

"No, but sweet little Charlotte Burke passed away at 6.27 today."

TWENTY-SIX

I go numb. It feels like someone has placed a fish bowl over my head. I can see the photographer taking photos, but it doesn't register. I can see Tommy's lips moving, but I can't make out what he's saying. My mind swims with images of Charlotte Burke, surrounded by doctors and nurses, desperate to keep her alive. I can imagine her mother's frantic cries as she watches, helpless to save her daughter.

I can almost feel her suffocating fear and panic when she realises her daughter's gone.

"So young. So pretty. So helpless. Such a tragic waste, wouldn't you say?"

Tommy's voice brings me back from paralysis. The photographer at his side continues to shoot, despite the best efforts of the maître d' to intervene. Everyone in the restaurant watches, waiting for me to respond.

But what can I say?

"I'll assume that's no comment," Tommy says in a loud voice, addressing his audience. "After all, you hardly knew the girl, did you? You only met her at your animal sanctuary when she was left unsupervised with your goats."

A hand on my arm restrains me. Yvonne whispers in my ear and pushes me towards the door. She drops some banknotes on the table and thanks the maître d'.

"It's not like Kent Fisher to run away," Tommy says as I pass.

I spin around. "But it's just like Tommy Logan to capitalise on the death of a poor young girl. Can you imagine how her mother must be feeling?"

"I'm sure she'll tell me in the morning when I interview her. In the meantime, perhaps you could tell me if you've tested your animals yet."

Yvonne drags me away, forcing the photographer to step back.

Tommy calls after us, unable to hide the glee in his voice. "I'll take that as a no, shall I?"

Outside, the damp air feels cool and fresh. Not that it makes any difference. My mind seems to be operating in a different world to the one around me. I'm aware of Yvonne, clutching my hand, leading me through the fine mist of rain, visible in the headlights of passing cars. I can't hear the cars though. The only sound comes from the noise in my head.

"Why didn't your boss tell you the kid had died?" Yvonne asks, cutting through the noise.

"Her name's Charlotte. Charlotte Burke."

She releases my hand and steps back. "Hey, I'm not the enemy here. Chill out."

"Chill out?"

"It's not like you know her, is it?" She shivers, her flimsy jacket offering little protection from the cold rain. "You're angry about how this will look when word gets out."

"I'm angry because a young girl should never have died. It's my job to protect vulnerable people. That's what I do."

"You think you're Mother Theresa?" She stares at me, shaking her head. "What about the kid's mother? Isn't she supposed to protect her children?"

I feel my fingernails digging into my palms. I want to hit someone or something – anything to release the pressure inside. "What if my goats infected Charlotte?"

"What if they didn't?"

"I need to ring my boss," I say, reaching into my pocket. "Damn, my phone's in the restaurant."

Yvonne pulls my phone from her bag. "Maybe she left a message."

We duck under an awning and I check for calls, messages, texts or emails from Danni. But there's nothing. She must know. Public Health England would notify her first and then me. So, why haven't I heard anything?

How did Tommy know? Who told him?

I spot him with his photographer on the opposite side of the street, heads bent against the rain. The younger man bounds up the steps, two at a time, to the first floor office of the *Tollingdon Tribune*. He unlocks the door and strides into the illuminated room, not waiting for Tommy, who struggles up the steps. As he stands on the landing, sucking in air, our eyes meet. With a sly smile, he turns and heads inside.

Thankfully, he's too late to get the story into tomorrow's edition, but that still leaves the website and social media.

Yvonne, who's also watching, takes my arm and snuggles up. "My flat's around the corner."

"When I walked past earlier, the lights were off," I say.

"What?"

"Tommy said he was on his way back from Jevington when he spotted us in the restaurant. Who turned on the lights in his office?"

"The cleaners? Another reporter? Who cares?"

"He returned to the office," I reply, thinking it through. "That's why the lights are on. Then he came across to La Neapolitan. He knew we were there. Someone tipped him off."

"We had a window seat. He spotted us."

"Not from his office. He would have to walk past and the only person who did that was a wino."

"He spotted you earlier, walking to the restaurant."

I shake my head. "The offices were closed when I walked past. No, he knew I was in the restaurant with you."

She steps back, her eyes cold and angry. "Are you saying I tipped him off?"

"Why was the photographer dry if they'd been out in the rain for four hours?"

"Maybe he was in the office."

"No, Tommy had a photographer lined up," I say, watching her closely. "All he had to do was get me out somewhere convenient, in full view of the street."

"You think I set you up?"

I ignore her incredulity. "Who else knew where I would be?"

"I didn't know if you were coming to the restaurant. I didn't know the kid was going to die, so how could I set you up?"

"The story was about me out enjoying myself while Charlotte fought for her life in hospital. When she died, Tommy must have …"

Yvonne stares at me, shaking her head. "You think I played up to you in there, knowing that kid was dead? What do you think I am?"

When I don't answer, she spins away, her heels pounding on the paving slabs. She pulls her jacket tight, dislodging her bag, which slides off her shoulder. For a moment she wobbles on those precarious heels before striding out of sight around the corner.

I look up and see Tommy at his office window, towelling his grey hair.

Back in my car, I switch the fan on full blast to clear the condensation. Maybe the rush of air will clear my head too. I don't know why Yvonne set me up, but who else could it be? I suppose Tommy could have spotted me on my way to the restaurant, rang his photographer and caught me in the act.

I shake my head. Yvonne chose La Neapolitan, only yards from Tommy's office.

Why didn't I go home after my wasted journey to Belmont?

I look at my phone, ready to tell Danni the worst, but wanting to know why she didn't ring me with the news. She can't have rung the sanctuary or Niamh would have contacted me.

Either Danni didn't know, like me, or she didn't tell me.

No, she'd tell me. She wouldn't want me doing anything that could harm me or the council, surely?

Of course not, I tell myself, staring at the photo of the dismissal letter she produced and signed ahead of the formal hearing.

At home, I can't sleep. Neither can Niamh. It's 2.15 and she's wrapped in her dressing gown, staring at a mug of cold tea in the kitchen. Her reddened eyes fill with more tears as I hug her, wishing I knew what to say. But what can I say? I screwed up.

"If only I hadn't taken Frances shopping," she says, scooping up Columbo, who immediately licks her face and tears. "It wasn't as if she wanted to go. We walked from shop to shop, me getting her to try on something different, and she bought more combat trousers."

"We could all do with some of those when the media arrive tomorrow."

Niamh shudders. "Don't. I should have made you test the goats sooner."

"It's not your fault. We'll get through this."

"Not if we have to close. Where will the animals go? What about Frances?"

"It won't come to that," I say with more conviction than I feel.

"But our reputation will be damaged. People won't trust us."

She's right. Not only do I need the goats to test negative, I have to prove Charlotte's infection came from somewhere else. That's not going to be easy. With an outbreak affecting lots of people, it's easier to identify common foods or sources of infection.

I make tea, not sure what to say to fill the silence. Columbo's back on the floor, asleep under the table, but I won't sleep a wink, so I might as well make plans for tomorrow. It should be simple as I know exactly what I'm going to do and say – nothing. The goats will be tested, the media will drift away when they realise no one's talking, and I'll go for a long run to allow plenty of time to beat myself up.

"Go to bed." Niamh puts a reassuring hand on my shoulder and gives me a grim smile. "We'll survive. We're Fishers, remember."

"I'm not."

"Oh yes you are." She kisses me on the forehead and squeezes my shoulder before returning to her room. I remain at the table for a little while, thinking about alternate futures where I design eco villages or set up my own detective agency.

"Maybe not," I say, aware that Columbo's awake and looking up at me. "Daphne Witherington was lying three miles from her husband as the crow flies and I went to Glastonbury. What kind of detective does that make me?"

Back in my room, with Columbo curled up by my feet, I spend some quality time with Kinsey Millhone, wondering how she would have investigated the missing wives. Would she have rushed to Glastonbury to confront Miller? Of course she would. What about the letter from Stacey Walters, arriving a few days after? Would Kinsey have believed it? I doubt it. Would she have looked for a connection between Marcie Baxendale and Miller? Kinsey would record the details on index cards, using them later to review her progress. She would never trust to memory like me.

I turn off my Kindle and search through the storage boxes on top of the wardrobe for my old clipboard and pad. Inside the bedside cabinet, I unearth an old fountain pen and a pack of cartridges. In the bathroom, I rinse the nib under the tap, insert the cartridge, and eventually coax the ink to flow.

Columbo gives me his full attention, placing his paw on the clipboard to tell me he's ready to share my thoughts and deductions. As he can't read my scrawl, he soon goes to sleep beside my legs while I record everything I can remember about Daphne Witherington. I repeat the process for Stacey Walters, stopping only to visit the bathroom and then make another mug of tea. Finally, I write down everything about Kirk and Marcie Baxendale. With the help of another mug of tea, and a treat for Columbo, I review my notes.

"Well, matey," I say, ruffling the fur behind his ears, "do you think Daphne Witherington's the body in the freezer?"

He takes another treat and reserves judgement.

"She disappeared on a day when her husband and Alice were out. As she didn't take her paints, she knew the killer and thought nothing of going out with him. The tenant, McGillicuddy, knew her, maybe had an affair with her. But," I say, having Columbo's full attention now, "why would he kill her and keep her in his freezer for 12 months? Wouldn't he get rid of the body and move on?"

Columbo paws my arm and I slip him a final treat, until the next one, of course.

"Agreed, the Colonel's the more likely suspect."

But if the Colonel killed his wife, why did he ask me to investigate? Was he hoping I'd blame McGillicuddy? Or Miller, who took £20,000 to dump Daphne. If his story is true, of course. Miller also had a history with Stacey Walters, who disappeared while her husband was off on a hoax delivery.

The Colonel knew Marcie Baxendale, who deserted her beloved spaniel. All the wives are connected, but only with the killer, it seems.

"I wish you could talk," I tell Columbo. "I wish your namesake was here because I'm missing something. Something obvious."

I flick back through the pages of scrawl, looking for the killer detail. I'm almost back at the beginning when I remember something.

Councillor Rathbone and the man at the printers gave a different description of Miller to Davenport.

I tap the pen against my lip, trying to coax more from my weary thoughts. Miller said he reneged on the deal with Colonel Witherington because someone threatened to kill him. While Miller's a compulsive liar, what if he told me the truth? What if he fled and someone else took his place? That could account for the different descriptions.

It also rules out Miller.

So, who killed Stacey? Who killed Marcie?

I'm back to the Colonel again. Or am I? McGillicuddy left a couple of days before the body in the freezer was discovered.

Eager to share my breakthrough, I ring Gemma. The phone rings and rings. I'm about to hang up when her bleary voice answers.

"Do you know what time it is?"

"6.19," I reply, glancing at the clock. "Someone put the body in the freezer after McGillicuddy left."

It sounds like she's shuffling about, trying to get comfortable. When she giggles and says, "Not now," I almost end the call.

"Who did?" she asks. "Why?"

"Someone's tracking our investigation," I reply. "Someone with a freezer. Someone who produced a letter from Miller a couple of days after my trip to Glastonbury."

"Todd Walters? Are you sure?"

"He's been clearing out his shop and freezers, hasn't he? He could easily move a body from his freezer to the one at Meadow Farm."

"To make it look like McGillicuddy killed her," she says, moving about again. When I hear the sound of running water, I hope she's not in the bathroom.

"They would have known each other," I say. "McGillicuddy supplied him with game, told him how Daphne Witherington visited Meadow Farm, eager for company and love. Walters has an affair with her and makes it look like she's sleeping with his old enemy, Miller, who's sniffing around Stacey. Walters can't believe his luck."

"But why would he kill Daphne and Stacey?" she asks.

"Maybe Daphne wanted to end the affair. Maybe they argued, he lost his temper, and hit her. He didn't mean to kill her, but … Then Stacey finds out or tells him she's seeing Miller and Walters kills her."

Gemma's silence lasts for half a minute. "So, who's in the freezer – Daphne or Stacey?"

"Don't forget Marcie."

"How did Walters know her?"

"Didn't Baxendale say she lived with her father outside Mayfield? Walters probably delivered sausages to them."

"Todd Walters," she says, still sounding surprised. "Are you sure?"

"You've seen his temper. And who better than a butcher to remove someone's head?"

"That's not funny, Kent. You should tell the police. Walters might run."

"No, he thinks he's safe. He's kept one, two, maybe three bodies in his freezer for a year and carried on as normal."

"If you can call keeping bodies in a freezer normal. Why didn't he get rid of them?"

"Chop them up, you mean? He could have run them through the mincer, I guess. But if he had there wouldn't be a body at Meadow Farm. Unless he couldn't bring himself to mince Stacey, which means it's her in the freezer."

Gemma groans. "I think I'm going to be sick."

"Not as sick as Walters when he discovers I'm onto him."

TWENTY-SEVEN

It's amazing how quickly everything falls into place once you solve the puzzle.

"Poor Colin Miller," I say, ruffling Columbo's fur. "He was trying to make money selling dodgy sandwiches and ended up running for his life when Walters threatened to kill him. Walters then disguises himself, meets Daphne, his former lover, and spins some tale to make it look like they're running away together. Once he's killed her, he can deal with Stacey, who's been seeing Miller on the sly.

"I'm still working on why he killed Marcie," I add, watching Columbo trot over to the door where Niamh's standing.

"So, Todd Walters did it," she says, picking up Columbo. "Why would he put his wife in McGillicudy's freezer? When the police identify her they'll go straight back to Walters."

"He'll claim McGillicuddy had an affair with his wife. Or Walters points a finger at the Colonel."

"At which point, you stroll in and solve the case," she says, as if I make a habit of this. "I hope you're right."

I follow her to the kitchen. “What do you mean, you hope I’m right.”

“I don’t know Walters, but from what you’ve told me, he’s more likely to punch someone than plan an elaborate set of murders.”

Frances rushes in. Charlotte Burke’s death has made the local news. “There’s worse on the internet,” she says, thrusting her tablet at me.

Thomas Hardy Logan has posted a damning story on the *Tollingdon Tribune* website. Below the sensational headline, the photos show Yvonne and me chatting, smiling and looking intimate while a poor, helpless child dies in a London hospital.

“So that’s where you were last night,” Niamh says, shaking her head. “I thought you went to see the Colonel.”

“I didn’t know the daughter was about to die,” I say.

“All the same, Kent, was it wise to be out enjoying yourself with all this going on?”

“It’s just bad timing,” Frances says, coming to my defence.

“No,” I say, “it wasn’t one of my better ideas.”

I hand the tablet back, not wanting to read Logan’s gloating narrative. No doubt he’s sent it to every editor he can think of, hoping one of the nationals will come rushing down. If they do, I hope it’s not when Sarah arrives to test the goats.

I ring her, knowing she gets to the surgery early. She sounds a little breathless when she answers. “I know it’s a big ask,” I say, “but could you do the tests now? I have a feeling the press will be descending on us today and …”

"I can't possibly come until after surgery. I'm sure Brian would though. He is your vet, after all."

"Only because you walked out."

"Can you blame me after you seduced my little girl?"

A dirty mist clings to the South Downs, obscuring the hills and the sky. The humid air seems to press the moisture to the ground, weighing down the leaves and cobwebs. I pick my way through the relentless bramble that's determined to overwhelm the delicate plants and flowers in the shorter grass. I need to cut it back, but like the jagged nettles that narrow the path, it simply reminds me how much I've still to do.

"We only need Birchill to give us the land and enough money to run the place," I tell Columbo while he sniffs among the grasses. "Then I could pack in the day job."

He looks up at me, decides there's nothing of interest, and wanders on, nose to the ground.

He's right. It's not going to happen.

Half an hour later, I go with Frances to the entrance and close the gate for the first time since I moved in. It takes a few clouts with a lump hammer, a can of WD40, and a rusty squeal that disperses the nearby wood pigeons, to move the gate. Once in place, I wrap a heavy chain and padlock around the post to secure it.

"Shouldn't we put up a closed sign?" she asks.

"We don't have one. We're only closed to reporters. You rang everyone who needs to know?"

She nods. "No one's calling today except for Sarah. I thought you were taking the day off."

"If I'm not here, the reporters will go away."

"And you can avoid Sarah."

Frances and Sarah go to the same fitness class at Downland Leisure Centre. Of course they talk. Why wouldn't they, sharing an interest in animals?

"I always thought you and Sarah would get together," she says as we walk back to the barn. "You were always protesting together, fighting the same causes."

"We were friends, Frances. Partners in crime."

"What pushed you apart?"

Niamh calls down from the kitchen, saving me. "Alice just rang. The Colonel wants to see you."

Twenty minutes later, parked halfway up the hill overlooking the hospital, I discover I've no umbrella or coat in the car. The brooding clouds gather and darken, waiting for me to make a dash for it. The wind, growing stronger by the minute, encourages me down the hill and across King's Drive into the grounds of the District General Hospital. My shoes squeak on the polished vinyl tiles as I make my way to the stairs at the back of the building to the rather swish Michelham Unit, where patients can pay for private rooms.

I find Alice, dozing in an armchair at the side of the bed. A huge monitor hangs over the bed, showing details of heart rate, blood pressure, oxygen saturation and who knows what? I don't need a machine to tell me the Colonel's ill. The oxygen mask, his grey, lifeless face and stick-thin arms tell me all I need to know. He's aged 20 years since I last saw him.

Over at the window, I look down into the enclosed atrium with its trees and shrubs. Though pleasant enough, it's not much of a view for the amount of money it must be costing the Colonel.

A nurse comes in to check on the Colonel. She looks at the monitors, checks the pulse clip on his finger and straightens the oxygen mask. She takes a long look at his notes before replacing the clipboard in the slot at the end of the bed. The noise wakes Alice, who starts when she sees me.

"He's very weak," the nurse says.

Alice yawns and stretches her arms and neck before getting to her feet. She points to the door and leads me across the soft, green carpet into a small rest room, closing the door behind her. The beige upholstered chairs are low but comfortable, separated by a table, containing various magazines to help me spruce up my mansion home with its seven-acre garden.

"He woke up in a bit of a state," Alice says, whispering for some reason. "He kept saying your name, over and over. Then he drifted off again, waking with a start a few moments later. The monitors started to bleep and two nurses rushed in to calm him down."

She fiddles with a button on her beige cardigan, looking tired and lost. "Is it Mrs Witherington? The body they found."

"I don't know."

She looks up, her eyes wide with worry. "Will they ask me to identify her?"

I can't tell her the body has no head. "I don't think so."

"But he's in no state to do it," she says, gesturing towards the Colonel's room. "I don't think he's got much longer."

She begins to sob and I sit there, not sure there's anything I can do. I check my phone, wondering whether Danni will call as I've not shown for work. I ought to tell her where I am, but I can't be bothered. Having seen the Colonel, lying there, helpless without the monitors and machines, my problems at work seem petty. In London, Charlotte Burke lies in the mortuary, her future stolen by a microscopic bug. Her family will never get over her death.

"Let's see how he is," I say, taking Alice's small hand.

When we enter the room, his eyes flicker open. He looks through us at first, unable to focus or make sense of where he is. His mouth opens, but only a trickle of saliva dribbles out. A tired hand rises and flaps at the oxygen mask, failing to move it.

Alice hurries over. "Let me."

She takes a tissue from a box on the bedside cabinet and then lifts the mask. She dabs the saliva from his chin, talking to him in a soft voice. Then she pours a small amount of water from the jug into a plastic cup and raises it to his lips. Swallowing seems painful, but he's fully conscious now, staring at me. A crooked finger beckons me closer.

His voice is little more than a hoarse whisper. "Is it my Daphne?"

"It might be," I reply, close to his ear.

His hand grips my arm. "Do you think it's her?"

When I hesitate, his grip tightens. "I need to know," he gasps, turning his head as Alice tries to replace the mask. "Find out!"

She slides the mask back and gradually his breathing slows. His grip weakens until his hand falls away. His eyelids drop, obscuring the defiance in his eyes. I know it sounds crazy, but I'm sure he intends to stay alive until I uncover the truth.

Outside the room, Alice turns to me. "You don't think it's Mrs Witherington, do you?"

I'm about to shrug when my phone rings. Gemma's voice is quiet but clear.

"Chloe Burke's in reception with a film crew."

TWENTY-EIGHT

"What does Chloe Burke hope to achieve?" I ask Gemma.

We're in the post room on the ground floor to avoid Danni.

It's a cramped, windowless room that smells of stale photocopier. The tired machine rests in a corner beneath an extractor fan that whirs and occasionally whines. On either side, wooden pigeon holes, dedicated to every team in Downland District Council, huddle above counters heavy with plastic baskets, crammed with franked envelopes bearing the council's crest. Most of these rolled off the letter-folding and envelope-stuffing machinery that covers most of the floor.

"Isn't it obvious?" Gemma brushes some dust from the sleeve of her cream polo neck sweater. "She wants your blood."

"Why isn't Danni dealing with her?"

She laughs. "Why do you think?"

"Someone's got to do something. A media release from Geoff Lamb won't solve anything."

She puts a hand on my arm. "You can't go out there. It's not your problem."

"Then why did you ring me?"

"You always know what to do." She looks at me the way she did when she believed in me. "Management are hiding in their ivory tower, scared shitless. They sent Chloe Burke a message to say she should contact you at the sanctuary. Can you believe it?"

Of course I can. "It's not their fight, Gemma."

"They could at least defend you." She bangs a fist down on the counter, raising more dust. "I know the poor woman's lost her child, but it's not your fault."

Let's hope not.

"How does charging into the town hall with a film crew help?" she asks, her voice rising. "Is she trying to humiliate you?"

"She wants to know why her daughter died," I say.

"Then why doesn't she ask?" Gemma stares at me, bristling with frustration. "She won't like the answer though."

"What do you mean?"

Her hands fall as her tension melts into a smirk. "I'm getting just like you," she says as if it's an incurable disease. "When I went to collect the poo samples for Samuel and his grandfather, they'd gone out and left the pots in an envelope by the kitchen door."

"What have you done?"

"Used my initiative," she replies. "I spotted some fresh bags of manure by the fence, so I went into the back garden and found more manure around the vegetables, along with a couple of children's spades."

"You sampled the manure, right?"

"We're waiting for final confirmation, but it looks like the E. coli strains match. The bug came from the manure, not your goats. Isn't that brilliant?"

It's hardly the best word to use under the circumstances, but I don't care. "Thank you," I say, hugging her as a mixture of relief and pride overwhelm me. "Thank you!"

My goats might yet yield the same strain of E. coli, but I don't mention that.

She eases out of the embrace. "We're not there yet."

"What do you mean?"

"Danni went ballistic when I told her. She said the results were invalid because I'd obtained them dishonestly."

"That doesn't change the results."

"I know, but she's refusing to release the results in case the Burkes sue the council. She's forbidden me to tell anyone – especially you, but we need to take more samples, Kent."

"If the manure's contaminated, other people should be affected, but we haven't had any more cases, have we?"

"I spoke to the lab about that. They said people can become resistant over time like farmers do. Charlotte, being young and vulnerable, couldn't fight the bug, unlike her brother."

"Do you know where the manure came from?"

"A smallholding outside Tollingdon with a few pigs, some goats and a cow. And get this," she says with a grin. "It's owned by Stephen Burke's brother, Martin. He was out, but one of the neighbours said he gives the manure to his brother. That's why no one else is affected."

"You need to confirm that, just in case," I say.

"I'll check when I take samples this afternoon. Danni can't object to that, can she?"

"That's what you think?" Danni steps into the doorway. I don't know how long she's been listening, but the glint in her eyes worries me. "My office now," she says.

I shake my head. "I'm talking to Chloe Burke."

"You'll do no such thing."

"Why, are you going to talk to her?"

She sighs. "Kent, we're dealing with Miss Burke."

"By ignoring her? How does that help?"

Danni folds her arms. "If you want to confront her at your sanctuary, be my guest. But not here. This is not the council's fight."

Gemma cuts in. "But we can prove where the E. coli came from."

"From samples obtained by stealth?"

"By initiative," I say, losing my calm. "This isn't a court case, Danni. This is about a four year old girl and her distraught mother."

"So distraught she marches in here with a camera crew?"

"Don't you mean desperate? She wants to know why her daughter died and we're not telling her."

Danni folds her arms. "Have your goats tested negative?"

"I'm still waiting to hear."

"Well, until they test negative, Kent, you could still be responsible. Do you want to tell Miss Burke that?"

"We can't leave her in reception, Danni."

"We never asked her to charge in here with TV cameras."

"We could at least talk to her."

"And tell her what? You can't bring her daughter back, Kent. You can't prove she got the E. coli from the manure." She glances at the clock on the wall and turns to leave. "Go home, Kent before you do something we'll both regret."

She leaves just as she arrived – without a sound.

"Maybe she's right," Gemma says with a helpless shrug. "I should never have called you. I was angry because she wouldn't release the sample results."

"Not as angry as Chloe Burke," I say, pushing through the door.

It's a short walk to reception down a long corridor. By the time I reach the door to the foyer, my palms are sweating. I've no idea what I'm going to say, but I know I have to face her. Anything else will only confirm what she and the media are thinking.

Trial by media, where you're guilty until the papers print a tiny apology on Page Seven.

I peer through the small glass panel into the foyer with its ornate high ceiling, chandeliers, and sweeping staircase, ideal for wedding photographs after a visit to the registry office. Chloe Burke and her parents are standing against the far wall. Nearby, the TV crew wait and watch. One man holds a camera, panning up the staircase. A second adjusts his microphone. The young, vaguely familiar woman, dressed in a dark trouser suit and spike heels, paces up and down, glancing at her watch.

No one's talking or looking at each other. They seem lost in this grand, pompous vault with its sumptuous carpets, polished marble banisters and handrails, and the portrait gallery of aldermen and mayors from the past to the present. Long velvet drapes, tied back with gold braided rope, hang either side of tall Gothic windows that cast a rather gloomy light.

If the surroundings intimidate Chloe Burke, she's not showing it. From the way she chews her nails, I imagine she's dying for a cigarette. Dressed in a black trouser suit and grey blouse, she looks painfully thin, her face white and drawn. Her eyes hold a sadness and grief that's drained the life and soul out of her, leaving only anger and confusion.

Her mother and father look no better.

I recall some of the aggressive encounters I've defused over the years, but none of them compare to this. None of them were captured on video. After a deep breath to calm the jitters in my stomach, I push open the door, retreating when I spot Tommy Logan, Adrian Peach and their photographers enter the foyer. They look around, nod to the TV reporter and take up a position beside them, ignoring the Burkes.

I glance back, half expecting Gemma to be there to wish me luck, but the corridor's empty. I adjust my chinos, straightening the belt buckle, and raise the zipper on my fleece to hide the stain on my polo shirt. After a final deep breath, I'm about to enter the foyer when I spot Gemma and Danni, sneaking down the staircase. They stop of the half landing, keeping out of sight of the reporters.

I step back and flatten myself against the wall. For a moment, disappointment overwhelms the thoughts and fears churning in my head and stomach. I feel betrayed as Gemma exchanges a few intimate words with Danni.

Did Danni ask Gemma to call me to the office, knowing I'd confront Chloe Burke?

I push open the door and step into the foyer, surprised by the quiet. No one notices me at first, apart from Danni and Gemma.

Then all hell breaks loose.

People come to life. Fingers point. Reporters move forward. Photographers shuffle for the best position, their cameras whirring. Chloe wrenches her hand from Stephen's. The determined click of her heels on the tiled floor echoes through the vast space, silencing the murmurs behind. She strides into the middle of the floor and stops, her eyes focused on me like malicious lasers. She's shaking, pain and fury tearing her apart.

Two security officers by the entrance hurry up the steps and then stop, not sure what to do. They glance at each other and then spread their feet, standing there like officious guards with their chests puffed out.

Chloe's fingers curl into fists and uncurl as she watches me approach. Her chest rises and falls. Perspiration beads on her forehead. Her unblinking eyes stare into mine, focusing her anger. Her breathing increases as I stop about a yard from her.

For what seems like minutes, we stare at each other, oblivious to everything around us.

I clear my throat. "I'm so sorry about Charlotte."

She doesn't move. She doesn't blink. Her eyes seem empty, like her soul maybe. Time seems to stop as I wait.

A strange, almost eerie smile starts to form on her lips. She takes a step closer. The smile transforms into pure hatred as her hand swings through the air. The slap stings my cheek and knocks my head sideways. I wobble, but stand firm, looking straight back at her.

"You killed my baby. My poor, sweet, innocent little baby."

Her voice sounds hoarse and empty, trembling with emotions she can barely keep in check. I don't know how she's holding herself together, but I admire this young woman. I wish I could help her, ease the pain a little by giving her the answer she needs.

But how will condemning her father and uncle help her?

"Don't you have anything to say?" she cries.

"Do you want to talk about what happened?"

"Talk?" She shrieks with hysterical disbelief. "I don't want to talk! I want you to kill you!"

This time, I catch her wrist before her hand makes contact with my face. I hold it there, a few inches from my face.

"I hope someone you loves dies," she says, her voice as chilling as the ice in her eyes. "I hope you have to watch someone you love fade away while you stand there, helpless to do anything."

She wrenches her hand away. "Maybe then you'll know how I feel."

She strides straight for the exit, head high, tears running down her pale cheeks. Her parents rush across, but she brushes them aside and hurries down the steps, almost colliding with the security officers. For a moment, the reporters and photographers have a dilemma. Do they follow her or turn on me?

As I'm rooted in the middle of the foyer, they press forward, hurling questions at me. But all I can hear are Chloe Burke's words, pounding inside my head. 'I hope someone you love dies', she said. 'Maybe then you'll know how I feel.'

Peach's voice breaks through the haze. "Mr Fisher, Have you anything to say about Miss Burke's allegations?"

"Do you refute them?" Tommy asks.

I look up to the half landing. Danni shakes her head.

"Gentlemen, please," I say, raising my hands to calm them. "Chloe Burke lost her daughter last night. She's suffering more than you or I can ever know or imagine. Our thoughts should be with her and her family."

"Yes, but do you refute her allegations?" Peach asks.

"Have your goats tested negative?" Tommy asks. "Or positive?"

I turn and head for the door, pursued by the pack.

Peach tries to push in front. "She's accused you of killing her daughter,"

"While you were entertaining an attractive woman," Tommy says, struggling to keep up.

Peach reaches the door first and blocks my escape. "What do you have to say about that, Mr Fisher?"

One of the security guys belatedly strides over, but I raise a hand to stop him.

"Mr Peach, you've just witnessed the devastation E. coli can cause."

"Sure, spread by animals like goats," Tommy says.

"What about undercooked meat and poultry, vegetables and salads contaminated by faecal matter?" I ask. "As an environmental health officer, I need to be sure of the facts before I make accusations."

Tommy moves closer, sweating more than usual. "Are you saying your goats didn't cause the infection?"

Suddenly, everyone's closing in, waiting for my answer. I glance up at Danni and Gemma on the half landing.

"I'm asking you to wait until you have all the facts," I reply.

Tommy smirks. "Yeah, like you do."

Peach steps aside, realising I'm not going to say more, and I slip through the door.

The reporters drift away, but the TV crew remain. The presenter talks to her colleagues and then starts to talk to camera. In the surge a moment ago, I didn't notice her or the cameraman, who must have been filming from the side. She's already interviewed Chloe and her parents for her feature on this evening's local news.

She has footage of Chloe Burke slapping me. What else does she need?

I return to the second floor. The atmosphere in the office chills to sub-zero when I walk in. Lucy and Nigel look away, clearly uncomfortable. Gemma ignores me, busy tapping away at her keyboard.

"Okay, what's wrong?" I ask.

Silence.

"You clearly know what happened, so what's your problem?"

Gemma's chair tumbles to the floor as she springs to her feet. "Why didn't you tell Mrs Burke about the manure?"

Nigel and Lucy nod their support.

"When we've sampled at the smallholding and have positive results, we will. And we'll tell her in private, not with cameras rolling."

"You bottled it, you mean."

Normally, I'd expect Lucy to make such an accusation, but Gemma seems to have taken my actions personally.

"Gemma, you heard Danni," I say.

"Since when did you listen to Danni?" She moves in between Lucy and Nigel's desks. "The papers will say we're incompetent. They'll claim you're protecting your sanctuary."

"Is that what you think? All of you?" When no one answers, I sigh, more annoyed than disappointed. "Clearly you do."

"You had a chance to show everyone we weren't at fault," Gemma says, arms folded.

"How would that have helped? Hasn't Chloe Burke suffered enough? She was falling apart in front of me."

"Yeah, especially when she slapped you."

"What, you think I should have slapped her back?"

"The samples I took saved your sanctuary, Kent. Why couldn't you save us?"

She brushes past me and storms out of the office. Nigel and Lucy look away, but I know they agree with Gemma. Maybe they're right. Maybe I should have defended my team. But if the Burkes find out how Gemma obtained the manure samples …

Outside the office, Kelly's neutral smile and silence confirm I'm in the brown stuff.

As I reach the stairs, Gemma comes out of the toilets. She dabs her mouth with a tissue and strides past as if I don't exist.

I can't face returning to the sanctuary and a frosty reception from Sarah, so I drive to Mayfield. On the High Street, I stop and take a closer look at Walters' shop. The closed sign is on the door and the drawn curtains upstairs suggest he's still in bed. Further down the High Street, I peel off and follow a narrow road, peppered with parked cars. I squeeze into a parking space and walk between the old cottages and houses, turning left up a steep lane that leads back to the High Street.

My calves and quads feel tight when I reach the High Street and it takes a few seconds to catch my breath. I peer through the window of Walters' shop. With no meat or food on display, he's clearly closed, but he could still be around.

I walk back down the lane, stopping at the double wooden doors that access his rear yard. With a glance each way to make sure no one's around, I turn the wrought iron handle and lift the latch. Again, I check each way before slowly pushing the gate open. Inside, I close the gate behind me, scan the yard, and head for cover between the red Nissan Qashqai and the wall. From here, I look around me, surprised by how many stainless steel units Walters has dumped. Tables, shelving and under-counter refrigerators teeter in stacks, ready to topple onto the white delivery van that looks like it screeched to a halt in the middle of the yard.

From the steel plated back door, which is locked, a narrow passage follows the back wall to the corrugated lean-to that covers the walk-in chillers. I negotiate several piles of cardboard, which are turning to mush as they absorb the grey, fatty pond around the gully that can no longer drain the sink waste. Once past the sludge, my route to the chiller remains clear. Like many older models, the door slides to one side. I will have to release the lever and heave the door towards me before I can slide it open.

Only the sound of traffic penetrates the yard. The compressors for the chiller are not running. Whether they're between chill cycles or shut down, I won't know until I go inside. The iron lever remains firm, defying my efforts to move it. I spread my legs, brace myself, and then pull again. With a creak and a groan, the lever moves towards me and the door seal breaks. I drag the door toward me and then across a few feet on warped and corroded runners.

Next time I'll come armed with WD40 and a crowbar.

The air inside's warm and smells rancid, which doesn't bode well. I peer into the empty space, clad with plastic sheeting and a pressed steel floor. A rusted hanging rail weaves its way across the ceiling, finishing its journey adjacent to a braced steel shelf. The hole above, masked by cobwebs, heavy with dust, reveals where the compressor once sat. A glance to my left reveals two chest freezers, hiding in the shadows along the side wall. I reach up and flick the switch on the wall, but the light doesn't come on.

I open the camera app on my phone and take a couple of shots, recoiling from the brightness of the flash. Then, I walk over to the chest freezers and I slide my fingers around the handle of the first. I take aim with my camera and lift. The lid resists for a moment and then lets out a long groan as the rusty hinges lose the battle.

Inside, it's empty and clean, though the air smells stale. Even the plastic seals are spotless. I look again and can't help laughing. Like I'm going to find a body, right?

I move over to the second freezer. The moment the seal breaks, a putrid smell knocks me backwards. The lid thuds down. Coughing and choking, I stagger back.

Then I notice Todd Walters in the doorway, cleaver in hand.

TWENTY-NINE

"I thought I saw a rat."

It's feeble, but better than a quip about chilling out.

Walters remains in the doorway, his face in shadows, his silence unnerving. Will he lock me inside and leave me to rot until I smell like the contents of the freezer?

Walk-in chiller doors have an internal release in case you get shut inside. During hygiene inspections, I never enter a walk-in unless I've checked the release works. Some need a little coaxing. A few are broken, damaged or missing, usually on older models.

It's impossible to tell with this model from where I'm standing, back pressed against the wall. I'm trapped inside a small room with nothing to hide behind. I scan the hanging rail, hoping for a forgotten meat hook I could use to defend myself.

"You're probably wondering why I'm here," I say, sliding my phone into my pocket. "My friend, Mike – he's the burly Jamaican guy who runs Mike's Mighty Munch on the Uckfield bypass – runs a second hand catering equipment business. I'm sure you've come across him on your travels. He's parking the van down the lane and should be along at any moment."

Walters remains silent and still.

"I knew you were having a clear out, so I thought I'd check to see if there was anything we could buy. These two units look fine. You'll need to clean this one out," I say, wishing I could get the stench out of my nostrils. "How about fifty quid for the pair?"

He lumbers inside, blocking out a lot of light. "Do you think my Stacey's in there? Isn't one body in a freezer enough for you?"

I sidle along the back wall as he strolls up to the freezers. He grips the handle and raises the lid, oblivious to the putrid stench that fills the room, clawing at my nose and lungs. He beckons me over with the cleaver.

"It won't kill you," he says. "I didn't know the power had gone or I'd have moved the stuff inside. I paid good money for these plucks. Come and see for yourself."

The cleaver makes a sloshing sound as he disturbs the contents, releasing another wave of nauseous fumes. Though I'm tempted to run, Walters is hardly acting like he's about to chop me into little pieces.

I walk over and stretch my neck to peer inside. A tangle of bovine hearts, lungs and spleens swim in their putrid juices. As nausea turns my stomach, I rush outside.

"He joins me a few seconds later, closing the door with ease. "You look like you've seen a ghost."

For a moment in there I thought I'd become one.

"Thanks, but I need to go."

"Not before you tell me why you're sneaking around my yard. You think I've done my Stacey in, don't you?"

He sounds intrigued rather than angry. Then again, he's holding a cleaver, dripping rancid blood over the concrete. Wedged into a narrow passageway between old catering equipment and the back wall of his shop, I'm going nowhere fast.

"I don't think you've told me everything," I say, wondering if my theory's in tatters. "You knew Daphne Witherington, right?"

He grins and rubs his thumb across the cleaver blade, checking how sharp it is. "Miller bragged about fleecing Witherington and setting up as a promoter. He had contacts at the Glastonbury Festival and was on the lookout for talent."

Walters turns the cleaver in his hand. "He meant my Stacey. He knew she'd love to sing at Glastonbury. When I told him, he laughed. Said my Stacey should stick to pubs and clubs."

He slams the back of the cleaver down on a stainless steel table. The noise reverberates through the enclosed yard, startling a couple of doves on the wall. Several fridges and units tremble and sway, ready to fall.

"That's why I beat the shit out of him." Walters' grim smile is tempered with regret. "And then a month later, he takes off with my Stacey. He took her to get even, didn't he?"

I wish I knew. "I have to go," I say.

He pushes out his arm and blocks my escape with the cleaver. "What were you looking for in the freezer? You think I chopped someone up and made sausages?"

"Colonel Witherington was a magistrate. So was his wife, Daphne. You were prosecuted for assaulting –"

"A tax inspector. I know. I would have gone down but for that woman. So, why would I want to kill her?"

"I had to make sure, Todd."

"Then why didn't you ask instead of sneaking around?"

He lowers his arm and shuffles along the back wall, walking through the fat oozing out of his drains. When he reaches his Qashqai, he stops. "Would you be interested in this?" he asks, patting the bonnet. "Three years old, one careful driver."

Though tempted, I'd prefer blue not red.

Then I realise what a fool I've been. When Daphne, Stacey and Marcie disappeared, a black car was spotted nearby, not a red one.

Trade remains brisk at Mike's Mighty Munch from my arrival at midday until I leave a little after one. While Mike serves his large portions, I devour a bacon and egg roll, followed by a chocolate-coated flapjack, and three mugs of tea. We manage to squeeze in ten minutes together during two cigarette breaks.

He listens to my summary, making no comment other than a chuckle at my recent encounter with rotting tripe. Then, with a final pull on his cigarette, he homes in on the headless corpse and McGillicuddy.

"Doesn't that strike you as a bit convenient?" he asks.

"What, the corpse or McGillicuddy?"

"You identify a third victim and almost immediately a body appears, just after McGillicuddy disappears."

"You agree the three women are connected?"

"I didn't say that, pal. I'm saying it seems too convenient."

He returns to serve a couple of plumbers and three men from the Environment Agency. While the burgers are cooking, he hands me another mug of stewed, lukewarm tea.

"Are you saying someone knows I've linked Marcie's disappearance to the others?" I ask when he joins me for a second cigarette break.

He rolls his shoulders. "Perhaps your killer's closer than you think."

That's when I realise how many people know what I'm doing. Those around me, like Niamh, Davenport, Gemma and Richard, to Miller, Walters, even Baxendale. It has to be someone who knew Daphne, Stacey and Marcie – someone who drives a black car or cab.

Mike nods when I explain. "Now you're starting to think like a detective, pal. Now focus on the motive. Why were these women abducted and killed?"

"No idea. I've only just established a connection."

"Your caterer," he says, pulling out another cigarette.

"No, they all left personal possessions behind. They left without warning but thought they'd be returning, which is why they didn't take anything with them."

He considers this for a moment. "They knew their abductor and went willingly, blindly even. Something connects them to the killer. Something in their history perhaps."

I smile, impressed by his logic as much as I'm dismayed at how dense I've been.

"Or they all ran off with secret lovers," he says with a grin.

"Don't do that," I say, making no effort to hide my irritation. "For a moment there, I thought you were talking revenge."

"I'm trying to demonstrate how flimsy theories are without facts. Either the abductor is the connection or your three women have something in common."

"They're so different, Mike."

"How do you know? They were all unhappily married, weren't they? They share something in common. Or someone." He pats me on the back and grins. "And that's before we even consider the fourth victim."

"The headless corpse? You think it's another missing woman?"

He flicks his cigarette into the gravel. "Why not?"

"Then why cut off her head? No, it has to be one of the three."

He pats me on the back. "So, find out if McGillicuddy drove a black car."

I stroll back to my Ford Fusion, eager to speak to Alice or the Colonel. I'm hardly back on the main road when Niamh calls. "Are you on hands-free?" she asks. "Only you sound like you're in a tunnel. Pull over and ring me back."

I stop in the next layby, occupied by one of Mike's competitors, who has no customers at the moment. Mike will be delighted.

"Sarah's tested the goats," Niamh tells me. "She left five minutes ago and not a reporter in sight, so you can come back now."

"I'm not hiding from Sarah."

"Of course you are. Anyway, that's not why I rang. I forgot to mention I'm off to Charleston this afternoon. You can update me on the headless body this evening."

I settle back in the seat, realising how easy it is for someone to keep track of my investigation.

Too easy.

I reach the DGH in Eastbourne at around one thirty, parking up the hill as usual. With my telescopic umbrella in one hand, I set off, buttoning my jacket with the other. I want to know why neither the Colonel nor Alice mentioned McGillicuddy, but it seems I'll have to wait a little longer. I duck into a bus shelter to take Gemma's call.

"Have you seen the Tollingdon Tribune website?" she asks.

"No."

"I don't know what you said to Tommy Logan, but he's going for the jugular. He's got you having a night out with stunning blonde, Yvonne Parris, while poor, vulnerable Charlotte Burke perishes in hospital. There's even a photo of you with your head under the table, looking up Yvonne's skirt."

"I dropped a bottle."

"As opposed to your guard?"

"Someone's trying to discredit me, Gemma."

"Chloe Burke?"

"Why not?" I ask, sounding like Mike. "You saw her this morning."

"How would she know you were going out in the evening?"

One day I'll stop jumping to conclusions. "Yeah, you're right. Are you feeling better?"

"Why shouldn't I be? No one's calling me a heartless, self-centred rat."

I end the call, wondering if there's something she's not telling me. Then with a smile, I stop speculating. She'll tell me when she's ready.

No, she'll tell Richard, of course.

I push the thought from my mind and ring Tommy Logan. He picks up straight away, announcing his full name in his pompous drawl.

"It's the heartless, self-centred rat here, Tommy. Let's talk about last night."

"It's always a pleasure to discuss your less than admirable behaviour, dear boy, but I gave you an opportunity to comment last night and you didn't take it."

"Who told you I'd be in La Neapolitan? And don't say a little bird."

"You were sitting by the window. How could I possibly miss you when you were with such a ravishing young lady?"

"Come on, Tommy. Charlotte Burke dies and you just happen to be passing the restaurant where I'm eating?"

"You're starting to sound paranoid, dear boy."

"Who told you Charlotte Burke had died?"

"You know a reporter's sources are as sacrosanct as the confessional. You should be asking your people why they didn't tell you. Then again, you were removed from the investigation."

I cut him off before I say something I'll regret. Someone tipped him off and as only Yvonne knew where I'd be, the choices are limited. So are mine when I reach the Michelham Unit. Alice has returned to Friston.

"Does that mean he's better?" I ask the nurse.

"He's stable at the moment."

That means he could go downhill at any time.

I head uphill to my car, pursued by a howling wind that turns my umbrella inside out. Drenched, and in need of new umbrella, I slide into the car. When a little life returns to my fingers, courtesy of the heating system, I ring Alice, but there's no answer. Twenty minutes later, after crawling behind the bus along the winding road to Jevington and Friston, I reach Belmont. She's coming out of the door, but beckons me inside.

"How's the Colonel?" I ask, wiping my shoes on the thick mat.

She looks as tired as her crumpled blue slacks and white blouse. Dull eyes peer through strands of hair that have escaped her tight bun.

"I don't think he'll last the night," she says, her voice filled with resignation. "He's clinging on for news about Mrs Witherington. Is she the woman they found?"

"It's too early to tell. Shall I make us a cup of tea?"

She shakes her head and fetches her raincoat from the back of an oak chair. "I must return to the hospital."

"Before you do, would you tell me about McGillicuddy?"

"Ross? You don't think he has anything to do Mrs Witherington's disappearance, surely?"

"I'm asking you, Alice."

She laughs as if my suggestion's ridiculous. "They liked to walk on the Downs and along the coast, but who doesn't?

He taught her to use his fancy camera so she could take photographs to help her with her paintings."

"How did the Colonel feel about that?"

Her back straightens. "Are you asking if he was jealous?"

"Was he?"

She shrugs the coat over her shoulders as she talks.

"Colonel Witherington worshipped his wife, Mr Fisher. He fell in love with her the first time he saw her, even though she was married to Spencer Ellis. He was a renowned author and a magistrate like Daphne. They'd moved to Sussex from London and joined the local bench. That's where Colonel Witherington first met her."

"Did they have an affair?"

She laughs. "My, you do have a suspicious mind. Be careful it doesn't bite you."

"Too late for that, Alice. So, tell me about them."

"Mrs Ellis – Daphne – was devoted to her husband. He had motor neurone disease, which eventually reduced him to an invalid. He died about eight years ago and the whole of Pevensey came out to watch the procession. She took him to the cemetery in a horse drawn carriage. It was so beautiful and dignified."

"I assume the Colonel attended."

She nods. "We were both there. Colonel Witherington wanted to help, but I rather got the impression someone else was looking after her."

"Who?"

She leads me into the main reception room, decorated with Regency red and yellow wallpaper above the low level oak panelling. Enormous leather sofas congregate around a sturdy oak table that sits a few feet from a huge brick fireplace. Alice's shoes squeak on the polished boards as she navigates to a dresser in the far corner. She points out two gold framed photographs among the porcelain figurines.

"Colonel Witherington married her about nine months after Spencer's death. They held the reception at Birling Manor in East Dean."

The first photograph shows Daphne in an elegant cream dress, trimmed with lace, while the Colonel's in full uniform, medals gleaming. She's certainly an attractive woman with a distracted smile and big blue eyes that seem focused on a dream. The second photograph shows the happy couple with Alice and Davenport, who's standing next to Daphne.

"Davenport was looking after her," I say, impressed by his tailored suit, straining over a stocky chest. "He's lost some weight since."

"Alasdair gave her away," Alice says, taking the photograph from me. "Her parents died when she was young. When Spencer died, Alasdair became a great comfort. "That's why he's so good at his job."

"Didn't his wife die recently?"

"So sad," she says, straightening the photographs. "Angelina was a lot younger, something of a wild child, I'm told. Some say she married Alasdair to escape her domineering father, but on the occasions I saw them, they were so in love it made me feel uncomfortable."

I've met couples who can't keep their hands to themselves in public.

"Her parents are hot blooded Italians. That didn't help," she says, shaking her head. "They never took to Alasdair, especially when they married in the registry office. When Angelina became ill, they blamed him, of course. There was a terrible argument and she refused to see them again. Mind you," she says with a wry shake of the head, "that pales in comparison to the kerfuffle over the funeral."

"What happened?" I asked, following her out of the room.

"The family wanted a big church ceremony, as you can imagine. She'd asked to be cremated, so Alasdair went ahead, despite threats from the family."

"Threats?"

"Abusive calls, solicitor letters. Alasdair had a breakdown and Colonel Witherington stepped in to keep the business ticking over."

"I didn't realise they knew each other so well."

"They've been friends for years. Colonel Witherington advised Alasdair when Angelina's family continued to hound him. Ghastly people," she says with a shudder. "They live near Sovereign Harbour in Eastbourne in a house that looks like a castle. It has turrets and towers at each end. Colonel Witherington would never have permitted that in Downland."

"No," I say, wondering why he never opposed Birchill's planning application to build Tombstone Adventure Park. "The Colonel was vigorous in defending our landscape."

"He's vigorous about everything. That's the trouble." Alice picks up a hessian bag and walks to the front door. "Mrs Witherington thought the strain would be too much for him, what with his council work and commitments, but he told her to stop fussing. Then she went missing, as you know."

"Presumably Davenport had returned to work by then?"

"Of course," she replies, opening the door. "They discussed her disappearance at length when the police couldn't find her. He suggested Colonel Witherington ask you for help."

"Davenport recommended me? He never said."

"Oh, he's far too modest," she replies, waiting until I've followed her outside before slamming the door.

I'm still parked in the drive ten minutes after she drives away, wondering what else the Colonel kept from me – like a copy of Davenport's police statement. Had Mike not uncovered it, I would never have known about it.

Eyes closed, I think back to the conversation in Davenport's antiquated office, trying to recall what's bugging me. What did he say? That's right. He said he didn't understand how I could help Colonel Witherington.

Then why recommend me?

Davenport's mobile goes straight to voicemail.

"Hi, Alasdair, I understand you recommended my services to Colonel Witherington. Why didn't you tell me?"

More to the point, why didn't the Colonel tell me?

Shortly after three, I pull up outside Tollingdon Funeral Services. The blinds on the front windows and door are down, but there's no CLOSED sign. I jump out and take the stone steps two at a time. The front door's locked. After rattling it a couple of times I retreat down the steps, pausing when I spot light escaping through a gap in the wooden cellar flaps.

Maybe someone's working after all.

I drive around the block and down the narrow lane to the rear entrance, pleased to find the gates open. Yvonne's red MGB almost collides with mine as I drive in. She reverses back into her parking space, while I take Davenport's.

She winds down the window. "Have you come to apologise?"

I let my window down, squinting as the drizzle hits my face. "I'm looking for Davenport. Do you know where he is, when he's due back?"

"If I did, I wouldn't tell you after the way you treated me last night."

"The way I treated you? Have you any idea how much trouble you've caused?"

"Me? You're the one who accused me of setting you up."

"You booked the table," I retort, starting the car.

"I didn't book the table, Alasdair did."

Finally, I ram the gearstick into reverse. "What, he's your social secretary now?"

She screeches her car forward and across mine to cut off my escape. She hauls herself out of the car, slams the door, and strides over, her expression darker than the clouds overhead.

"I don't know what's going on," she says, bending till her face is inches from mine, "but I didn't think you'd show, so I never booked a table. Then Alasdair offered to join me if you didn't show and said he could get us a good table, okay?"

She gives me an angry glare and returns to her MGB. As she screeches off down the lane, I don't move, barely aware of the rain that's hitting against my face.

“When Charlotte died, her mother didn’t ring Tommy,” I say, thinking aloud.

Chloe Burke rang Davenport. Or her father did, probably to arrange for the body to be collected.

Then Davenport tipped off Tommy.

THIRTY

Sometimes my mind works so fast it's frightening. It's not inspiration. There's no such thing. It's the culmination of a subconscious process that takes pieces of information over a period of time and works out how they all fit together. And when it does, the mind serves up the answer with a triumphant shout.

When Todd Walters doesn't answer his phone, I drive to Mayfield, wishing the rain would clear. It's only four o'clock and it looks like dusk. The High Street's deserted and many businesses have closed early, leaving me a choice of parking spaces. Walters lumbers up to the front door within seconds of my knocking.

"You had second thoughts about the Qashqai?" he asks, letting me in. "Only someone in the village took her out for a drive earlier."

"I'm here about Stacey. Did she lose anyone close in the last couple of years?"

"Dead, you mean?"

I nod. "Someone in her family, a close friend."

"No, she didn't have much family. There was the bloke she shacked up with before we met. The drugs got him," he says, miming an injection into the arm.

"When was this?"

He scratches his head. "Eight, maybe nine years ago. He lived in Brighton, but his family came from near here. Cross in Hand, I think. Stacey said they bought a load of sausage rolls and savouries for the wake and we used to laugh about it because we could have met a couple of years before we did."

"Do you know who did the service?"

"The funeral? Sure, Tollingdon Funeral Services. When my mother died a couple of years ago, Stacey recommended them. She said Alasdair Davenport was a great help when her bloke died. He even popped round a couple of times to check on her, make sure she was all right and that. Now, that's what I call service."

I'd call it something else, but Walters doesn't need to know that.

"So, what's this got to do with my Stacey?" he asks, looking expectant.

"Loose ends," I say, with a nod to Lieutenant Columbo.

As I turn to leave, he grabs my arm. "Is she dead?"

I don't know what to say, which tells Walters all he needs to know. I feel awful, watching the hope drain from his face, but I can't lie to him. Neither can I prove she's dead.

Not yet.

In the car, I make some notes. I'm about to drive off when Gemma phones.

"The E.coli in the manure matches the strain that infected the family," she says. "Nigel and I have just come back from the smallholding. He won't be selling any more manure."

"Serve a notice on him," I say, "just to be sure."

"Kent, he's absolutely gutted. He's infected his niece. Once the family find out, he's … He wasn't to know his manure would infect Charlotte, was he?"

A small light flickers in my mind and then goes out.

"Anyway, you're off the hook, Kent. Why don't I come over with a curry to celebrate?"

"Sure," I say without thinking.

When I reach Tollingdon and join the rush hour traffic, I'm still going over what Gemma said, trying to figure out what sparked off something in my head. I'm still searching when I reach Baxendale's house at a quarter past five. He's in the bedroom, wandering about in his underwear, holding a shirt against himself as he sways his hips in time to the music that spills out of the small casement window.

I ring the doorbell and step back, head bowed against the rain. My damp trousers stick to my knees and thighs, while my fleece has lost the battle. Wrapped in a bathrobe, Baxendale opens the door and looks at me in surprise, clearly expecting someone else.

"I thought my taxi was early," he says, stepping aside. He glances down the road before closing the door. "I'm off out with some mates."

"Bit early, isn't it?"

"We're off to Brighton."

"By taxi?"

"No, only to the train station." He pulls a blue and white striped scarf from a coat hook and holds it above his head with both hands. "Seagulls!"

"You're off to watch Brighton," I say, calling on my miniscule knowledge of football. "In which case, I'll get to the point. You told me Marcie's father died."

"Yes, about seven years ago."

"Do you know who organised the funeral?"

"Your council. Marcie's dad had nothing, just the rags he lounged around in. And Marcie was a kid. She couldn't afford to pay for it."

When someone dies without money, or relatives who can arrange the funeral, the council steps in. Tollingdon Funeral Services have held the contract for welfare burials for as long as I can remember.

"Why are you interested in Marcie's dad?" Baxendale asks.

"I'm interested in the undertaker, Alasdair Davenport."

"I remember him. He steered Marcie through the worst, arranging everything, popping round to see her and that. At first I thought he was a letch, but –"

"What do you mean?"

"Well, Marcie may have been fifteen and a bit overweight, but she was as sexy as hell. She dressed like a punk, but that only seemed to exaggerate her appeal. She had a gleam in her eyes when she looked at you and …"

"You thought Davenport couldn't resist."

"I should know. I lost count of how many times I got aroused in class." He blushes and drifts into an uncomfortable silence.

"Enjoy your football," I say, moving towards the door.

"Hang on," Baxendale calls. "I'm not saying he did anything."

No, but he's thinking it.

I'm still thinking when Baxendale's taxi comes and goes. His neighbour arrives home, glaring at me to let me know I've parked in her space. And the rain continues to fall, drumming on the roof of the car like frustrated fingers.

Davenport met the three missing women at funerals seven or eight years ago. His concern for them may have extended beyond the professional. Nothing came of this because he later married Angelina, whom he adored. Now she's dead and three women are missing.

What am I missing?

Then there's the headless body at Meadow Farm. If it's a fourth missing woman, why remove her head?

Maybe the police will find more bodies on the farm and arrest McGillicuddy – when they find him, of course. He must have realised his days were numbered when I made the connection with Marcie.

So, who told him?

I'm back to my list of people who know more than they should about my investigation.

I stare at the misted windscreen and turn the fan to full blast. Maybe it'll clear more than the windscreen.

So who's the woman in the freezer? She can't be the only body, but the killer wanted to disguise her identity, presumably to delay the trail to his doorstep. It's as calculated as the abductions, as the fake letter from Stacey Walters that was meant to throw me off the trail.

Then I start laughing.

The headless body has nothing to do with Daphne, Stacey or Marcie. It's meant to throw me off the trail, but it's identified the killer instead.

There aren't many people who can produce a body at short notice.

Half an hour later, thanks to more rush hour traffic, I reach the Sovereign Leisure Centre in Eastbourne. I take a left at the roundabout and follow Prince William Parade towards the harbour, wondering how long it will take me to find a house that looks like a castle. As I pass the sewage works, hidden inside a large brick fort, I realise the modern estates cover one, maybe two or three, square miles.

As I come around the small roundabout into Atlantic Drive, I spot a couple of dog walkers. Dressed in waterproof coats and trousers, and bent against the rain, it takes a toot of the horn to get their attention.

"I'm looking for a house that looks like a castle."

"You mean Castello Mia," the woman says, pointing. "Drive down until you reach the close on the left, just before the roundabout. You can't miss the house."

A couple of minutes later I'm parked outside a detached house with a stone clad front elevation that rises above the eaves into a crenellated parapet wall, complete with small turrets at either end. One has a flagpole, flying the Italian flag. All it lacks is a drawbridge and a moat, though it looks like the rain has created a new pond in the middle of the lawn.

I nip past a blue Fiat Ulysse on the driveway and step inside the arch to an enclosed porch with an oak door, lined with riveted battens. I glance around for a metal pull, attached to a church bell, but find only a video intercom. I press the button, listen to the static and then hold up my ID card.

"Kent Fisher, environmental health officer. Could I have a quick word?"

Manfredo Tucci turns out to be a short, stocky man with dark, almost black eyes that brood beneath bushy eyebrows. He has thick, wavy hair that's turning silver, and a solemn face, dominated by a large nose. Though I estimate he's in his fifties, years of smoking have aged him, if his nicotine fingers and stained teeth are anything to go by.

"To what do I owe this visit?" he asks in a heavy Italian accent. "My wife only make pasta for the church. It's not a business, no matter what these …" His hands waft about in the air as he speaks. "… neighbours tell you. They don't like my castle, no? It's a magnificent, don't you think?"

I'm not sure whether mediaeval castles had surround sound and a bar in the corner of the living room, but what do I know? The living room has a warm, traditional feel, thanks to the brown leather three-piece suite, chunky oak furniture and a wood burning stove in the stone hearth. I'm drawn to the large dresser, filled with shelf after shelf of china ornaments and figurines. Many are bride and groom, holding a cache of sugared almonds in white netting.

"We give to the guests at the wedding as a keepsake," he says, walking behind the bar. "You look like a man who would enjoy Peroni, or perhaps you'd prefer some Chianti?"

I shake my head and sidle across to the family photographs on a sideboard unit. Mr and Mrs Tucci have two sons, one daughter and plenty of grandchildren.

I point to a photograph of a serious-looking woman in her early 20s. She's wearing tight jeans, a blue fitted top and high heels. Her thick black hair cascades over her shoulders, almost hiding her small face. She has a cheeky smile, wide, olive eyes, and a prominent nose that may account for her self-conscious air.

"Is this Angelina?"

"How do you know her? Who are you, Mr Inspector? What are you doing here?"

He's in front of me, trying to force me away from the photographs. I stand my ground despite the nauseating reek of cigarettes.

"Fredo, let him speak." His wife, dressed in a black dress with a matching scarf, walks in with a tray of espresso cups and saucers. Short and overweight, she walks with a stoop. Her tanned skin looks ready to crack open along the many lines that score her cheeks and forehead. "If he knows Angelina, maybe he's here to help."

"Or cause more trouble."

When we're seated, she asks me why I'm interested in Lina. "She's dead almost two years," she says, making the sign of the cross. Then she hands her husband the sugar bowl. He tips four heaped spoons of sugar into his coffee.

Manfredo stares at me. "Why are you interested, Mr Health Inspector?"

"I believe she was ill for some time."

"She wasn't ill," he says, unable to speak in anything other than an agitated voice. "He made her ill. Every day I curse that man for what he did to my angel."

"Fredo," his wife says in a soft voice, "she was always weak as a child, getting every infection. If someone at school had a cold, she would get it. And always you pamper her, Fredo, letting her stay home from school."

"Mama, didn't I let her stay out late when she was a teenager? Did I criticise her friends?"

His wife snorts. "No one was good enough for you."

"Especially that man, Davenport." For a moment it looks like he's about to crush the small cup between his fingers. He turns to me, finger jabbing the air. "He made her ill."

"How did she meet him?"

"Work experience," Mrs Tucci replies.

Fredo snorts, his arms are on the move again. "Would you let your daughter work in a place full of dead people? I forbid her to work there, but would she listen to her papa?"

He slams the cup on the table, spilling coffee into the saucer. "No, she stays out late, coming home drunk and giggling," he says, on his feet now. "Then she tells me she make love to Alasdair Davenport."

"You accused her, Fredo. She said it to spite you."

"Mama," he says, taking her face in his hands, "he got her drunk. She was so young."

"No, Fredo. She was a woman, not a child."

He steps back, tears of rage in his eyes. "He take advantage of her. He never deny it."

"He married her, Fredo. They were happy together."

"Until he poisoned her."

I watch as his anger melts into sadness and despair. His wife goes to him and squeezes his hand. "She was ill, Fredo. So ill. Why are so interested?" she asks, turning to me.

"Davenport's interested in my stepmother."

Fredo laughs. "See, mama. The inspector doesn't like him either."

"Fredo, tell him about Lina's illness. Tell him what you saw when you visited."

He sits, his fingers hovering close to the packet of cigarettes in his breast pocket. He takes a while to compose himself, staring at the floor when he speaks.

"I visit Angelina about three months before she die. She was so thin, like a ghost. She laugh, she joke a little, but she wanted to sleep. All the time, she yawn and doze off."

He sighs and looks up. "I beg her to come home. I go on my knees, but she says her place is with her husband. She says he's looking after her, but he's not a doctor. What does he know about pneumonia? If he'd taken her to hospital she would never have died."

He closes his eyes against the tears and rises. "He killed her."

Moments later, the front door slams after him.

"Lina hated doctors and hospitals," Carmela says. "I don't know why, but she get hysterical. That's why she never go to hospital. When her husband took her, they said it was too late, they couldn't treat her."

"Davenport told you that?"

She nods. "She looked so weak – more like a little girl than a woman. Because she hated hospitals, she never get the antibiotics. Fredo blames himself. He thinks he let his little girl down."

She looks lost for a moment, staring into space. "I always hoped they'd have a little girl because Lina wanted children so much. She tell me they try, but … I don't know what was wrong," she says, looking back at me, "but Lina changed. Maybe she could not have children. Maybe she dies from a broken heart."

Mama blinks back the tears, determined to remain resolute. It must be difficult, losing her daughter and trying to placate her husband. I want to ask more, but I'm clearly intruding. I slip away, not sure she hears me. Outside, Fredo's in the porch, blowing smoke into the rain.

"You're a health inspector," he says as I pass. "You tell me. How does a young woman die from pneumonia? Old people die from pneumonia. Homeless people, alcoholics, people who take drugs - they die from pneumonia because they don't have the strength to fight it."

Charlotte Burke died because her immune system couldn't fight E. coli.

Back in the car I phone Niamh. Her mobile goes to voicemail. "Ring me," I say, starting the car. "I need to tell you something about Davenport."

Though the traffic's thinning, the relentless rain slows my journey out of Eastbourne. Finally, the traffic speeds up and I'm back at the sanctuary, surprised to see Gemma's Volvo parked by the old caravan. I find her on the kitchen floor, playing tug-the-towel with Columbo. The aroma of chicken jalfrezi seeps out of the oven to fill the air.

"Is Niamh with Alasdair?" she asks, rising.

My stomach tightens. "Isn't she back?"

"What's wrong, Kent?"

I ring Davenport. He picks up straight away. "Good evening, Kent. Good of you to ring."

I can hear country music in the background. I try to speak, but my mouth's so dry, it takes me a few seconds. "Can I have a word with Niamh?"

"She's indisposed at the moment," he replies, "but I'm taking good care of her."

That’s what I’m afraid of.

THIRTY-ONE

I grab my raincoat from the back of the door. "Davenport's got Niamh," I tell Gemma.

"What are you talking about?"

"Columbo," I call, turning off the oven. "Here."

I scoop him up and tuck him inside my raincoat, despite his attempts to wriggle free. "Gemma, tell Frances we're taking Columbo," I call, hurrying down the steps. "I need something from the barn."

I put him on the back seat and collect a crowbar and pickaxe from the barn. Gemma jumps into the passenger seat moments later, shaking the rain from her hair.

"What's going on, Kent?"

"Davenport killed Daphne Witherington, Stacey Walters and Marcie Baxendale," I reply, accelerating out of the yard. "He left a body at Meadow Farm to throw us off the trail."

"He did?" She places a hand against the dashboard to steady herself as we swing and bounce along the lane. "Slow down, Kent, or you'll kill us both."

I hold on tight to the steering wheel as the car grazes the verge. Though I know the twists and turns of this lane intimately, I can hardly make out the hedgerows. Even on full speed, the wipers can't cope with the rain that's battering the windscreen.

"Thank you," Gemma says, settling back when I ease off the accelerator. "Now, tell me why Davenport killed those women."

"It was something you said earlier."

"Me? What did I say?"

"Remember Martin Burke, the man with the smallholding. You said he wasn't to know his manure would infect Charlotte."

"What's that got to do with Davenport?"

"His wife, Angelina, died from pneumonia because her immune system couldn't fight the infection."

"You think he infected her with pneumonia?"

I brake hard as we approach the junction with the A27. "No, Gemma, HIV. AIDS."

"I thought there were treatments." She stares at me, looking both doubtful and puzzled at the same time. "People don't die from AIDS, do they?"

"They do when they don't know they're infected," I reply, pulling out and into the stream of traffic heading for Tollingdon. "Angelina had a phobia about hospitals and doctors. She wasn't diagnosed until it was too late."

"How do you know?"

"Her parents told me. They didn't know she had HIV, but it explains why Davenport killed Daphne and the others."

"It does?"

Her sarcasm's starting to irritate me. "Davenport believes one of the women infected him," I say, unable to keep the impatience from my voice.

"So why hasn't he died? Or anyone else?"

She has a point. Without tests, I can't prove anything. "Maybe he's dying, Gemma. I saw a photo of him, taken eight years ago, and he was much stockier then. He's thin and pale now, like he's withering away."

"Maybe he's stopped eating ready meals."

"Will you cut it with the wisecracks?" We jerk to a halt at the traffic lights and I turn to face her. "He's got Niamh. I don't know what he's done to her, but if we don't get there soon, she could be joining the other women he's killed."

"Then you'd best get moving," she says, gesturing at the space that's opened ahead of us.

The driver behind me sounds his horn when I stall the car. I draw a breath and start the car, pulling away smoothly to join the traffic crawling into Tollingdon.

"Look, I'm no expert on HIV, Gemma, but I imagine it's like any infection – some people are stronger and resist it better and for longer."

"I know, but how do you know he had sex with Daphne and Stacey?"

"Don't forget Marcie."

We slow to a halt again. "Come on!" I call, drumming my fingers on the steering wheel. Columbo barks and leaps down from the parcel shelf, panting as he peers between the seats.

Gemma reaches across to still my fingers. "You don't know if she's dead. It's all supposition."

"Deduction," I say, inching the car forward a few yards. "All three women lost someone close seven or eight years ago. Davenport did the funerals. And I checked," I say, before she can challenge me. "All three women also benefitted from his unique aftercare."

"Okay," she says, twisting to tickle Columbo behind his ears, "but if one or all of the women had HIV, how come no one else has been affected?"

"Maybe they have. Maybe they got treatment." With a sigh of relief, we reach the mini roundabout that's slowing the traffic. "And maybe there's a much simpler explanation."

"Go on, Holmes, the suspense is killing me."

With no sign of an end to the stream of traffic around the roundabout, I accelerate into a small gap, forcing the car coming around to brake and slow down. The insistent sound of his horn follows us down the road.

"Davenport embalms the dead," I say, accelerating away. "All it takes is one infected body, one careless moment where he cuts himself, and he's infected."

"He must know the risks, Kent. He'd wear gloves."

"But what if he was rushing, or complacent? It doesn't matter really because he blamed his infection on one of his lovers. He passed it to Angelina without realising until years later when she became ill with pneumonia."

"Then, after his wife died, he took revenge, starting with Daphne." Gemma frowns, looking thoughtful. "Bit extreme, don't you think?"

"Not if you won't accept it's your carelessness that caused the infection."

"Denial, you mean? To avoid accepting the blame, he turns on his former lovers."

"Starting with Daphne. He knows the Colonel's routines and picks a day when she's alone in the house. He calls under some pretext and takes her out for the morning."

Gemma gasps. "That's why she left her paints. She thought she was coming back."

The traffic slows once more as we reach the town centre. I don't know why I glance at the clock, because Davenport's not going to harm Niamh until I'm there. He knows I won't ring the police because he'll kill her the moment he spots a patrol car or an officer on his CCTV.

With razor wire and security cameras, his yard's well protected, like his embalming room.

"How does Colin Miller fit in?" Gemma asks, breaking into my thoughts.

"He was a bonus because he had a history with Stacey. I don't know the exact details, but Davenport tells the Colonel that Miller and Daphne are sleeping together. Davenport knows Miller needs money and sets up an elaborate sting. All Miller has to do is take Daphne out for a meal, drink too much, and tell everyone they're running away together."

Gemma nods. "Davenport sits at the next table to witness everything."

"No, that's what Davenport wants you to think. Miller told me someone threatened to kill him if he went to the restaurant, so he fled to Spain. That was Davenport. Having frightened off Miller, Davenport takes his place and meets Daphne for dinner."

Gemma shakes her head. "Why would she play along if she's expecting Miller?"

"Davenport tells her that Miller's run off with the money and dumped her. He takes Miller's place and persuades her to have something to eat. Then, a week later, Davenport gives the police a false witness statement."

"If Miller went to Spain, how did he buy meat from Walters after Daphne disappeared?"

I smile, enjoying her puzzled frown.

She sighs. "Davenport pretended to be Miller."

"Walters had already caught Miller sniffing around and sent him on his way."

"Davenport sets up Stacey and …" Gemma stares at me. "When did you work it out, Holmes?"

"Much too late."

I drive past Tollingdon Funeral Services, knowing Davenport wants me to enter through the yard, where he can track me on his cameras.

"Davenport laid a trail to Miller," I say, "knowing he was safely tucked away in Spain. Only Miller blew the money and returned to Glastonbury. When I found him, Davenport had to act quickly. He sent the letter from Stacey."

Gemma shudders. "He was planning that letter while we ate dessert."

"It gets worse," I say, turning into the lane that leads to the yard. "Davenport set me up. He told the Colonel to ask me to find Daphne. Alice let it slip this afternoon. Once the Colonel hooked me, all Davenport had to do was stick close to Niamh and follow my progress."

"He was taking a chance, wasn't he?"

"Not really. He'd already disposed of the bodies. That's what undertakers do."

I stop at the gates and dive out into the rain. Inside the car, Columbo barks and paws at the window, eager to join me. With my hood over my head, I peer through the gap between the gates and spot Davenport's black Ford Mondeo in its parking space.

The gates are unlocked.

"In a minute," I tell Columbo, who licks my ear once I'm back in the car. "We're going in through the cellar."

Gemma pulls out her phone. "We should call the police,"

"He'll kill Niamh before they break down the door. He's got cameras everywhere."

"And if you don't call the police, he could kill you."

I speed back up the lane, preferring not to think about it. Once back on the main street, I park a couple of doors up from Tollingdon Funeral Services and retrieve the pick axe and crowbar from the boot.

"Stay here with Columbo," I tell Gemma. "And no matter how much he paws the window, don't open it. Keep him dry."

I pull the hood over my head and make for the cellar. Kneeling on the wet slabs, it takes me seconds to force the padlock and latch. I look around and get to my feet. Thanks to the rain, the streets are empty, except for an occasional taxi flying past. After I dump the tools in the boot, I fuss Columbo.

"I don't want you barking," I say, wishing he'd calm down so I can pick him up.

"I'll bring him," Gemma says. "When you're in the cellar, I'll hand him down. And I'll keep him dry," she adds as I start to speak. "Even if I get soaked in the process."

He settles inside her coat without protest. Mind you, if I was nestled in there, I'd be more than content. He gives me a bark, reminding me to get on with it.

I grab my Maglite and head back to the cellar. I pull back the flaps, hand the Maglite to Gemma, and lower myself into the opening before dropping to the floor. Columbo wriggles as she lowers him into my raised hands, but once I pull him close to my chest, he relaxes. When I set him on the floor, he rushes into the shadows to explore.

"I still think we should call the police, Kent."

I shake my head. "He's got Niamh in the embalming room. She'll be dead the moment they arrive."

"What's to stop him killing her the moment he spots you?"

"He won't get the chance to gloat," I say, hoping I'm right.

She pulls her coat tighter. "Haven't you forgotten something?"

"I don't think so."

"Isn't this where you tell me you're hopelessly in love with me?"

"Not now, Gemma."

"That's what you claimed when you abandoned me at Tombstone," she says, shining the Maglite in my face. "Or have you forgotten?"

How could I forget? "Give me the torch, Gemma."

She lets it go. I just grab it before it smacks me in the face. I'm not so lucky with the cellar flap. It catches me on the head as she closes it with some venom. Thankfully, it's only a glancing blow as my reflexes save me. Seconds later, the second flap thuds down, shutting out the light and the rain.

I congratulate myself on another emotional moment well handled.

I shine the beam around the whitewashed walls, black and blistering with damp. Rows and rows of grey filing cabinets, twisted and rusting, fill half the space. Tables and chairs with musty smelling upholstery, cover the remainder, leaving a passage to a panelled door in the corner. Columbo sniffs the base of the door, his tail wagging hard.

The door opens into a corridor. At the end, brick steps lead up to a door. Nose to the ground, Columbo finds another door to the left and nudges it open. The smell of something like disinfectant seeps out of the room. I recall Davenport telling me the cellar flooded with sewage and call to Columbo.

When he doesn't respond, I go after him. "Shit!"

Columbo's by a four-poster bed, pawing the mattress and whining. It could be a child propped up by pillows, but it's an emaciated woman with lifeless olive eyes. Foundation and rouge colour her sunken cheeks, while her scarlet lips look thin and shrivelled beneath her prominent nose. Thick, black, wavy hair cascades over bony shoulders, protruding into her pink nightdress.

Poor Angelina, embalmed instead of cremated.

When Columbo leaps onto the bed, I snap out of my daze and rush over, grabbing him as he places his paws on her chest. He wriggles and growls when I carry him out of the room and close the door behind me. I lean back against the wall to catch my breath, not sure whether I feel sick or sad.

At the top of the stairs, the door opens into the funeral parlour. On the other side of the door, I find a key in the lock.

Davenport anticipated me entering from the cellar. As usual, he's one step ahead.

I leave Columbo to explore while I make my way to the embalming room, across the corridor from the small kitchen. An intercom on the wall bursts into life as I approach, startling me with the sound of country music.

"Better late than never, Kent."

The lock clicks and I push the door open a few inches. I peer into a storage area lined with tall metal cupboards and shelving. Glass jars, some labelled and filled with a brownish liquid, mingle with empty ones. Boxes of latex gloves, stacked high, fill another shelf. On one side there's a stainless steel bench, where a pump lies prostrate among coils of rubber piping.

At the end of the room, a second door summons me.

I beckon Columbo, who follows me in, nose to the floor, sniffing under the shelves. I wedge the door open with the Maglite and I nip across to the kitchen for the biscuit tin. Armed with digestives, I return to find Columbo, determined to burrow beneath the shelves. He soon comes out when I crumble the digestives and scatter them across the floor.

While he eats, I grab the Maglite like a club and open the second door, quickly sliding through the gap. I pull the door behind me to stop Columbo following. My heel stops the door closing, letting it rest on the latch.

I look up at a gun, aimed at my forehead.

"You're lucky I'm a patient man," Davenport says with a smile.

"You won't mind waiting for the police then."

"Take a look at the screen on the wall behind me."

The monitor shows views from four cameras, one at the front of the building, two in the yard, and one on the deserted lane beyond. Gemma's pacing up and down at the front, glancing at her phone every few seconds.

"Lose whatever you're hiding behind your back and put your hands on your head."

I place the Maglite on the adjacent bench and raise my hands over my head. As he backs away, he reveals Niamh, lying under a white plastic sheet on the ceramic embalming table. She looks so peaceful, it takes me a moment to realise she's naked under the sheet.

"Stay calm," Davenport says from the other side of the table. He smiles and pushes hair back from her face. "I sedated her."

"Before or after you removed her clothes?"

He runs his fingers along the rubber tubing that runs to a pump beneath the table. "Do I detect a hint of jealousy?"

"I'm talking about decency, but you don't know anything about that."

He laughs and holds up a monster stainless steel needle, about four inches long and almost half an inch wide. The sharp point at the end sends a shudder through me.

"It's a trocar, used to remove fluids from the body. Don't worry," he says, running the needle along Niamh's cheek, "she won't feel a thing."

"Is that what you did to Daphne Witherington?"

I look around for something to use against him. Maybe I could batter him to death with the docking station that's playing the rather ironic, *Stand by your Man.*

"Does my music offend you?" he asks, following my gaze. "I can turn it off if you prefer."

"No, no," I reply, aware of Columbo sniffing at the base of the door. "It helps with the ambience."

"It helps to have the right music. When I cremate you on Monday, I'll play *Burning Love* by Elvis."

"I'd prefer *Funeral Pyre* by the Jam," I say, aware of the sweat running down my back. "Or you could bury me to the strains of *Going Underground.*"

"I'm glad your wit hasn't deserted you, Kent."

"Do you mind if I take my coat off? I'm overheating."

"Be my guest. You won't need it in the chiller."

I unzip the coat, sensing I need to make a move. Columbo's getting restless and could bark at any moment

"How did you dispose of the bodies?" I ask, shaking the water from the coat. "Did you put two together in a coffin?"

"You can't squeeze two bodies into one coffin. Think about the health and safety implications of all the extra weight. No, I added a leg here, an arm there, and a head when space permitted."

I fold the coat with the fleece lining on the outside and toss it onto the embalming table next to Niamh. "Who's the woman at Meadow Farm?"

He sniffs and wipes his nose on the sleeve of his lumberjack shirt. "I don't remember. I kept her in reserve, in case I needed her." He uses the tip of the trocar to lift the plastic sheet. "Such a pity," he says peering inside. "Still, I've enjoyed watching you fumble around, wondering if you'd stumble on the truth. It allowed me to spend more time with Niamh."

"Planning a ménage â trois with Angelina downstairs?"

He drops the trocar and strides around the table. He pushes the barrel of the pistol into my chest, his eyes narrow with rage. "Those filthy bitches poisoned me. They robbed me of children and then my wife. Now, we're all going to die long before we should."

"That's not Niamh's fault."

He starts to blink rapidly as his eyes redden. "No, the fault is yours, Fisher." Then he starts to sniff. "Have you brought that wretched dog of yours?"

"It must be his fur on my coat," I reply, enjoying his discomfort.

He steps back, wiping his nose on his sleeve. He grabs my coat and hurls it at me. "Time to say goodbye," he says, taking aim.

"I lied," I say, pointing to the floor. "Columbo's behind you. Bite him, Columbo!"

Davenport can't help looking down. I hurl the coat at him and push open the door. His arms flap as the coat smothers his face. By the time he throws it down, Columbo's biting his ankle. With a sharp cry, he looks down and tries to swat the dog with the gun.

But I'm already on him, grabbing his gun arm and forcing him back against the bench. He smashes into the docking station, ending the music. But he manages to push a hand into my face, forcing me back.

I feel the embalming table against the back of my legs. I cling onto his gun arm as I struggle to remain upright. My other hand tries to fend off Davenport, who's forcing me back. When Columbo bites him once more, he freezes for a moment, wincing with pain. Then I hear a yelp. He pulls back and swivels, wrenching his arm so he can take aim at Columbo.

I kick him hard enough to spoil his aim. The sound of the shot echoes off the harsh surfaces, followed by a second. Somewhere in the confusion, I hear a whine, but I can't see Columbo. My momentary distraction allows Davenport to grab my throat and forces me back until I'm lying across Niamh. He swings the gun round and points it at my head.

I close my eyes a moment before he sneezes over my face. A second sneeze gives me the chance to grab his wrist and force the gun away.

"It wasn't the women who infected you," I say, my fingers tracing along the rubber tubing on the table. "You cut yourself in here."

Another shot rings out as he sneezes again. His grip on my throat loosens. My grip on the trocar tightens.

Davenport now has both hands on the pistol, forcing it towards my head. He squints, barely able to see out of his red, swollen eyes drowning in tears. Then they bulge open as the trocar plunges into the side of his neck.

For a moment he stares at me, looking confused. Then he staggers back, crashing into the bench, a wild hand trying to grab the trocar. The docking station clatters to the floor. Then the pistol as he grabs at the trocar with both hands.

With a cry of agony, he pulls it from his neck.

Blood spurts from his wound. Blood trickles from his mouth as he wheezes.

I grab the pistol as he collapses to the floor.

Then Columbo charges out of nowhere, lips drawn back over his teeth. Davenport raises the trocar.

I fire the three remaining bullets.

THIRTY-TWO

In Colonel Witherington's conservatory, Alice serves tea and fruit cake. Outside in the garden, Columbo pesters Monty, who just wants to lie in peace. I'm delighted the dogs get on so well, especially since Columbo's assumed the role of pack leader.

Alice takes her seat in the final wicker chair and gives me a smile. "Have you taken it all in yet, Mr Fisher?"

I'm still speechless.

Two weeks ago, I spent several hours in the Custody Suite in Eastbourne, answering questions about the incident in Tollingdon Funeral Services. For a while it looked like they would charge me for shooting Davenport in the arm and shoulder. I didn't tell them I was aiming for his heart in case they realised what a lousy shot I was.

Well, I'd never fired a gun before.

Though Davenport couldn't be questioned for another five days due to his neck injuries, he soon confessed to killing Daphne Witherington and Stacey Walters, claiming they poisoned him with HIV. He claimed not to know the identity of the woman in the freezer, though the police soon discovered her head in one of his chillers. He also denied all knowledge of Marcie Baxendale, but confessed to another murder in the Tunbridge Wells area.

The day after my tussle with Davenport, I went to see the Colonel. Though weak, and unable to say much, he thanked me for finding his wife's murderer. When Richard arrived, I left, sensing I wouldn't see the Colonel again.

That night, he passed away in his sleep.

We've just returned from the funeral, arranged by one of Davenport's competitors. Niamh claims she fine, making a show of her bruised shoulder, sustained when I fell on her in the embalming room. It gives her and Gemma the chance to compare injuries, joking that I've left my mark on both of them.

But Niamh knows how close she came to death.

Richard leans forward to take another slice of Victoria sponge. "Do you have any plans for this magnificent house, Kent?"

I still can't believe the Colonel left me his estate. Alice can continue to live in the annex over the garage for as long as she likes, enjoying the substantial legacy he left her.

"Are you sure there's no family?" I ask again.

"Positive," Richard replies. "It's yours."

"But I don't want it."

"Of course you do," Niamh says, having spent all day yesterday touring the house and gardens with Alice. "I'm moving in tomorrow."

"Monty and Columbo get on," Gemma says, glancing out of the window. "It's perfect."

"Maybe you'd prefer Meadow Farm," Richard says.

Niamh agrees. "You can move the sanctuary and tell Birchill where to stick his land."

"You can tell Danni where to stick her job," Gemma says, following me into the garden.

I sit on the stone steps and savour the view across the Downs, knowing I should feel grateful. Columbo trots up, lies down and rests his head against my thigh. His dark eyes look up at me and I know he's all I need, along with my flat, my sanctuary and the job I love.

"Mr Fisher," Alice calls from the conservatory. "There's someone to see you."

I rise and greet Kirk Baxendale, who's gained a few pounds and looks good in a navy blue suit. No wonder, he's found a slim woman with short brown hair, beautiful eyes and a demure, but incredibly sexy smile. It's only when we shake hands that I realise who she is.

"Where did you go, Marcie?" I ask. "I thought you were dead."

"I went to a retreat to work out what I wanted," she says, clinging to Kirk's hand. She looks into his eyes and smiles. "Bit of a no-brainer really."

Gemma gives me her best 'told you so' smirk. "You got that wrong, Super Sleuth."

Like a lot of things, it seems.

Kirk slides his arm around Marcie "We're leaving for the Peak District tomorrow. New school, new home, new start. A bit like you," he says, looking at the house. "From what I hear, it sounds like your problems are over."

I have a feeling they're just beginning.

THE END.

About the Author

Robert Crouch spent almost 40 years working in environmental health, mainly as an inspector, checking hygiene and health and safety standards, but latterly as the manager of a team of officers.

While he enjoyed modest success writing articles and columns for national and trade magazines during the 1990s, it wasn't until he turned to writing crime that he found his true niche. He now writes full time from his home on the South Coast of England, drawing inspiration from the beautiful South Downs and his former job.

If you enjoyed *No Bodies*, please consider leaving a review at

Amazon UK
Amazon US

If you would like to learn more about Kent Fisher and the mystery novels, or keep up to date with new releases from Robert Crouch, please visit http://robertcrouch.co.uk, where you can also sign up to his email newsletter, *The Tollingdon Tribune*.

AUTHOR'S NOTE

Most people are unaware of the work environmental health officers (EHOs) carry out on a day-to-day basis.

With each Kent Fisher Mystery novel, I hope to explore different areas of environmental health to reveal the depth and breadth of the important work carried out to protect public health.

I should also tell you that the setting, Downland District Council and the events in my novels are fictional. Tollingdon exists only in my imagination, as do many of the pubs, hotels and food businesses. And as the saying goes, all characters appearing in this book are fictitious. Any resemblance to real persons, living or dead, is purely coincidental.

KENT FISHER WILL RETURN IN *NO REMORSE*.

Can murder ever be justified?

Printed in Great Britain
by Amazon